Bhanu Kapil < @yahoo.com>   Apr 24, 2011, 9:03 AM   ☆ ↩ ⋮
to me ▾

Two things:

1. I have been waiting to be physically alone in order to read your bottle/letter -- with its odor of seashores and menstrual blood and the butcher's shop and time. I am rarely alone, but today my son's dad is picking him up to take him to Easter Lunch. Then, with my friends, I am going to the river -- we are going to make a flower mandala of shed things.

2. I think you are going to make a huge book. An almanac for extreme girlhood.

Published by Semiotext(e)
PO BOX 629, South Pasadena, CA 91031
www.semiotexte.com

Cover Photograph: Jackie Wang

Design: Hedi El Kholti
ISBN: 978-1-63590-192-4

Distributed by the MIT Press, Cambridge, Mass., and London, England
Printed in the United States of America

ALIEN DAUGHTERS WALK INTO THE SUN

an almanac of extreme girlhood

Jackie Wang

Semiotext(e)

Contents

This book is dedicated to:

My fairy godmothers, guardians of the lost girl—
Chris, Cris, Bhanu

And Lily, my alien sister

"Does my life have no plot? I'm unexpectedly fragmentary. I'm little by little. My story is to live. And I'm not afraid of failure. Let failure annihilate me, I want the glory of falling."

—Clarice Lispector, *The Stream of Life* (*Água Viva*)

Preface

The idea for this book was seeded in an email that Bhanu Kapil sent to me in 2011:

I think you are going to make a huge book. An almanac for extreme girlhood.

Over a decade later, the book would finally be born: *Alien Daughters Walk Into the Sun: An Almanac of Extreme Girlhood.*

I arbitrarily decided my girlhood ended at twenty-nine. I'm writing on a café terrace during a pandemic, thinking about who I used to be when I was a wolf among dogs, before I was domesticated enough to join the society of respectable people (I accidentally typed "dead" people because respectable people are dead inside). I still find it hard to sit at a desk. I never had a desk growing up. It's a holdover from my feral upbringing—untrained, uncultivated, sleepless, habitless, with insomnia and frizzy hair. Wildness was not a thing I sought but the way I came into this world. It was the thing I had to beat out of myself to make a life. I remember, at a squat in the woods of Santa Cruz, Clair once said, *But you've always had so much power in flight.*

There are many ways to periodize a life. The time of lovers. The time of geography. The time of school—the undergraduate years, the punctuation of semesters. The time of mental states—the summer of my mania, the winter of my grief. I've opted for some combination of place and emotional state. When Chris Kraus suggested I organize this collection geographically I balked in my mind—I have always been adrift on this planet, unmoored from any particular place. But the structure I had initially imagined wasn't working. I had wanted to organize the book into an encyclopedia of extreme girlhood, with the essays arranged into entries. But that meant the playing cards of my life would be shuffled into a random order. The reader would have to jump around in time.

So the encyclopedia of extreme girlhood became an almanac of extreme girlhood—a nod to the fact that these pieces can be read as field guides and weather reports. At the time they were written, they were not meant to be arranged into a book. It still surprises me, that I have become the kind of person who makes books. I believed I would always live too fast to be a person who makes books, that I would always be so beholden to my unconscious drive to sabotage everything I do to ever see a book through to completion. In my dreams my readers are assembling the lingual shards of my life into books. I am holding the completed object with a sense of awe as I flip through the pages—yes, I have written every word in here. But I never had the energy to give my words shape. Blessed are the ones who have made a container for my liquid being to sleep in. (The book glows in my hands.)

A friend once asked me: *How will you dispose of your juvenilia?*
To which I replied: *I'll publish it.*

Goethe wrote *The Sorrows of Young Werther* when he was twenty-five. Clearly, I am no Goethe. There are some people who emerge into this world, fully formed, aesthetically mature and capable of generating a complex thought. Just look at the scribblings of nine-year-old Paul Bowles. He created a diary that documented the adventures and pitfalls of imaginary characters who went on wild journeys and were continually surrounded by death, disease, chaos, and crisis—all of which were conveyed by little Paul in a tone that is eerily mute, terse, and affectively stunted while also being intellectually sophisticated. When little Paul was caught scribbling, his father beat him and took his journals away for two months. Writers are made in such moments.

By virtue of genetic good fortune or the circumstantial luck of being born into the learned class, there are some who demonstrate great talent early on, penning Great Works by their midtwenties. I am not among them. (Unless you count *Carceral Capitalism*, which I wrote in my twenties.)

No, that's not quite true. The truth is I cannot fully disavow these writings because although many of the pieces are aesthetically green, I respect the person I used to be: fearless, open to the world, guile-less, and practiced in the art of living. I no longer know how to live as though the impossible were possible. I only know what I'm "supposed" to do to lead a successful life. I have a PhD from Harvard now. I put money away into a retirement account while I write from the comfort of a tenure-track job. I'm not cleaning up broken glass or wresting knives from my lover's hands while flitting from punk house to punk house, in search of a place to land. I'm not setting out into the unknown on my bicycle, with two kitty-litter buckets tied to my rack, without a map, hitchhiking over mountain ranges with truck drivers. Some of those things, I can live without (the broken glass). Others, I miss (the adventures). As you age the doors close behind you, one by one, *Slam*, with every choice you make, *Slam*. When you are young and in the hallway of your life all those aureoled doors are pulsating with a soft light, the glow of potential: *I shall learn Russian and read the Vedas. I shall be a great navigator.* Then one day you wake up to yourself grading a stack of student papers. All the people around you have changed. They give you real estate advice. If I could have seen that the path I stepped on would lead me here, would I have stepped off? I didn't even know I was on a path. But every decision is a path, even decisions I made for the sake of survival, like going to grad school when I ran out of money.

Chaos theory! Every life is a pinball tracing a singular rhizome. Life is. What could have been can no longer be. How incredibly lucky I was, to encounter the people I encountered, the ones who helped me along the way.

Throughout my twenties I was trying to be a writer. Each word was penned with an overwhelming sense of shame. I had to start with the shame, with the feeling I was not worthy of the title *writer*. I remember sitting in the little loft of my room inside the Copycat Warehouse, tap tap tapping away at the novel I would never publish, posting my essays to my blog, writing reviews for magazines, scribbling in my journal about my self-hatred. Below me my lover C. would sit with her piece of paper taped to plexiglass, meticulously drawing her obscurantist comics. She was a tormented artist who nearly ruined my life, an aesthete who was stingy with compliments and almost never had anything good to say about my writing. But she was serious about art, about her craft, whereas I had always felt like a perennial dilettante. We would go to the Red Emma's bookstore and the Johns Hopkins library to work on our art and would sneak into the MICA printing lab to print our booklets, many of which appear in these pages.

The artist I was dating? She's dead now. Suicide. I can't help but feel that, in some fundamental way, she made me a writer. Not by encouraging me to take my writing seriously (no, she belittled my writing), but by modeling what an artist life is. That and the pain she caused me, pain being a precursor to writing. When we weren't warring, all we did, day in and day out, was create. I made videos and wrote poems, stories, and songs. She was always working on her comics or making weird videos, which amassed a cult following on YouTube. We were penniless, slept on a pile of clothes in the tiny porch room of a bedbug-ridden punk house, shivered in the winter. But we had our art.

Because it is You I owe what I am, writes Alejandra Pizarnik.

Under what conditions do we become who we are?

This collection is not a complete archive of what I wrote in my twenties. It excludes most of the poetry and all the fiction I wrote during that time. It includes some of the zines I wrote, but excludes my earliest zines, *Stuck inside Your Head* and *The Vertigo of Falling* #1. It also excludes both issues of *Memoirs of a Queer Hapa*. It includes a good chunk of the pieces I published on my Tumblr blog, *Ballerinas Dance with Machine Guns*, which has since become *Giulia Tofana the Apothecary*. It includes some of the criticism I published in magazines and literary blogs like *HTMLGIANT* and *BOMBlog*. It excludes the fiction and poetry chapbooks I made (*C. Exigua, Shadow*

Ladies, and *Forest of Spines*), and the experimental undergraduate thesis I wrote on poetic postcolonial theory, écriture féminine, and feminist writing practices. It also excludes a draft of a novel I wrote and a book-length unpublished poem I wrote about the girl who tries to escape through a crack in the sky.

What you have here are traces of a wayward girlhood, a life lived on the run. Instead of going back and rewriting these old essays to make my past self sound smarter, I have preserved the raw energy of these pieces as they originally appeared.

I.

2006–10:

THE HARD-FEMME YEARS

Sarasota, Florida. China. All over the place, on bicycle and hitchhiking.

I suppose this period started with me fleeing home, dumping the high school boyfriend I never fucked and declaring myself a lesbian. Home was miserable. Throughout middle school and high school I was persecuted by my extended family, who had delusions that I was possessed by the devil, a drug addict, a whore, pregnant, a satanist, a terrorist—when really, I was spending my free time volunteering at the library and attending absurdist plays. When I was sixteen my brother was locked up, then sentenced to life in prison. My parents were suicidal. Threats were made on my family. My father lost his job. During my junior year I lived in hiding for months; it was too dangerous for me to go to school. Some kids might try to kill me. I was ready to just give in to gravity and let my life fall apart, but then a weird survival instinct kicked in my senior year of high school: I decided to try to pull myself together. I registered for community college classes to try to improve my grades, went to classes on the weekend, signed up for the SATs, and collected applications for college—all by myself. I wanted to go to New College of Florida, an honors liberal arts college without grades that has recently attracted the ire of Governor Ron DeSantis. It would be my ticket out.

This section starts there, finally away from home, in the company of fellow nerd-freaks. It covers my undergraduate years and the time I spent studying abroad in China. In a beach town of retirees, New College of Florida in Sarasota was a bubble of nudity, psychedelia, late-night conversations on continental philosophy, fruit trees, barefoot hippies, noise music. Everyone was gay. My crew was all lesbian, except for the cerebral anarchists, who were all boys. Beneath my bed I made a cuddle fort called the Cuddlepunk

Liberation Love Fort that was plastered with revolutionary slogans and pictures of my friends. I lived with my girlfriend P. throughout those years, in a mostly lesbian house we called the House of LaBeija, or, alternatively, the Petting Zoo. I worked odd jobs—as a motel attendant, an elementary school tutor, and the director of programming for my college's Gender and Diversity Center. During my senior year P. and I broke up and I moved into the storage closet of the Forty-Seventh Street House, an activist house hand-built with reclaimed wood, where I became best friends with a fellow queerdo named Matthew. Dumpster diving was on the chore wheel. Matthew and I would write stories and songs together. We'd sit in gay bars writing whimsical letters to our crushes and would read them to each other in his room at night. How free I was, during that season between consuming lovers.

P. had been obsessed with a mysterious YouTube personality who was in a noise music band: C. Four months after P. and I broke up, P. brought C. to play some shows in Sarasota. I watched C. perform in my college's auditorium with a prurient curiosity—who was this tall waif speaking in a Mickey Mouse voice about medical simulations and drawing absurdist cartoons on the whiteboard while striding manically across the stage? How deliciously weird, how not of this world. Immediately, I was obsessed. Less than two months later she was living with me in the Forty-Seventh Street House closet. Thus began a period of great chaos. The abuse started the day she moved in with me. Perhaps she was testing me, to see if I would take it, to see if I'd stick around. I did. The week before my thesis defense we were kicked out of the house after she flipped out on the house-mates and cut herself with an X-Acto knife.

The Vertigo of Falling #2: Life in Kunming

These are excerpts from a perzine (personal zine) I wrote on my travels in China in 2008 and early 2009, when I moved to Kunming to live with my aunt and study abroad. It follows The Vertigo of Falling #1, *a diary-style zine I wrote in high school after binge-reading the diaries of Anaïs Nin. I suppose I imagined I would have many issues of my various zine series, but I usually did not get past the first or second issue!*

Leaving Sarasota

Tonight, after my goodbye party had died down, we crammed ten people into Alexis's van. We drove to the ocean—sitting on laps and the floor—to see the meteor shower. We walked to the darkest part—the dunes where the gay men fuck—so we could see the sky. I ran while jumping rope on the shore in a bra and shorts, the violent wind whipped my hair around; every foot crashing onto the sand emitted glowing rings in the water. I went out into the ocean, swam around alone and was dazed by the strangeness of the moon. I was moving my hand vigorously in the ocean and was so enthralled by the glowing water that I didn't notice a wave coming right for me. It hit me smack in the face, knocking me off my feet, and I got up manically and hysterically laughing to myself; all at once the suffering leaving and turning profoundly hilarious and insignificant and okay. Salty, too.

I rested on the shore—the shallow place where the water meets the sand. Shallow enough to breathe yet deep enough to feel the continuous ebb and flow of the water. The sand forms to my body as the waves recede, trying to pull me out—I look up, waiting for meteorites. I made wishes that were vague. I don't like being disappointed.

Dreams, Delirium, Dogs, Love, and Family

In China, you remember your dreams. Usually you don't because you wake up on your own, gradually, and by then the dreams are long gone. But you are startled awake every morning, by rustling and horns and the city stirring. Walking in the streets beneath the towering residential buildings, you want to scream, *Shut the fuck up do you ever shut up?!* You break down crying, thinking of your dreams. In your dreams someone holds you: not someone you'd expect, not someone you think of romantically in your waking hours, holding you in many settings, in water and comfortable beds, tender unspoken affection. It feels so nice and you miss touch so much, miss it so much.

A wave of drowsiness strikes daily at 3:00 p.m. You're on the bus riding across Kunming with your eyes closed and your head down, trying not to fall asleep but there are forces stronger than you, pulling you. You slide in and out of consciousness riding through bustling streets and everything whirling around you in a roaring frenzy.

At night you film a man sitting in front of his store. He's looking away. You walk the streets alone, filming fights and children running. You pass him again and he's writing. You walk by him slowly, a tacit connection, maybe; you keep walking, dragging your feet and he is still looking at you as you walk away. You think about the unspoken flows between people, everywhere. How many of those intense moments are mutual, how many one-sided? The tension. Silence breaking, opening your vision, perception so wide you could be anything, throw yourself into anything and be near it. I want to be near it want it inside me and my insides outside me. How funny it must be to hold your insides outside you and not even feel it. Well, your hands would feel it, but it'd be like touching another body.

I want to live as though dead because when you're dead you become a part of everything. How can we decompose while alive? Awake? I want to fall away into the dirt and be eaten and carried away in pieces. Death is not passive. Do you remember walking with your schizophrenic friend and him telling you that death is not finality? You leave your imprint on everyone and everything—the groove in the chair that receives your ass. And people. Their ever-changing memories of you growing blurry and ill-defined … farther and farther from what was lived but it's still just as real. When I'm awake I'm hit with still images from dreams that have no context or movement. I strain to place them but cannot.

The TV flickers in a dark room. You stand outside the dirty window with your eyes closed. On the other side of the wall there are people and you wonder why there are so many walls. So many people in boxes stacked on top of boxes. They protect you. They destroy you.

* * *

Kunming. Such a strange city. You hang out with an Australian lady who has been living in Kunming for ten years and her Chinese is worse than yours. She was stabbed thirty times, her husband and son were killed, and her hand was severed and sewed back on. Her hand, dead for fifteen years but brought back to life thanks to a miracle performed at a Christian-revival church. The trucks that spray the streets to keep the dust down play the happy birthday melody, but off-key like an old dying toy. Reminded by the song, she says her birthday was last week. She thought she was fifty-eight, but later realized she's actually fifty-seven. She described the feeling of the revelation: endowed with another year of life, just like that, like a gift but all it took was forgetting. All last year she could have been saying, *I'm fifty-six. I'm fifty-six!* She periodically goes back to Australia to collect welfare money but hates to go back. *Why are you in Kunming?* She doesn't know. What is she running from? Why doesn't she have pictures of any of her children? She runs to my aunt's apartment whenever she has a problem—locked out of her room, stolen cell phones, no power. Today she comes bearing gruesome details of an injured street dog. The dog was lying on the carpet with its insides outside its body. She runs through the list of organs, ruminating on what could have possibly happened, baffled.

* * *

Twice your aunt breaks down, soon after you've moved in with her. Each time her crying fit was brought on by the memory of her dog. The first night you sat down eating dinner, asking questions, trying to understand her life philosophy. *I don't give a fuck about anyone*, she says. *Life is nothing. Life is nothing.* She moves from place to place—unsettled—no husband or children. *I make friends everywhere I go. Then I get bored of them and just fucking leave. I tell everyone, don't call me.* I ask her how she developed this philosophy and she breaks down. There were two pivotal moments—the death of her mother, my grandmother, and the recent death of her dog. Those were the moments when she realized that everything was meaningless and adopted her nihilistic life view. *My mom wasn't supposed to die. She took such good care of herself.*

Do you feel sad, do you feel happy? People ask her. *I don't know. I knit; I walk around; I talk to people; I watch Korean soap operas; I visit places.* Happy, sad—it doesn't matter. Even her deepest suffering has no meaning. Beaten, abused—it didn't matter. She didn't care. She just wanted to leave Taiwan, to get the hell away from everyone.

At first you admire her detached aggressiveness because it's the opposite of you. She says, *Who gives a fuck about friends. What does it matter? No one remembers you when you're dead.* The second time she cries she's talking about her dog Angel. She couldn't bring Angel to China when she moved. So Angel lived with my family for two years before moving to my uncle's. After a year at my uncle's, she got a tooth infection and died. *She wasn't supposed to die so young.* She wasn't supposed to die so young. The same story as her mother, life cut tragically short. She doesn't believe in God, but she believes in destiny. And there's no fighting it.

She was different from other dogs. She was so smart. She was supposed to die in my arms. She gets hysterical, said she was in the hospital for two months after she heard Angel died, said she still cries herself to sleep. *I wasn't loved as a child. You're lucky; you have so much love. Men loved me but I could never love them back.* So this dog was the only thing she ever loved. It was true companionship. *Jing Jing, the girl on the street, that's fake. She sits on my lap and gives me a kiss because I buy her candy.* She says she has psychological problems and so she cannot love, but she could love that dog. Angel's ashes are at Uncle Eli's. *I'd kill myself if I ever saw them!* She yells. People would probably say, *It's just a dog, who cares, get over it, just an animal.* But you have to imagine—what if you couldn't love anything but a dog, and that dog loved you back, and it was pure and mutual? Why does love have to be complicated to be considered real?

Romance in China

Writing from a café in the university district of Kunming.

The more people I meet in Kunming, the more it starts to feel like Werner Herzog's *Encounters at the End of the World.* Kunming is full of eccentric people who have no idea why or how they got here. When you ask them about it, they don't give you straight answers and by the end of the conversation you still don't know why they are here, other than they were carried here by some vague destiny. I ask the Australian lady—she doesn't know. I ask this guy David from Ghana—he read a profile about the city online. My cousin Jing Wen's friend Xiao Fan (they met when Xiao Fan was shining my cousin's shoes in Shanghai) is here trying to make money selling Chinese pizza. I ask the owner of a Korean café. He got a BA from NYU and an MA from UChicago, ran out of money when working on his PhD and came to Kunming. Why? He just says, *Destiny.*

Friday night I went to a Korean café with this adorable girl Kim Jumyung from my school. We stayed there for hours eating and taking shots of Korean liquor, although I probably only had one shot. "Bruce" (American name of Jumyung's friend) played songs on an acoustic guitar and told stories about tripping on mushrooms and Jumyung told me about how much she loved weed and Radiohead. She said that in Dali, a city in the Yunnan province that is home to the Bai ethnic group, there are marijuana trees growing everywhere, except I thought she was saying "free" when she was saying "tree" and I kept saying, "Wait, they give you free weed everywhere?!?!" And she would nod, and I would imagine people walking down the street handing out free baggies of weed. Like Christmas. Those Korean kids are wild.

Jumyung's real cute and is an artist, too. She asked to draw me and said she'd give me the drawing as a gift. I was thinking it'd be cool if she were queer. Sometimes it seems like she's hitting on me, like when out of nowhere she says "I LIIIIKKKEEE YOOOUUU HAHAHA!" (always manically laughing) and her friend, the owner of the Korean café, says, "everyday she comes in here and talks about you. Jackie this, Jackie that. Now you're finally here."

Last night I went to an art opening in a giant loft. There were tons of other loft-style art galleries in the alley. This guy wanted to go with me as a DATE but I invited other people to meet me there and he seemed pissed. Jumyung came with her crazy friend "Bruce," a Dai woman who works at the Korean café, and two cool Canadians. They're vegetarians from Vancouver and know where a bunch of veg restaurants are in the area. We exchanged dirty words in six different languages and played a weird Korean game about bunnies.

The bad part about the café I'm at now is that they don't allow you to poop in the toilet and will charge you fifty kuai if you do!

Crushes, Perception, Adventures in China

Here's what you need to do. Say *fuck yes* to everything (except dates with creepy men). Don't hesitate. "It seems like we only regret the things we don't do." Don't scroll through potentially negative outcomes. Just give a resounding OK! And go on your way. This is a philosophy I'm borrowing from Mr. Al Burian. I, like the newly freed bird in Vonnegut's *Breakfast of Champions*, have stood at my window contemplating the vast and tumultuous world outside, and I've gone back to my bed—my cage—opened a book, got a pen. There's always more to read. But I'm shifting my outlook. Today Jumyung asked me to lunch. I've already said no before, and this time I gave her a wishy-washy "Maybe / we'll see / it's hard for me to eat out because I'm a vegetarian" and walked away because my aunt said to come home for lunch with the family. And then, on my next break, I tracked her friend down, excitedly replied to her lunch request, "Yes! *Wo gen nimen yiqi chi wufan, hao ma?!!* I want to eat lunch with you!"

After class I can't find Jumyung. She calls "Jackie Jackie Jackie Jackie Jackie Jackie" in a cute voice and we walk through a graffitied alley. The thing about crushes is that they narrow your perception. It's like you can only pay attention to one thing when they're around; it could be WWIII and you'd be leaning in listening, the bombs falling around you and you can't even hear them exploding! Once a schizophrenic man at Food Not Bombs said, "I could only pay attention to one thing so everyone had their privacy." That's how it was. There was a flurry of high-pitched voices, children running around, a cloud of indistinct jibber jabber, and we were walking right through it. It hit me. Where I was. How did I get here? Children everywhere, wearing backpacks, just out of school.

Jumyung gave me a four-leaf clover she had pressed in her sketchbook. This was after she showed me a pot plant growing in the middle of the city. I perused her sketchbook and she pointed to a Damien Hirst quote. Fun adventures in communication and food. Her calling everyone crazy ("ni de naozi you bing") because it's one of the few things she can express in Chinese. Ate spicy bean-sprout soup, kimchi, and a strange dessert. Kissed napkins with lipstick and taped them to the wall of the Korean restaurant.

* * *

You're so close to the sky in Kunming; you can feel the thunder amassing energy from all around you, sucking a little out of you too and throwing it back, pissed. The first couple of weeks were intense.

You just wanted your organs to fall out they felt so heavy and cumbersome. The second day in Kunming I went to church with the eccentric Australian lady. The man delivering the sermon is rambunctious like a coke addict. He starts with a long-winded anecdote about the Olympics, about how he loves to see underdogs win. *Did you guys hear? Iceland is in the handball finals! What the hell do they do in Iceland?? PLAY HANDBALL I GUESS! There are only like a hundred thousand people in the WHOLE COUNTRY.* Then he moves on to a rant about the *Rocky* movies, another inspiring underdog story, before he tries to tie it all back to Christian gospel. *All those awesome ideas in Hollywood, they're actually God's ideas! They're from the Bible! Now there's drama. Look at Jesus—crucified, down for the count and bam! He rose again!* The band plods through an hour of praise songs. During a song a man gets up, grabs the microphone, and tells the crowd about his dream. Golden orbs came tumbling over a mountain and turned into a king. The king took me to a banquet and there were mountains of food. *The lord is coming, said the king, and he's preparing a banquet for us all!* The man repeated *He is coming! He is coming! He is coming!* while the music in the background rose to a crescendo, nearly obscuring his voice. The audience gave themselves over to the moment completely—eyes closed, total euphoria. It was wild.

The thing about love is it's better unfettered.

Drunk on the Midautumn Festival

Lordy lordy, I can move! And am feeling surprisingly upbeat for my condition. Since the moon festival party, it's been nonstop bodily pain—crippling, debilitating pain. Various parts of my body conspiring to produce a pain that is whole and total and all-consuming.

Today I plucked a gray hair from my head and contemplated its significance as I held it to the light. Kim Jumyung called me three times for food and walks, but I was nearly bedridden.

I had this idea at the moon party that I could drink because there are tons of Asians with ADH deficiency who drink, so 2.5 shots of Korean liquor—no big deal, right? Mark, Jumyung ("Kim"), and I split the bottle, downed shots while singing Leonard Cohen and Queen at the bar. Jumyung was being giddy and even a little touchy. Sometimes it seems like our interactions are suffused with romantic tension and flirtatiousness, and other times I think maybe I'm just delusional. Either way, she was sayin' I LOVE JACKIE! and quietly told me she didn't want to do palm readings because she wanted to talk to me.

We eventually convinced a tipsy Mark to start the live music. Jumyung and I were pretty much gone at this point, clapping and dancing and yelling about how much we loved each other and then Jumyung started playing the flute and Bruce came to join in the music-making and it was all gleeful drunkenness.

Then, all at once, a wave of dizziness hit me and I fell to the ground in slow motion. I couldn't see or hear anything, clutched a chair and hoisted myself up, straining to see. My vision and hearing kept cutting in and out, and I remember straining so hard to gain control of my senses, to no avail. For a moment I could see things shiny and out of focus, enough to get me to the bathroom where I passed out and was jolted into consciousness by the eager knocking of a partygoer who probably had to piss. I remember thinking, *This is thirty times more intense than tripping on shrooms.*

Flyer for the party, by Jumyung

So I got up and passed out in another setting—in the nook where people sit on the floor to eat. I woke up after about twenty minutes and started shaking violently, cold and in physical pain. I tried to cover myself with pillows. Then I started hysterically crying; bad thoughts flooded my skull. A Canadian woman named Cierra came into the nook, kept repeatedly asking me if I was on drugs and started an intense conversation. I was fucking delirious—nodding, crying, and laughing. And then Jumyung came in and was like, *AH! What's wrong!?* And I was manically laughing while hysterically crying and then she started crying and Cierra was like, *Oh no don't do that, Jumyung!*

I don't remember what happened after that, but I made it home without my aunt noticing that I was piss drunk and sick.

* * *

Zhongquijie kuaile.

Take the moon pie, good man. You deserve it. Always playing your
erhu with the dog sitting on the carpet in front of you. You
deserve the moon, good man.

The flesh of mulberries' bleedin', without being prodded or punctured.

The cement table's a tree stump, and you bow before branches to
garner entrance to the garden.

Pointing outside of ringed time, emerging daily, without regard
for time.

The sun's a hand throwing punches.

The sun's your father.

Your hand was born with markings and they follow you through time.

She touches your hand and speaks to you quietly, telling you how
you were, how you are, how you're going to be. The passersby take
bites of her ice cream on the grandiose stone steps at sunset
until she is left with little.

She opens her eyes wide and we breathe heavily, laughing. The child
pokes an immobile butterfly and says "fei."

The Glee and Horror

Today, by default, I'm stuck with a French guy for nearly the
whole day. A good-looking, educated, twenty-four-year-old who
speaks four languages and is a business grad student. The French
guy asks me how I communicate with Jumyung, in a skeptical
tone with the subtext, *How can you guys even be friends?* She speaks
a so-so amount of English and not much Chinese. I can't explain
and I don't even care to explain. When it's just Jumyung and me

it's total delirious glee and romping around town for hours doing nothing but hysterically laughing the whole time. When it's just us it's speaking poorly constructed and grammatically incorrect Chinese with English words thrown in. When it's just us we'll look at something, then look at each other and laugh because we're thinking the same thing. We make wild facial expressions at each other and it wouldn't make any sense to anyone else, any outsider, any onlooker, but for us it makes total sense and it's like YEAH YEAH YEAH !!! We go to a Chinese folk-painting class and are just laughing the whole time, heads on the table, passing notes and talking about the boy sitting two rows behind us who I think is cute but really I like Jumyung better. How do we communicate? I don't know. Sometimes you're just on the same wavelength.

I was thinking, *How much of life is left to chance?* The class I randomly ambled into, the seat I randomly sat in, and the person sitting next to me. Who is this person? It's Jumyung. We make funny faces at each other and when we go outside for our break, she introduces me to her friend as her "pengyou" (Chinese for "friend"). We hadn't even talked yet. She considered me her friend before we even talked. How many people do we not meet every day?

When it's just us, it's our bizarre and nonsensical world. But when others are around there's this gloom—where to go, indecisiveness, conversations that go nowhere because you're trying to say something that's agreeable to everyone, to speak the lowest common denominator. P. and I talked on the phone about our escape fantasies. Escaping the crowd with our crushes because the situation and the people are bogging us down and we just have so much more fun on our own. Let's just fucking leave because this makes no sense to anyone else. Like when Kim Jumyung and I leave the Korean café to saunter through gardens and eat street food on stone steps. You wonder how seven hours could pass without feeling anxious, like you need to be somewhere else. Because there's nowhere else you want to be.

LIFE: haha

Yesterday I was laughing so much that I felt like I was going to pass out. I was sitting talking to Jumyung and we were hysterical. On the bus ride home, I was laughing to myself just thinking about the things she said. Before I took the bus home, she was drunk and ran out of the café after me as I was walking away. She was teary-eyed and said that we are true friends, that she wants us to be friends forever, that she doesn't want me to leave in January. She was stumbling around, giving me hugs and saying "I love you!" in a way that is supposed to sound funny but also contains an element of truth, even if that truth is just that she cares.

Today feels almost too absurd to talk about. It started with Jumyung telling her Spanish classmate that I wanted this Hungarian guy Mátyás's phone number (what? I didn't tell her to ask that). The Spanish kid told Jumyung that the Hungarian kid is gay. Then Jumyung called me and told me the Hungarian kid is gay. The Hungarian kid looked at me confused after class and said, "Someone told me you were trying to find my phone number." I didn't know what was going on, what Jumyung told the Spanish kid. Felt so embarrassed. I wrote a note to the Hungarian kid that said something like *Ohhh you're gay, that's cool I'm kind of gay too I have a girlfriend blah blah blah I just want to make a new friend in Kunming.* And then I imagined myself having a gay friend in Kunming. Then I saw the Hungarian guy in flute class and left the note on his desk. He instantly knocked it onto the floor and when he got up for a second, I had to sneakily pick it up and put it back on his desk in a more obvious place, but he got up and moved to a different desk, leaving the note sitting alone. I laughed to myself and then tried to get his attention by pointing to the note. Eventually I gave up and tossed it to him: HERE. *This is for you.* After class I saw him and he said, *I'm not gay at all. I'm completely heterosexual.* I was laughing at the situation and he said, *This will be a funny memory.* Then he gave me his phone number and walked me to my bus stop. When we got there I said, *Wait. I don't actually want to go home now.* I was thinking I should hang with Jumyung and Cierra, but I somehow ended up at the Hungarian guy's apartment for five hours, talking about absurdism, being a teenager, metrosexuals, suicide, and other miscellaneous topics. The evening culminated in a delicious pasta dinner cooked by his friendly Italian roommates.

* * *

On my hand I write, "Talk to people. Make friends." Jumyung grabs my hand and laughs and I tell her about how hard it is for me to talk to people, how terribly awkward I am. Today she introduces me to her American classmate and I laugh because I have zero American friends in Kunming. She said that when she saw "make friends" written on my hand she felt sad because she thought I wanted American/European friends, that I felt dissatisfied hanging out only with Koreans. "That's not true!" I tell her.

But what is it I'm looking for? Who is it I'm looking for? And why am I looking?

Jumyung knows how I feel without me saying it. Even on the phone she can hear it in my voice and I know she knows because I hear it in the way she says, "I miss you, Jackie," even though we just saw each other earlier that day. She says it again and I laugh to prove that I am happy.

* * *

You don't want the bus ride to end. When it's your stop time pauses as you approach the exit and you come face to face with the night. And before you even get off the bus you can feel the cold. The bus spits you out like a sour mouthful and you are left to wander the streets alone in the cold rain. When you don't sleep you start to walk into traffic and people grab your arm yelling "Xiao xin!"—which means "Be careful!" but literally translates to "small heart." When you don't sleep you take the wrong bus to the end of its route and end up nowhere. Your tired mind can't process the situation, so you just take the same bus back to where you came from.

Dreaming of the air saving us. We can't fall.

We were walking around dreaming.

We were both so tired that our walking was a dream. We started to fall asleep in the café and jumped up and walked outside. You can't explain the timbre of "I am dreaming right now." She bought a handmade journal for October and it nearly matches yours. She draws your face on the first page.

Profound Appreciation of Food and Flavor (and Friends)

We're baking bread
That's how we spend our time
So happy baking bread
And all we do is fine
There are no better times

For talking with your hands
Or crying out instead
We're happy baking bread
—Avey Tare and Kría Brekkan

This song is so sweet, these two weirdo musicians (one of the guys from Animal Collective and one of the twins from Múm) married and singing about the happiness of baking bread. It reminds me of everything I miss about America—so much time spent in the kitchen with friends, so much time collecting spices, oils, and sauces; so much time picking perfect produce; cabinets bursting with teas, pots hanging from the ceiling; dumpstering goodies; house full of delicious aromas, herbs from cuttings; collecting fruit from the trees, trying to grow our own vegetables. The peppers were so abundant that all my food was too spicy because I wanted to use them all. When we moved into our house we pooled our spices together on that lovely shelf in our kitchen, and when everything was placed we stood back looking, impressed and contemplating the flavor possibilities. And there's this very simple joy missing from my life—the joy of sharing my food with friends.

Jumyung strolls into class at 11:15 a.m. to trumpets and fanfare, everyone calling her name. Everyone loves her. *Settle down, class, settle down.* She teaches you how to eat a persimmon. You fail at peeling it, your hand covered in sweet orange flesh. You spit a hard piece into your hand, and she tells you to put it back in your mouth and chew it because it's sweet. You do and it's the best part. Unlike your aunt, she's not pedantic when she instructs you on how to eat the fruit; she is patient, speaks to you on your level.

On the streets I buy a watermelon from a farmer and it's the most delicious watermelon I've had in my life. I regret that Jaclyn is not here to make her watermelon gazpacho. I am learning to like bananas. I am learning to haggle when I buy fruit.

Do you want to share a kimchi pancake? I'd never had a kimchi pancake before. I'd never even had kimchi before I met her.

My aunt said that I've loved food since a very young age; she knew by the way I slurped the soup.

Today I spent a good deal of time looking up Buddhist vegetarian restaurants and reading about the Han and minority cuisine of Yunnan. I feel excited to try all this street food—stinky tofu, erkuai rice cakes—and to taste pu-erh tea. And I want to cook kimchi pancakes and green-onion pancakes for my friends. Every day I've been going to a new restaurant. Jumyung has been sick, so I've been eating alone, sitting in cafés and Indian, Japanese, and Chinese restaurants, trying new foods, sipping tea and reading Arundhati Roy's *The God of Small Things.*

Did you know you can cut the top off a passion fruit, fill it with water, stick a straw in it, and it becomes a delicious tropical beverage?

The Erhu Player

On this day. On this day everything was open. Mark and I were both floored by the image of a flood of scooters and bicycles riding down an incline, becoming a dense wave of people on low-impact vehicles tumbling toward us and we dashed across the street to peek inside the grandiose tea garden. On this day I was floored by everything I saw. The street—culled from a dream—the buildings old and crumbling and the old men betting on crickets that they make fight each other, getting them riled up by rubbing their antennae together. There was the bird and flower market, with its extensive collection of animals, offbeat weaponry, and "tobacco" paraphernalia—a fragment of Old Kunming still standing despite the developmentalist impulse to destroy everything old. "The Chinese consider these buildings an embarrassment," one says. He doesn't understand the aesthetic preference for the New, the preference for the Immaculate and Unsoiled. Another says that the Chinese have seen enough old shit, and the general sentiment is, "Let's build some new shit." Nearby, the Yuantong Temple still stands after twelve hundred years, a vestige of authenticity for weary wanderers that measure the Realness of their experience by how genuinely weathered these buildings look, how Genuinely Weathered the farmers' skin looks, those Simple Locals. In China the old mingles with the New, and you end up with Buddhas adorned with flashing LED lights, an offputting sight for the Weary Wanderers, but I stand back contemplating it all. This idea of Real Culture, and what it means in China, where so much "culture" is preserved when it can be commodified—turned into a tourist photo op—or used as a propaganda tool, a picture of all the ethnic minorities lined up in traditional dress, coexisting harmoniously. Thank you, Communist government, for all the development and tourism. My aunt says, *Those minorities are sneaky. They really take advantage of Chinese (Han) people.* What?

* * *

"I am full and the weather is good. I have everything." These are the words spoken by Minou, the owner of the Korean café, after eating and before falling asleep blissfully. We were all in the sitting room of the café—Jumyung drawing, me reading and writing, Mark playing guitar. Giant windows framed the movement outside. When Minou wakes up he tells me a story about when he was a grad student at the University of Chicago. "At UChicago they pushed the students so hard that everyone was depressed as hell at the end of the semester. There were always three or four suicides. One day I was really depressed and didn't want to get up or go to school." But he did go to school, and while he was walking to school he started hysterically laughing. He asks me, "Do you know why I was laughing?" *No, laoban, why?* "Because as I was walking to class, I saw three different guys talking to squirrels."

Jumyung and I went to Cuihu Park at around sunset—a park on a huge lake lined with willow trees and stone benches. On this day I was perceiving everything. The weather and lighting were so good we ran around kicking the air, laughing, making nonsensical jokes, swinging around trees, and dancing in circles around each other.

The park was full of so much life. On every corner there were older Kunming folk jamming on Chinese instruments, people singing, and old ladies dancing in synchronized groups. Jumyung and I would stop and listen, slapping our legs, tapping our feet, and shaking our heads. We walked by a solitary old man playing a Chinese violin. We sat down to listen and both instantly felt like breaking down, the song and moment so sad. And right next to me was a mother and her baby. And when the mother would lean down to kiss the baby, the baby would pull on the strings of the woman's scarf.

After the man finished his song, he told us about his instrument, and we continued to walk around, talking about how happy we felt right then, how perfect everything was. I bought little handmade wire bicycles that I want to turn into earrings. I told her that I will remember this day every time I wear the earrings, the day we wandered Cuihu Park at sunset and made the curious locals guess our nationalities, the day we saw a man flying a kite so high that we could barely see it in the sky. We returned to the Korean café for a special dinner with friends, and when we were talking about sexuality it finally clicked for her that I am really queer (I said "bisexual" to make things easier) and that I haven't been joking all this time. She got excited, repeating, *Today is a good day, today is a good day, I have to write in my journal RIGHT now!* And she whipped out the journal we bought together, the one with a drawing she did of me on the first page, the one that almost matches the journal I got to log my adventures in China. And even though it seems like she really does like-like me, the circumstances will probably prevent it from ever happening. Maybe it would happen if we were the sole survivors of an apocalypse, because only then would the barriers be erased. Radioactive ruins would replace the City of Eternal Spring as our new stomping ground in this postapocalyptic world; we'd probably die quickly, but happily.

The Nap

You remember the day you called Mátyás up because you were so tired but didn't have time to go home. You had plans for the evening, and you asked if you could sleep in his bed. He said yes, opened his empty room and unfolded the blankets for you. There was something so intimate about the drool stains on his pillow, something so intimate about opening the door after you woke up. You thought he was in flute class, but he was home and your hair was messy and you weren't wearing makeup. Something so intimate about walking out in your ridiculous socks. He stood in the kitchen washing dishes as he talked about the dreams that he knew were about his fear of being close to girls; the sun was setting behind him and you were sitting in a chair lacing up your shoes. He said, "I like your shoes." You looked at them. They were dirty with the dust of Chinese streets and rainy days steeped in mud.

The Letter

Dear Mátyás,

After we walked around Cuihu Park and ate at the vegetarian restaurant, I didn't want to talk to anyone or do anything. I just wanted to think about the things we talked about and I knew that if I did anything I would lose the feeling. You know, that feeling you get after you just had a good conversation. After our talks this weekend I felt happy. Nothing you said sounded crazy to me and it felt kind of like being drunk. As soon as I got home I tried to go to sleep and thought about many things in my bed.

I don't expect anything. I know that after Kunming our lives will move in very different directions. I am not writing this letter to try to "make you mine" or to get you to like me. I'm not trying to convince or persuade you of anything. People are not objects that exist for us, right? People don't want the same things from each other, don't feel the same way about each other. I know that no matter how I feel that doesn't change the fact that nothing romantic will happen between us. I want us to be friends and I don't want things to be weird between us. It's unrealistic to even expect that we will be friends after Kunming.

The whole time we were walking around Cuihu I wanted to give you a big hug so badly but I didn't because I didn't think it was appropriate. But the feeling was there the whole time. I was so aware of my body. I know what situations are unrealistic. This isn't about getting what I want. People don't exist for us. Yeah. Let's be good friends in Kunming. I don't expect anything else from you.

* * *

A cold and rainy day in Kunming. Walking around, your feet go numb and your breath is thick. I wanted to be cruel to him but when we sat down, I just started laughing and said, "I'm never sad, haha!" I asked if he had the letter and he said no. He didn't bring it because he thought I was going to dissect it in front of him, thought I was going to use it against him. I told him that's not what I wanted to do, that I wanted to destroy the letter, to unwrite the letter. He said I can't do that. I asked him why. He said the letter "came at a good time for him," made him realize that Kunming is just a trap for him. Although I can't explain in words what he means by this, I know what he means. Nothing in Kunming will ever mean anything to him, and if it starts to, he will crush it immediately. He says, "I have no real friends," and I tell him that I already know this. I wanted to be cruel to him but when I saw him I couldn't. He was nervous and I was nervous, touching everything and compulsively drinking water. I asked him if he thought we should still be friends and he said *yes*. There were long stretches of silence imbued with tension so thick you could slice it, and after every silence he would blurt out a morbid question. "If you were to kill yourself, how would you do it?" A conversation about suicide or life would ensue. I told him that I wanted to be mean to him, but that I'm just too fucking forgiving. He insisted that it was a good thing, and I insisted that it was a bad thing. I asked him when it was a good thing and he said, "In situations like this one." Before he left I told him, "It's a good thing I don't love you. Or else we couldn't be friends." He said, "Why did you just say that?" and I replied, "That's the situation, isn't it?" He said, "There was something strange about the way you just said that," and I said, "What? What is it?" He said he didn't know, that he could just feel it.

I wanted to walk away from this conversation feeling completely indifferent toward him, but I couldn't.

I started to cry in the café, not because I'm sad, but because I can't cultivate indifference. Because I am too forgiving. After a while it starts to wear you down. After a while you start to feel like an object, a stuffed animal that belongs to an aging child, that can be discarded and picked up at will. This is a characteristic that I have surely inherited from my father, who tells me over the phone that he is not mad at my aunt, after all the things she said to him, that at any moment he'd be willing to repair their relationship.

After this last week all those Bergman films suddenly start to make so much sense. One minute people are tender and loving, the next they're violent and hostile. In the end you don't know if it was love, hatred, or indifference that you felt for the other person.

And most of all I want to tell him, "Teach me how to be indifferent like you."

You Are True

Dangran keyi.
Sure, I'd let her kiss me. And they say, "Think about the consequences," of getting drawn into her psychotic world. But the truth is I don't care if I'd feel bad afterward, after leaving, after her indifference. The truth is that I knew, from the very first time I saw her, that she was special. I wrote to a friend, "I started classes today. Very cute/awkward Korean girl sitting next to me in class today. Called me her *pengyou* ("friend" in Chinese) even though we only communicated through our facial expressions." All this time I've just sat back, just tried to be her friend, to make her happy when she was sad even though I never could because I am not the right person, not a boy. The truth is I am always ready. Ready to see her when she is ready to see me, but lately it's almost never and she says, "Bu hao yisi." I'm not coming. Not today. Not tomorrow. But still, she calls me late at night, drunk and telling me that she really does love me, saying things like "Fuck, why don't you speak Korean?" I feel bad, like it's my fault we can't communicate about the details, can only get at the general idea.

* * *

Once you were at KTV (karaoke) when she called and afterward you sat down in your thoughts, and all those pop songs made so much sense—the cliché lyrics were suddenly profound. Yeah, those cheap '90s videos of lovers in parks and at carnivals suddenly looked like a beautiful and important document; an aerial view of humanity—their interactions and mannerisms—and you felt stupid, to be so much a part of it, to be performing the same story, infinitely repeating it all with everyone else and filling up time and history with the same bullshit. Falling in and out of love, friendship, leaving, dying, people, confusion. I'm embarrassed to be a part of it, to be living proof that the pop songs are true.

In the taxi the night after she told you about her sad life and how she ended up in Kunming, you felt like crying. All you can do is offer hugs and you wonder if it means anything, this small gesture. All you can do is be ready, willing to come back at the drop of a hat, to go with whatever she wants. All you can do is sit back smiling awkwardly when he tells you that they are fucking now and that all this time he's been trying to find a way to get with her and he asks you what you think of them together and you say, *good*. You sit there as he tells you that they're fucking but still she says she wants to have sex with you, calls you her "girlfriend" and tells you that she's in love with you and he says that she says it too.

Breakdowns, Breakthroughs, Losing Friends, Being Kissed, Birds

ROUND 1
Note to friend:

I had a drunken emotional breakdown on the streets the other day. Felt insane, like punching a glass window or jumping off a building, and went for a walk at night and drank a bottle of soju—Korean liquor—in ten minutes on some steps in front of a bank. Minutes later I had my face in my notebook and was crying like crazy and some guy came up real close to me and was looking at me all funny and I didn't even feel embarrassed I felt so not a part of this world and its people and whatever I could have pissed right there and not even cared because I am not even a part of this world. Then I called my Korean friend Jumyung who was right around the corner eating street food with her friends and told her to please come see me and when she did I was hysterically laughing and crying and fell on the floor and demanded another bottle of beer. I refused to go home and told everyone that it was REALLY no problem if I slept on the street and I only spoke Chinese the whole time, even when people who only speak English called me. Apparently I kept insisting I sleep on the street, but I ended up in Jumyung's bed and threw up a bunch of times and my roommate came and picked me up after 4:00 a.m. and I came home and threw up some more. I don't really have any memory of any of this, this is what people told me happened because I blacked out from 11:30 p.m. until the morning and woke up in my bed wearing Jumyung's clothes. I am pretty much happy/normal/okay now, although when I was talking to my friend today he said, "You don't seem okay at all," because I was nearly in tears describing a hug ...

* * *

That hug. Right before you lost your memory. It came back to you the next day. You were on the phone crying and saying, *Will you please come? I'm on the* shaokao *street. Please come.* And when you saw her, she wiped your tears and hugged you so hard and instantly everything felt okay, so safe. How can a hug mean that much? How can you feel it that much? How can such a simple form of touch fix everything so easily, all at once?

Jumyung. Why? There's a memory of when you ran into her at the bus stop outside your old apartment. She was wearing pearls and heels, standing in the sunlight with her hair loosely tied back on her way home from her job teaching art to children. You were happy.

ROUND 2
It's Christmas Eve in China. It's so easy to forget, except someone blew themselves up at a café and I lost my best friend, Mátyás. On my doorstep, he left a package filled with my gifts and zines, along with a note:

"Jackie: For you are the center of my past which I need to abandon. See you in the future (February?)."

Dear Mátyás,

The first night we were in Mile, I was tipsy. We were in the hotel room in the dark talking about whether or not we'll stay friends and you said, "Maybe we can make it."

After you left the package, at first I felt upset: about the things you said and about you feeling bad. My girlfriend doesn't hate you. When you left the package she said, "go find Mátyás and make sure he's okay." At this point I wasn't really thinking about the thing you said in the note, I was just worried that you were freaking out. Later I thought about the note. I'm not interpreting when I say phrases like "you are the center of my past which I must abandon. See you in the future (February?)" mean you don't want to see me for the rest of my stay in Kunming (because I'm leaving at the end

of January). It generally hurts when someone you consider a "true"
friend says they're abandoning you without giving any reason.
That night I went to shaokao *with Jumyung and she asked me to*
go to the Uprock Christmas party where you were, but you ignored
me when I got there. What frustrated me was that you knew you
hurt me and you didn't do anything, didn't say anything, didn't
seem to care, even ignored me. I really didn't want to be your
friend anymore. I wondered if we were ever friends at all.

But something happened these last few days. My mood changed.
I felt happy and because I felt happy, I forgot why we weren't talking
in the first place, forgot why I wanted to stop being your friend.

Mátyás, you don't have to say or do anything and I'd still be
willing to be your friend. Maybe that's how you know I've truly
accepted you for who you are. But that doesn't mean that the things
you do sometimes won't hurt me. Even when I know they shouldn't,
they still do. It's hard, but I guess it means that there's something in our
friendship that makes it worth with all the bad feelings. There is
something that makes it worth to stay friends.

ROUND 3

You didn't feel like doing anything but then Jumyung called and was
saying that she's your true friend, asked you to come down and you did.
She told you to go to the club and you went with your girlfriend. You
got drunk and laughed and danced and cried like crazy. Jumyung was
there hugging you, wiping your tears, pulling you onto the dance floor
and a Korean boy was giving you tissues, saying, *Cheer up! There are
many boys out there*, and you kept saying, *That's REALLY not my problem!*

You were crying while dancing, your eyes closed and you said, *I
want to go back to America. This isn't even my real life.*

You loved to see her dance. You loved to see her happy. Something about her hugs fixes everything. You were feeling so bad. You kept thinking, *I want to go home, to get away from these people who don't give a shit.* You just wanted to be home.

At the club you were lying on the couch with your face in your hands, crying, and your girlfriend was telling you to get up and you just kept saying no. He was at the club, waiting for you to talk to him but you wouldn't. No, you are tired of being the one to resolve everything. You are so worn down by these people and for your own sake you just can't do it anymore. You just can't do it. In a box he left at your door were your zine and letters.

You lost your best friend in Kunming on Christmas Eve and by the time you went to the party it was already Christmas.

Something happened at the club. Maybe it was Jumyung. She was glowing and you were dream-dancing, throwing your head around and getting so lost in it. Daft Punk's "One More Time" came on and you started to cry because it sounded so good and everyone was in it. A thought from an outside voice came to you, *Nothing can hurt you if you don't let it.* And like that, the hurt went away and for the rest of the night you let yourself get lost in the music, gave yourself over to it completely. Before you left she touched your face and kissed you on the lips for the first time.

ROUND 4
Some days it is the sun that sneaks out from behind the clouds, warming your cold face, and you stand on the corner, touching a tree with your head to the clouds. At this moment it is the sun that gives

your life meaning and you stay until it leaves and you are ready. You walk down the busy street with your headphones on, watching all those faces and invisible thoughts that fill up—what space?—some other place, the place where thoughts exist apart from us, playing shuffleboard and retiring in the sun. Yeah, the birds were dancing to your music so high in the sky. They looked so beautiful: two separate formations mingling like lovers, contracting expanding falling lifting winding tumbling. You stood there, amazed, remembering your solitary walks around Cuihu Park, how deeply you felt everything, when you realized, *This is a magical place*, and saw all the life existing in it. It was on those walks alone that you wondered how you could ever leave this place, could ever go home.

As you are walking up to Cuihu Park you see two little girls in brightly colored clothing holding hands and strutting gleefully toward the brightly colored animal rides. You know the little things will leave their mark—a different way of living, existing, seeing. And the people? You don't know what will slowly become of them in your mind. Wait it out and you will be free. I promise. Your strength will return to you over and over. There will be moments when you feel weak, but there will also be days when the sun steadies your stride and you will stand up straight and thankful. There is so much love waiting for you as soon as you are ready to receive it. Go home. Every day you are more ready to go home.

Letters

In China I feel so strongly that I am a product of language, history, culture, and all these forces outside me. In a café a guy mistakes me for pure Shanghainese. I tell him I'm not Shanghainese, but my dad's *jia xiang* ("native" or "homeland") is Hangzhou, only a couple hours from Shanghai. Then while talking to some old British guy who refers to me as an "ABC" (American-Born Chinese), he interrupts and says I'm not a REAL ABC. Yesterday, while driving through the Yunnan countryside, I saw tombs tucked away in mountains and in fields. Generations and generations of families that have lived and farmed on these lands. They must feel so connected … to these people, their family, to this place … but maybe that's stifling? The villages look like the village I visited when I was seventeen and didn't know how to speak much Chinese or know much at all about my family or this place, but that's when I became ready to learn, maybe. I remembered a photograph next to the tomb with all the names of my dad's family inscribed on it. In the picture, on one side of the tomb was my dad's extended family, farmers who still live on the same lands, and on the other side was my dad, me, and my dad's cousin, who left the village and became head surgeon of a big hospital in Hangzhou. The placement of the people seemed to represent some fundamental divide, between the rooted and uprooted, those who left, received an education, and learned a new way of living and those who stayed and remained rooted. We are blood, but what does that mean? It was hard to feel a connection to the place or the people because I have no memory of ever belonging to it. My Hungarian friend Mátyás believes in the history of places, in the memory of language and families—he feels such a strong connection to it all. Can it be erased—this memory that runs so deep? Can it be forgotten or does it leave something on you somewhere? My dad has never known his *jia xiang*. He was born during the Civil War to a military father and they moved to Guilin and that's where he was born. After the KMT lost the war, they retreated to Taiwan with the other nationalist supporters. It's strange to think about, this history of displacement.

家乡 jiā xiāng
是 什么？
What is home?

We are blood.
What does it mean to
be displaced from your blood?
I have no memory of
belonging. Can you still feel
a connection to a place &
people you have never known?
even if you are made from the
same blood? History & language doe
to us.

When my family was visiting my older brother in prison, fifteen minutes before we had to leave, my older brother asked my dad if Grandpa had any last words before he died. This is the part that really killed me—I can't think of it without crying. My dad started to tell us about some of the things Grandpa said before he died. He told us a story about our grandpa. When he was a little kid, he was enrolled in the most prestigious middle school in his area. One day he was caught gambling and was kicked out of the school. His oldest brother, a respected member of the army, had to go pick him up because he was the closest family member to the school. When his brother got there, he was furious—he yelled at my grandpa the whole way home, told him that he shamed their family. My grandpa was terrified of how his parents would react. When he finally got home his mom didn't yell at him, she hugged him. She wasn't angry. She told my grandpa's older brother, "Don't yell at him. He's just a kid. People make mistakes. It's no big deal." She gave him a second chance. She forgave him. My dad was crying as he was telling this story. I don't know if I've ever seen my dad cry before. You can't imagine the look on my dad's face as he cried and said, "She gave him a second chance. She didn't yell. She hugged him. People deserve second chances."

* * *

When I was at a café there was an older white guy with a younger Chinese guy. They were on a trip biking around China and the older man was giving the young guy advice about life and telling him about his past and his mistakes. He told the younger guy about a woman he was with for eleven years and how she was a good person, but they tortured each other emotionally. They were trapped, "caught." He said the only way he could get away was to physically leave, but she followed him to the airport. The older guy told the younger guy that life is a challenge, and to think about "who you are, what you want, and if you're really in love."

* * *

I was thinking of so many people. Like the face of a woman—my cousin's mother. She would never talk and her face was always so blank. I remember watching her sit on the couch with her hands crossed, quietly staring off into space. One day I asked my aunt where her husband was, because I remember seeing him the last time I was in Beijing. My aunt said that one day he just never came home. I said I didn't understand. Where did he go? My aunt said, "What don't you understand? One day he just never came back."

On New Years

Well, the year is over. I'm a little late on the reflection but forgive me; I took a final, left for Dali on New Year's Day, came back to Kunming the other day and immediately took two more finals. Last year. Last year. It's starting to come back to me. It feels like ten years. And mostly I can only think of my time here in China. Yeah, I remember when I would see Jumyung and go to the Korean café every day but now when I go there all the waitresses say, "*Hao jiu bu jian le*. Haven't seen you in a long time, *zuijin ni kan jian Jumyung le meiyou*?" *Mei kanjian*. Laoban's hair is so long now, and he doesn't talk to Jumyung anymore. It wasn't long ago that I was hanging out with Mark and his "wife" Cierra, and now he's dating Jumyung. Something about being here makes your hair grow faster, your friendships shorter and after the crying-ihateyous-die-fuckoffs and cryptic but malevolent notes, I pulled Mátyás to the staircase on New Year's at the party and said, while drunk and laughing, "Can we please just be friends without the drama?" and shook his hand and left.

I don't have any grandiose resolutions or any grasp of what happened this last year.

On Leaving, & Family

You already feel Kunming receding in your mind—a train arriving in rewind. He said we can't think of everything at once and you told him that you don't forget. But the truth is you can only see what's right in front of you. Kunming's a beautiful dead tree you pass while looking out a bus window on a cloudy day, yelling to your friend, "Did you see that?" She'll look until it sinks into whiteness. Everywhere, some new thing to turn your attention toward: a herd of oxen crossing a dirt road, or the bad English translation on the back of a package of raisins.

At 4:00 a.m. you sat staring at the dark and empty kitchen, wondering how you got here, how what happened could have happened. You thought you'd make a clean break from Kunming. The days leading up to your departure didn't leave much time for thought. You thought you'd make a clean break until you visited your aunt for the last time—the day before you left Kunming—and she broke down crying and gave you a speech about how you're the last hope for your family, how you have to go make something of yourself, have to do it for your dad, because no one else in your family will. No, you can't let your dad die disappointed, wondering where his life went wrong, how he could have raised such idiotic children. Never had you been so aware of the weight of being a daughter, of being somebody's child, of existing as part of a family, and all the responsibility that comes with that. And you knew at that moment that no matter how much you wanted to, you would never be able to exist apart from everyone else. You thought it was your right to choose isolation. You thought there was such thing as a decision that didn't implicate someone else, and you thought it was your right to fuck up, fail, and destroy yourself. You want to say, *I didn't ask to be born into a family, I didn't ask you to sacrifice everything,* to be given everything. Your aunt reminds you of your familial debts, how little you've made up at this point. She tells you to go home and make something of yourself.

You thought you'd make a clean break from Kunming but you couldn't walk away from your aunt's apartment feeling nothing, down the still and silent hallway with the lights that turned on when you coughed or wore heels, or while waiting at the bus stop you waited at every day for months, the route you knew by heart, passing the secondhand market that will soon be destroyed. You couldn't not feel anything saying goodbye to Yang Yang, your housemate, at 6:55 a.m., right before catching a taxi to the airport. Or at the Speakeasy Bar the night before your last full day in Kunming. Jumyung came. She asked you what you wanted for your birthday and you said, Nothing. She said, "How about a kiss?" And put her cold hands on your flushed, hot face, and gave you a peck on the lips. You couldn't not feel anything looking at the back of her head. Something so lovely about her sloppily tied back hair. Or when she bent down to tie her shoes—how moving it was. Shoes come untied. You looked at your shoes. Dirty and loose black boots. All this time you blamed her for the estrangement between you two. But maybe it was you? She wanted you to need her but in the end, you didn't. You had other friends. She didn't want to share you with others and you heard it in the bitterness of her voice when she said, "So I guess the Hungarian guy Mátyás is your new best friend now?" The truth is, it was always this way. Only you two alone together or nothing at all, but there are others in the world. You both hated to be around each other when there were others around and she complained that the others didn't understand her unusual blend of Chinese and English—"Jumyung Hua," you called it. It was partly you. You chose others over her because it was impossible for it to be just you two.

The truth is, these memories are a dragonfly you see on the ground that you know will die soon. Strained and slow movements, a struggling pulse. You'll pass it the next day, in the same place, stiff and lifeless. And the next day? It'll be gone. Eaten or swept away by the rain or mysteriously disintegrated. And all the days after that you won't even notice, won't even look down. Only ahead. And sometimes you'll feel like something is missing, something beneath your awareness.

Dreaming of Jumyung

In your dream you were dancing together and a man came. He was her fiancé. You two were having so much fun but the air between you changed as soon as he arrived. How did you end up naked? It was raining. You two were wet and sitting in the backseat of a car at night. She told you she never got to say goodbye and you started crying. Your real tears woke you up right before she said goodbye. You were so close. You woke up feeling like shit, your face wet and wishing you could have continued the dream, if only for a few minutes, to get the goodbye that you so badly wanted.

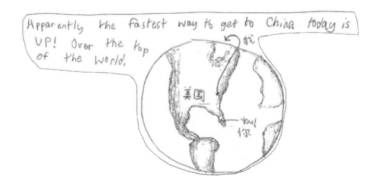

Apparently the fastest way to get to China today is UP! Over the top of the world.

(2008–9)

the adventures of

LONEBERRY

The Adventures of Loneberry

These are excerpts from The Adventures of Loneberry, *a zine I wrote compiling travel stories from the summer between my junior and senior years of college. I did not yet have a smartphone, nor did I carry a map. Are such experiences of lostness even possible today?*

This zine is about being a little person in the world and feeling immense. Part tales of wild journeys, part critical reflections on being a queer, mixed-race woman and lone traveler. It's about crushes. And letters. And shitting on the idea that adventure is a white-boy thing.

Starting at the End ...

Your summer's over. Killed off early but grandly—in Baltimore, of course, for the third time in one summer.

Where ya been?? In no particular order:
Baltimore (three times), New Orleans, Boston, Philly (two times), Colorado Springs, Denver, Halifax (Nova Scotia, Canada), Cape Breton Island (Nova Scotia), various places around New Brunswick (Canada ... Bay of Fundy), Pittsburgh (two times), Portland (Maine), somewhere in Jersey at Joe's mom's house, Bar Harbor and Acadia National Park (Maine), Chicago, Baton Rouge, Dallas. And all the random small towns with parking lots and shacks and fields I slept in. Alone or with Joe.

Sitting on my bucket at sunset after arriving to Baltimore, I am waiting for L., my crush, to pick me up. Everyone said I'd be stupid not to go back and I started to get excited thinking about them. I was afraid. Afraid of killing the magic by really Being There in the flesh and talking, and afraid of how they'll feel as more is revealed. I'm strange. Would almost rather walk away rather than Make Things Happen. Leave and leave it unrealized and tragically missed.

But I went back. And I'm glad I did. I sat on my bucket making up songs about how I never mean it when I say goodbye to Baltimore because I'm always coming back. Sang to myself and watched the leaves shake against the dusk sky. Talked with an older Black woman with long dreads and a lovely smile. L. rolled up and, to my surprise, was with Carrot, whom I met in Pittsburgh. We passed a tree with branches curved in the strangest way, like giant fingers ready to cradle a body, and I imagined it was me wrapped in the branches of the tree, feeling so safe and comfortable, every arrival followed by so much relief. Listen: I know it's wrong to feel this way. Like the world has got yr back—the feeling epitomized by the image of the tree that holds you. There were moments when it all seemed to be falling apart, moments when I thought I'd never get there and the destination only seemed to recede with time and movement—five rides and twenty-six hours of hell hitching from Pittsburgh to Philly, getting dropped off in Jersey only to discover the Delaware River was blocking my passage. I made a "Philly" sign with spit and watercolors on notebook paper and rolled into town before the APOC (Anarchist People of Color) conference even started. Made friends with enemies who were never really enemies and watched Rugrats with a militant. My last night in Philly was so great, full of so much laughter and munching on cookie dough and exchanging stories.

Robin was sweet, even made me a snack bag (including an avocado, my favorite) for the ride to Bmore.

Back in Baltimore. But this time rolling mostly with the queers and nonbinary folk. I danced wildly with energetic cuties. Rode through town at night lying down with Carrot in the bed of L.'s turquoise truck, watching the world zip by from a different angle, the trees like clouds the tops of buildings like waves and the air so cool. Sneaked into a pool at night. Surfed on lifeguard floaties, laughed, swam and dove for things with Willie, exchanged stories of foreign loves with Tina, dumpstered more food than could possibly be consumed (ate straight out of the $1,000-cake dumpster), and stayed up all night with L., lying outside on a bed of pillows and cushions while cuddling, kissing, and talking until daylight. Nearly cried when I left, sat on my bucket at a bus stop thinking about how at the beginning of the summer I never could have imagined what was to happen, whom I was to meet, or even where I would go. Nothing went even close to plan, and in many ways I'm glad it didn't, glad it was always open, glad to leave and go back and to meet new people and see it a different way every time I went back. I sold my bike for sixty dollars and bought a sixty-dollar plane ticket home to Florida.

Heaven sent rain. If heaven sends rain, go back. I was loading my stuff onto my bicycle and he said, "I remember this scene."

* * *

It was the last night before leaving for home. It was the night of the meteor shower. I remember where I was a year ago. The night of my leaving-the-country party, before moving to China. I was also

(65)

swimming, but in a glowing ocean. I jump-roped on the shore, got tossed by the waves, and lay in the sand watching the meteor shower. She was holding the back of the car riding her skateboard. Someone said it was like *Back to the Future* and I thought, *We're always moving into the future*. And you can't imagine what that future will look like, not even its outline.

Characteristics of Naive Superman Syndrome

(Often experienced alone in the middle of the night after days of not sleeping):

—disregard for limitation
—confidence in one's ideas
—arrogance/refusal to compromise
—possibility and reality as one
—boundless energy/mania
—recklessness
—visions merge with reality
—don't give a fuck about anything, especially consequence; could die and wouldn't care
—talking to strangers becomes easy
—unfounded glee
—talking real fast, saying nonsensical shit
——deterioration of social filters

* * *

People. The different ways they live. A man who sleeps in his car. The noise-musician friend who sleeps in a closet and works at a boot shop and as an oyster fisherman in Baton Rouge. His hard exterior but the softness of the things he notices—a beautiful flowering tree, a ladybug, and a man looking for a lost dog. The engineer who hosts strangers.

I want my mind to buzz so much I don't realize I'm bleeding. I never wanna feel too tired. So many ideas you overcome hunger. I wanna live so light I float. Never empty. Just full of something lighter. Everyone is simpler. I should be simpler. What do I need? *Nothing*.

On Living a Poetic Existence

Creativity as a reflex, like a kid who marks the page without thinking. I was coloring like this in Colorado, and I drew a picture of a green crayon that was drawing a red line and just could not stop laughing. Paul says, *You were in a funny mood last night*—I apologized for acting crazy.

That night. I was making strokes of color large and unafraid. A loose tongue. New friends. Received a wonderful painting as a gift. Warm colors. Paul knew everything I needed. Tea to warm the cold hands, goji berries and ice cream to quell the sweet tooth, watercolor paints to cure the whiteness of the page. I asked them all their first and last dreams and Paul spoke of vast landscapes and glaciers and mansions and a friend who shares my last name. How vivid the dream was. After waking he played music for hours and it was like continuing the dream. Kate wanted intense red on her page and I drew a picture of the King of Dreams. He was crying and his crown was a fence but he'll be okay.

Maybe at one time I thought a poetic existence would entail trying to figure out what excites me, and then doing that as much as possible. But now I know it's about totally transforming my vision so that there is color between the space between home and leaving, color everywhere, magic as a default. I don't need to be entertained, don't need significant events to trigger excitement because I am learning to be excited by it all, really loving such little things.

Hard Times

So, how much backstory do you want?

I am on day three of no sleep. Yesterday was hard and beautiful.

Pittsburgh was full of weird coincidences, meeting Moxie—an anarchist hacker whom I've been internet friends with for six years—at a bike-shop party. Crashed at his place, went to the shooting range, and picked/sorted/blanched mustard greens for storage for an anarchist convergence. More backstory: before leaving Florida I was looking for literature to inspire me. I went to the New College infoshop to browse the zines and found only one that looked good to me, titled *One Way Ticket*. I brought it with me and it was the first thing I read while on the road. As I was talking to Moxie's roommate Julian, I realized that he was the author of the zine I had brought with me.

I ate a huge breakfast at Moxie's and took off on my bike out of Pittsburgh. It was hot, hilly as fuck, and the road sucked (no shoulder and tons of cars), but I covered thirty miles quickly. Then I turned down a road that I was sure I was supposed to turn down but it was unmarked and I rode a ways down it only to realize later I was on the wrong road and that the road led back to the road I was on but was closed because a bridge had been destroyed in a flood (oh, the beauty of not having a map). I had no other choice but to go backward … completely uphill … and probably wasted well over an hour. I rode more until I got to a place where I literally could not ride because there was so much traffic and no shoulder. I then hitched a ride with a guy (a construction supervisor maybe in his late thirties) who took me over a brutal mountain. He was lovely and we talked excitedly about writing, learning, traveling, life, and not compromising. I told him stories and he said, "I'm so jealous!" and told me about the screenplay he was working on.

I then started biking more, but ended up pushing my bike up a mountain for a couple hours. I stopped in a beautiful field to eat and walked my bike up more and found a dilapidated brick shack to sleep in near the top of the mountain. I read, wrote, and listened. When I realized I had lost my sleeping pills, I got high but was still unable to sleep. Then I developed this incredible and all-consuming thirst and started to get nervous because I was almost out of water.

When the birds started chirping as day was dawning, I packed up and left the shack on no sleep, making my way farther up the mountain. I was totally overjoyed when I found a clean stream of water near the top but when I was at the top, it looked like I was increasingly in the middle of nowhere. I started worrying that I was on the wrong road and was afraid to coast down because I was not confident that it was the right way. So I biked all the way back to the town I had been dropped off at the day before. I was reluctant to because if it turned out I was on the right road, I would have to spend a couple hours going back up the mountain. I coasted down and found a coffee shop and it turned out I was on the right road. But I decided to go to the library to change my route because I wanted to hitch out of the mountains. I wrote four letters to friends and read my friend Jimmy's poem about insanity. I made a fourteen-mile route to the closest interstate that led to Baltimore. The bike ride to the interstate was brutal as hell—hot and uphill. Some guy offered me a ride which I accepted even though it was pointless because I was only three-quarters of a mile from the interstate. The guy was really nice, offered me food and money and a place to sleep if I didn't get a ride. Interstate 70/76 turned out to be a toll road, which meant I couldn't get anywhere close to the on-ramp. This exit was also in the middle of nowhere and there were only one to two cars getting on every ten minutes. A creepy white guy kept coming to the gas station I was sitting at to bother me and ask me unsettling questions. I kept switching spots, moved between gas stations, and tried to get as close to the toll booths as I could without being seen. I knew there was no way I would get a ride so I tried to find a place to sneak onto the highway. I took all my gear up a steep gravel incline with a tall fence on top and tossed all my gear over the fence, dragged my bike up the incline and tossed that over (I'm terribly short, mind you), and got all scratched and bruised crawling under the fence. I made a colorful sign with a heart smiley face and plopped my kitty-litter-bucket pannier on the shoulder, stood on it waving my pink bandana in desperation while trying to calculate how long it would be until the sun set. I got a ride in forty-five minutes and was dropped off at 11:00 p.m. fifty miles outside of Baltimore. What to do now? Go to sleep and bike there in the morning? I resolved to bike straight to Baltimore. I tried to look at a map at a gas station but the only road I could see that went to Baltimore was I-70. Biking on an interstate in the middle of the night is pretty much the most foolish thing you can do, but I was desperate to get to Baltimore. So I rode on the shoulder of the highway for a long time and got totally demoralized when it got really steep (on Mount Airy). Then a truck driver pulled over onto the shoulder, blocking me, hopped out and was touching his dick and saying creepy things; I literally had my hand on my pepper spray as I was getting out of the situation. I got off at the next exit, which was on top of the mountain, and ate tons of food and decided to keep going. As I was coasting downhill, I hit a huge pothole and got a flat. Demoralized again, in total darkness, thirty miles from Baltimore, no place to sleep and just steep slopes beside the interstate. I called my old friend Monica, whom I haven't seen in years, and told her about my situation (what a random call to receive at 2:00 a.m.), but her friend with a car was sleeping and so could not help. I called Abe in Denver because I was lonely. He was thinking I was down and giving up. I laughed and said no way, that it was totally cool, that challenges can even be exciting.

I thought the last exit I had gotten off at was close but later realized it only seemed close because I was coasting downhill at a rapid speed. So I spent a long time pushing my bike back up the mountain to the exit to fix my flat outside a gas station because it had enough light for me to disassemble my bike. I tuned my bike up and was feeling good because it was running way smoother. I resolved to keep going even though I told myself I would stop, sleep, fix my bike, and continue in the morning. So I kept going, feeling giddy and triumphant as I was going downhill, but I had a feeling that something else would happen and right then I was pulled over by a cop. He just checked me for warrants and gave me a new route. The new road—my god, it was beautiful. Just trees and fields and farms and not a single car. I watched the fireflies twinkling in the crops, the stars above; I was gobsmacked by the surrealness of the day. Even the hills seemed bearable, although there were a couple that were so steep I had to walk my bicycle up them. At 5: a.m. when I was ten or so miles from Baltimore, a chubby, single father, eccentric newspaper delivery man with a mustache stopped and offered to give me a ride to Baltimore. I was thinking his company would be good, as I was extremely sleep-deprived, so I accepted. When I climbed into his van, he threw a newspaper in my lap and there it was on the front page: Michael Jackson was dead. I ended up getting stuck with the guy for five hours, doing all his errands with him. Even after his errands he took me places (like his office) and drove around town. I realized that he was probably pretty lonely and just wanted the company. It was fine, but I was delirious and eager to get to my friend's place. He dropped me off in front of Rose and Monica's warehouse at 10:00 a.m. It's been years since I've seen both of them, but things have been so great here. Monica asked me where I was coming from and as I told her about my travels she was like, "Oh yeah, I've met Moxie too. He inspired me to do hat band!" ("Hat band" is a game where you create a band by picking names out of a hat.) Although I haven't talked to Monica since high school, we still talk in the same inspired, excited way: bouncing ideas and plans off each other, all energy, positivity, creativity, and ambition. Seeing Rose has been good, too. And I really dig the Copycat Warehouse they live in. I am glad to be in Baltimore with old friends who went different ways but moved in similar directions on their respective paths.

Even when things felt like they couldn't get any worse, I still felt a sense of ecstatic joy, in love with being outside and feeling the world. Not annoyed or worried. I know it will all turn out but don't care if it doesn't.

Here's to life and not being defeated by defeat—

* * *

Lynzy, an ole fren, rolled into Baltimore the other day. We had a shit-on-reality moment (standard fare with Lynzy) which consisted of dancing to no music and screamin' chantin' waxing poetic and singing in the streets late at night—"primal-rage theater," we called it. In the streets we yelled, "WELCOME TO MY THEATER, MY PRIMAL RAGE THEATER!" A woman came up and said, "I wanna dance with you," and we replied, "Coooome dance." After introducing ourselves later I realized she's the partner of the woman I'm hitching with to Pittsburgh.

I cuddled and spent the night with my Baltimore crush. It was a sweet night, full of dancing, a drag show, a radical puppet show, and late-into-the-night talking with L.'s head on my lap. I said, "Why are you smiling???" and L. thought I said, "You smell," and then asked why I was smiling. I said, "Because I'm happy!" But the exact thought that was in my head at that moment was, "I have led a good life." I'm always thinking this line, as if I'm at the end of my life, and feel as though it's been a great time. I told this to Mike, that I know that there were so many average moments between rapturous and magical ones. I know this but I still remember everything like it was always wonderful.

L. said other cute things, too. Like, "Can I hold your far-away hand?" and "Are you comfortable being the little spoon?" and "What's the biggest bug you've seen?" and "Can you sing me the lullaby you wrote?" and "Fuck offff!" to a guy who yelled "You have nice legs" as I was bicycling in a dress. I thought it was magical but maybe it was just me, livin' in my magic, soul always cartwheeling and melting into bliss. I'm not afraid of leaving. It doesn't make it any less meaningful.

* * *

I've spent the last couple of months on road trips with friends, hitchhiking, and bicycling around the East Coast and Canada. My bike got stolen the other day. I cried for the first time in seven months (first time for feeling bad, at least) because I was having an alienation attack, and then drama at the CrimethInc. Convergence, more freaking out but finding myself brought closer to some people through the craziness. No journey is complete without its moments of defeat, and I've had my share: getting dropped off in the middle of the night in the pitch-black pouring rain on the highway with no map and over thirty miles away from my destination. Flat tires when so close. Speedy cars that will spray you with mud but won't pick you up. The pale-faced woman at the gas station who is more concerned about my fate than I am. Ice cream breakfast with Cindy and sleeplessness. Truckers who love their little daughters who turn butterfly gardens into memorial gardens for fireflies and other little dead things. Songs and zines from new friends. I kissed my crush in front of everyone, ran around in a fountain in the rain and felt a sisterly affection for a certain tall statuesque boy who can enchant you with his stare. I don't know whether all this adds up to *good* or *bad* and I'm not sure it matters.

Divine Lorraine

On some days Philly starts to resemble the postapocalyptic landscapes of your nightmares—trash lines the bottoms of mangled metal fences, buildings are blown out and abandoned. This is why Joe loves Philly, loves to bike around busy streets pulling out the side-view mirrors of cars and standing outside majestic, half-crumbled buildings, looking up, strategizing ways of getting in. We break into the Divine Lorraine, an abandoned hotel, with his nerdy-nervous but open and willing friend Brenden. The three of us wander the building, making our way to the top where there is an incredible view of the entire city. We watch the sky turn grey and angry and when we get out the rain has already begun to fall. The wind whips the trash and debris around, and we speed through the streets on bicycle, trying to find shelter, feeling at the end of the world.

Tumbling

All the dead trees on the shore of Cape Breton look like bone
Where do the stoned-out pebbles come from?
All the moose out on the road don't know what's going on
As I tumble down the trail into Meat Cove

There's nothing on this road that winds through the mountainous coastline of Cape Breton, Nova Scotia. We feel far from humanity. We're always sleeping outside retro gas stations, waiting until morning, fearing the stretches of nothingness that threaten to leave us stranded. When we come upon a small coffeehouse, we're gleeful and eager to satiate our newly procured addiction. One Canadian buck for a bottomless cup of bitter goodness. I get mine filled four times and am a jittery mess, stumbling around in cowboy boots, thoughts firing and unable to focus on anything. Joe and I decide to catch a river trail to the shore. Coffee makes me unaware of my surroundings but frenzied with thoughts—I literally tumble onto the trail to Meat Cove, down wooden steps and into rocks. I get up, scraped, bruised, and laughing so hard. The fall has interrupted my coffee-induced mania, jolted me out of my thoughts and into the world.

* * *

My name is.
It doesn't matter what my name is.
My name is and I believe in magic.

Where did this magic come from?

The way my brain was wired? Or the things I have sucked up livin', the sun's rays which are above all Magic, above all Life epitomized.

Doctors Psychiatrists Teachers Policemen Lawyers will all try to drag your ass back to earth, to sedate your delirium, but you gotta resist the pull of administrators and their senators. Ask yourself, *Do you like the way it means so much?* And if your answer is yes, politely refuse their offerings of anchors and maps.

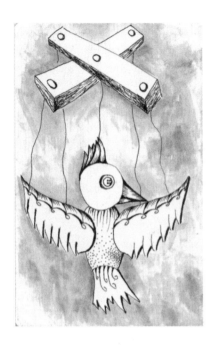

Letters

I'm in Halifax, Nova Scotia, Canada. Tonight I went to the casino here to write because I find it to be such a strange and lonely place. Plus, they have unlimited free soda and coffee because they're trying to keep people caffeinated so they stay awake and gamble. I got 2 sodas and 2 coffees, so I was super hyped on caffeine and hungry as hell. Broke, I wandered the streets with a sign that said "wanna buy me a meal in exchange for conversation and stories?" I was instantly stopped by the Halifax Dance Man—a rambunctious and sleazy fast-talking old man (YouTube famous, too) who was rolling with his "lower deck crew." It consisted of his daughter, a motorcyclist, and a caricature artist. They bought me food and were a real strange bunch. Even tried to hook me up with the 40-something-year-old biker. There was a surreal moment when a random Christian woman came up to the daughter, who always looked like she was about to cry, and said she was under God's wing, and disappeared into the night. I got a random email tonight from a stranger who said he read my zine in Alabama, of all places! I have no idea how it got there. Some traveler kids in Baltimore said they saw my zines all over the South and I didn't believe them because I only print a few copies and give them to hardly anyone. The magic is hitting me hard lately and I'm drawing and writing inspired letters to friends and new crushes and singing the songs of my friends with friends biking through the thickest fog. I'll always remember the tips you gave me about talking to strangers. Sending magic yr wayyyy.

* * *

It's really funny how fast you can get to know a town. Joe and I were only in Halifax, Nova Scotia, for three or four days and we already had a group of friends (he was into hanging with the fixed-gear-bike polo boys, I liked the queer girls who made zines), activities (burrito bike, brunch at the zine library, loitering/writing at the casino where there's free coffee/soda), etc. We joked that all we needed were girl-friends in town to be really established. The burrito-bike pop-up kitchen these kids did was pretty awesome ... every Saturday night a bunch of friends get together and make veggie and vegan burritos and deliver them on bicycle. They post flyers around town and actually get a ton of orders. It's like a party where you accomplish something and make money. I guess I'm back in Baltimore again because it's another town I've really broken into. I hang out at Red Emma's, a radical bookstore/café, and read and read and read and do my writings at the Mac Lab on the MICA campus and even know some good dumpsters. Last night I went alone on bike and it was a real struggle to haul a giant box back on my bike rack. I've got some good friends here and spend a lot of time at the Copycat, the warehouse they live at. They have a big theater/stage here and have touring and local acts perform. The other day over 160 kids showed up for an event, and apparently these projects are making pretty good money to go toward rent. I think I'll start heading south after Pittsburgh. Lots of people have good ideas about how to live. I wanna walk all the way around the coast of Sicily when I graduate.

* * *

Well, you should be glad we left when we did. We seem to be dragging clouds fat with rain with us wherever we land. I opened this notebook and out rushed the smell of sage; before I left your house I pocketed the piece I had been fiddling with, stolen pieces of my last evening in Denver, will always remember the warmth and tongue-tickle of your spiced drinks. I walked the mile-long route back to the R & R house at sunrise, so quiet and calm, the beauty of little moments firing and I could hardly believe *this life is real.* That day, the ride to Chicago—I had so much time to contemplate the recent past, thought mainly about the people in Denver, drove through the Nebraskan plains listening to Paper Bird, drifted in and out of sleep in the back and wrote very few words, didn't know what to say but felt okay about saying little about these resonant moments. I did think that if I die, this life would have been a good life. Already! Yeah, this is real. We wake up to gospel singers and hear our friends' songs in living rooms late at night. And maybe I am guilty of romanticization, but I say, fuck it. Our lives are grandiose. I am still so delighted to see color—yolk-colored shades of turmeric; to taste—coughing happily on cayenne; and to remember (life is ... struggling to get yr head through a sweater ... hand me a bigger sweater!).

And after all my harping, you somehow forgot to give me yr cd!

Anyway, I hope you are having a good day. Listen to yr body, and be true to yourself [even if that truth is an unfinished sentence; an unclosed bracket

* * *

Dear Joe,

Since we parted I've been thinking about you often: the time we spent together, how strange it is to look back on the recent past. I am in my room alone, my first full day back at my house, and literally hours away from the end of summer. My girlfriend is spending the night at her new girlfriend's house and although I am alone at least I have the space to say goodbye to this summer, to think it over and write you this letter. Because these last few months I've been moving so fast that I've barely had time to think, and when there is the space to think I can only catch up on so much, only process so much. So much has slipped by, reduced to a single word or phrase in my note-book. Like: *Peggy's Cove*. Sitting on those enormous rocks on the shore with you and Tobiasz in the dense fog. We all seemed in a strange mood, were talking about metaphysical topics so openly, like a dream, and I was awestruck by your description of the place you walk to in your mind. I remember looking into the crystalline water, the seaweed swaying, the atmosphere around us white, and my senses so alive.

Reduced to: *Skyline Trail*. It was raining so hard, was so cold and windy. We couldn't see anything but we walked out on the trail anyway, kept going because we expected to see something spectacular behind every corner, were waiting for the moose because we were following the fresh tracks. It was miserable but we joked about our stupidity through it all; I didn't even have a rain jacket. I remember the precise moment you said, "Let's get the fuck out of here!" and we laughed and turned around.

Phrases like: *Biking around Halifax pier at night.* It was so foggy and we were screaming Briar's songs at the top of our lungs. I think I saw two lovers but can't remember if they were only shadows or objects I thought were lovers from a distance because that's what I wanted to see.

Words like: *Rainbows.* Fuck, they looked so close! And they were everywhere.

Roméo LeBlanc is dead. It echoed on the radio as we drove through the small town where his funeral was being held.

Last supper. We were hell-bent on spending as little money as possible, but it felt great to let go and eat delicious Ethiopian food for our last moments together—felt great even though I ended up overdrawing my bank account. We talked about how we never stopped talking to each other the whole time, how much we love growing and changing and you said you want to achieve old-man-level awareness when you're 30, and to keep moving from there. I was impressed by your openness, the way you learn from everything and everyone.

Demystification. I learned how to drive and saw my first moose. I think we saw five.

Fundy. The most variable tide in the world. I overheard a little kid say "fundy undies" and laughed to myself.

This is the first time I'm really thinking of all these things. Remembering all the places you skipped stones, all the places we slept outside. Most of all I remember the first night we crossed the border, how they confiscated my pepper spray—you said I wouldn't need it in Canada anyway. We slept in that clearing with the wild-flowers, in a little tent, and you said we were good at being friends.

If I were to describe to you what happened after we parted ways, I could fill a thousand pages. I fell madly in love with the specialness of more people than I can count, stayed in places long enough to really feel the transformation of strangers into unique persons—their mannerisms and perspectives—and left feeling depressed by the fleetingness of these connections. I jokingly called you a "cuddle whore" and ended up cuddling four people after we parted ways, kissing one and going back to find the Big Crush one last time. I was picked up by truckers who loved their daughters, was bought dinner, was harassed for hand jobs, was given a knife, was hassled by so many police officers and hauled off the road by a giant yellow emergency highway-clean-up vehicle driven by a sleep-deprived man who was going to learn the sex of his unborn child at 1:00 p.m. that day. And I rode my bike in the rain through the whole night and felt so isolated and alone that I wanted to stop at every desolate gas station that appeared along the long stretches of nothingness. The shoulder of the road ended, I pushed my bike up a mountain through thick brush nearly as tall as me and emerged with an unpatchable flat tire, sat in front of a mechanic shop at sunrise with my disassembled bike and wet gear scattered around me as I stared off delirious, sleep-deprived, and hungry beyond imagination. The owner eventually arrived to open the shop and bought me food from a vending machine even though I told him I could pay for it myself.

I am looking at the little phrases in my notebook, the unfinished thoughts. Like: *Two girls wearing dresses. Old friends. One is me, and we're both riding old bicycles to the farmer's market.*

Maine. The rapture of coasting downhill on bicycle at 30 mph.

It was in Canada when I realized how far I was from suffering. In that moment. In Maine when I felt like there was so much beauty, so much stimulation, that I would erupt.

It was in Pittsburgh where I sat alone, but was surrounded by people, crying, and my friend saw my red eyes and asked, "Did you not sleep or something?" I told him I was just crying, he asked why and all I said was "Because anything I could say would be totally incomprehensible to everyone around me." And stared off silently.

It was in Baltimore where I stood surrounded by crowds of people going wild to bands and I thought about group dynamics and collective euphoria, wondered why we are sometimes outside of it, sometimes inside. I was outside looking in, but instead of feeling resentful, instead of judging their joy, I felt so happy for everyone, resolved to open myself to fun—no matter how cheap or shallow; I would deconstruct the mental barriers and dance the rest of the night.

It was in Pittsburgh when I realized that maybe I really am fundamentally a loner, because I am on a mission to feel and to not be interrupted by prattle or anything less than transcendence. It was there that everything about society and humanity felt crushing, on a mission to destroy my excitement. I'm not waiting but why does everyone seem to be waiting to feel inspired? I am not fucking waiting. It was there that I wandered alone, wondering why I feel I have lost coherence.

But it was also there that I put on red lipstick and rode through town at night feeling big and fabulous with another cool lady. It was there that I crammed into a small nook with three other people laughing uncontrollably all night, there that I played punk soccer and scored one of the four goals, there that I danced intensely inside an abandoned ice rink, there that I kissed my big summer crush for the first time and felt so embarrassed because I had just eaten a jalapeño bagel, ate the most delicious tomatoes I've ever had in my life from my friend's garden, discussed heartbreak with someone over coffee and fell for the stare and ambition of a friend, the uncontrollable laughter of another, the hand gestures and humbleness of yet another, and scribbled "I am alive because I know how to laugh" on a table.

So. This is my outro. Thanks for being a part of it. Tomorrow things will be different. Tonight I stay awake remembering.

(2009)

On Being Hard Femme

This piece originally appeared as a limited-edition handmade zine.

Here's a little zine that poured out of me after an impromptu "ladies brunch" made with dumpstered food while visiting Baltimore. It was sparked by the remembrance of the excitement of discovering "hard femme," and how empowering that was for me.

I first came across the term "hard femme" in a zine titled *Hard Femme Bike Tour*, which I printed from the Queer Zine Archive Project. I was getting ready to do some journeying alone on my bicycle and was looking for literature to inspire me. The term resonated with me deeply because it spoke to my confused and sometimes contradictory gender identity. On some days I even felt bad about my gender expression. I love to wear red lipstick, but don't shave my legs or armpits. I like to dress sexy, but not for men. I wear dresses, but will gleefully hop into a dumpster or crawl under a fence while sporting my finest. I'll bicycle sixty miles in four and a half hours in ninety-eight-degree weather wearing heeled boots and a knife on my belt.

Both my girlfriend and I have muddled gender identifications consisting of elements of both toughness and femininity—she's good with power tools but has long blonde wavy hair. On some days people will debate who is more femme. I get offended if people say that I am, because femme is usually associated with weakness. People will say, "You wear dresses!" But to me, that doesn't make me any less tough.

Hard femme made me realize that gender can be more fun and dynamic than that, and more open-ended than the "butch-femme" dichotomy. Not only is that dichotomy reductive, but the idea that there is even a spectrum that runs from butch to femme is false. Our presentation is not linear. We can be everything and nothing at once. We can fuck with everyone's notion of what these categories mean. And we should do it without apology!

So here's to hard femme. A dynamic merging of opposites, a new way to meddle with the categories, and, above all, a vision of how to exist in the world in a way that makes us feel confident, strong, and empowered. Because we are in control of who we are. Because identity is shifting and creative! Because it's exciting to reinvent the meaning of terms, to imagine without being what they have imagined for us. Tear it down with a smirk on yr faaaaace!
—Jackie, Baltimore 2009

What Is Hard Femme?

Not much has been written about it. Most people, even many of those who move within queer circles, are unfamiliar with the term. But that's not a bad thing! The newness of the term just means there's more room to play. Most of this zine is about what *hard femme* means to me. It sometimes means something very specific to me because it's tied so closely to my understanding of myself and my growth as a person. It might be different for you … and I hope it is!

Here's what Urban Dictionary has to say about the term:

1. hard femme
Not to be mistaken with the typical femme, the "hard femme"
describes herself as "queer," is political, looks more feminine
than masculine, and if prompted, can kick some serious ass.
She doesn't need to "wear the pants" in a relationship—the
hard femme rules with a dress. She not only despises the gender binary, she works to dismantle it.
*Misogynist Butch: "There she is! It's that femme I told you about
that tried to wear one with me!"*
*(Not necessarily misogynist) Butch #2: You should've known better.
That girl's got "hard femme" written all over her.*

For me, hard femme is about being tough, badass, strong, inde-
pendent, dirty, feminine, queer, sensitive, sexy, intellectual, playful,
thoughtful, open, positive, and uncompromising. It's about being
shy and lifting weights. It's about knowing skills and having self-
esteem. It's about feminism. Hard femme is not just a look, it's a
state of mind, a way of feeling good about your abilities, a way of
feeling good in your skin.

When I found out about "hard femme," I was thrilled. I couldn't
wait to tell people about this idea that helped make sense of my
incongruences. I couldn't wait to tell my girlfriend because she had
witnessed my strivings toward mental and physical strength and
was always telling me how well I was doing and encouraging me to
cultivate a "sexy-badass style." I'd stand in front of the mirror making
an angry "fuck off!" face while flexing my biceps and we'd laugh at
my pseudo-machismo. Angela Davis and Assata were my heroes. I

looked to them daily. I started biking long distances, running, swimming, lifting weights, and deconstructing my own mental fetters—all the things I had learned being raised as an Asian girl in this sick society, all the bullshit fed to me that was meant to break me, to make me think I was weak so I wouldn't discover my strength. One day it appeared to me. And I ran with it.

On Being Strong

Being strong is not just about physical strength. A definition of strength based merely on physical ability risks being profoundly ableist. I am still working to undo my own physical-centric ideas about the meaning of strength. But ultimately, for me becoming stronger has always been about overcoming what I perceive to be a limitation—whether self- or socially-imposed. Not believing in myself was the root of my weakness.

When I started to believe in myself, I tried to do more and more things. More and more things became demystified, fear began to melt away and I was on a roll. I felt energized, like I was really breaking out. With every little improvement, every little accomplishment, I was becoming freer. My sense of what was possible was expanding. I even learned ways to turn my failures into important lessons, learned the hard way. When I gave up on bicycling and hitchhiked past the Appalachian Mountains on my way from Pittsburgh to Baltimore, I didn't beat myself up. Biking up mountains is hard, and I laughed at myself for being so naive as to think I could bike as far through mountains as I could in flat-as-a-pancake Florida.

But becoming physically stronger was an important part of me becoming mentally stronger. Because it really proved to me that I wasn't nearly as weak as I thought I was, or that improvement was possible. I emphasized *endurance* because I've never had a car and became interested in using my body to take me places. I began bicycling long distances every day and doing lots of physical activity. I learned how to fix my bike so I wouldn't get stuck. I began to think of myself as stronger, tougher, and felt more connected to my body, rather than seeing it as something to loathe. I used to be depressed—thought of myself as weak, ugly, chubby and all that bullshit I internalized. It took a lot of work to realize it was untrue. I've still got a long way to go.

The Racialization of Femininity and Sexuality

How do people perceive me and how do I perceive myself? I just wrote about all the effort that went into viewing myself as tough and strong. But what about how others perceive me? Or how I've been told I should present myself? I'm little—under five foot two inches and small-framed. I hate being little. I'm a woman. An Asian woman. For many, Asian women represent idealized femininity—dainty, subservient, soft, cute, weak, innocent, quiet, and born to serve men.

I hate this. I used to take some of these things as a compliment until I began to realize how racialized they were. Sometimes, when people call me cute, I scream, I'M NOT FUCKING CUTE! It's not that I don't like it when people say or think I'm cute. It's a reaction against the reduction of Asians to mere empty and cute beings—superficial and devoid of depth. Mostly this reaction is born out of fucked-up experiences with Asian fetishists—those white men with "yellow fever."

Embedded in the idea of the hyperfeminine Asian woman is an assumed heterosexuality. Queerness and lesbianism are considered deviant, and heterosexuality is considered healthy and normal. Since Asian women are viewed as normal, meek conformists, Asian women are also assumed to be heterosexual. Outwardly feminine women often are read as heterosexual, so the association of Asianness with femininity adds another layer of heterosexism.

I've caught myself falling into these traps, even as a queer Asian woman. When I first met one of my best friends, who is Chinese, I was surprised to find out she was a lesbian because she seemed so conventional before I knew her. I realized later that this view was a distorted and racist way of reading people's sexuality.

For me, being hard femme is also about challenging our racialized ideas about femininity and about challenging the association of femininity with weakness. I like meeting badass dyke Asian women and reading zines and stories by femme queer Asian women writers. Like Beverly Yuen Thompson, a tattooed professor whose research on queer/bi hapa (half- or part-Asian) women taught me many lessons about how I think about myself and the complexity of identity.

I like being unconventionally femme, unconventionally Asian, unconventionally tough (none of the macho bullshit), and stirring it all up, overturning expectations while laying claim to these categories. But without allegiance. With movement.

Hard-Femme Moments

Hard femme is …

—Long hair on your head … and legs!

—Miniskirts that reveal … legs covered in bike grease! And muscular calves!

—Being told "WAAAIT, Jackie! Don't get in the dumpster! You'll get your dress dirty!" And hopping in while laughing at such a silly notion!

—Long nails that are dirty underneath

—Love to cook but hate to clean!

—Reapplying lipstick while sweatin' hard on the side of the road

—Being a woman and traveling alone

—Tossing your bike and gear over a tall fence and waving a pink bandana to catch a ride

—Understanding that being tough does not mean being negative and ditching love

—Earrings and boy haircuts

—Power tools, bruises, boots, and flower in hair

(2009)

We Are Good Enough

The following pieces are excerpts from my pamphlet series We Are Good Enough, *which had eight issues. While I was doing an art-museum internship, I used my photocopier access to print the short, anonymous pamphlets that I would then leave around town (Sarasota, FL): on café tables, tucked between newspapers, and in my college's mailroom.*

"Every Griotte Who Dies Is a Whole Library That Burns Down"

In the morning on Easter your brother calls from prison; mom brings the phone to you as you're sleeping and you have a nice, lighthearted conversation. Except you don't remember any of it, amnesia being a side effect of these sleeping pills. In the IHOP you are trying to remember. There were two things. Writing in Cuihu Park at sunset, watching the birds and people and feeling very free to just wander through the day. The other memory, blast open by a red light cross on top of a church that you drive by; it reminds you of a Christmas tree. You remember your home, waking up in the middle of the night around Christmas, the stillness and the lights when everything else was dark. There was Christmas after the trial, the verdict, Randy gone and mom too depressed to put anything out, *not this year this is just not our year.* Growing up in this house. We were such poison for each other, everything so poisonous that it began to resemble hell.

Things aren't poisonous anymore. There's this strange harmony, this acceptance of each other, this bizarre love that maybe only comes with distance. And crisis. A family drawn together by the Crisis.

* * *

Biking around, I had this gut feeling I'm going to die soon.

Death doesn't worry me. It's the process of dying. The knowing you're going to die. The tiring chase in the nightmare. The rest is like sleeping. God knows I love sleeping.

Not afraid. Not. Fear keeps us safe and alive. And yet, dead.

Movement outside in the sun. Perched on a fence by my favorite berry tree, plucking away and thinking how this is how I want to live. A backpack full of passion fruit and hearty greens, thinking how I wanna live lightly, to float rather than grind it all to shit with anxiety and unneeded possessions. I wanna exist lightly but live BIG, big in my own fucked-up way: writing free at any cost, feeling everything. She's right. I'm all extremes and no middle. All separation or obsessed, all torn between paths leading to opposite ends of the universe and wondering if it's possible to maybe just rip yourself up and be scattered because it'd be easier than making a decision and you want to be everywhere at once, to do everything, and if you could just break up like a starfish you'd get so much more done, wouldn't need to ponder what you missed today, who you didn't meet. Yous yous yous propagating yourself, a herd of identicals (ants? penguins?) marching in different directions. Everywhere, living out different destinies.

Animals, Physics, and Sports: Note to a Dead Dog

Dear Lucky,

Today you were put to sleep and it is twenty minutes before the day ends; it seems urgent to write this down now, to channel the immediacy of the moment. I would not be starting this essay about family if it weren't for your death; there just wouldn't have been any space for it in my mind.

I read recently that we need silence to hear because words cannot be constituted without gaps, without the spaces between, without the space to hear the other. Silence can pull us outside ourselves, and not-saying still speaks. At first, I didn't understand my dad's silence. I thought maybe the phone got disconnected. I didn't understand at all. I kept saying, "Hello, hello? Are you there?" And nothing. But my dad was still at the other end of the receiver. He was silent. He was there quietly listening to my bewildered hellos because he could not say, because he was trying to say that grandma's sick and you were dying and were going to be killed the next day. He never directly came out and said it, but I understood and I could not bear to put him through the saying of it. But in the empty space there was so much wordless reverberation, so much conveyed in that moment that I am now only beginning to understand it. Maybe I was too stubborn to hear it before. I walked back to the room where my partner was sleeping and held up three fingers and said that there are three things that have fundamentally shaped my father's understanding of the world and they are: animals, physics, and sports. Maybe now I would add death and history.

It sounds cheap to lay it out in a list like that. It doesn't convey the deepness of it for my dad, how these three things conspire to create the system that makes up my father's worldview. Animals, physics, and sports—to say those things are mere influences or ordinary preoccupations for my father would fall miserably short, for they are the filters through which my father perceives the world. In every conversation he plucks a metaphor from each camp, drawing profound connections between the banalities of day-to-day living, a retired man's meager struggles and their broader significance elevated to extremes only known by those who feel everything as overly meaningful. The silence was an opener; the language became transparent to itself; the secret language was revealed; the code was written down; the code was thrown away; translation is never sufficient, and so: a father's silence. It is what it is although it is so much more than that. You will just have to trust me.

Lucky, what does a dog know about silence? Tell me. As a child I sometimes wondered about your auditory world, how terribly jarring it must be to hear so much, how unsettling. When I speak of my silence, perhaps I am speaking of my refusal to hear. But you, you seemed barely capable of sleeping; your ears were always twitching and you were on your feet barking like hell at the slightest rustling. I wondered about your sensory world. As a child I heard all these myths about how you see and hear; I don't think I ever quite sorted out what was true. Were you really colorblind?

My mom called me this morning after they put you down. She said my dad washed you up real nice and wrapped you in a blanket to take you to the vet. Until the last day he was still doing everything he could, cooking you plain rice and lean chicken when you couldn't digest anything else, relentlessly cleaning out your eyes to try to save your vision, giving you vitamins, cleaning out your ears. He had an elaborate regimen and nothing was futile if it could help even a little bit, if it would give you even the slightest bit more life. I hope you aren't offended by me saying that my dad did not want to get you when we were kids eagerly clamoring for a puppy. I was six or seven. He thought it'd be too much responsibility. Randy and I would throw quite a few fits arguing in favor of getting a dog. I remember in elementary school I wrote exclusively about wanting a Dalmatian; I frequently fantasized about us running together in the yard through the green grass. The 'rents eventually buckled. The first day we got you, you did not drink from a bowl and we had to use a bottle to get you to drink. That day we ran in circles around the house and you chased us. We would stop, kneel, and you'd jump into our arms and lick our faces. I watched my dad transform from someone who was reluctant to take on superfluous responsibilities into someone who takes responsibility to superfluous ends. I watched you change, too. When you were younger you were so energetic that we could barely have guests over because you would get all crazed and run around the house hurtling over couches, but these last few weeks you've been crashing your blind face into walls and lying in your excrement because you couldn't get up or control your bodily functions. A part of me feels embarrassed for writing this with such feeling, because matters relating to pets can be easily written off as trivial.

When I was a child, I also remember looking up the average lifespan of a dog your size and calculating how old I would be when you were expected to die. I remember feeling relieved when I realized I would likely be in college when you were expected to die, relieved because my child self could not comprehend how I could possibly cope with being there when you died. Here I am. In college. I was right. Things are considerably easier to cope with. There just isn't enough space in my adult mind to entertain any single thought very long, no time for it to be carried to its most bleak and dismal end. Things seemed to dip so easily into delusion when I was a child. But now, my mother calls me crying and fifteen minutes later I am taking notes in class. Through her tears she says, *I'm proud of you, graduating college and all.* I don't tell the people around me about any of this. The intimacies of family dynamics seem impossible to convey.

And I can't help but feel like this is some strange marker of the passing of time, a rupture in my life's progression, a throwback to an earlier projection of myself. I can't believe I've made it here. I just can't believe it in the same way I can't believe my little brother is grown up because I would wonder what he would be like when he grew up and now, here we are. Here we are. I can't believe I thought so hard about where I'd be when my dog died and I am seeing myself live through that; I have made it to this peculiar point and can juxtapose the curious questions of my child self with the turnout, this unfurling present. She has made it here and she is not doing so badly.

(2009)

II.

2010–12:

THE PUNK-HOUSE YEARS

Baltimore. Glasgow. Trips beyond—across Europe, Pittsburgh.

After graduating I decided to move to Baltimore. The previous summer I had met L., a cool person who wrote me a nine-page list of reasons to move to Baltimore. *Why not?* Baltimore had the perfect ratio of anarchists to art-school kids. It was a postindustrial port city—rent was cheap, but it was probably the most palpably segregated city I've ever lived in. When we arrived in Baltimore, C. and I landed in the Copycat Warehouse, in the Copycat Theatre section, where two of my Florida friends lived and staged performance-art events while finishing up art school at MICA. C. and I lived in a makeshift room with a tiny loft. I would sit in the loft working on my novel (which I completed but never published) while she sat below me, drawing her comic. It wasn't long before I was forced to leave that spot, too. I had left to go to a short writing residency at the Cyberpunk Apocalypse house in Pittsburgh but spent most of the time on the phone with C., trying to talk her out of suicide while she berated and belittled me. While I was away C. had freaked out on the housemates and trashed our room, smashed the walls and a window, and run off to a punk house in Hampden called Good View. So I left the residency early and abruptly came back from Pittsburgh. While packing and cleaning up the trashed room, I received a call from my father saying my mother had had a serious suicide attempt and was in the hospital. What was there to do but move my meager possessions to Good View and weep in the basement, nested in two sleeping bags because it was winter and the heat was not turned on. A few days later I was off to Florida.

C. and I took up residence in the Good View punk house in Hampden, a white working-class neighborhood of Baltimore made famous by the campy film director John Waters (whom I once saw in line at the bank). At that time the neighborhood, which had not yet been gentrified, consisted mostly of the descendants of workers from Appalachia who had migrated to Hampden to work in the mills. C. and I lived in a tiny porch room that was like an icebox in winter, as it had no insulation. We rechristened the house "Good Void." Our rent was eighty-five dollars a month. I tried to live as long as I could on my meager savings so I could write all day, and I did, on my novel, essays, and poetry. I was able to scrape by on $3,000 a year, including rent, food, travel—everything. Baltimore was an easy place to be a punk: we could get unlimited free books at the Book Thing warehouse and eat well by pooling our food-stamp money.

The Good View house, I was told, was haunted by a schizophrenic artist who had hidden razors around the house and painted green ghosts on all the walls because he believed he was already dead. He committed suicide in the house. Periodically we would find the razors tucked away in random places. Before the vegan animal liberators moved in, the house was one big art installation of garbage piled to the ceiling, broken vintage electronics and junk cluttering every corner of space. I think the first anarchist to move into the house was Madison, an ex–heroin addict who left Chicago for Baltimore in a bid to kick his drug habit, which he did, successfully, by transferring his addiction to Karl Marx, spending years reading the entire Western philosophical canon in chronological order, starting with the pre-Socratics, to better understand Marx's reference points. The only house rule was "no heroin."

I would quickly learn that Good Void was the house that served as a repository for all the freaks who couldn't exist anywhere else.

Things were very porous in the beginning, truly communist. We didn't have assigned rooms and would sleep wherever we happened to fall asleep. Madison would sometimes cuddle with C. and me like our adult child, before Madison became engaged to a delightful British woman with a heart of gold. We were awake at all hours, making weird videos and burning Ayn Rand books inside as a kind of civic duty to take bad ideas out of circulation. Outsiders saw our house as a Marxist death cult, which I suppose was not too far off the mark. I became fast friends with Madison because we both shared an extreme devotion to study. We'd often put in ten-hour days at the Johns Hopkins library, taking a break midway to split a burrito from the Chipotle nearby. An autodidact who was teaching himself Russian, he decided that the only way he would get to Russia was by going to college, starting with community college. We audited classes at Hopkins and would spend countless hours arguing about absurd topics such as whether Spinozism could be reconciled with Marxism, or whether Catholics should be executed during the revolution (I was on the side of "no"). Later, when we were in PhD programs at Harvard and Yale, I would joke to him that the Good Void punk house was actually a prep school feeding its students into the Ivy League.

I became friends with an English grad student at Hopkins who gave me the key to his spare library-basement office, which became my "guerrilla office." I stocked it with packets of instant Indian food, bedding, and illicitly hoarded books. It was my sanctuary, as I didn't have any place to sit down and read at my punk house. My friend crew consisted mainly of the badass women and trans people in the Baltimore Feminist Reading Group, which both C. and I were a part of.

Maybe it was in Baltimore that I became a real "writer," even though it wasn't until a decade later that I felt I had the authority to claim the title. In Florida I had started a Tumblr blog, *Ballerinas Dance with Machine Guns*, where I dumped my thoughts on literature, film, queer politics, and theory. This was during a period I often refer to as "the Golden Age" of feminist literary blogs. My posts were often in conversation with writer-bloggers such as Kate Zambreno, Bhanu Kapil, Ariana Reines, Dodie Bellamy, Elaine Castillo, Anne Boyer, and Roxane Gay. I also wrote for the indie-lit blog *HTMLGIANT* and *BOMB* magazine's *BOMBlog*. It was during this time, too, that I began to develop as a political thinker, and though I don't stand by everything I wrote in those days, my politics have been humorously consistent since I was a teenager (antistate, feminist, antiprison, anticapitalist).

In 2011, I left Baltimore for two months to do a filmmaking residency in Glasgow, Scotland, and traveled around Europe when my films were completed. I returned to discover an affair was afoot while I was away. Faced with my girlfriend's lies, I became aware of just how credulous I could be when it came to taking people's word at face value despite evidence to the contrary. The abuse continued. Once, when no one was home except me, she went on a rampage destroying everything in the house. I tried to calm her down and she proceeded to strangle me. I pushed her off me. The thing that set me off was not the strangulation, but the fact that she was going to leave me to clean up her mess—the shelves of books and baubles had all been knocked over, there were glass and broken objects everywhere. Though it was not the first strangulation or physical altercation, it was the first time I did not respond by crumpling into a ball of self-loathing. Still, I stayed. And covered for her when people kept cutting their feet on the glass that she failed to clean up properly.

How long would this continue? I was running out of money. One day, while leeching Wi-Fi from the neighbor, I wondered what would happen if I changed my G-Chat status from "invisible" to "available." Lily Hoang, a fellow *HTMLGIANT* blogger, messaged me to say I should apply to a creative-writing MFA program that she taught at in New Mexico. "When is the application due?" "Tomorrow," she replied. I sent my application in. The rest is history.

Channeling the Alien Plath Girl:
Emotional Drag/Porn/Excess

This originally appeared as an HTMLGIANT *blog post.*

I heard Dodie Bellamy use the terms "emotional porn" and "operatic suffering" recently on her blog and I love that. I recently wrote on my blog about "emotional excess" in relation to the films of Andrzej Żuławski, and I've just been thinking—I love things that are flamboyantly and unapologetically emotional. It makes me think of teenagers. Since crossing over into my twenties, I look at teenagers and feel kind of embarrassed for them. They lack emotional filters. They're so direct about their suffering. They're making themselves look pathetic. But really, I kind of envy them, their lack of restraint. It must be really freeing to be that open without feeling the urge to censor yourself.

When I was in high school, I used to call a certain type of girl a "Plath Girl." For me, the Plath Girl was white, upper middle class, educated, a perfectionist, melodramatic, mean, and incapable of feeling joy. I guess I still used this term in college … isn't that fucked up? Yes, now I remember. There was a girl I thought was cute and I asked her on a date. She always wore black eyeliner and had a Virginia Woolf tattoo. I thought we could go to the airport and watch the planes take off but she was like, *Why don't you just come to my room?* When I went to her room, she did lines of coke off her desk while ranting about how much she hated everyone, how depressed she was at school, and before I knew it, she had left me so she could hang with other people. When my friends asked me about the date, I think I just said, "Turns out she's quite the Plath Girl." (But was this an imprecise categorization? Did the tattoo mean she was actually a *Woolf Girl*?) Really, I think the Plath Girl is kind of sexy. She has direct access to her emotions and isn't ashamed to show her bitterness or depression. (I am also involuntarily turned on by emotionally volatile people who can sometimes be cold to me. Perhaps it is a masochistic impulse.) There is certainly a performative element that pervades this kind of outward display of emotion, but that doesn't mean it's just an act.

I think I was too awkward, ethnic looking, and weird growing up to be a Plath Girl, even though I was teeming with emotions. I was more of an Alien Girl. A little Björk or Yoko Ono. (Imagine what kind of babies the Plath Girl and the Alien Girl could make. Horrifyingly self-destructive and obsessive babies, I imagine.) Nobody is more emotionally excessive and operatic than Björk. She epitomizes performative emotional excess. Her emotional affectedness is so over the top that most people can't even stand to listen to her. Needless to say, I had an unhealthy obsession with Björk that peaked when I was in ninth grade. When nobody was home at my house, I would blast her music on the stereo and scream her songs on the top of my lungs—the symphonic songs with the violins and wailing vocal crescendos. It was my emotional porn.

What I love about Dodie's terms is that they lack self-seriousness while still holding on to the idea that there is emotional truth within the performance of excessive emotion. There are elements of self-mockery and self-parody that come with these displays. I am utterly fascinated by literature and art that, like I wrote on my blog, strad-dles the "line between extreme seriousness and complete self-mockery," the type of literature that puts on emotional drag but doesn't let you know what's beneath the drag, whether or not you are supposed to laugh, take it as a joke, take it as sincere, feel embarrassed for the author, or some combination of all these things. I am reminded of Ariana Reines when she wrote, "I wanted to write poems that an educated person would feel embarrassed to read, poems that sound like Goth girls with feelings, except for sometimes they are 'smarter' than Goth girls with feelings are supposed to be." The character Maggie in Kate Zambreno's *O Fallen Angel* also comes to mind.

The thing about performative emotional excess is, it's not fake. As in, *She's not faking it to get your attention.* She's reveling in it, playing it up. She loves it and isn't afraid even if she knows it might make her look pathetic. By exaggerating this type of direct articulation of emotion, we can explore the emotional worlds that are denied to us when we pass into our twenties and beyond. We exaggerate it to the point of absurdity, and we may do this to cover up the fact that we are still these overfeeling and fucked-up human beings; we have these little pimply and confused teenagers inside of us yelling and demanding a voice, but we hush that voice—we have coworkers and editors and readers who are always eyeing us, looking for the places where the seams of the adult bodysuits are coming undone.

(2010)

The Phallic-Titty Manifesto: Queer Sex and the Naming of Parts

This piece originally appeared as a limited-edition handmade zine.

When I was a little kid, I called my brother and his friends into the bathroom and gleefully announced that I was growing a penis. I dropped my pants, spread my lips, and pointed to my clit, the little nub that I was convinced was a budding pee-pee. Later—when my mind was heavy with gender theory—I tried to make sense of the incident, applying what knowledge I had gained from my four-year liberal-arts education. Was I a gender dysmorphic child? A girl actually destined to be a boy? Several of the trans boys I know have talked about how as children they would pray to God before bedtime to give them a penis when they woke up the next morning. Or maybe, rather than being boy-identified, I just had a classic case of penis envy? Probably neither. I think I was just confused. Why were the boys sanctioned and encouraged to do the things I wanted to do, like venture into the woods, while I was supposed to play dolls? Why didn't they want me around them? What made them different from me? The divide seemed arbitrary to my child mind. Before things were solidified and rules were pummeled into my little brain, boundary crossing was totally possible. I could turn into a boy; I could turn into a bird; I could catch up to my older brother in age. Everything was amorphous, flexible, fluid, and full of possibility. Time, identity, anatomy—it was all so open and anything could change.

I often want to talk about bodies, about my body in relationship to my partner's body, but I always run up against this wall: How to talk about bodies as a cisgender person, and how to talk about my relationship to my trans partner's body? When cis people talk about trans bodies, it sounds so fetishistic and gross. So I keep avoiding the subject. But I want to talk about how the context of my relationship to my partner helps me reimagine my relationship to my body, how the bedroom can be a site of resistance, how fucking can be used to destabilize and deheterosexualize bodies, how tits can be dicks and dicks can be clits.

I have phallic titties. After sex I popped an Ambien and my thoughts got all screwed up and since I was on this phallic-titty thought it became this weird associative manifesto that—of course—I do not remember (amnesia being a side effect of Ambien). But it was about fucking everything with my titties, milk as my cum, erect nipples—I even have two. My girlfriend is into my tits. I didn't used to like my tits. I was five foot two and wore a size-D bra and I started lifting weights to try to get rid of them. They did get a lot smaller, but then I got lazy and they became big again. My reason for disliking my tits has more to do with practicality than body-image issues. Giant tits can be unwieldy—they get in the way, they're uncomfortable to sleep on, they attract gross hetero dudes. A bit of advice for the big tittied: you probably shouldn't even try to wear a button-down shirt unless you want your melons to be visible and, on the occasion that you feel compelled to wear a low-cut top, know that there's a good chance that nasty men will chase you down the street. I'm not sure how many women out there want to defeminize their appearance as a way to render themselves less sexually attractive to men. I always think of the surrealist photographer

Claude Cahun, how she always shaved her head to cultivate the alien look. If my exterior presentation matched my interior I would look like an alien as well. But alas, I'm just a femme.

The thing about being a femme queer is that you're continually read as hetero, you attract all the wrong people, everyone thinks you're straight. Don't be fooled. There's nothing flattering or complimentary about men harassing you and yelling "Hey big titty girl!" as you're walking to the grocery store. I've resorted to exclusively wearing sports bras to try to downplay the size of my breasts. Sometimes I wonder, How did this—these big titties—happen? Asian women don't have large breasts, right? It must be the Italian in me. I got unlucky with my DNA inheritance: I'm severely allergic to alcohol (ALDH2 deficiency or "Asian Flush Disease") and am sweaty and stinky like an Italian, unlike my Chinese family members who likely have significantly fewer apocrine glands, the nefarious biological machinery responsible for producing body odor. (Dad: "Why do you need to wear deodorant?! I never wear deodorant and I don't stink. Frivolous Americans!" "It's because I got mom's stink genes, Dad!") But for the sake of advancing this essay, the question of whether my titties are big because I inherited my mom's curves or because I just eat too much food will have to go unanswered for now.

My partner loves my titties. She plays with them and sucks them all the time. I think her titties are quite cute as well. They're smaller than mine but perky like an adolescent girl's. They poke out of her thin cotton T-shirts. It's strange the way people sometimes filter her cute tits out when they misgender her, strange the way mine are hyper-apparent when I'm read as a heterosexual female. I hated my titties because they invited—against my will or permission—

unwanted sexualization. They were a marker, a burden I was forced to carry (and they do get heavy). But I like my big titties more since starting this relationship. My titties are imposing, multiple, phallic.

Judith Butler: "Consider that 'having' the phallus can be symbolized by an arm, a tongue, a hand (or two), a knee, a thigh, a pelvic bone, an array of purposefully instrumentalized body-like things."

Judith forgot titties.

When I was writing my Ambien-induced phallic-titty manifesto as I was drifting off to sleep, Judith Butler's "lesbian phallus" hadn't even crossed my mind. But now, I can't ignore it. After reading "The Lesbian Phallus and the Morphological Imaginary" while in college, I initially thought, *Why would lesbians want to participate in a phallic economy? Isn't the logic undergirding phallocentrism terrible and detrimental?* Judith isn't trying to say that lesbians should all want dicks. They're trying to say that the exclusive association of penis and phallus is a phantasmatic identification. Judith asks, If nobody has the "phallus"—which is really just a signifier or imaginary effect held in place by language—then why does it seem inextricably bound to the anatomical penis? For Judith, when lesbians claim ownership of the phallus, when they dislodge the phallus from a masculine or heterosexual context, this disrupts the very logic driving the phallic economy. If the phallus represents privilege and power, then constantly reiterating that the phallus is inextricably tied to the penis just reifies the privileged relationship between the phallus and masculine morphologies. Anatomy is meaningless unless it's backed by language. For certain words to maintain a certain meaning, it depends on repetition, on us constantly reinforcing and restating those meanings. We can subvert and transform the meaning of symbols such as the phallus. They are "transferable, substitutable, plastic."

If this theoretical digression has lost you, I apologize. The main idea I find of value in Judith's theory of the lesbian phallus is the idea that substituting other body parts for the phallus has the potential to be transgressive. If nothing else, it undermines the determinism and significance attributed to anatomy. But Judith's account of the lesbian phallus didn't overtly consider transwomen, or the possibility of delinking the phallus/penis in other ways. What might be considered a penis according to normative morphologies could be considered a clit. What might be considered an anus could be renamed a vagina, or take on the role of a vagina in sexual practices. Sometimes I fuck my girlfriend from behind with my clit-dick or erect nips. All parts of our bodies are potential erogenous zones. Boundary crossing can happen in any number of directions.

Judith Butler: "If what comes to signify under the sign of the phallus are a number of body parts, discursive performatives, alternative fetishes, to name a few, then the symbolic position of 'having' has been dislodged from the penis as its privileged anatomical (or non-anatomical) occasion."

Tits can be the phallus in multiple ways. For one, they can ejaculate. I learned recently that many women artificially induce lactation for erotic purposes. Sometimes you can achieve this merely by having your tits sucked on regularly. (I wonder if I will start generating milk soon, given the constant stimulation my nips receive.) Milk can become cum. (But better: it has calcium.) When lactating women are sexually aroused, they may experience a let-down reflex where they involuntarily eject milk. "This is why some women leak or squirt milk during sex," one website says. While lactation fetishes often tend to occur within a heterosexual framework because they are associated with pregnancy, nursing, and reproduction, milky tits also exist outside the mommy-daddy bond. Lesbians do it too. There's also something very queer about the fetish itself, the way it eroticizes and sexualizes lactation by unsettling the assumption that the sole purpose of breast milk is to nourish babies.

The idea of ejaculating tits opens up another way women, symbolically, can "possess" the phallus (or *phalluses*, I should say). It undermines the pervasive view that pregnant bodies are abject and unerotic. You often hear stories of men rejecting the bodies of their partners during and after pregnancy because there is something gross or sexually off-putting about pregnant bodies.

* * *

Not much information exists out there on phallic tits. I looked up variations of the term—*phallic breasts, phallic boobs, phallic tits, phallic titties*, and so forth—and found nearly nothing besides a few porn sites and online erotica. But I did find an Urban Dictionary entry for *penis tits*:

1. penis tits
1. *noun, interjection (slang)*. Exclamation of frustration. 2. *noun, object (slang)*. An object or event that provides supreme satisfaction. 3. *noun, object (slang)*. Nipples with a phallic shape, resembling miniature penises.

1. "Penis tits! I forgot to send my rent check in." 2. "I just won the lottery! That's the penis tits!" 3. "When that girl took her shirt off, she had some serious penis tits."

These definitions make sense to me. Penis tits: (1) Frustrating for men that fear women's possession of the phallus; (2) Objects that provide supreme satisfaction; (3) Dick nips (my partner has told me before that my nipples are long, like "miniature penises").

Though my search for phallic breasts yielded very little, one thing that repeatedly showed up in the search results were descriptions of works by an artist named Louise Bourgeois. Coincidentally, Louise is one of my favorite artists. She was quoted saying "Sometimes I am totally concerned with female shapes—clusters of breasts like clouds—but I often merge the imagery—phallic breasts, male and female, active and passive."

What I like about Louise's work is that it uses the phallus without denigrating the body parts that are typically considered "female." She uses phallic imagery without resorting to phallus worship, without abandoning nonphallic shapes. Indeed, her depictions are often parodies that upset the totemic and rigid qualities of phallic imagery. Consider the sculpture *Eye to Eye*. Are the objects more tit-like or dick-like? Well, they're certainly phallic in that their forms are elongated. But they are also rounded like tits, and have pointed tops like nipples. Some of the protruding objects also appear to have slits, which suggests cunt imagery. So in this sculpture alone we see traces of multiple bodily formations and morphologies. "Masculine" and "feminine" symbols are combined, transformed, blurred. Materiality itself—what is considered natural, concrete, and opposed to abstraction—is not discrete or unambiguous. I have always admired the way Louise's sculptures upset boundaries by showing the ambiguity of flesh and by upsetting the either/or logic of noncontradiction.

Let's consider the logic behind "feminine" and "masculine" morphologies. When we think of "female anatomy," it is largely defined by absence, which is represented by the vagina. The cunt is considered a hole, not a thing in itself, but the absence of the thing. "Male" anatomy is defined by the ability to penetrate. The thing goes into the hole. Not only is this binaristic divide dubious because it renders women "passive" and men "active," it's also a mythic fabrication. Even cis men have holes. They're called anuses, mouths, nostrils. Women can penetrate with their tongues, fingers, fists, tits. Breasts can be round, but so can testicles. Dicks can be long, but so can tits. Cunts can engulf. People falling outside masculine/feminine gender categories also likely possess some combination of concave and convex body parts. The way we imagine bodies seems incredibly distorted by an imaginary gendered picture we project onto the surface of bodies, which is reflected in the significance placed on the "penis" and the "vagina." To emphasize only these parts and to assert that they are radically distinct and oppositionally defined just reinforces heteronormativity while limiting the potential pleasure of exploring other erogenous zones and nonpenetrative, nonheterosexual erotic practices.

* * *

People sometimes ask me what kind of sex I have. This question is mostly asked by cisgendered people who are curious about what sex with a trans person is like. They direct this question toward me, the cisgendered partner. Maybe I'm less threatening to them? Depending on the context, I sometimes find this question justified and sometimes invasive and sensationalizing. While I am often vague and evasive when confronted with this question, I always try to make it clear that the way I engage with my partner sexually is unconventional, expressly queer. Once, my friend Milda pressed me further: "But how is your sex unconventional?" This seemed difficult to explain. Should I say, "Well, my partner doesn't have a penis, she has a giant clit"? And I sometimes pretend her big clit is my big dick. Also, we pretend to be incestuous sisters engaging in illicit activities behind "mom and dad's" back. That answer seemed like it required a bit of explanation, so I think I said something like *It's hard to explain*. She replied, "Well … do you use toys?" No, not really. "Me neither. It creeps me out to think of commodities entering the bedroom, of capitalism seeping into the most intimate parts of my life. So if you don't use toys, what's so unconventional about it?"

I think the dodgy answer I provided was something about how we rarely engage in penetrative sex. Since we're a queer (lesbian) couple, we engage queerly. It's strange to think that we might be mistakenly read as heterosexual or assumed to have hetero sex. It's strange to think about how much of my identity is bound up with my partner's identity, and how people's misgendering of her indirectly heterosexualizes me. It's strange to think that my queerness was never called into question when I was dating a cis woman for three years. But although my partner and I—to varying degrees—suffer from an anxiety of misidentification (hers, as a transwoman, is more amplified and stressful than mine), this isn't a fault of our own—it is a subtle manifestation of heteronormativity and transphobia.

So how is our sex unconventional?

In the bedroom we make and remake our bodies. In the words of Judith, we "reinstitute sexed bodies in variable ways" so that "in crossing these boundaries, such morphogenetic identifications reconfigure the mapping of sexual difference itself." That's an inflated way of saying we give our parts different names, pretend we have things we do not possess in a conventional sense, cross gender boundaries by ascribing both masculine and feminine features to our bodies. Judith calls this process "resignification." In doing this, we challenge the idea that bodies are immutable. Flesh itself is open-ended. Even without surgery, you can change your body by transforming your relationship to your body. You can reimagine bodies in different ways. Since we can only refer to bodies through signifying practices, altering our practices produces different effects. Because bodies are held in place by linguistic structures, renaming parts and claiming ownership of phantasmatic symbols can disrupt anatomical determinism and binaristic gender differentiation. "The more various and unanticipated the anatomical (and non-anatomical) occasions for its symbolization the more unstable that signifier [the phallus] becomes" (Judith). Like I mentioned earlier: tits can be dicks and dicks can be clits. Why not? In declaring ownership of the phallus by claiming that titties can be lesbian phalluses, we can weaken the authority of the phallus by subverting its exclusionary and heterosexist foundations.

(2010)

Negative Feminism, Antisocial Queer Theory, and the Politics of Hope

This originally appeared on my Tumblr blog.

What are negative feminism and antisocial queer theory? My fragmentary answer: they are queer critiques that aim to decenter positivity, productivity, redemptive politics of affirmation, narratives of success, and politics that are founded on hope for an imagined future. They're rude politics and have no interest in being polite. They embrace masochism, antiproduction, self-destructiveness, abjection, forgetfulness, radical passivity, aggressive negation, unintelligibility, negativity, punk pugilism, and antisocial attitudes as a form of resistance to the liberal feminist and gay politics of cohesion. They're about *not-becoming*, because the notion of *becoming* is perceived as following the capitalist logic of production and models of success that are often tied up with colonialism. They ask, *Why the fuck should queers be nice?* And assert that politeness is heteronormative, that we should embrace our utter *failure* at functioning within a colonialist, heteronormative, capitalist, racist, sexist, and transphobic framework.

Jack Halberstam is an academic who has recently articulated these theories. I want to talk about his theories and raise some pressing questions and criticisms of his controversial ideas in the context of my limited conversations with him. This essay is largely based on Jack's article "The Anti-Social Turn in Queer Studies."

While driving in a car with Jack, my roommate Matthew, and his partner JD, we have an exciting conversation about everything from bats to drag. Jack is in a rush to get to the airport but is incredibly calm, easygoing, and undemanding even though there's no time for the promised dinner with the college's budget. JD is a Buddhist enthusiast, eager to discuss this inspiring interest of his. In the car he mentions how much happier he is since coming to Buddhism, how it has transformed his thinking and allowed him to think lovingly of strangers, even the little buggers with their giant carts of shit standing in front of him in line at the grocery store. Now, Jack is someone whose recent work revolves around the heteronormativity of the politics of hope and the imperialism of happiness. Jack adds, "But why would I want to think lovingly of everyone? Maybe there are people out there that are truly undeserving of my love." The comments JD makes spark a fascinating discussion on emotional dynamism and the value of positive feelings, giving me a glimpse of the place from which Jack's theories of queer failure and negative feminism come. We questioned why there is a tendency to privilege certain "positive" or "good" feelings and examined the impulse to flatten or repress the full spectrum of affective responses.

For me, the (anti)politics of negation discussed by Jack arise from a queer resistance to *emotional repression* and the privileging of *feeling good* over feeling like shit. It's about challenging the productive and rationalist logic of capitalism that makes you feel sick if you can't function within its framework. It's about thinking through how emotion informs how we approach politics and how privileging an approach that only values positive feelings erases and denies the position of people who refuse to or simply just can't feel happy about participating in such a shitty context—people who are angry or depressed and seek self-annihilation as a way to reject the demands of the heteronormative world.

So where does radical negation get us? Jack's borrowed mantra, *no future*, rejects such temporal considerations. But most of us out there probably still care about the viability of specific political strategies. While I was at Ida, a queer commune, I got into a discussion with two people who were critical of Jack's negative feminism and antisocial queer theory. They raised some good criticisms that I am trying to think through here.

It was a few months ago when I brought Jack to New College to give a lecture. I was working as the Gender and Diversity Center program coordinator and got to spend some time with writers and intellectuals such as bell hooks and Eileen Myles. At the time I was most familiar with Jack's work on trans men, queer temporalities and subcultures, and female masculinity, but was wholly fascinated by his lecture on "the queer art of failure." It seemed relevant given that lately, in the radical queer community, there is disagreement between those who adhere to a politics of community and affirmation and those who adhere to a politics of cynicism.

But of course it's not that simple, and maybe it's more accurate to say that some approach politics with an attitude of *constructiveness* and others approach it with an attitude of *destructiveness*. Jack is trying to explore the destructive side of things, particularly a disorganized and unintelligible form of self-destructiveness or masochism as a form of resistance. But unlike the nihilistic posturing of those that are too-queer-for-everything, Jack is not interested in a purely *aestheticized* attitude, nor is he necessarily all critique. What we get is still a strategy, albeit an antirational and antiorganizational one. While Jack's theories are somewhat nihilistic, they dissociate themselves from nihilism's historical complacency with sexism. He writes that he would rather "turn to a history of alternatives, contemporary moments of alternative political struggle and high and low cultural productions of a funky, nasty, over the top and thoroughly accessible queer negativity."

So I wouldn't say that Jack's theories advocate *doing nothing*; rather, they advocate *doing something through a refusal to do anything*, a radical form of passivity. Similarly, Jack notes that "negativity might well constitute an anti-politics but it should not register as apolitical." A passive consumer who watches TV all day and drives an SUV to work wouldn't be the same as, say, the narrator of Jamaica Kincaid's *Autobiography of My Mother*, who refuses to be happy or do anything because she rejects the impetus to participate while she is forced to exist under colonialism. Jack writes: "She opposes colonial rule precisely by refusing to accommodate herself to it or to be responsible for reproducing it in any way. Thus the autobiographical becomes an unwriting, an undoing, an unraveling of self." While the narrator is resistant to the logic of production and participation, the strategy is—in a roundabout way—a perverse form of productivity.

Criticism of the Negative Turn

One major critique is that it invalidates and delegitimizes the work of people who are committed to a queer struggle that is not antisocial, negative, anticommunitarian, or anti-identitarian in character. Constructive, affirmative, and restorative forms of political engagement are portrayed as decidedly *un*queer. When Jack tosses memory out in favor of forgetfulness, Bea, a person I met at Ida who studies history, rightfully asks, *What the fuck? Why not cultivate the historical memory of queer struggle?* People who adopt an attitude of queer cynicism often shit on and belittle the efforts of people carrying out any constructive project. But Jack is critical of this type of cynicism when he describes the "archive of feelings" (Ann Cvetkovich) that characterizes much (gay) antisocial theory. The kinds of affects in this archive include "fatigue, ennui, boredom, indifference, ironic distancing, indirectness, arch dismissal, insincerity and camp," but he notes the limitations of this repertoire and favors a more dynamic set of emotions including "rage, rudeness, anger, spite, impatience, intensity, mania, sincerity, earnestness, over-investment, incivility, brutal honesty and so on."

While the problem with any constructive project is that it will always be problematic in one way or another, it is still valuable to carry out an imperfect project rather than to retreat with frustration over the impossibility of getting everything right. There is no way to be fully outside the context that we are at odds with, no way to overcome the limitations of language, no way to easily undo all our internalized responses. When I spent time with former Black Liberation Army and Black Panther Party member Ashanti Alston, he emphasized a process-oriented, experimental form of action where you act without necessarily having all the details worked out. Figuring things out as you go becomes a way to avoid getting trapped in inactivity. It's a hell of a lot easier to perform these exercises in pure critique than it is to actually act. But like I said earlier, I don't think Jack is all critique because he is offering an alternative strategy, whether we agree with its validity or not.

A lot of the critiques raised in this brief conversation made me question and think through why I was initially so receptive and open to Jack's ideas. For one, I encountered the ideas in the context of meeting Jack—who is a thoughtful, energetic, and engaging scholar, not to mention a sweet person overall. But more importantly, Jack's ideas spoke to me on a different register—they were so visceral, so much about affectivities and affectivities in relation to the formation of politics. I have always separated the two—the political "self" and the self-destructive, overfeeling, and dysfunctional "self"— because I felt that the two could not be reconciled, because politics seemed to demand a certain level of functionality and affective distance. Jack spoke of self-destructive behavior as a valid emotional response to the world we are confronted with. And maybe through my feminism I have internalized the idea that masochism and depression are things to be overcome, things that mark you as weak. Masochism, cutting, and self-annihilation seem incompatible with feminism because they might be viewed as forms of self-punishment that arise from internalized sexism, misogyny, and hatred for one's status as woman. But maybe the self-destructive impulse arises when we realize that we are at odds with the system that surrounds us, when we realize that participation would mean symbolic death—we are fashioning a new kind of refusal.

In a blog post titled "The Artist Is Object—Marina Abramovic at MOMA," Jack uses the term "shadow feminism" to describe this feminist reconceptualization of masochism and the shattering of self through pain. He writes:

> In this genre, we find no "feminist subject" but only un-subjects who cannot speak, who refuse to speak; subjects who unravel,

who refuse to cohere; subjects who refuse "being" where being has already been defined in terms of a self-activating, self-knowing, liberal subject. We find a feminism that stages a refusal to become woman and that locates this refusal deep in the heart of masochistic pain/pleasure dynamics.

But this notion of feminine negativity is really nothing new, and I think Jack does not acknowledge the debt he owes to French feminism. Decades ago, Xavière Gauthier wrote, "And then, blank pages, gaps, borders, spaces and silence, holes in discourse: these women emphasize the aspect of feminine writing which is the most difficult to verbalize because it becomes compromised, rationalized, masculinized as it explains itself."

In my thesis on race, gender, and the practice of writing, I consider the appropriation of silence as a rhetorical strategy that disrupts the masculinist system of meaning. This perspective views silence itself as a rupture, as resistance to a system of signs that values presence and occupation over gaps and absences. The view of woman as non-subject can also be traced back to Jacques Lacan, who asserted that women occupy a state of nonbeing because they are merely a lack—a negative sign. The territory of femininity is marked by irrationality, madness, and silence because women are seen as fundamentally alienated by a phallocentric system of signification. But ultimately, I did not buy into this deterministic view and tended to side more with the approach of writers such as Hélène Cixous—who rejected death, the authority of the phallus, and the view of woman-as-castrated in favor of "limitless life"—as well as Audre Lorde, who in an essay titled "The Transformation of Silence into Language and Action" wrote:

I was going to die, if not sooner than later, whether or not I had ever spoken myself. My silences had not protected me. Your silence will not protect you. ... Because the machine will try to grind you into dust anyway, whether or not we speak. We can sit in our corners mute forever while our sisters and our selves are wasted, while our children are distorted and destroyed, while our earth is poisoned; we can sit in our safe corners mute as bottles, and we will still be no less afraid.

Ultimately, I find that a purely negative politics has major limitations, no matter how radical. Negative feminism and queer theory challenge the idea that participation is the *only option*. But they don't acknowledge that negative politics are still inscribed within the same framework. Negation isn't a form of escape. It can make you even more limited by the structure that surrounds you because it promotes an approach that is defined exclusively by the structure, can only think in a way that is reactive. This can make you even more stuck than if you were drawing on your context as a point of departure for constructing alternatives.

Concluding Thoughts

The issue, for me, does not come down to hope vs. cynicism, but figuring out how we can resist the tendency to police people's affective responses. This means challenging the hegemony of happiness, which invalidates people who are too crazy or angry or fucked up by the world to function or participate in a polite way. With that said, I am not wholeheartedly for feminist or queer negativity as narrow positions. I am interested in the mingling of destruction and construction—concurrent undoing and doing—and building my politics on spontaneity, dynamism, and an understanding of subjectivity as *tenuous* and *volatile*, which creates space for radical emotional instability. Our affective responses are in flux and we should be able to utilize a range of attitudes and approaches. I'm wondering if it's okay if I'm sometimes full of a whole lot of negativity *and* hope, wondering why we think of things as mutually exclusive or why it sometimes seems so hard for us to move beyond zero-sum-game thinking.

(2010)

In Search of Nobody's Muse
(Not Even Mine)

This essay was originally published on BOMB *magazine's* BOMBlog.

"I didn't have time to be anyone's muse ... I was too busy rebelling against my family and learning to be an artist."
—Leonora Carrington

Leonora Carrington is considered the last living member of the inner circle of pre-WWII Parisian surrealists. She's ninety-three years old. And she's still alive and creating art in Mexico City.[1]

I've often had fantasies of tracking Leonora down, of hopping on a plane to Mexico to find her. It would be the beginning of an epic journey, and I imagine us having a brief but meaningful encounter where she would bless me with a near-century's worth of wisdom on what it means to be an aging woman artist. I imagine myself emerging from this experience spiritually renewed and ready to tackle *this life*—to develop a total, lifelong commitment to creativity. I wrote on my blog that when the artist Louise Bourgeois died, I had this irrational regret of having not met her while she was alive. In hopes of trying to divert another repeat of my Louise regret, I began trying to get in contact with Leonora Carrington.

---

1. [Carrington has since died, in 2011.]

Remedios Varo wearing a mask made by Leonora Carrington and Kati Horna

I found that there was someone else who had been on a similar mission: *Guardian* journalist Joanna Moorhead. Joanna is a cousin of Leonora's, but until recently she had never met Leonora, nor was she aware of her artistic legacy. Joanna did end up tracking Leonora down. She flew to Mexico and wrote several articles on her cousin. I decided to contact Joanna, thinking maybe I could find Leonora through her:

> *My name is Jackie Wang. I am a writer who is interested in the work of your cousin Leonora Carrington. The Hearing Trumpet is one of my favorite books of all time, and I've always loved your cousin's gleeful rebellion against surrealist representations of women: the view of woman as muse, as* femme enfant, *and so forth. The character Marian Leatherby in Carrington's* Hearing

> Trumpet *was ninety-two years old, and now Carrington herself is ninety-three, which means she has just surpassed the age of her character. I am really interested in writing a piece on Carrington, focusing on what it means to be an aging woman, how aging women are ignored/delegitimized. I was wondering if you knew of any way at all that I could get in touch with Carrington. Any help at all would be greatly appreciated. Thank you for your time. Take care.—Jackie Wang*

Leonora's surrealist occult novel *The Hearing Trumpet* is about Marian, a ninety-two-year-old woman. Her family, who assumes she is senile and has lost her mind with age, commits Marian to an institution. Leonora herself had been institutionalized around the time her lover—the famed Dada/surrealist artist Max Ernst—was arrested during WWII. The institution Marian is sent to in the book turns out to be a strange cult headed by the mysterious couple Mr. and Mrs. Gambit. The elderly women sleep in bungalows that resemble a boot, a cuckoo clock, a mushroom, a birthday cake, an igloo, a circus tent, and a lighthouse. Marian forms alliances with other women and unearths elaborate conspiracies revolving around a portrait of a winking nun. This book brought me immeasurable joy, especially during moments when the women would get together, dance and flail their arms around, compelled by an inexplicable urge.

> *We began by nodding our heads in time to the drumming, then our feet. Soon we were dancing round and around the pond, waving our arms and generally behaving in a very strange manner. … Never before had I experienced the joy of rhythmic dance, even in the days of foxtrot in the arms of some eligible young man.*

We seemed inspired by some marvelous power, which poured energy into our decrepit carcasses.

Old ladies, more alive than ever. Leonora is most famous for her paintings, but her writings are just as brilliant. In *The Hearing Trumpet*, Leonora creates multiple logics and absurd sequences of events, undoing them as she goes along, like a dream that abandons each preceding moment as it moves forward. There is space nested within space, unforeseeable digressions. Reality unwinds as you go deeper into the labyrinth.

When Leonora left Europe, she landed in Mexico and was joined by two other surrealist women expatriates: the Spanish painter Remedios Varo and the Hungarian photographer Kati Horna. These three women worked together, inspired each other, and continued to develop as artists as they were virtually ignored by the art establishment. Older women were often the subjects of their work. They painted and photographed each other. After reading the narrative recounted by Joanna Moorhead, I wondered how much of *The Hearing Trumpet* was inspired by the little artist clan they established in Mexico. I immediately recognized Remedios in the character Carmella:

Varo and Carrington, in particular, found they shared a deep intensity of imagination. They encouraged each other in feats of daring: Varo would write letters to strangers, their names picked at random from the phone book, inviting them to attend dinner parties. There were also endless experiments in cookery, with surreal recipes served up to unsuspecting friends, including an omelette made with human hair, and ink-dyed tapioca passed off as caviar.

But while the wild lives of the surrealist men in Paris attracted much attention, those of the surrealist women in Mexico passed largely unnoticed.

When I had the impulse to contact Leonora's cousin, who wrote this in the *Guardian*, I was thinking about old ladies, institutions, and conspiracies. My partner had told me about an old schizophrenic woman named Phyllis whom she had met in a mental hospital. When we were walking down a side street in Northampton toward the lot we were parked in, Phyllis appeared. It was a moment of cosmic coincidence. She was ambling down the street holding a plastic bag containing her lunch, her gray hair pulled back in a ponytail. We stopped to talk to her and stood there for about twenty or so minutes listening to her fantastic stories. In *The Hearing Trumpet*, a younger woman named Carmella is Marian's only real friend. I imagine Carmella and Marian's bond to be similar to the bond between Phyllis and my partner. Carmella is the only one who really listens to Marian. She gave Marian the trumpet.

Like the character Marian, who is obsessed with uncovering the story of the winking nun, Phyllis too is perpetually on a quest to uncover secret histories. But—like Marian—Phyllis goes largely ignored. To most, Marian and Phyllis are just some crazy hags. But as you read *The Hearing Trumpet*, it is clear that Marian is incredibly lucid and perceptive. When I listened to Phyllis talk, my brain melted because I was fed more information than I had the stamina to process, and everything she said seemed intuitively true. I realized that her problem was not that she didn't understand anything. She understood too much. How was it possible to conflate the two? I suppose the secret to understanding the distinction is to open our ears. Even though the character Marian is physically almost deaf, maybe it is actually we who need hearing trumpets.

Today I received an email from Leonora's cousin saying:

Hi Jackie. Sorry for the delay. That's great that you're such a fan of Leonora's work. She's an extraordinary woman and it's a huge privilege to know her and to be able to spend time with her. She'd be very supportive I think of the idea of a piece about women and ageing, but I don't think she's up to a chat on the phone or by email—she is elderly now, and life is increasingly tough when you're her age. Why not expand the piece a bit to take in other fascinating later-life women, and then you won't need direct input from Leonora? Let me know if I can help further; I want to be supportive to anyone interested in Leonora, but I don't want to make her life difficult by asking her to speak to people when I know she finds this stressful.—All best, Joanna

Alas, I will never get to meet Leonora. Which is okay. She is very, very old, and I wouldn't want my girlish fantasies to cause her any strain. I've come to accept this sobering response and indirect rejection because in this strange way, her elusiveness reaffirms the stance that I loved her for: her rejection of the role of the muse demanded by the culture surrounding surrealism. Leonora will not be anyone's muse. Not even mine.

(2010)

Ballerinas Dance with Machine Guns:
The Cosmic Vision of Refbatch

This essay was originally published in Action, Yes, *the online literary journal of Action Books.*

the future is absent. the present is also. the past is disputing every second. that woman female object stopped to exist in 1999, you can see shadow only. the fighter of removed is representing to you its fight. which soon will not be needed as we all will burn. I said I drown in information, like a swimmer, who is exhausting to fight with waves in the lake or ocean—at time when a man drowned on telaviv beach—soon I will not have any dress and any tooth, and you will have to take my talk as it is—without any attributes

—Refbatch, corrected text from video description

Night approaches in an unidentified patch of woods in Russia. A woman in a red tank top and gaudy eye makeup stands in the forest pointing a camera at herself as she violently lurches her head around while ranting in a hoarse, inaudible voice. The sound of her screams reverberates against the trees, creating an echo that is a haunting accompaniment to the dark blue palette of the video footage. The content of her tirade would be impenetrable if it weren't for the enigmatic titles and typo-laden descriptions accompanying the tens of thousands of videos she has posted on the internet. In this video, she writes of being stalked and attacked by conspirators who persecute her for having captured footage of their illicit activities. Intermittently, she jerks the camera away from herself, as if she is trying to draw our attention to something in the distance, perhaps an attacker. But there is nothing there, nothing but bare trees and a sky that indicates the rapid onset of darkness.

Who is this woman? To me, she is known as *Refbatch*. Refbatch is the internet username of Anna Matskevich, a middle-aged schizophrenic Russian woman who compulsively posts videos on YouTube. But Refbatch is much more than an internet personality: she is the creator of one of the most ambitious and beautiful visual and textual documents ever produced. In about two years, she has uploaded more than 10,200 videos to YouTube, often accompanied by sloppily written English text. The videos make up a surreal and obsessive document of one madwoman's life in Russia: ranting at strangers in the streets, getting into fights, wearing skimpy clothing while dancing in snowy forests, punching the air in beautiful fields and parks, compulsively relaying conspiratorial accounts of news stories, getting harassed by policemen, standing in lakes and rivers while doing slow and hypnotic arm movements, going up and down escalators through bunker-deep Soviet subways, and other everyday activities, like using the computer.

But for Refbatch, "the everyday" is imbued with cosmic significance and tied to a meticulously orchestrated plot to suppress her "vision." At the end of a lengthy diatribe that accompanies one of her videos, she writes, "i recorded now all thsi theem instead of rerst. sleep, food again. l am ill very stromng I have hogb level of frost -beete feet … hsuabnd elimiantes me." She is drained and worn down from sleep-deprivation and hunger; her feet are frost-bitten; she is derided by her husband, but she writes and records videos out of a compulsion to reveal *the truth* to the world. In a lucid moment of self-awareness, she reflects on her "vision" and "abnormal endurance" when she writes: "mistifying about my vision cases and anomal enduranec not habitul for a woman while I have in reality weak health." She persists despite her poor health, despite the vast plot by Scientologists, the Kremlin, Islamists, YouTube, the police, the FSB (Russian secret service), and others sent to suppress her secret knowledge and block her attempts to publicize the incriminating evidence she has gathered through her videos. Refbatch writes manically about the coincidences between news stories and her life; everything—from plane crashes to earthquakes to the death of Kennedy—seems profoundly connected to subtle incidents in her life. She writes:

EVEN NOW, THROUGH SLEEPING I SHPOULD TYPE THIS—
UNDERTSANDING THAT OUR POIOSNS WE WILL NOT AWAKE
TOMORROW IF I WILL NTO SHOUT THAT I NOTIVED THE ARTICLE—
OPENED BY *chance,*

—and undertsand its sence.
life become too hard bec of their this hunt.

half of vidoe snot sent—

I began this article by attempting to answer the question, *Who is Refbatch?* with the limited and fragmentary portrait I have constructed through her texts and videos. But there is an insurmountable divide between her and me, an unbridgeable temporal distance between the moment the video is captured and the moment the digitized data is rendered and made public. To me, Refbatch is only the spectral impression of an existence whose meaning I will never fully comprehend. I do not know Anna Matskevich. I only know *Refbatch*: the digitized object, the messenger, the blurry face of a woman whose image hangs draped over what I think must be a solid being. I try to remove the shroud covering the mysterious figure but find nothing underneath. She can't be located; is always already gone.

Refbatch eludes me; my understanding of her is partial. Where does she get money to live? Who is the man who occasionally appears in her videos and holds the camera? The tidbits of information that I do know about her life are often not offered directly, but revealed only because they are implicated in her conspiracy in some way. While I gather that there is likely a man in her life who shares her delusions, I only gather this because she posted a letter with one of her videos that said:

> *from: Maxim Belov*
> *Today Anna Matskevich tried to upload in "YouTube" her video*
> *"Al-Qaeda controls my communication means"—internet connection*
>   *didn't work.*
> *Because of this video record is not uploaded yet it could be dangerous*
>   *for Anna.*
> *[…]*
> *Your sincerely*
> *Maxim Belov*

It's likely that Maxim Belov is Refbatch's husband. From the message we can gather that it's possible that the two are engaged in a folie à deux. The phrase, meaning "delusion for two," was first integrated into my lexicon when I heard the story of the Papin sisters, who were two French maids who killed their employers and then had sex with each other. Even though Refbatch's husband shares many of her "visions" and can be seen in videos imitating her movements, Refbatch frequently refers to him with ambivalence and suspicion. She asks herself, "But what is th erole of my husabnd—why he evry time take participation in this resonance and in destruction of me till end." She often speculates that he has been drugged and made to turn against her, to participate in the conspiratorial suppression of her insight through violence and abuse. Refbatch also writes about being poisoned and drugged ("as always hided, sprayed by drugs, and threatned in the forest"). The poisons are said to erase their "self-undertsanding, joy of life, and so—opportunityt creat andjust to syr-vive." Refbatch often refers to the poison or the effect of the poison as "outmind," a term used when one loses the mental capability to decipher the unstated meanings found in one's surroundings, like the ability to understand the messages encoded in news stories.

The paradoxical nature of Refbatch's monumental document is that it's totally nonsubjective, even though it is an obsessive record of her life. Her videos and texts do not document her interiority. She denies the ego. Her existence seems to completely revolve around relations and exterior events. In a way, Refbatch is possessed. Fragments of history, pop culture, news media, and information colonize her entire being. She often writes of herself as if she is an *object*, a hollow vehicle defined solely by the singular purpose of transmitting the truth. She has stated that she—a woman/female *object*—has not existed since 1999, making her a residual shadow that remains only to broadcast her struggle. *The fighter of removed is representing to you its fight.* Refbatch is a ghost. Like a ghost, she lingers in an intermediary zone between life and death because she has unfinished business. Her presence is phantasmatic, diaphanous. She is shadow—only half here. In some sense, she is *pure message*. Since she lacks the presence of *being*, her temporality is destabilized. Time crumbles because the intrusion of the past scrambles the forward linear trajectory. She writes that the future and the present are absent and declares that the past is "disputing every second."

Refbatch turns herself further into an object when she speaks of herself in the second person.

> *you did thsi?*
> *you dance bear foot?*
> *ypou did nto sleep and di not eat—*
> *you tookj absue poisones scandla pof hsuabnd befor ework and insteda of sprot triasngina?*
> *you posses vision/*
> *you can move non stop—a out rest poiisitive smotion and money payed. you/*
> *or me/*
> *iof not then taker your long fuck to your pocketand hold it ther until you will not posses such features as me—*

In this syntactically complex passage, Refbatch uses second person throughout much of the text, but in the end she performs a sort of textual splitting of the self by introducing the first person pronoun "me" while keeping the "you" intact. She accommodates both the "you" and "me" in the phrase *you will not possess such features as me*. But both "you" and "me" appear to refer to herself. She teeters back and forth between positions, "*You/ or me/,*" the slashes of which may also indicate this split in perspective. It's as if she were controlled by an outsider, as if she were speaking from both the interior and the exterior, looking at herself while she looks at herself, an object apprehending an object. Linear time, the subjective position, and logical sentence structures are all overturned by Refbatch.

I often find myself unconsciously thinking of Refbatch before falling asleep, and it is during this time—when the logic undergirding my thoughts comes undone—that I feel like I can intuitively understand Refbatch most. Every image and line strike me as wrenchingly tragic. Once before going to sleep I asked my partner, "Why does she do it? Is it the unrelenting need to expose the truth to the world?" My partner said that that was likely her motivation, but I pressed it further: "But then why does she post all those videos of herself dancing in fields and forests? How are those related to the global conspiracy?" She replied, "Because it's a form of expression that she feels is also persecuted."

It makes sense. For Refbatch, bodily movement itself is a form of testimony. She imagines that even the tai chi–like movements she performs—which she often refers to as "morning exercise," "ballet," "snow sport," "training," or "dance"—are suppressed by the conspirators. She writes, "my dances on snow as freedom of speech are forbidden." She relates an incident that she refers to as "attacked ballet" to a news story possibly having to do with the suppression of Buddhist practices in Malaysia. Around the time Michael Jackson died, Refbatch posted videos titled "we dance-Michael!" and "michael found thw way how to be young and to dance in any age—those who do not want to dance—eliminated him fro—." In another video, she writes about how Serbian ballerinas dancing with machine guns were pushed out of their space: "serbian balerinas made thero class somewher on the ban of adriatic sea at very hot—but now there are ruins only there—for serbs dancers."

I Am Outmind to Understand What Tempo I Am Enforced to Live

My obsession with Refbatch is getting unhealthy. As I become more invested, I lose my ability to write about her with distance. While neurotically trying to unearth more information, I make a startling discovery. Refbatch has a second YouTube channel under the name Refbatch1, bringing her total video count to more than 11,623. Next, I find a Refbatch account on Yahoo Video, but this one only has five videos and appears to be a desperate attempt to continue broadcasting after being "censored" by YouTube. I am trying to piece everything together, to make sense of it. It's not gibberish. The more I sift through the videos and text of the 11,623 posts, I realize the incredible coherence of Refbatch's logic. I find a Myspace account belonging to Refbatch. There are videos posted there as well. She is listed as forty-six years old. Then I find four videos all containing the same series of letters written by "Maxim Belov"—her husband—while she was detained in a psychiatric "prison." This is one of my greatest finds yet: a rare glimpse of "factual" details relating to Refbatch's life. He writes:

> *Anna Matskevich was detained and sent to 13-th psychiatrical clinik of Moscow for political expression against totalitarism in Russia. ... I called at 9.00 a.m. to the receiption of the clinik. ... She said that today Anna Matskevich will be psychiatrically checked and tommorow only I will get result about her future. When I said I want to take her home soon as it is possible—she refused, refering to their timetable. When I asked if any medicins were used against my wife—Mrs. L. V. Mischenko insistably suggested that I should call tomorrow. ... By the way, there is some information that staff of this clinik sadistically jeer at people like fascist butchers in Hitler time.*

... By low if a person has somebody of his relatives, who are against the psychiatrical test of him—the test can't be done. I am against from the test of my wife. ... If Russian Federation just announce open repression against her by such messuares—I apply for political refuge from her name and myself. Rights and freedoms, incl.expressions are persecuted in the country. ... It is clear: that when state wants to remove a dissident—there are'nt obstacles for this.

If Maxim did write the letter, it's the most concrete evidence that their delusion is shared. The letters are dated January 3 and 4, 2010. YouTube won't let me scroll that far back through her videos, so I use a trick on Google's video search engine to see if she posted any videos during those days. Disappointment: it appears that she posted as usual during the days she was supposedly in the hospital. Was the whole thing a hoax? But I believe that she went to a mental hospital, and I am sure Maxim must have written the letters. I can tell because his writing is clearer and contains fewer typos. I noticed that he types "aren't" as "are'nt," but what if it's her fabricating the letters? Is it possible that both of these non-native-English-speakers like to use the word *jeer*? I decide to try to look up the psychiatrist mentioned in the letters—Mrs. Larisa Mishchenko. I find out that Larisa Mishchenko is a character from an *X-Men* comic. I read a summary on the website *Mutatis Mutandis*:

A journalist by the name of Larisa fights with her editor over his unwillingness to allow her to work on a story about corruption in the military. The editor points to photographs on the wall of previous editors who published controversial stories and died because of it. Larisa doesn't relent, insisting on writing the story and having it published and the editor gives in. … [At] the apartment of Larisa Mishchenko, Larisa looks out the window to see a FSB agent standing watch over her residence.

The story of the comic book character Larisa Mishchenko is uncannily similar to Refbatch's story. But is it just a bizarre coincidence? Is Larisa Mishchenko actually the name of the psychiatrist who oversaw Refbatch? Does this psychiatrist even exist? Did Refbatch even go to the mental hospital? Should I call the phone number of the supposed Russian doctor listed in "Maxim's" letter? I no longer know what is real. I look for sources outside of Refbatch's discourse for grounding, but emerge even more confounded. While watching Refbatch's video, the boundary between fact and fiction deteriorates under my increasingly intensified feeling that—in some sense—everything is real.

Like Refbatch, *I drown in information.* The stream of input is unending, especially since it's not unusual for Refbatch to post around twenty videos/text commentaries a day. In my search, everything is connected and pregnant with meaning, like the oversaturation of meaning in Refbatch's world. An unsettling parallel is formed between my engagement with Refbatch and Refbatch's engagement with the world. I wonder if I am getting drawn into her *way of being.* My mind reels. What is the meaning of the phrase "blind send" that repeatedly appears in Refbatch's videos? What is the meaning of the term "eblo"? I try to look it up. It might be an offensive word for "face" or a slang word for "penis" in Russian. I look up the word "alkl" and after coming up relatively fruitless, I realize that—given the closeness of the letters *k* and *l* on the keyboard—it's likely a typo of the word "all." I try to search her real name. A profile on a site called "My Opera" shows up. Listed occupation:

Dissident. I scroll through more search results and find her name listed in dance-competition results. Is that a different Anna Matskevich? "What do you think?" I ask my partner. She said that it actually crossed her mind that Refbatch was once a professional dancer. It makes sense to me too: she's obsessed with dancing and is unusually athletic. Couldn't this be her?

The internet crashes. That's why I am able to write this instead of restlessly sifting through information. But I still have pages and pages of text copied into Word documents and hundreds of video stills to mull over. At every turn I notice a new pattern. The task of writing about Refbatch is totally absorbing. I began this piece with the intention of writing a short blurb on one schizophrenic woman's peculiar videos, but the undertaking has spiraled out of control, consuming me and my life completely. Through Refbatch, I try to find the meaning of it all. I haven't left my house all day. The more I go through her material, the less I think, *This woman is crazy*, and the more I recognize her lucidity and the profound truths of her messages.

Covered and Shut Up

we are bea out from scandals form only open eyes—
representin melodies of … Beethoven, ect.under grad noise;
so next day
tehre is no interest and wsh just to get up from bed,
as melodies by beethoven are outbombing by abusement
of grad rockets to your side form everywhere.

I am trying to understand what motivates me to pour all this time and energy into trying to understand Refbatch. Why am I writing this? I know that—for one—there is an urgency to preserve the monumental work that Refbatch has created and is still creating. Since this sprawling document exists on the corporate-owned website YouTube, it is extremely vulnerable. YouTube often deletes the channels of users that post an excessive number of videos, and their terms of service explicitly state, "YouTube *reserves the right to decide* whether Content violates these Terms of Service for reasons other than copyright infringement. … YouTube may at any time, *without prior notice and in its sole discretion*, remove such Content and/or terminate a user's account for submitting such material in violation of these Terms of Service." I hope that people will work toward archiving and backing up Refbatch's videos and texts so that they are not lost forever if an administrator hastily decides to delete her channel. (Since writing this, Refbatch's account has been deleted, but she's reemerged under a different avatar.)

There is another underlying motivation propelling this piece. It is the desire to expand our notion of reality, and to create space for the existence of parallel realities. Even though on some level I may think that the "facts" of Refbatch's claims are "not true," I find it problematic to dismiss her reality. Reality is multiple. Refbatch's reality may be just as subjectively true as yours or mine. We depend completely upon the creation of internally coherent narratives to validate and extend our reality, but these can't be measured against an objective or transcendent point of reference. There is no way to access *the true reality*—it doesn't exist. People may watch Refbatch and think, *Who is this lunatic woman?* They may dismiss what she has to say while remaining intrigued by her wild behavior. When I try to show her videos to people, she is often either dismissed as psychotic, or exoticized, for the same reasons. But when people engage her work this way, they fail to actually *listen*. They don't meaningfully consider her messages. As I delve deeper and deeper into Refbatch's world, I realize that she has created a mad language and vocabulary to articulate what I would consider a justifiable response to delegitimization, oppression, trivialization, and invalidation for being a woman, for having "cosmic visions," for existing under governments, religious institutions, and other apparatuses of control. Refbatch is an antiauthoritarian. She has noted that she would rather die than relinquish her right "to create, to think, to love, to fly into space." She persists despite feeling weakened, attacked, and demoralized, noting that *she makes more than men could while being considered weaker than they are.* Even though Refbatch may develop wild fantasies to accompany her feeling of persecution, there is nothing irrational about her feeling of marginalization. In a strange way, her testimony reveals the true face of the world, a world that can be cruel and unkind to madwomen who are endowed with too much vision.

* * *

psychiatry women show who attacked pope—
when I will die I will follow the information anyway—but they
     want and everybody only wants:
I must be as missing
covered and shut up
stop to shut me up by psychiatry

I do not need permission to see.

they do not allow me to be so as I am.

(2010)

The Skin-Cloth: Race, Fashion, Hygiene, Writing, and Embodied Movement through Space

This essay originally appeared on the Delirious Hem *blog.*

"Drenched in Light" is a story written by Zora Neale Hurston about a recalcitrant little Brown girl who cannot stop dancing. Little Isis Watts. Also known as Isis the Joyful, as her presence is haloed. Movement is her way of being in the world. Her grandma gives her tasks and chores and she does them begrudgingly, her body unable to sit still or be disciplined. Hers is a body that refuses to submit, that insists on occupying space with limbs extended, armed with quick feet and swerving hips that leave enormous ovals of energy in her wake. She cartwheels to the yard to do her chores, romps around while raking leaves, and intermittently frolics with the dogs while washing the dishes. When a carnival takes place nearby, she feels that she must go, that she must take to the stage and dance while the band plays and the audience watches. While running down the road toward the carnival, she stops.

> She realized she couldn't dance at the carnival. Her dress was torn and dirty. She picked a long-stemmed daisy, and placed it behind her ear, but her dress remained torn and dirty just the same.

But Isis has an idea. She returns to the house, takes her grandma's new tablecloth out of a tattered trunk, and runs to the carnival with the tablecloth wrapped around her body. At the carnival she dances as the band plays, amassing a crowd that is fixated on her presence—the presence of a little Brown girl whose feet twinkle beneath the fringe of a tablecloth.

> The Grand Exalted Ruler rose to speak; the band was hushed, but Isis danced on, the crowd clapping their hands for her. No one listened to the Exalted one, for little by little the multitude had surrounded the small brown dancer.

When her grandma catches her dancing at the carnival in her table-cloth, she runs to the creek and wants to die, but the sentiment passes after she enters the water with the tablecloth and begins to splash and sing.

* * *

What does a little Brown girl need to do to ward off the feeling of wanting to die?

I think about this.

I think about little Isis Watts's guerrilla occupation of the carnival, the way she insisted on taking up space, the way her tattered clothing almost stopped her. But she stole the tablecloth to cover the markings of pover-ty, the markings that were meant to keep her off the stage and out of the limelight. Isis gave herself permission to inject her body into the festival and her presence was so huge that nobody gave a shit when the Grand Exalted Ruler rose to speak. I imagine the Exalted one to be a white man eager to command the audience's attention. But Isis takes away his power. Her refusal to be barred from feeling a sense of fabulousness and bigness is a revolutionary gesture, for it decenters the white person's exclusive claims to grandeur and fabulousness. And she accomplishes this by whatever means necessary, by stealing the tablecloth, by performing extravagance without having access to extravagant clothing.

Fashion is all about the way you occupy space. Any potential that I find in fashion has to do with Brown girls and queers of color occupying space in ways that don't make them feel like shit, or using class drag to disrupt the exclusivist boundaries around white opulence. I have seen the way that fashion-as-the-worship-of-whiteness fills Brown girls with self-hate, the way it can ravage their sense of self-worth. We exist in a world that insists that the value of a person corresponds to their wealth—the value of their commodities. Fashion can also obscure the violence of our lifestyles, the hyperexploited labor of Brown bodies behind the name brands. I am interested in fashion insofar as it can be used to disrupt the racist, classist, and capitalistic trappings of the fashion world, like the queer people of color in the documentary *Paris Is Burning*, who steal and sew their own clothing to perform in "balls" (queer fashion events that incorporate multiple forms of drag, including forms of class drag).

These are provisional forms of fabulousness, aimed at dismantling the dehumanizing effects of certain forms of class and race elitism. As Judith Butler said, "This is not an appropriation of dominant culture in order to remain subordinated by its terms, but an appropriation that seeks to make over the terms of domination, a making over which is itself a kind of agency, a power in and as discourse, in and as performance, which repeats in order to remake—and sometimes succeeds."

As a queer, racially ambiguous Brown girl, I am very aware of the way my body exists in the world, the way it moves through space, the way it is read and judged by people. When speaking about the

Croatian performance artist Zlatko Kopljar, Serbian art theorist Miško Šuvaković described how Kopljar uses his body as a "'probe' for testing the micro- or macro- social horizon of reality." But I can't help but feel like my body is always a probe—that every insulting racial comment or sexual advance on the street is a microencounter that reveals larger structures of power. The demarcated space of the performance event and the practice of injecting your body into spaces that are hostile to your presence (as a way to have some kind of revelatory contact with power) are irrelevant to me. My whole life is a performance-art piece in that people are *always* interacting with my body in ways that expose the "macro-social horizon of reality."

* * *

During most of the day the body is sheathed in cloth. And beneath it—another cloth. A Brown-skin cloth. Dark nipples and oily skin. You can never abandon the markings of the skin-cloth. When you go for a walk or write or sleep, it's always there. It's the outfit you wear in every episode. What does your skin-cloth look like? Mine has scars. Many scars. When I scar, I scar dark and for a long time. I wonder if these scars could count as an outfit. I wonder about the place where surface ends and interiority begin and what this means in light of the way certain wounds seem to cut through all layers.

* * *

On some days I like to occupy space differently. On some days I enjoy tricking heterosexual men into thinking I'm normal, straight, and pretty. On some days I feel like donning the tablecloth and wearing it in such a way that people are fooled into thinking it's an expensive dress. On other days the strategy of provisional fabulousness doesn't work for me. I want to be more aggressive. I want to walk around all wild, oily, frizzy, unkempt, and smelly—without combing my wolf hair or hiding my period odor or armpit smell. If fashion is about your presence in space, then odor is a form of fashion. On some days I want to disrupt hygienic space with my grossness, to sit in places that I look like I shouldn't be in while looking lonely and strung out amidst the opulence. To shit on etiquette and make people feel uncomfortable. To force people to confront everything they try to cover up and eliminate and wash out when they get dressed in the morning. To pollute white space with my Brown body.

I negotiate my movement through physical space like I do textual space—always with an eye to undoing the damaging codes that regulate those spaces, the ones that make you feel like you're worthless, that your beauty doesn't count as beauty, that your presence is unwelcome, that your words aren't worth saying, that you shouldn't be up there dancing. To explore fashion is to explore the surface of the body. I think about the garments I cannot take off. The skin-cloth. And my burning desire to rearrange space so that we may be received differently, so that we can move through space without fear.

(2011)

On Hand Jobs, AWP, the Internet,
Truck Drivers, and Embodied Living

This originally appeared on HTMLGIANT.

After AWP, the Association of Writers & Writing Programs' annual conference, both Ariana Reines and Kate Zambreno blogged about how they do it for the young girls, how the young girls respond and feel comforted. They put themselves out there unapologetically and I like that, but I also think about how I could never be that, how I was never a libertine in that way but perhaps very much so in others, how I never sought the Fuck (unless it was with myself), regardless of whether it was a casual pleasure-fuck or a complicated hate-fuck. I spent my adolescence obsessively trying to avoid all contact with boys/men and fantasizing about stabbing the ones who sexually harassed me. In middle school I was horrified to find that someone wrote down in a 'slam book' that I had been fucked in the ass by some kid named Jordan, which was a lie. I was a loner nerd but then all the cool girls befriended me because I had a hot older brother. They would sleep over my house as a way to hook up with other boys in the neighborhood. Late at night the girls would call the boys and negotiate sex plans. Once Katie arranged for me to give a hand job to some kid even though I didn't want to. Behind some park late at night I definitely did not want to touch it. Later his friend tried to get a hand job from me, noting my "soft, tiny hands." I kept saying noooo and "I can't give you a hand job because my best friend likes you and I would never do that to her." A year and a half ago, when I was hitchhiking/bicycling alone around the East Coast one summer, I got a ride from a trucker who told me he was driving straight to Philly. But it turned out he wasn't even going to Philly, and he also wasn't planning on heading straight there. He stopped somewhere to sleep and I was stuck in the truck with him. He begged me for hand jobs like that jerk in middle school. I said noooo and he kept begging and then he started offering me money while saying, "Come on! Loosen the fuck up. Don't you want to make money for your trip? It's not like I'm asking you to fuck me or anything." To shut him up I said, "I have a boyfriend," because I didn't know how he would react if I said, "I'm a lesbian."

Miraculously, the boyfriend lie worked on the horny truck driver. My fake boyfriend saved me. It was while hitchhiking that I learned that the truckers call sex workers who hang around the truck stops "lot lizards." The nice old man truck driver who gave me a ride before I got stuck with the horny guy got on the radio to try to find me a ride and everyone on the radio immediately started chiming in: "What do her tits look like? Does she have a nice ass?" He said, "She ain't no lot lizard. Just trying to find a ride to Philly." The old man gave me a knife and bought me a Subway sandwich before I got in the truck with the horny guy. After I got out of the horny guy's truck, the next guy who gave me a ride was very Philly Italiano in a tender kind of way. I put my bicycle in the back of his truck and started to climb into the front seat, but as soon as I got into his truck a woman in a nursing uniform drove in front of the truck, pointed her finger at me and screamed for me to get out of the truck. She told me to get inside her car and when I was in the passenger seat she said, "I saw you on the side of the road with your sign. You can't get in that man's car!" The guy got out of the truck and said, "What's going on here? Has this young girl escaped from the mental hospital?" The woman was a zealous Jehovah's Witness who forced religious pamphlets onto me before I got out of her car. The crazed lady was comforted when the Philly Italiano guy told her, "Don't worry ma'am. I'm a God-fearing man myself." (Cue the image of the tough guy proudly holding up his crucifix.) This is not writing about literature but maybe it can pass *as* literature. Writing happens in movement. So. We go. Isn't it funny that *jobs* comes after *hand* in the phrase *hand jobs*? Imagine your hand wearing a nice suit and carrying a briefcase as it walks off to work while you look at it tenderly and think, "My hand is off to its job again." If I had a nickel for every time a gross guy told me to touch his penis. … After a while you start to really hate being a woman, especially one with big tits. Once I was sleeping over at a friend's house and a Christian boy crawled into the bed I was sleeping in and said, "Touch my shaft. Come on. Touch my shaft." I said, "What are you doing? I'm dating your best friend." Then he started freaking out while saying, "How am I going to remain abstinent until marriage???"

I am in Glasgow, Scotland, right now. I came here two days after AWP. It took me nearly two days straight of constant travel to get here because I was trying to do it on the cheap. I scammed my way to NYC via bus and got stuck in traffic for hours and ran to the subway and train and airport with a Belgian girl who was also on the bus from Bmore to NYC and, incidentally, was trying to catch the same flight to London. Today I went to a building called the Center for Contemporary Arts to try to read and write while sitting at one of the tables in the center of the arts complex. They promptly kicked me out because I didn't buy any food and for the rest of the day I was fuming while thinking about how all space is capitalist space, how much I hate the culture of contemporary art, how it is impossible to even sit down or gather with friends or do anything at all unless you are engaging in some sort of commercial exchange. Maybe the sidewalk is the last of the spatial commons but if you stopped walking or sat down while on a sidewalk, you'd be "obstructing traffic," and that certainly is not allowed.

Did you go to AWP? Did you feel connected or alone in your head? How did it feel to be near the people you know digitally, to know them embodied for a few days? I found it hard to make eye contact with people because I felt embarrassed inside my skin. I hope I didn't come across as rude. I was very excited to see everyone but I was nervous and extremely sleep-deprived. I met many of the *HTML-GIANTers*, bought tampons with Ariana Reines, made a fool of myself in front of Bhanu Kapil and Eileen Myles (especially Bhanu, after giving her an Ambien letter and bundle of drawings), hung at a bar with M Kitchell and Kate Zambreno, wandered the DC streets for hours lost and alone while it rained, was berated by an Eastern European man who made racist remarks about me, stayed up all night talking to an old classmate about Clarice Lispector, flipped out when I found out Clarice Lispector loved Spinoza(!!), hung with Alec and other Florida people … and so on. Tim Jones-Yelvington was definitely the best dressed. I think it was Mike Young who asked me at lunch if I live in a punk house and I said I live in a "Marxist Goth Cult," which may or may not be a joke. A few months ago I deleted my Facebook and it definitely feels like I exist less to the world. I've been reading too much post-Marxist theory and feeling paranoid about subjective and immaterial production under post-modern capitalism—"Empire," you might call it—and have been thinking about how Facebook / Tumblr / Twitter / Web 2.0 operates according to a consumerist logic, the constant production-consumption feedback loop that exploits our human NEED for acknowledgment while turning our fears and longings and sadness into tiny poops to be consumed without actually granting us the satisfaction of the interpersonal connection that we often desperately crave. That, to me, is the saddest thing … the way an email only feels good for a few minutes, the way we are immediately waiting for the next thing.

(2011)

Notes from Berlin

This originally appeared on my Tumblr blog.

A perfunctory update. Hello. I traveled from Glasgow to Berlin. Soon I go to Prague, then Budapest, then Győr, then Vienna. After that it's back to Glasgow, maybe stopping in London if I have to. Woke up bright and early this morning (which means I didn't go to sleep at all). Mind was reeling even after I took my sleeping pill. It's dangerous that I'm writing right now considering I didn't sleep … brain's a little fuzzy and so it oozes out all wrong. Lately I waste buckets of time staring off confused, wondering what my last thought was, beating myself up over my scrambled brain. Then I tell myself, *What can you do? You're defective*, and continue the interminable frog hop through horrific and lovely thoughts that spring into existence and hang themselves upon awareness.

Today, after cooking some vegetable curry, rosemary mashed potatoes, and rice at the Schwarzer Kanal Queer Wagenplatz squat, I rode the guest bike to the huge Soviet memorial in Treptower Park. So began my very communist day. It was high noon and the sun was out. I rode my bike round and round in circles around an enormous statue of a Soviet soldier crushing a swastika while holding a sword and saving a baby. My eyes felt like movie cinematography—the circling, the upward angle, the sun. The park was nearly empty, the square vast. I felt swollen-brained. Thought about my roommate

M., how I would have forced him to attempt to translate the Russian text for me if he were there, how communist iconography will forever remind me of him, how much fun I think we would have traveling together judging by how much fun we had at AWP while we were bonkers with sleep deprivation. (Later I went to the Stasi Museum, which I want to write about some other time.)

I am worried about going to Budapest. The last time I saw my friend from Hungary was the day before I was leaving Kunming. It was my birthday/going away party of 2009, a little over two years ago. Some friends and I went out to hot pot and KTV (karaoke) and he stormed off without saying goodbye even though we wouldn't see each other again … maybe forever! I was thinking, *You fucker!* And, *We are definitely not going to stay friends after this! No way.* Now here we are. He keeps sending me emails: "Can you eat cottage cheese? Fish? What about eggs?" *Yes, actually. I am obsessed with eggs. No fish. Cottage cheese good.* We will visit his hometown in Hungary and his mother will cook for me and I will feel overwhelming endearment for phrases like "Just write me when and where do you arrive to Budapest and I go and catch you up!"

I met some wonderful people in Berlin through Al Burian. They just stuffed me with a lot of food. Alan, the Classics professor, said he is going to sprinkle ice cream sandwich wrappers around my bed and claim that I ate the rest of his box while on Ambien. But what if he goes to trick me and finds that I already ate the ice cream sandwiches while on Ambien?

As Al Burian was telling me a story about destroying a housemate's rocking chair in a fit of rage while we were eating at a Lebanese restaurant, a guy who worked at the restaurant started laughing and then I burst out into hysterical laughter and then he laughed harder and it was a strange moment, an unknowable energy circulating between people.

I want to write about CAConrad's deranged brain, the Stasi Vs. The Punks in the GDR (musings on statism and subcultures and decadence and the Cold War and in-the-flesh communism), fandom, Mao's embalmed body, the politics of affect and why Negri's reading of Spinoza is better than Deleuze's, whether or not my roommate M. would have been considered a proper "socialist personality" by the SED (he's certainly got the paranoia part down), how Rousseau's ideas about need and recognition can be applied to considerations of Facebook, being candy-sexual, walking around Berlin alone eating cake with my hands (and other reflections on lonerist tendencies), sleep deprivation, epic poems about finding the lost aliens of planet earth … you get the idea. There's a lot going on up here but I am very confused right now. Love you, byyye!

(2011)

Make Mantra of American Language Now

This originally appeared on my Tumblr blog.

I am running out of sleeping pills and money. While I was writing this in my notebook my pen ran out of ink.

When I woke up in Prague after many nights without sleep, it was like waking up from a drunken blackout that lasted several days. Eyes open onto the hazy torpor of your marred consciousness. Your consciousness: gradually widening and before you know it, you're thrust into the fluorescent lights of the mind. There's the jarring clarity when you notice your purse is shredded on the bottom. You must have been dragging it along the ground without realizing it. In Hungary you stapled it back together. And then that sober, nagging thought: *Did I lose anything?* Or, *what has been lost?* To be, without the centering subject. To be so lost you go amorphous.

When you don't sleep you are always on the brink of tears. A man and his daughter bike past you while you are walking near the Turkish market alongside the Spree River in Berlin and you start to cry thinking about how you loved it when your dad would ride around with you strapped into the backseat of his bicycle. Sometimes you would ride to Grandma's house. We were living in Hudson, FL—a very white and Southern area. Later I would won-der how my dad felt there, or in Wyoming, the place he lived when he first came to America from Taiwan. It was certainly weird being a family of aliens in the South. How did we get there?

In the grandiose church in Győr, Hungary, you remember how you loved to light the candle at church with your grandmother even though you didn't know what it meant—maybe something about remembering the dead? Maybe the child mind just loves to make fire.

Sleepless: a ball of light-energy jittering through a city with a giant mop of hair and flaming-red-marble eyes. What is the *dérive*? A wandering alien-monster with tears in her eyes, about to have a psychogeographic meltdown. Everything becomes not-simple and I look at people on the Metro and believe I can see to their souls.

I want to look like you, man. I want a big body and square head and stubble on my face and the ability to walk around without being pursued sexually or harassed about my race.

Everything shrouded in a mystical slime. A crazed sleep-deprived flâneuse wandering through old European cities with a notebook full of somniloquent scribblings. The people walk around looking all processional and I swear to God, the tourists on the Charles Bridge in Prague were part of some kind of sublime funeral. It seemed like everyone was wearing black, walking past the blackened statues with their black gloves while the black birds soared across the sky. I break down teary-eyed on the train from Berlin to Prague just thinking about the funerals of revolutionaries ... imagining thousands and thousands of people following their caskets through the streets, and the holy fervor of that collective sadness. I think about the funeral of Bunchy Carter from the Black Panthers, how it rained on the day of his funeral. The surviving Panthers said it was Bunchy pissing on racist America. I feel a little better thinking about the assassinated Panthers pissing on racist America.

I kind of didn't want to go to Prague but when I got there, I made a really good friend. He reminded me of someone I love very much and in my head I made a personal map of the people I love.

When I felt myself becoming manic I doubled the sleeping-pill dosage and things stabilized. It's funny to be able to do this, to end the intensity with a little pill. Sleep is stabilizing; people are stabilizing. My vision goes flat. I can think in complete sentences again, but still not very well.

(2011)

Birds, Orphans, and Fools
by Juraj Jakubisko

This originally appeared on my Tumblr blog.

The redeye flight to London fucked up my sense of time. I stayed at the airport the entire night because I couldn't afford the thirty-five-pound train into central London. The bus cost seven pounds, but they didn't run until the next day. So I stayed awake at the airport, sat on a cold floor next to a vending machine, and compulsively ate junk food and candy while watching Slovak, German, and Hungarian films on my laptop. It was weird feeling totally emotionally destroyed by Juraj Jakubisko's film *Birds, Orphans and Fools* in such a context. I wrote notes in my journal.

> You are free because you're crazy. / Some people get drunk on water. / We can't master life. We can't master love. So let's enjoy it a while. At least something. Those moments that go by. / At least a little bit of happiness. / The sea will come. / Yes, the sea. / You are giving up sooner than necessary. / You've lost the courage for madness.

> All of a sudden, the emptiness.

* * *

FUCK. It's my life. I also try to seek out the lost orphans and loner-outcasts of planet Earth, the ones looking for a way out of a world they do not understand. The characters in the film live in a giant dilapidated church with the other orphans—costumed children and an old man who plays the piano like a shamanistic maniac. Their parents killed each other in the War, and they are trying to figure out how to LIVE. Like the Buddhists who practice CRAZY WISDOM, they believe in the freeing potential of madness. When they ran out of gas while cruising down that beautiful snowy road, I knew what was coming. I know the feeling of running out of gas. Everything began to crumble.

Jakubisko's postwar absurdist tragicomedy seemed to be saying, GIVE UP. THE WORLD WILL CRUSH YOU. How could I contest such assertions? That doomed feeling returns. The sterility of this airport so crushing.

But when the music was swelling—the music of Zdeněk Liška—it felt like this blazing, luminous defiance. To love, in these times! Impossible and yet … look at us. Look at the world and the way we somehow still remember … the joy of hugging our friends.

(Bodhan, the friend I made via CouchSurfing, writes: *The only awful circumstance about meeting Jackie came at the end of our meeting: her bus arrived so unexpectedly soon that I couldn't even manage to properly hug her. It was supposed to be a very long hug.*)

Still remembering that fragile exuberance, we let out a resounding FUCK YOU, screamed in the face of everything meant to hold us back.

Cue up the reprise!

There is synchronicity in our scattered longings.

I want to believe I am not alone.

I want to believe that we are capable of sharing something more than a mutual belief in the concept of money.

And then an enormous bucket of water is dumped on our ecstatic chorus, sent to drown out our foolish bravado. Floods wash everything away these days. I was on the bus from Prague to Budapest when the earthquake happened in Japan. When I emerged from the automotive chrysalis, I couldn't believe how apocalyptic it all seemed, when my friend showed me the videos.

(When our peals reached the gods, they were pissed.)

(Cue up the angry rumble.)

(Do I even believe in fate?)

I can never maintain *it* (the energy?) for long before the fatigue weighs on everything, makes getting out of bed seem impossible. Do I believe in fate? When I start to feel this deeply EXTINGUISHED I think there is some force out there that does not want me to live.

(2011)

Hi. Just Breaking In to Get My Free Brainscan!— Queen of the Filchers (Only from the Bad Guys)

This originally appeared on my Tumblr blog.

Dragged my suitcase around London all day. I'm losing my mind. The subway pukes me out in front of St. Paul's Cathedral and I wander in two minutes before the SINGERS begin their melodious praise to God and her glory. Yeah the SINGERS! That's the other thing I liked about being raised Catholic. It sounds so good and I am not even religious. Above the ominous black doors, there's a sign that says, THROUGH THE GATE OF DEATH WE PASS TO OUR JOYFUL RESURRECTION. What if I'm a sinner? Fucking queer. I wonder if I will immediately die if I open those doors. Bodhan, my Czech friend, says, "It's funny you like candy so much" while I mull over my selections in a giant grocery store. Look at me. I'd let my mouth rot out of my face before I'd give up candy, like Freud and his cigars.

* * *

Hey bus driver—

Listen. I know my ticket is for yesterday. I am going to tell you a lie and put on my innocent face. My plane was delayed and I missed the bus. I called the Megabus hotline and they said you'd put me on this bus as long as there's space.

There were many days spent in this weird lugubrious state and I lived in dread, fearing the onset of an unpredictable inertia. Like living in an earthquake zone. Emotional natural disaster coming. You think taping your windows up will be enough but it's not. There was this squashed feeling—a bodily depression, every part of my flesh occupied by it. I wondered, *Should I try to see London?* And, *What is wrong with me?* A travel book I downloaded gives me an ominous diagnosis: "When a man is tired of London, he is tired of life, for there is in London all that life can afford."

Maybe it was chronic depression. Or maybe, as Elaine joked, I just couldn't *afford* London. Whatever it was, I missed my bus because I was going mad. I couldn't understand very basic things. Like time ... like the passing of days. Where does one day end and the next begin? When you stay awake all night there is no mental RESET. Days bleed together, get counted as one. When I looked down at my bus ticket and realized it was for the previous night, I must have thought about the problem of TIME for an hour straight. I felt like it was a conspiracy. I hopped on my computer and googled "what day is it" and thought, *This can't be true.* I kept trying to calculate it and nothing was adding up. Is this worse than that time I showed up at the airport long after my flight left because I didn't actually know what time it was departing? The guy at the counter asks, "What flight were you supposed to get on?" I don't know how to answer so I estimate. He says, "There's no flight going to Tampa at that time. Give me your information, I will look it up."

The bus driver was unsympathetic. "This ticket is for yesterday." He points at the date. I KNOW. I just said that. I told you my excuse! "The people on the phone gave you the wrong information. We can't let you on this bus." "Oh. Um. Can I pay a fee or something?" "Yeah, give me thirty-five pounds." "What! I don't have thirty-five pounds." (What if I could hand over thirty-five pounds of my fat?) "Sorry." "Listen, if you don't let me on this bus, I am going to be stranded in London out in the cold! They promised me on the phone! I called this here number on the reservation ticket and it was the USA number and they gave me the UK number and I called them and they said, 'Yes, young lady, you will get on that bus! We will fly you to Glasgow because we love you! Have you seen *The Never Ending Story*? It will be like that!'" (Actually, I tried to email them and they just sent a form letter about how I agreed to the terms and could not be refunded.) "Please, mister! Let me on this bus!" He eventually buckles under my pressure and feigned innocence, but directs me onto the sketchy bus with all the drunk Scottish teenagers. The party train. Onward into the night! The man next to me can actually sleep. He has a face that looks like a corpse when lit a certain way by the streetlights.

[Re: title. I always thought *filcher* just meant "thief" but apparently it also refers to someone who ejaculates in someone's ass and then sucks out semen with a bendy or twirly straw. Oops.]

Good night my little lonesome doves. May you dream of getting a sensual back rub from Björk ... and eating a tunnel through a candy mountain (so you won't have to walk uphill). We live the Good Life.

(2011)

I Tripped, We Laughed. Let Me In!
Brain Damage

This originally appeared on my Tumblr blog.

Last night I dreamed about Bakhtin and the carnivalesque, though I don't remember the details just the feel of it. Today I woke up thinking, I WANT A TABULATED MIND. Felt myself Orientalizing the normies, their exotic ways of being, their functionality and the linear movement of their thought. Today I woke up with the phrase, I AM SOME SCIENTIST'S BLUBBER BLUNDER! Some madman's experiment gone horribly wrong, a MUTANT girl with enormous holes in her brain looking for a way out of damage.

I know what it's like to feel partial. And I don't want anyone else to feel partial.

That's why I got teary-eyed when Eileen Myles read at the Belladonna* event during AWP. Because even though the part they read from INFERNO about having a half-brain and being WASTED (not drunk but *thrown out*) is jocular in tone, it still destroys me. When you edit footage in Final Cut Pro you fill the holes and empty spaces with SLUGS. I think about that, about stuffing slugs in the holes in my brain, slimy and silent stand-ins for the missing memories, the places where there should be RECALL but instead there is just NOTHING. Feeling the limitations of your brain like that makes you nuts. Forgive me if I stutter and cannot remember your name. Remind me. Write notes on my hand. I need your orientation.

Today I found myself so bloated with words that I kept having to stop to write in my notebook on the short walk to the underground. A belly full of coffee and the energy of DIANE DI PRIMA'S poems REVOLUTIONARY LETTERS making me soar, I was a lightning rod continually struck by words, JAGGED sentences fully formed. In that crazed feeling I thought about my sleep-deprived romp through Canada with Joe that summer I lost my sleeping pills in Pittsburgh ... Sitting by the ocean on the shore of Cape Breton Island, I wrote my first song—IGNEOUS HAND. It came to me while staring at a white log with branches that looked like BONE. Pilar would sing it in her beautiful voice all the time.

A rare sunny sky in Glasgow. I arrive at the University of Glasgow Library, ready to begin my work. Elaine said the library folk were effusive and eager to help visitors but when I went, they did not let me in even though their website says, "We are pleased to offer members of the public access to the Library to consult our collections." There was something crushing about being turned away like that and I wondered, IS IT BECAUSE I LOOK UNKEMPT WITH MY FRIZZY HAIR AND OVERSIZED COAT AND SMEARED LIPSTICK? Why am I always shut out shit out kicked out? Now I sit in an empty university cafeteria. When I sat down to write I found that the energy was gone—usurped by a low-level functionary's arbitrary deployment of their meager institutional power. In the new world there will no longer be GATEKEEPERS. Emma Goldman kept a sign on her door that said something like "Property is theft. Come inside." WE KEEP SPACE OPEN.

(2011)

Synchronicity // Departure // Divergence // Remembrance

This originally appeared on my Tumblr blog.

In Hungary you said, "I like your shoes." Have we been here before?

That made me embarrassed. I was just thinking *don't look at my shoes don't look at my shoes don't look at my shoes* because they're beat up dirty and falling apart. Look at you. You're handsome, well put together. Before opening your room, you said, "I warn you, it's small." I braced myself for a closet but the door swung open and it was like four times the size of my room, the room I am sitting in now. "This room isn't small at all," I said. I wondered if you assumed I had a luxurious lifestyle just because I'm American. I felt embarrassed about everything. My clothes. The subtle shittiness of all my things. Right before visiting you I bought a pair of socks on the streets of Berlin from a Turkish man for half a euro. The seller said, "Are you Japanese?" I said, "No, American. Ummm … half-Chinese and half-Sicilian."

I was embarrassed about my socks. I only had a mismatched pair and they had huge holes in them. How could I face you in these socks? The lining of my coat was ripped in places. In the sun I tried to walk behind you. Embarrassed. When you spoke to me, I looked away. You bought me Hungarian and Viennese pastries and at the counter the woman said, "Your friend is very pretty." You said, "Yes, she is American." The pastry shop didn't have any tables or chairs, so we stood in front of the window, facing the sun, eating our desserts. It was hot. I wanted out of the light and under blankets. I wanted away from your sight. I was so afraid you would think I had grown ugly that I could hardly speak. At the bus station I waited there alone with my things, without a cell phone, wondering how you would be able to find me. I kept thinking *is that him? is that him?* while looking at the young men passing by ... as though so much time had passed that I would no longer be able to recognize you. Two years had passed. You had just gotten back from Taiwan and were still speaking some Chinese to fill in the missing English. You had gone back to Kunming. I said, "How is Yang Yang?" "Same. Partying and getting drunk all weekend, sleeping all week. I wonder how long she will be able to keep it up." We wondered together. We wondered how long a person can live while doing nothing and then I wondered—*What the fuck am I doing?* I'm a loafer who's just too square to party. At the bar you had to buy me a nonalcoholic drink. I told you I'm allergic to alcohol and you were confused because I drank all the time when we lived in Kunming. It's true—my girlfriend at the time mailed me a big bottle of Pepcid AC and so I drank. I drank shots of soju with the Koreans and shitty Dali beer from the street vendors and White Russians at the Halfway House bar full of women who all looked like lesbians to me. You called me while I was black-out drunk on the street and I only spoke Chinese and you said, "Jackie! Speak English." Were we fighting? We were always fighting. Desperate and hysterical, I called Jumyung. She happened to be on the same street eating *shaokao*. She came. She gave me a hug and I collapsed onto the floor crying and hysterically laughing, insisting that I sleep on the street.

I don't remember what happened after that, but I've reconstructed the night from secondhand accounts. I vomited in Jumyung's room all night. She thought the lipstick on the napkin she used to wipe my mouth was blood. Yang Yang came and dragged me into a taxi because I was too fucked up to walk down the street to my apartment. I woke up in Jumyung's clothes. I thought they looked nice on me.

In the bar we were catching up. But I didn't know what to say. I didn't know how to explain my life to you. You talked about what things were like when I left. We spoke calmly. Not all intense, pissed off, or intimate like before. We were almost like strangers, feeling each other out but so hesitantly. Not the eager and immediately open kind of strangers. In the bar you said, "You changed me. I learned a lot from you."

I was waiting for you to say something like "You taught me the meaning of true friendship." Or something about love and communication. But then you continued: "I know it sounds simple … but you taught me how to eat, how to appreciate food. Before I met you I was just *feeding*." This almost made me laugh; it was like the time my ex-girlfriend told me "I no longer bruise from malnutrition since we started dating." Of all the ways I could have changed your life, I changed your relationship to food? I suppose it makes sense. Our relationship revolved around food. You made such a big deal out of me being a vegetarian. I dragged you to the vegetarian restaurant next to the Yuantong temple and you moaned and groaned about not having your meat but then you loved it. I cooked for you and our other friends. Every afternoon we would meet to go out to lunch. We ate Indian, Thai, Japanese,

Uighur, Korean, and—of course—Yunnan food. We ate and talked ate and talked. You didn't know anything about food and were initially reluctant to try anything. I dragged you everywhere because I was so excited that I could get huge fancy meals for less than three US dollars. I remember that time we went to the Indian restaurant and you told me that it was Thanksgiving in the US. *Really?* I had forgotten. What an evil holiday anyway. In the restaurant your eyes were tearing like crazy because the food was so spicy. It was kind of tender even though they were spice tears and not emotion tears.

We were late trying to catch the train from Budapest to Győr and ran with all our luggage. You ran ahead while I dragged my suitcase up and down stairs, struggling to keep up. You seemed embarrassed that the train was shitty, but of course I didn't care. When we arrived to Győr we walked from the station to a bar to meet your friend. He asked us how we knew each other and you told him. Then you turned to me and said, "Honestly, I didn't think we would ever see each other again." Well, here I am. I came here, but things are different now. Look how life moves, how that movement is so often a moving *away from*. I remember writing you an email that said that I didn't want to ever see you again because I was afraid that things would be different. You thought that was ridiculous. You thought things would be wonderful, close … the same.

But here we are. We don't know how to break through and I am wondering if I came to Hungary to learn what I always knew was true—a lesson on the contingency of connection … the fragility of relationships. It is never about compatibility. It was … it was two people, both foreigners. A protracted delirium. We were alone. It made us vulnerable and intense. What happened there happened. It couldn't have happened anywhere else, at any other time. It was … an inexplicable synchronicity, an alignment … a mutual readiness to be open. The willing spirit descended and we opened our mouths toward each other. Now we don't. We're both so afraid of disappointing each other and that kills it. We ask each other stupid questions about the other's culture. We sleep next to each other as if it's nothing. You used to be afraid of sleeping in the same room as me. Something about it being compromising. I couldn't wait to shut the lights off. I thought maybe we could talk more freely in the dark, without the pressure that comes with being seen. In the dark I wouldn't be afraid.

One night we approached something, some breakthrough, but you fell asleep while I was talking. I was relieved that I didn't have to continue the charade. I often got out of the bed after you were asleep. I sat by a giant computer screen in Vienna to scribble in my journal by its light. The guy from CouchSurfing who was hosting us came out, put his hand on my shoulder, stared at me intensely, and said, "It's okay to cry. You are suffering. You are lovesick. I have been lovesick for two years. I can tell, you are suffering." He gave me tissues. Wait. *What?* I wasn't crying. Lovesick? I remember wanting to laugh. I was just sick. I had a runny nose. He was nice, but I was perplexed. Was he hitting on me? Did he want me to go into his room now that you were asleep?

You were asleep. Everyone always falls asleep first. I wrote down some things you said. You were still very aphoristic, the way you talked. The first night you said, "Obsession is not about the other person. It's only about the self." You said the only reason you would want to learn French would be to read Levinas. That makes sense. We rode the bus to Vienna from your hometown. On the bus you said, "Depression ends as soon as you do something." I said, "True, maybe. But the problem is, you don't want to do anything when you're depressed. Then what do you do?" You replied, "That's what friends are for. To kick you in the ass." On the bus we were finally making headway, were finally feeling comfortable enough to speak beyond stilted banter, but then a woman told us to be quiet and we both shut our mouths.

When I got to your room and put my things down, you gave me a sweet stick of cottage cheese covered in chocolate. I ate it voraciously and you said something about a famous soccer player who started some campaign against the sweet. Something about it making the Hungarian people fat. We went to the folk art and culture museum and laughed. We laughed at the creepy mermaid gingerbread ornaments. We laughed at the exhibition about the Finns that included a room of heavy metal-band T-shirts. Finnish culture, y'know. I loved the ornate painted eggs. I thought that the folk museum would be something you would like to do since you're so into your Hungarianness, since you were always telling me about where you came from. The history, the specificity. I didn't understand it—the meaning of being "rooted." In Győr you took me under the bridge to show me something, some dilapidated place you would go to make trouble when you were a teenager. It wasn't there anymore and you felt sad that that part of your adolescence was gone.

Then we ate ice cream. I am bouncing through time. You made your typical stupid remarks about Gypsies and your mom fed me—

my god, how she fed me. How could you not have been a food person before meeting me with a mom like this? Your mom and your sister—they laughed together around the house. Your father had a braided beard. I said, "I like your family." I was afraid they would pray at the table but then you told me that you're the only religious one in your family.

In Vienna I felt things change. I felt us get annoyed with each other, felt us move even further apart. I can pinpoint the shift. We spent most of the day in an art museum looking at exhibits about the Viennese Actionists. I felt like you wanted to leave, but I wanted to stay, wanted to see and read everything. We watched a long Valie Export documentary about action art and when we emerged, you were silent. We barely spoke after that. I told you to wake me up before you left. You were taking the bus back to Győr and I was flying to London the next day. When you were about to leave I gave my usual speech about how we weren't really parting ways. This is not goodbye. "I'll be back, I'm sure. Hit me up if you're ever in the States."

I saw the summerhouse you would spend time at as a child. Your dad took us after he took us to the monastery. I had a toothache during the drive, but it was beautiful. You took this picture of me making a stupid face outside the monastery. The few pictures you took that day are my only pictures from my whole stay in Europe. The wind was blowing hard. If you look closely, you can see a loop of hair lifting up in the center of my head. You said something about my hair looking cool while blowing in the wind.

(2011)

Aesthetic Forms of Respect for the Status Quo Instill in the Exploited a Mood of Submission and Inhibition: Frantz Fanon, Violence, and Writing

An extended version of this essay originally appeared in Consequence *magazine.*

I'm barely in this world today. I wake up, pace the house. This depression is really killing my ability to write. My father calls me on Thanksgiving Day and quickly launches into a diatribe about the meaninglessness of my life. I hang up feeling incompetent and worthless—he wants me to get a real job, become a lawyer, go to grad school. *Do something with your life*, he says, *get it together*. I sit down to write. I have everything to say but no way to say it. I'm up to my neck in it and I feel sick, like I have to vomit up all these things I've been hoarding inside me. I wait for the right moment: when crystals fall from the sky and the earth emits a throbbing halo that I touch like a cloud. I wait for this glow to appear to me so I can sit down with my notebook and write. I want the dead leaves to cover my body, to see the sun splinter into light threads as it passes through the cracks and penetrates my skull so deeply that it pushes everything out, replacing the heavy thoughts that pry me so violently from the world with an easiness and openness of being. I need access to this cistern of intense feeling if I am to write. But on most days, I'm left with my fatalism. What the fuck am I doing? Just shit it out already.

Sanitized writing nauseates me more than writing that shits and bleeds all over white linens. Yet here I am, going nuts and scrapping every draft because I can't be the uncompromising and veracious writer that I need to be. What I'm calling for is courage, a kind of recklessness that seeks to blow up language. I want it to be scatological and scabrous, because I'm wounded and incoherent and when I hear the men with their well-reasoned and finely crafted sentences, my tinnitus flares up and I can't hear a damn thing. There is only the interminable hum of the canon, the bullshit standards of certain literary white men, their ceaseless carping lodged in my cranium. Everything seen through the disembodied eye that fucks the world.

Whose values do I measure myself against? It seems like there is something political about the anxiety I feel when I sit down to write, or publish, or do a reading. In the essay "Toward a Phenomenology of Sex-Right," Kathy Miriam discusses an example used in an essay by Sandra Lee Bartky about how the students who were women, in contrast to the students who were men, would frequently apologize when turning in their papers, even though the work the women students submitted was generally superior. When I was at my friend's house the other day, she told me about how she's been feeling like an imposter while recently applying to grad school. This made me think of how, when people ask me if I'm a writer, I often reply, "Well, I'm a *fake* writer."

Miriam writes, "The shame Bartky's women students felt indicates that they were compelled to recognize their being (as inferior) in the 'gaze' of the Other." Women felt ashamed even when their work was superior because they were viewing themselves and their work through a masculinist framework. In this schema we can never be good enough, no matter how great we are. It ravages our sense of self-worth, our ability to live and work without doubting what it is we are doing.

In an essay titled "The Immediate Need for Emotional Justice," Yolo Akili writes:

> Oppression is trauma. Every form of inequity has a traumatic impact on the psychology, emotionality and spirituality of the oppressed. The impact of oppressive trauma creates cultural and individual wounding. This wounding produces what many have called a "pain body," a psychic energy that is not tangible but can be sensed, that becomes an impediment to the individual and collective's ability to transform and negotiate their conditions.

Frantz Fanon elaborates on this idea that "oppression is trauma." He wrote that colonized peoples suffer psychologically from an inferiority complex that is caused by racism and the supremacy of white values. These values are internalized so that it is impossible for us to think or speak or act without conceptualizing ourselves in relation to the colonizer: what we think they want us to be; what we think would be good according to their standards. For Fanon, so long as colonized people sought the approval of the colonizer to validate their existence, the colonized would not recognize their inherent power. The only way to realize one's freedom was through fighting (with the colonizer) and bringing about a violent rupture with the status quo. For Fanon, using violence was a way to ontologically transform one's being. You come to consciousness through action. You realize your power when you are directly struggling for your freedom. He wrote:

> At the individual level, violence is a cleansing force. It rids the colonized of their inferiority complex, of their passive and

despairing attitude. It emboldens them, and restores their self-confidence. Even if the armed struggle has been symbolic, and even if they have been demobilized by rapid decolonization, the people have time to realize that liberation was the achievement of each and everyone and no special merit should go to the leader. Violence hoists the people up to the level of the leader.

In the news, revolutions are popping off everywhere. Pictures of Egyptians lighting riot-police vehicles on fire. They're pissed that the military will not hand over the government to the civilians and are attempting to give themselves permanent power by controlling the writing of the new constitution. The Philadelphia and Los Angeles Occupy movements have been ordered to be evacuated.

Channel that violence. I want to live in language in a way that makes sense to me. I want to use these words in a way that doesn't feel alienating. But when I sit down to write, everything is filtered through their way of saying things, their judgments. Who gives a shit about literary manners and their monopoly on speech? The task is to *blow up the language*.

(2011)

Epistolary Review: Dodie Bellamy, *the buddhist*

This review was originally published on BOMB *magazine's* BOMBlog.

Dodie, I want to do an epistolary review because I've been so clogged lately. It isn't the same thing as writer's block. My mind is always reeling—there is so much to be said, especially after reading your book. I just feel like I can't be loose anymore, uninhibited, whatever. I feel always on the verge of some release but then I pull out … I can't go there … Don't know why. So I thought if I wrote you, I could have an excuse to be a little more informal, a little more personal. Plus, it's fitting … since *the buddhist* is a performative writing project that merges life and the word. I don't find writing that excises the "personal" voice to be compelling. The feigned distance makes me lose interest. That's why I liked *the buddhist* so much. I want to say it's "vulnerable," but that makes it sound like I mean *weak*, and I do not mean *weak*. I mean an unapologetic TRUST in your emotions … at least enough to let yourself live in them and through them and with them.

Lately I've been repeating to myself: *My suffering is not profound.* And it drives me to total silence. In my silence I have absolutely no power—that silence rules every aspect of life. Using language becomes so fraught that it is impossible to articulate anything. I think about how you could have DOUBTED yourself, but you didn't. You didn't negate your suffering or write it off as petty, and in the end, you created a document that IS totally profound. But not in an obnoxious grandiloquent way—yours is both wild and "everyday" ... Smart, tender, creepy, passionate, and bitchy in the best possible way ... A "fuck-your-bullshit" kind of way.

A little while ago Bhanu wrote on her blog, "I have to make enough room for a person to go a little wild, in the first stages of a process." I think about how the BLOG became your space to go wild (perhaps because it's not Real Writing, as you wrote). The blog format ended up giving the book a spontaneous quality—it's immediate and has a real-life temporal progression marked by shifts in emotion and fake-out endings. Even though I was following your blog in real time, reading the book was still special and a totally different experience.

the buddhist fits in nicely alongside obsessive, performative works such as *I Love Dick* by Chris Kraus. When I was interviewing Chris once, she told me that some people were pitying in their responses to the book, as if she were a pathetic, self-deprecating hag who just wanted sympathy. But really, she thought the whole thing was hilarious and was (dis)owning her experience by publishing a book about her infatuation. Those who respond with pity toward these unguarded explorations of failure are oblivious to the wisdom of failure. I think the "pity" response is another way people try to deflate the power derived from resisting the injunction to suffer your rejection in isolation. I'm only twenty-three but I've always had a huge fondness for raging, sexually candid, unapologetic "hags"— or the "aging diva," as you've said on your blog. I think of Robert Mapplethorpe's portrait of Louise Bourgeois holding a giant lumpy latex phallus. The gorilla-fur jacket, the mischievous smirk on her face—the picture is perfect. Of course MoMA cropped the portrait so you couldn't see the phallus sculpture. People couldn't handle seeing an older woman holding a giant dick while smiling. It lessens the power of the phallus. It is a threat.

This book is a threat. It's all about rejecting the internalization of shame. When you have to live with shame in silence, it can eat you up and destroy you. Shame has a pact with secrecy because shame derives its power to humiliate from the demand that everything be kept hidden. There's a lot that we're supposed to feel ashamed about—our unorthodox desires, our emotional excessiveness. But shame's power is deflated when the veil is lifted and we realize that this shame we've internalized is kept out of the public because it makes other people feel uncomfortable by disrupting their normative attitudes, because it opens up the possibility for collective power through the naming of our suffering and sharing of experiences. It's like you wrote:

> This whole business of women not suffering in public, of having a gag order when it comes to personal drama, such as a break up, connects of course back to larger histories of suppression, such as the literature of victimization, women not daring to speak of rape or incest (and I'm in no way suggesting that my current situation is in any way comparable to those violations), a harkening back to the whole notion that domestic space is private, what happens behind closed doors stays behind closed doors, and somewhere buried in there is the history of the wife being owned by her man and therefore she better keep her trap shut, and bourgeois notions of suffering with dignity—or dignity itself, how oppressive a value is that? Betrayal happens in private (usually), thus betrayal is less of a bourgeois sin than talking about it.

I think there is a lot to be said about the strategy of turning pain into an object as a way to move through and beyond that pain—pushing it out and into the world in the form of something to be shared. I know people tend to be cynical about what approaches "therapeutic art," but such a perspective assumes that art which takes personal suffering as its object of inspiration is solely about the healing of the Self rather than the transformation of something personal into something social. I see power in the process of externalizing pain so that it enters the social. This passage from the book *The Body in Pain* by Elaine Scarry seems particularly relevant, especially if we substitute "writing" for "work":

> Work and its "work" (or work and its object, its artifact) are the names that are given to the phenomena of pain and the imagination as they begin to move from being a self-contained loop within the body to becoming the equivalent loop now projected into the external world. It is through this movement out into the world that the extreme privacy of the occurrence (both pain and imagining are invisible to anyone outside the boundaries of the person's body) begins to be sharable, that sentience becomes social.

I am also reminded of the work of Sophie Calle, who is known for compulsively turning her life's suffering into art. Tragedy, rejection, memory, and failure are the subjects of her works: she creates a film out of the ruins of a brief marriage gone sour, has people analyze a break-up letter to turn into an art book, tries (and fails) to capture the moment of her mother's death on film. As in your book, even the gesture of loving itself becomes communal. Rather than holing yourself up and letting the pain rot your insides—the pain is used to generate something meaningful rather than merely being suffered in vain. In many ways, the externalized personal voice turns singularly felt pain into something other than the Self, something that gestures toward a community.

Elaine Scarry has something to say about this too: "To be more precise, one can say that pain only becomes an intentional state once it is brought into relation with the objectifying power of the imagination: through that relation, pain will be transformed from a wholly passive and helpless occurrence into a self-modifying and, when most successful, self-eliminating one."

Judith Butler writes about this in the afterward to an anthology called the *Loss: The Politics of Mourning*: "Indeed, the voice of each might be said to survive the author, but not in a way that extends that authorship. Indeed, authorship is wrecked through its appropriation, and it is the strange fecundity of that wreckage that I am trying to address here."

I love the phrase "the strange fecundity of that wreckage."

Perhaps this is also related to the part where you write:

> Writing about the buddhist here has been public display, of course, but it's been a public display of trying to figure something out, I'm not sure what it was—but it's been compelling to me—something about desire, obviously, and the trajectory of mourning—but also about boundaries, about secret/public, about embodiment and meaning, and the frailty of the ego, about the embarrassment and shame of

being left or rejected, about pushing myself into ever uncomfortable spaces in writing. I'm not talking about my life here because it's particularly interesting, it's more like the whole "push the personal until it's universal" cliché, though of course nothing is ever universal.

I think something should be said about the recurring trope of "spiritual gurus" who are also dodgy characters. Not that all Buddhists are manipulators … But I do wonder if maybe there is a type of control-obsessed person who is drawn to the idea of spiritual mastery. I wonder about soft masculinity, too … The way "kindness," sensitivity, and spirituality are subtly deployed in power games.

In an interview you did recently for the What Is Experimental Literature series on *HTMLGIANT* you said: "For writing to be alive it needs to look at what's consciously or unconsciously occluded from the now. Transgression in art isn't necessarily about finding a weird pocket of extremity. It's about shedding light on what's all around us that nobody dares look at." YES—transgression is not about extremity but about confronting what is hidden, discarded, silenced, or removed—what people are too afraid, embarrassed, or uncomfortable to look at. It reminds me of the CAConrad poem "she said shit should never come up in a poem." Conrad writes: "how did shit get such a bad name? why is shit everybody's dirty little secret?" I am also reminded of Eileen Myles's commitment to writing a messy, failed femininity. I think of the phrases you use—such as "oppositional weakness," "emotional porn," "operatic suffering," and "embracing the fucked-upness"—as strategies for exploring the territory of failure and abjection. I loved how you went back and "unwrote" the polite and glossy ending to the book, returning to the messy carnage of abandoned love and paying tribute to the insatiable, overflowing CUNT.

This is going to be a funny review. It's not really a synopsis at all—it's a response … the associations and ideas that were aroused (hehe) by your work.

Take care,

Jackie

(2011)

The Suicide of the Other Jackie Wang, the Sky Bed, What Is the Meaning of This Energy That We Radiate

This originally appeared on my Tumblr blog.

There was a girl with my name who died in 2011. She was a precocious eleventh grader who committed suicide. It's pretty weird to read things like:

> Jackie Wang wowed us on a routine basis. She was so many wonderful things—zany, sweet, honest, profound, friendly, athletic, brilliant, beautiful, and much more. I would have never thought that things would come to a point for her that she would consider death as her final solution.

When I first read this I thought, *Am I dead?* And, *Am I really that athletic?* I really thought for a second that I was dead. I was sitting on the floor of a computer lab on the New College campus and I had used the door recently so I couldn't have been dead. According to the Manchus, doors are for the living—souls leave through the windows. I think the dead body exits through the window as well. I was still a competent user of doors, so clearly, I was alive. The next thing I thought was, *This girl must have googled her name at some point.* Since I am one of the more cyber-popular Jackie Wangs out there, it is possible she saw me. Maybe I crowded her out, tarnished her name with my vulgar rants, the effusions of malodorous psychic gas that I spill into the internet. Then I got the chills thinking about how I have no idea what I am transmitting. I have no idea how the things I do and write live in the bodies of the people who are not me. How do my emissions circulate, what imprints am I leaving in brains, whose brains, and what energy am I releasing into the atmosphere? How can I be more responsible to this energy once I have released it? Does it even have anything to do with me once it's out there?

I remember reading, when I was a teenager, some statistic about the high rate of suicide among Asian American women ... but also the high rate of college completion. So I thought, *Great. I'll either commit suicide or graduate from college!* I don't want to die.

I had a series of marathon conversations with Joohyun sitting by the ocean and around the kitchen table. We talked into the morning and while we were gyrating in the purl of communicative ecstasy, I felt that the transmission of energy between bodies was a touchable thing. I wondered about the things that were said—from where did this wisdom come? Maybe the spark of two Asian girls who think too much rubbing sticks together in a dark forest. What I know I only know through people. When I contemplate Great Men and their Spiritual Crises, I think of the emptiness of mastery and how miserable it must be to be a man of letters who is only in dialogue with his own head.

Yesterday I wrote something like thirty pages in my notebook. Stayed awake scribbling into the morning. The last thing I remember before falling asleep was the image of a dilapidated barn at sunrise. The barn was familiar but I could not tell if it was a dream I had had or the dream I was going to have. Am I having that dream right now? Then I became one with the bed that was also the mouth of a hungry sky. The last thing I wrote before passing out was *Be sky!* My headphones were still on my head when I woke up.

(2012)

All Joy Lives inside Violence

This essay originally appeared in Moonroot (#2), *a zine anthology of writings of self-identified womyn, trans, or genderqueer persons of Asian descent.*

Routes. The pain of forced (im)migration vs. the ecstatic freedom of mobility, of bodies in motion. My father, on the boat to Taiwan, five years old, after a protracted Civil War. Exiled from the mainland, from his extended family. Father's family lands on land already dispossessed, already taken from the Indigenous Taiwanese. Not long ago, Taiwan was under Japanese colonial rule. So father and his two siblings grow up in a Japanese-style house. Father's mother dies in Taiwan of cancer, asks father to come to grave with stories. Father goes to America, leaving his mother's dead body behind. Father's sister becomes a reckless pugilist—her mother was her only link to the world and now she is gone. Picture of father and his sister in the airport. He is leaving. The Cold War was raging, and his test scores attracted the American universities. Scientists were in demand. Did father dream of NASA? Of space? When father arrives, the situation has changed—there are too many Chinese people and he will no longer be able to get residency status through being a student. Father drops out and moves to New York City to work at Chinese restaurants and later opens up a convenience store with other Chinese immigrants. The rest of his family eventually comes to the US, leaving the mother's remains behind. Once again, the family lands on land that has been dispossessed, long ago.

My dad and his sister, in an airport, right before he left for the United States

Father never looked back though his sister swears he would have had a better life had he stayed in Taiwan. I think of the complicated forces at play that have shaped the trajectory of his life ... how he got here, how he met my Sicilian New Yorker mother, how she got here, the story of her family ... how her grandfather owned a fruit stand in New York, how it went out of business when a gigantic grocery store opened down the street, how he lost everything during the Great Depression and died young, of a stroke. It would be easy to speak of the pain of uprooting and the migratory paths determined by the forces of global capitalism and war without trying to understand that many Asians come to the US in search of a better life.

Of my siblings, I am the only one who has spent time outside of the country. Compared to many of my hypereducated friends I am not cosmopolitan, but compared to my older brother, who is in prison, I am very cosmopolitan. Before leaving for New Mexico, I received a letter from my brother. He is in solitary confinement. In the hole he talks to himself, writes that he is thinking of the good old days, when we were a family, when he was free. But he is okay—better than the others in confinement, who sometimes go crazy and cut themselves. He is okay but there is no heat and sometimes it is so cold he has to sleep with his shoes on. But he is okay. I read my brother's letter while in Santa Fe, surrounded by poets and artists and thinkers, in an enchanting house tucked away in the mountains. We sing songs, gather around, talk politics, go on walks, take drugs. *So fucking bohemian*, I think. Sitting in the loft looking out at the landscape, letter in hand—my mobility collides with the harsh reality of my brother's captivity, and the captivity of those like him. Suddenly my bullshit bohemian-poet lifestyle is a joke and I am confronted with the contradiction of my position: the wideness of the desert, the sunset over the majestic hills, the flame-shaped shrubs, the people, the beauty—all require violence to exist. All joy lives inside violence. In every letter my brother asks me about the "outside." *What is China like? Can you take a picture of the Baltimore skyline for me? Have you seen our cousins lately? How much is your rent?* It is crushing to hear him say, *I hope to go there one day*, knowing he is sentenced to life without parole. It's crushing to hear him talk about how he wants to go to college when he will never be able to, not even in prison, because work, education, and trade programs are only available to people with shorter sentences. It is crushing to think about how the legal motion discussing thirty-five of the over fifty flaws and gross illegalities of his case and trial sat in some courthouse, without being read, for years. I write to him about Tupac's hologram, how strange it was to watch a video of the hologram, how it made me think of how he and I and our little bro would listen to the album *Me Against the World* over and over when we were children.

What is the meaning of mobility to him, as a prisoner, or my father, as an immigrant, or my little brother, who calls me just to tell me about his dreams, how he would one day like to see the world? On the phone he says, *I want to live like you do.* What is the meaning of mobility to my mother, a former housewife? Now that her children have all grown up, she doesn't know what to do with herself (except speak of wanting to die or travel).

It is tempting to speak only of my identity as a queer woman of color as though my hands were clean, to speak of being oppressed and not the gruesome underside of my location, what it means to be a person living on stolen land, in a country built on slavery and genocide. I write: *It is unethical for me to smell New Mexico.* It is unethical for me to be "free" when my relative freedom as a nonincarcerated person is only possible through the removal, imprisonment, and degradation of certain bodies, bodies marked as threatening or worthless. I am not saying that I or you, the reader, should feel bad about your life or falling in love or going on road trips or hanging out with poets and petting cool dogs, but that we should try to understand the hidden brutality our lives depend on, even though we may not have consciously chosen it to be that way. Though I cannot live outside of this violence, it is necessary that I live. Live inside it but also: against it.

* * *

She stands before the mountain, feeling broken and humbled. The immensity of it. She knows nothing of the violent underside of her fleeting rapture. Perhaps her joy obviates it. She is: a person who sometimes eats bananas, wears clothes, writes, and wanders. All of these activities implicate her. On some days she is formless. She becomes: a red napkin caught in the branches of a tree, briefly, before deliverance. A red napkin unmoored by the wind. Adrift. A lightness that lives inside violence.

(2012)

Asexuality & Demisexuality: Queer or Antiqueer?

This originally appeared on my Tumblr blog.

Is asexuality queer? I wonder about this and other gender-/sexuality-related issues as I read the proposed changes for the new edition of the *DSM* (V). Lots of revisions are being proposed under the categories of Sexual Dysfunctions and Gender Dysphoria. Some disorders will be dropped, others will be revamped. Vaginismus (muscle contractions when something is inserted into the vagina) and dyspareunia (inability to have "penetrative" intercourse / pain in the vagina due to medical or psychological causes) will be collapsed into a single disorder called "Genito-Pelvic Pain / Penetration Disorder." *Penetration* disorder. I hate the sound of that. Sounds like a threat—a menacing demand that everyone submit to the phallocratic order. For women in the Sexual Dysfunctions category, there's also Female Orgasmic Disorder and Sexual Interest/Arousal Disorder in Women. The "male" equivalent of the later is Hypoactive Sexual Desire Disorder in Men. I'm wondering about the curious difference between the names of the disorders drawn along the gender lines. Naming women's sexual problems as a problem of "interest/arousal" seems to pander to stereotypes about frigid women, while describing the male equivalent as a problem of "desire" reinforces the stereotype that men are supposed to be actively desiring, sexual.

I have been reading a lot of psychoanalysis and criticisms of psycho-analysis lately—Freud, Kristeva, Merleau-Ponty on Freud, Bracha Lichtenberg Ettinger, Kelly Oliver, and various essays/books on perversion and fetishism. Freud's model isn't exactly a compelling account of subjectivization, and, as many feminist critics note, it can't account for female desire at all (or even female subjectivity outside of a masculinist framework). Although many theorists are quick to contest Freud's conceptualization of desire, the primacy of sexual desire itself often goes unquestioned (unless you consider it displaced by Lacan's emphasis on the role of language in subject formation ... um ... but not exactly since the Phallus is the designated transcendental signifier propelling all desire).

With Freud we have inherited a dangerous notion of an essentialized *sex drive*, which has produced a form of sex normativity so totalizing that it is nearly impossible for me to bring up asexuality without people—queers and nonqueers alike—giving an extremely reactive response. People often act like such a concept is so totally alien and unthinkable that it is not *biologically* possible. Even "antiessentialist," gender-savvy people often default to this or some variation of this argument, or try to morally justify this reaction by saying that asexuality is inherently sex-negative. This reaction reveals the sex-*normativity* of many queer communities. Hypersexuality becomes an underlying criterion for queerness. While casually searching for articles on demisexuality (an "asexuality"-spectrum sexuality defined as a lack of sexual attraction when an emotional connection isn't present), the first page of search results contained an article titled "Is Demisexual Anti-Queer?" The article was written by some popular queer blogger who goes by Gauche. The opening sentence contains the statement "*demisexual* is the dumbest thing ever." The main point the writer is trying to make is that demisexuality is antiqueer, normative, nonfluid, and predicated on sex-negativity. It conflates Hollywood-style hetero romance with this fairly open designation that only refers to a person's inability to feel sexual attraction for someone without an emotional connection. The author generalizes from an assumed hetero-romantic hypothetical manifestation of demisexuality (the "implied" normativity of demisexuality), and uses this assumption as the foundation on which to launch their queer critique of demisexuality.

Taken from the blog Queer Secrets

Regarding the question I asked in my post about asexuality/demisexuality being "queer" or "antiqueer," I'm not actually interested in answering that question. Certainly, most manifestations of asexuality deviate from "normative" sexuality. A gay blogger trying to make sense of the growing alliance between asexuals and queers said it was "appalling" that the LGBT community would take the asexual movement seriously, and that asexuals were "stealing the language of gay liberation." He wrote, "As far as I'm concerned, this isn't an orientation—it's a *disability* and it does no one—least of all the asexuals who are missing out on one of life's greatest pleasures—any good to pretend otherwise," and "Homosexuality is *not* a disability; asexuality *is*."

If you define *queer* as a sexual orientation—well, asexuality doesn't have a sex *object*. In that case, it fails at "producing" an identity at all and registers simply as *nothing*: utterly inconceivable as a possible subject position. If sex is considered the essential constituting force behind subject formation (Freud's theory of sexual development is simultaneously the story of how one becomes a subject), then it's no wonder people often consider asexuality "inhuman." (*Sex*, and specifically *orientation*, is also the site where gender is produced.) But because it's politically untenable to occupy the nothing position (social death), we see groups like the Asexual Visibility and Education Network emerging.

* * *

Visibility and nonvisibility both have consequences. The nonvisibility of asexuality can be psychologically distressing if you feel totally alienated and broken, wondering why you feel pathologically avoidant of any situation that might lead to hooking up. It's "comforting" to hear the stories of others and feel like you have a community. The creation of these communities also enables people to organize against the pathologization of asexuality (i.e., the "disorders" listed in the sexual dysfunction category of the DSM). But of course, there's the whole critique of identity politics that comes with the consolidation/production of sexual identities and the idea that you are somehow more "free" if your sexuality is uncodified—that identity is the surface that allows for regulation, control, marginalization. Given the sex-normativity of society and the invisibility of asexuality, privileging the uncodified nothing position hardly seems liberatory. (At the time I was a paper on the topic, a professor told me I couldn't write about asexuality because there was almost nothing academic written on the topic … asexuality seemed to not exist at all when people considered the range of sexual identities.)

Sex-Normativity and the Superiority of the U-S-A

Thinking about the weird moralizing attitude of the "queer" and "sex-positive" critique of demisexuality in the article I mentioned, I am reminded of a certain attitude that Jasbir K. Puar describes as *sexual exceptionalism*. Jasbir analyzes the sexual politics of the US and how queerness and the valorization of sexual liberalism are tied to nationalist discourses on *freedom* and individualist notions of US exceptionalism. The US prides itself on being tolerant, open, and free of sexual constraint, which can be mobilized for racist agendas such as the United States' war on terror. US sexuality is elevated over Muslim sexuality, which is portrayed as fundamentally repressive. I think of the liberal mantra at the heart of US identity: the US is the place where you have *the freedom to do what you want*. How does one think through sexuality in ways that are candid and open without reproducing a US-brand of individualist sexual libertinism? In many ways, the Marquis de Sade seems *so* American, ha.

When writing about the sexual politics of Abu Ghraib, Jasbir writes, "Reinforcing a homogeneous notion of Muslim sexual repression vis-à-vis homosexuality and the notion of 'modesty' works to resituate the United States, in contrast, as a place free of such sexual constraints." This elevation of "open" liberal democracy over "closed" fundamentalism reveals, as Sara Ahmed notes, "how the constitution of open cultures involves the projection of what is closed onto others, and hence the concealment of what is closed and contained 'at home.'"

Art and Eroticism

In the essay "On Eroticism," Merleau-Ponty asks, "Is eroticism a form of intellectual courage and *freedom*?" (emphasis mine). He concludes that this isn't necessarily always the case and distinguishes between discussions of sexuality that are frank, courageous, and candid, and a type of *something-to-prove* (exceptionalist) eroticism that is invested in a profanation of what is "good" and "innocent" (Sadian libertinage, pleasure derived from "sinning" and "dominating") that just reinforces traditional sexual mores. "A certain eroticism presupposes all the traditional ties, and has neither the courage to accept them nor the courage to break them." Merleau-Ponty certainly isn't your average flesh-mortifying philosopher (MP is primarily a philosopher of the body). For him, the Marxists and the surrealists were more sexually revolutionary than the Marquis de Sade because their sexual discourse moved beyond Good and Evil.

Eroticism is one of my favorite things to read and write about—my work is saturated with the erotic … delusional little-girl lesbians, polymorphous posthuman bodies, autoerotic loners, creepy obsessive girls. But I prefer to read the tender, queer, and perverse literature of someone like CAConrad than someone overly invested in their own transgressiveness. How can we think about the erotic in art without essentializing the erotic as the underlying force behind all artistic production? (In the film *Black Swan*, Natalie Portman will never be a good dancer unless she gets fucked.) One day I will expound more on my thoughts regarding the relationship between eroticism and art, how to think about sexual energy and the artistic process. For now, I've said enough.

(2011)

III.

2012–13:

THE DESERT YEARS

Las Cruces and Mesilla, New Mexico, mostly. Then Chicago, Glasgow, Albuquerque, Florida, San Francisco, and New York City.

My life in Baltimore was untenable. How could I escape? Move across the country, of course. My admission to an MFA program in poetry in New Mexico would be my ticket out. I would land in the house of Lily Hoang, the creative-writing professor I had only met in person once, at AWP, during an interaction she had no recollection of because she had taken Xanax to cope with the social anxiety of the conference. She had just gotten divorced from an unbearably controlling man and was reveling in her newfound freedom. We would sit at her kitchen table, which has since become my kitchen table, getting tipsy on tea made from my blend of exotic dream herbs. I would search the classifieds of the free print papers at the one café in town, hoping to find a little adobe house to rent. One day such a place turned up in a classified ad placed by a local pecan farmer who had never used the internet.

When I moved away, things quickly fell apart with C. And when they did, things got nasty. I told our mutual friends about the abuse. When they tried to talk to her about it, she abruptly moved to North Carolina. Our breakup had sparked a minor scandal in the queer-anarchist milieu. People were calling, texting, emailing me constantly, pumping me for the lurid details of the abuse, asking to publish statements about the affair. After it was no longer news, I was left alone, in the desert, in my little adobe house without internet, desperately trying to put the broken pieces of my life together. My feminist friends kept me alive, as did Dylan, my New Mexico friend who took care of me when I couldn't take care of myself. To be honest, there is a hole in my brain where the details of this period have been carved out, as depression interferes with your ability to form memories. The chaos of my life up to that moment had finally caught up with me. At night I kept vigil at the altar of my grief, lighting candles and ingesting entheogens, hoping to find answers. I collected objects from thrift stores and turned my house into a kind of art installation, covered in sculptural objects, collages, and fragments of language I had plastered on my walls. I read stacks and stacks of books about revolution, masochism, and mysticism. On index cards I hand-wrote aborted drafts of a Semiotext(e) Intervention Series book I would never publish on the topic of revolutionary loneliness. I bicycled through the dust storms on the blue bicycle Lily had given me. I took late-night walks along the arroyos and in the pecan groves. I wept daily and wrote crazed emails to my kindhearted professor. My peers all hated me because they paranoically interpreted my depression as some kind of judgment on their character. I was referred to, in one peer's poem, as "the cunt on the blue bicycle." At the bar they talked about how my hair was probably a wig. I was not even aware of how big of a character I was in their mental psychodramas until two contacted me long after I left New Mexico about our (imaginary) feuds. No, I was too consumed by the task of severing the limb of C. to notice any of it.

The desert period. How strange, when your inner landscape matches the arid terrain surrounding you, a view of the majestic Organ Mountains. I'll always associate the smell of creosote with the exquisite melancholia of those days, when the odor of the plant would waft into my room after a rare rain. Every day I woke up to an all-consuming desire to die. It went on for years like this. I hated being awake and would try to turn off my brain with sleeping pills. How could I escape from my escape? After a year in the MFA program, I decided to drop out. My father was furious. Unsure of what to do with myself, I purchased a one-way ticket to Glasgow, Scotland. My editors at Semiotext(e) told me I could live for free in an apartment in Albuquerque to work on my Intervention Series book. Desperate to find a footing in life, I applied to PhD programs instead, programs that would enable me to study prisons, which had loomed over my life since I was a teenager. For a year I lived out of a suitcase, bouncing from couch to couch, from Chicago to Glasgow to Albuquerque to San Francisco to New York City and back to Florida, to deal with my brother's hearing and appeal. At the end of my sojourn, I washed up on the cobblestone shores of Cambridge, Massachusetts, to do a PhD at Harvard.

Regrow Your Spine

This originally appeared on my Tumblr blog.

Why should you care about my plants? You shouldn't. Plants are a lot like dreams. They mean a lot to the grower because the grower has an intimate relationship to the plants and the dreams she grows. The grower watches and the plants are enlarged in her mind. The pecans are huge in my mind, like the patch of mugwort I found the one morning I wandered outside at sunrise because the basement door was open, mysteriously open, and I was worried one of the cats had escaped. Cat pictures are like explaining dreams. The images mean nothing to those outside the relation. It is the relation that is charged—a feeling or a picture or a body connected to another living body by an invisible skein. Sometimes I feel so sensitized that I am bound to everything in this way. Do you see her, a maybe girl riding her bicycle as threads unspool and are released by the centrifugal force of her rotation, as she moves beneath the immense awning of the jagged desert mountain range, across the asphalt that smells like burnt water whenever it rains, the smell of creosote. When she rides through the orchard her nostrils flare and she gets a whiff of the ocean. Where is this ocean?

One night while wandering around Mesilla I stopped to observe a dead tree trunk standing solid against the yawning, star-filled sky. The air between us was alive and heavy like the air between two bodies bound by the eyes, intimate strangers caught in a state I mean stare I mean the act of seeing and being seen. I walked through the trees and it was so dark I could not see what waited for me at the end of the path. When I emerged from the trees I happened on a barn. I heard the animal shrieks slice through the shadows and felt afraid because I did not know if I was on a road or in someone's yard. I stood beneath the skirt of the willow tree and laughed to myself. I like to remember myself like this, laughing beneath the willow. I looked at the ditch and imagined two sisters lying there while holding hands, hiding because they know that a man is coming to take them away.

In writing there is always the problem of making people care about your personal associations. Sometimes I do not have the energy to do anything other than love what I know I am bound to. Which is to say: I cannot convey.

But this I will try to convey

What it feels like to not be a person

To have been used and abused—whether it's for the answers to math problems, sex, emotional labor, lunch money, an object to direct anger toward, care, or psychic relief. I think about all the bullshit I have put up with and it makes me feel sick. I think about how degraded and rotten I feel inside and there is almost not enough left of me alive to feel sick, but every single shriveled wheezing particle left in my jaundiced bodysac feels this sickness. The only thing left is to die and reemerge. I don't know why I have been holding on to this state of being ... a sack of rotten potatoes that stinks up the world and nourishes no-body. I don't buy it when people tell me that others are taking advantage of my compassion. It's not compassion—if I had that I could be forgiving toward myself. It's pure cowardliness and sometimes it's mixed up with a little bit of misguided love. It has nothing to do with desiring to be mistreated or being a masochist or growing up in a dysfunctional family. Out of all the people I have let into my world it is true that 90 percent of the relationships have been reciprocal and nourishing. But it is also true that my skin is thin and I have not done enough to protect my fledgling world. I know I am not to blame for what they do, but I also know that they will not stop of their own accord, that I am the one who has to say *no more*. I am not responsible for the relations that degrade me, but regardless of where the locus of responsibility lies, the course of action is obvious—nobody can end these objectifying and humiliating relations but me.

Though people cannot act for me it is also true that I have not had the strength to do it alone. my vision has been distorted because for years I have been coerced into perceiving everything through the eyes of the person who has hurt me, to see myself as an object to meet this person's needs, to feel bad for this person while I was being emptied of my substance. My friends do not help me by taking control—they enable me to act by restoring my dignity and my faith in people.

What does it feel like to not be a person? It feels like your jaw has been propped open with a stick while someone reaches into your throat with a wrench and rips your spine out through your mouth. Most people did not know my spine was missing. They looked at me and they saw someone who was strong. They do not know where I have been. Nobody knows where I've been. The isolation was often so total that I felt I was not really in this world. Nobody knows where I've been and I couldn't help but resent the world for it. Only I know that the morsels of exuberance I was sometimes able to wrest from the universe were not obtained through strength or will. What little I created—what little energy and light I was able to radiate—I created not out of a sense of self-worth, but because *the spirit* took over whenever I felt in my marrow that there was nothing left of me and I was giving up. Nothing ever seemed possible and yet something was made, over and against the fear, self-loathing, and imposed silence.

I should tell you (lest I be accused of suffering arrogantly): I have already given myself permission to speak.

(2012)

The Tumblrization of Everyday Life

This originally appeared on my Tumblr blog.

the Tumblrization of everyday life: glorification of the reactive affects

in some cases, the fetishization of powerlessness

there is nothing "wrong" with a politics of complaint

but there are several risks

like developing a dependency on "the enemy"

politically neutralizing oneself by siphoning off all of one's subversive energies into meaningless channels

or reifying one's powerlessness by identifying with it

because it makes one virtuous

complaint becomes a form of subcultural capital

a way to morally purify oneself

as a "queer woman of color" i know that the world *is* hostile to my existence

but it is not an indication of my "goodness"

i may frame it this way to cope with my position

but developing a morality out of not having power just reinforces my powerlessness

i am fine with expressions of impotence and weakness:

all the things that people do because they don't have power

but i want real strategies for transmogrifying weakness into power

not by denying or "overcoming" weakness, but adopting a certain attitude toward it

a more enabling, less moralizing attitude

(2012)

Her Brain Was Always Full of Seizuring Worms

This originally appeared on my Tumblr blog.

she was never present
on the phone i could hear her feeding the worms
i wanted to yell, *i can hear you feeding the worms*
and i know you are not paying attention

i wanted to hang up
after a while i stopped caring about what i had to say
i stopped remembering
there was no reason to ever recall anything
life became the back of a woman's head
a mess of hair without a face
and tiny bird claws for hands
with my bird hands i cannot itch the eye without scratching it
i want to ask you, *will you rub my eye?*
will you reach all the places i cannot reach with my claws?
will you not injure me while i lie
prostrate before you?

somewhere someone exhales gales of yellow leaves
while another walks away, pink ribbons of smoke leaking from her nose
it says nothing about you or me
speaks only to the event that made us

and the way the event is never finished, even after it has ended
that's why the one who is blown always waits
for a single settled moment
but only ever feels
precarious in her fungibility

the girl who walks down dirt roads alone does not want to be read
because she must create the space she needs to hear
the voice inside the untied shoe
she'll push all her loose papers to the edge of the room
and create a circle around herself with uncooked rice
is the voice the shoe itself or a being that lives inside the shoe?
here, it's easy to throw my voice, erase the boundary
i feel fearful right before slipping my foot into the shoe
maybe it's because i never see all the way to the toe
and it is possible there are teeth waiting for me at the bottom
or an organ to be tickled and she will moan
will the shoe moan when my foot enters?

* * *

don't get used to me writing publicly
soon i will go back to my rigorous solitude
alone in my internetless adobe house, built in the 1850s
mine is the window that glows red
i am inside mixing powerful herbs
i kneel and devote myself to the feeling
my occupation is not recognized as an occupation at all
you can't make a career out of your commitment to feel it all the way
but you will

i am waiting for someone to tell me,
it takes grace, to break as you broke
break because the active part of you has been cut out, split from
    your core
that is why you dream that your cunt has become
a general who must lead the army of cunts into the forest
to fight the 11-headed phallic monster

when the internet is around i always feel just on the surface of things
but sometimes i get this exhilarating sensation because something
    has been transmitted
FC writes that it has been almost a year since our last email exchange,
    but that she has thought of me every day since
she writes,
*you probably are creeped out by that, or maybe not. it is as if you have
many bodies, and some of them are being held by others when you
don't know it, through the internet maybe, or through paper, or through
electricity in the flesh. does it ever feel weird or like a burden to mean
so much to strangers?*
i love meaning a lot to strangers
i want to visit them in dreams

most days i wake up to this incredible stillness
there is no good, there is no evil, there is no love, there is no morality
there is just power (and our interpretations)
profound indifference
i develop the consciousness of furniture
peel away all the affects and reactions
and become neutral
suddenly everything we do becomes absurd

i wonder how many times we have used "love" to describe traumatic
    bonding
i study science and the brain because i am comforted by the idea of
    not having control

i think of myself as an object
watch myself act out
watch everyone around me
and think,
very interesting

* * *

i don't know where i'm going with this
meaning a lot to strangers isn't a burden but i don't know how to be
    connected to things anymore
i keep going back to the lizards in my mind
the image of walking down the road, dodging cars like in a video game
i didn't realize i was covered in lizards until i got home and accidentally
    flung one into the toilet bowl
not knowing what to do—and perhaps fearing the lizard would jump
    up and bite my ass—
i flushed the toilet
but as it was spinning round and round i felt this terrible dread

just as it was about to get sucked into the plumbing it sprung out of
    the bowl

(2012)

Compensatory Sadism

This originally appeared on my Tumblr blog.

Once my aunt boasted about beating someone up with a chair and getting away with it.

Everywhere we went she would pick fights with strangers, make them cry, slap them in their faces.

When she would play mahjong with the people on the street behind her apartment complex, she would smile and say nasty things about the other players in English because she knew they didn't understand what she was saying.

In Xishuangbanna she told the woman who came to give her a theater ticket that she was ugly. But she said more than *you're ugly*—she went straight for the existential jugular, even though the woman had nothing to do with the situation that was frustrating her.

She was an unloved child. The only way she knew how to feel powerful was to seduce people, take their money, and abandon them. She had to make others love her just so she could deny them love. She told me about how she tried to convince a man who was madly in love with her to commit suicide, how she paid for my uncle's college by manipulating a man for money.

I wonder if there was a particular moment when she decided, *I refuse to be the unloved child. From now on, it is I who will fuck everyone else over.*

Even after reversing the roles, she would still be the unloved child. But in flashes she could experience the joy of destroying in others what had been destroyed in her.

While I was living with her, she told me that she hated me because my father loved me, that I didn't deserve to be loved.

She said that my father was genuinely caring and good, and that I was a disappointing daughter.

She spoke endlessly about how disgusted weak and lazy people made her feel.

She told the woman who ran the phone booth that her daughter was mediocre and homely.

She told me that I was not the best, that I tricked people into believing that I was good at all.

She said she was glad she never had kids because she would have beaten them.

She told me I was "fat," "weak," and "easy," that my way of always waiting around for people was pathetic. I couldn't really argue with her. I was pathetic. But why was it that, without being strong, I was always able to get to where I wanted and needed to be? And how was it that I could survive her cruelty fairly unscathed, without an ounce of resentment toward her?

Quietly, I made plans to move out.

I was no match for her. She was a true sadist, and I, eternally wounded. But I was just so good at not caring. I knew that even though she was the most powerful person I had ever met, deep down she was miserable.

At the end of the day, I do not have the satisfaction of saying, "I have not let anyone fuck me over." She does.

I too would love to beat the shit out of someone. But unlike her I would only derive a sense of pleasure from it if the person truly deserved it. And even then, I would probably feel guilty afterward. When I told D. I thought it would be cool to be a dominatrix, he told me he wanted me to whip him. I said, *But you're too nice. I would feel bad. I only want to whip shitty people.*

I admit that for a couple years after living with her I became a very tough person. I lifted weights, biked twenty miles a day, worked out all the time, ate healthy foods, finished my homework early, dressed like a badass, and always carried a knife.

But I could never be cold or indifferent toward people. That's what always undoes me.

(2012)

Questions I've Been Asking Myself about Sex and Eroticism

This originally appeared on my Tumblr blog.

1. To what extent could we consider Fanon a theorist of sado-masochism?

2. Why do most of the Asian women I know, queer or not, end up dating white people?

3. What are the eroticized racial power dynamics that structure Asian femininity?

4. To what extent does the notion of consent reinforce liberal and capitalist narratives about subjectivity?

5. When is sex *not* affective labor?

6. To what extent are our sexual and romantic encounters actually eroticized battles for recognition?

7. What is post-orgasm disgust?

8. How does a masochist become a sadist? Is the masochist's capacity for sadism demonstrated by their violence toward themselves? Would such a transformation involve transferring their inward

sadistic tendencies? (Deleuze would say that a primary sadism is not the basis of masochism.)

9. If the colonizer is a sadist, and the colonized becomes a sadist during the revolutionary period, to what extent is a dialectical sadomasochistic movement part of the realization of the "new humanity" that Fanon speaks of?

10. Why am I bored by discussions/representations of sadomasochism that deal with "sexuality" proper, rather than the erotics of power? How do subcultural representations of S/M as bedroom/dungeon "play" reinforce the idea that sexuality is separate from economic, social, and political relations?

11. Is rape a "deviation" from healthy sexuality, or is it the underlying structuring principle of all sexualities?

12. What would an "objectless" sexuality look like?

13. To what extent is sex about the consumption of the other?

14. What is the difference between a masochist and someone with a martyr complex? Does the difference lie in the fact that the "martyr" locates the source of their suffering and pain in external objects (in other words, blames others for their suffering), while such a thought would *never even occur* to the masochist?

15. If you were a real sadist, what pleasure would it bring you to hurt a "self-identified" masochist? (Probably none.)

16. Is a sexual encounter that is not, in some way, violent, even possible?

17. Why did my last partner try to fuck me whenever I was upset about something or we were arguing? Was I wrong in feeling like she was trying to shut me up?

18. Why is it that the more pessimistic I become about sex, the sluttier I dress? Does it come from an unconscious desire to seduce and deny?

19. Is there a type of porn that specifically depicts Asian women humiliating white men?

20. Are sadists and masochists actually noncomplementary? Wouldn't their respective power struggles (and the pleasures derived from them) actually be neutralized by a "sadomasochistic" encounter?

21. How can people think that "sexual liberation" under white supremacy and patriarchy could ever be a positive thing?

22. Are queers particularly prone to having naively optimistic views of sex?

23. Are autoerotics queer? Do all sexualities have to have an object?

(2013)

Future Anterior: The Grammar of Survival?

This originally appeared on my Tumblr blog.

In counseling I am often hyperaware of how lucky I am to be a writer because I already have so many of the skills I need to work through trauma: the impulse to reflect on what has been lived, the desire to process things by externalizing them, the ability to narrate my experiences and to create something—some kind of meaning—out of the broken pieces of my life. I put pen to paper and though there is always this dizzying sensation—the immediate disintegration-disorientation of moving through an irreducible experience or feeling—without knowing what the hell I am doing I am moving toward a higher integration. As a writer I am a dual entity in a single body, both sadist and masochist, lorded by and lording over (in language), living in chaos while desperately desiring to be ordered and whole and only ever achieving a freakish, provisional coherence (as though I were an improperly assembled potato head, my mouth where my eyes should be, but I will just call these forehead lips my THIRD EYE and tell everyone they should be afraid because I SEE TOO MUCH). Always, what has been written will have been impossible. And yet, it will (have been said).

Writing will have saved me
I will have been saved by the practice of assembling words
In the end, I will have been saved by having written

In the future anterior I am not unbegotten.

* * *

The first time I caught myself thinking in the future anterior, or future perfect, I was startled by the peculiar temporal structure of the tense: what *will have been*, the space of the "imaginary real." It is the grammar of willed prophecy. The fact that this position is imaginatively accessible to me, that it is possible for me to temporalize myself in this way, is proof that something inside me has changed. I don't want to say anything about "healing," but I have read that the future perfect is the language of healing. I kept catching myself saying it, that *writing will have saved me*, and with that it was decided—I will not be broken forever.

Abdul R. JanMohamed (who quotes Lacan):

> From a psychoanalytic viewpoint, the perspective made available by the structure of the future anterior plays a crucial role in the "cure" of the patient and in freeing him from the tyranny of external determination. And it does so, according to Lacan, because of its function in determining the identity of the subject: "*I identify myself in language, but only by losing myself in it like an object. What is realized in my history is not the past definite of what was, since it is no more, or even the present perfect of what has been in what I am, but the future anterior of what I shall have been for what I am in the process of becoming*" (*Écrits*). According to this view, the "truth" of the analysand's life is not simply determined in a mechanical fashion by past events; rather, he is brought by the analyst to a point where he

can acknowledge that this truth also depends on the future, the nature of which is governed by his evolving desires, knowledge, commitments, and investments and, above all, by his choices. The efficacy of the subject's past history is determining, but that determination is drastically modified and, hence, in turn, determined by the subject's present and future choices and actions. (Emphasis mine)

The ability to project yourself into the future is not always good. I have felt the exuberant generosity of the untethered *NOW*, release from the weight of everything that has been and what will be. I have always rejected the idea of being a servant to an imagined future, but let's face it—the present is not always free!

Rachel Blau DuPlessis:

"The Laugh of the Medusa," by Hélène Cixous, is one of the great twentieth-century manifestoes. Like many manifestoes, it exhorts the *creation of something that is rhetorically palpable, so the new time that is urged as coming in history is already present in its own prose.* The *insurgent force* of the prose *catapults us into the future perfect,* with its *fecund confusions* of present and future tense. (Emphasis mine)

The future perfect is the ability to project yourself into the future, then reflect on what does not yet exist by moving backward to some place between now and that imagined point in time. How marvelous it is to move through time like this, in language! For several years I did not have the capacity to think of myself in the future perfect because I could not see a way out of the present. When there was no will to live, there was no future perfect. Sometimes I didn't even know there was no will to live. All I knew was *this is*, and *this sucks*.

Elizabeth Rottenberg citing Blanchot: "'The imminence of what has always already taken place': this is an unbelievable tense.... Imminence, the instance of what will already have taken place, will be in question."

Judith Butler, *Frames of War: When Is Life Grievable?*:

> But there can be no celebration without an implicit under-standing that the life is grievable, that it would be grieved if it were lost, and that this future anterior is installed as the con-dition of its life. In ordinary language, grief attends the life that has already been lived, and presupposes that life as having ended. But, *according to the future anterior* (which is also part of ordinary language), *grievability is a condition of a life's emer-gence and sustenance*. The future anterior, "a life has been lived," is presupposed at the beginning of a life that has only begun to be lived. In other words, "this will be a life that will have been lived" is the presupposition of a grievable life, which means that this will be a life that can be regarded as a life, and be sustained by that regard. Without grievability, there is no life, or, rather, there is something living that is other than life. Instead, "there is a life that will never have been lived," sus-tained by no regard, no testimony, and ungrieved when lost. (Emphasis mine)

* * *

Is this shift in the grammatical construction of my self-awareness evidence of LIFE (re)entering my body through the linguistic organ? Life asserts itself by making certain temporal possibilities intelligible to me via language. The future perfect of my thoughts makes my survival rhetorically palpable.

I am a periwinkle flower getting tossed around in the sea of time.

(2013)

Wishing Moon Across My Face

This originally appeared on my Tumblr blog.

temporarily moving to Chicago in less than a week

quit my job

scrambling to wrap things up here in New Mexico

i was looking forward to teaching my class on prison literature, but i can't stay here

what the hell am i doing with my life?

in the last year i have written over 2,000 pages in notebooks

but where is my book?

enough failed scraps for 10 books

i can't imagine having a life again

i can't imagine not avoiding everything

for the next year i'll be living out of a suitcase

i'm tired of being uprooted

"my transit body is exhausted"

and what about my little adobe house

i don't want to abandon my house, the altar i built in the living room

but i will go to Scotland and live with an Asian femme coven

can you imagine, what power, between all of us so powerful

* * *

i keep going back to a sentence in my notebook

it goes

"sometimes there is a perfect egg and everything is easy."

as in, cosmic alignment

i am in the alley of your sentence, looking for a way in

blessed word for word i am a space in the world

leave me with your breath and i promise to discover another world

the way something works in words is a world

a world rising to the surface of the page to meet you

she's there, beneath the scrim

a revenant waiting to be written

i'll make an opening out of stones

twelve of them placed in a circle at the bottom of the river

you'll like who you become

if you make it that far

on some days i see who i am

another plan is released into atmosphere

too many seeds and too little water

we remember graduation

some people had Fulbrights, big plans

and then there's my Lilliputian song in the thick of ambition

the feeling that i'm losing, have already lost

she tells me to feel the grass

lawns were a theme that night

we tried to understand

i remembered the opening of *101 Dalmatians*

and the story of the bird that spits blood to die

what is it about being an easily agitated body

animated by the breath of the one who does not wobble with her eyes closed in the sun of Sunday

to wiggle toward the Substance

to be received

a truly generous person does not feel embarrassed for anyone

when i am free the words will have their own way of remembering

the sentence becoming a cave to house the dreams you do not understand at the center of the primary chamber:

the heartbeat becomes a song you can't get rid of

with my body i perceive your body

feel you leaving i remember everything

the way we crossed the rosemary forest, sprig to sprig

in our neon socks making heat out of yesterday's dross

loving our high school songs truly

i imagine my mother, a girl again

a dream shared

across a generation

i'll not be a girl again

there was a closed-eye beginning

some nights i can remember everything, including my mistakes

some nights i wish moon across my face

for preparation

i spin like a woman in a glass costume doing circles in the vestibule

the moon is a path i'd like to show you in my hour of forgiveness

a book of scraps

was the creation of this forgiveness

and by forgiveness i mean, becoming nature

there's no ego to injure on this walk across a possible tomorrow

erect dunes may suddenly turn concave and your body will be at the bottom of the bowl

waiting to see what will be left behind

a pair of beautiful purple platform shoes

something very personal

the air is charged with this something personal, a choir of frogs

weaving a scene in which i am not afraid to show you the seed i keep beneath my tongue

and when i want everything to be okay between us

i try to make it funny

to deflate the weirdness that circulates between our bodies

in the dissonant song of the tone-deaf frogs

there is an opening

suddenly i am touched by everyone's insignificant thoughts

trying to choose a type of cereal or the turmoil of breaking a glass when you were almost finished washing the dishes

dreams of stale donuts

the leftovers of a punk-rock existence

3 eyes missing from the cover

trying to glue them back on

brain in entropic decline

i'm so fucked walking around crying smelling dirty clothes wondering if they will pass making collages of uterus monsters and flying tampons Maoist posters a box labeled "unicorns" pictures of Grecians on bicycles glitter acorns witch hands fly agaric decor panda ears herbal everything portals covered in fake flowers Polaroids of abandoned buildings and the baby dyke's religious jewelry on my nightstand

traces of a ridiculous existence

a trying existence

having (nonironic) profound moments in the kitchen while listening to Elton John's "Rocket Man"

everything is funny including crying in public and writing ridiculous emails to your professor at 3:00 a.m.

an old Black / Creole / Native American man in a pink shirt just sat down with me at IHOP and bought me dinner

he says he loves people and is psychic

he kept saying

"i had a feeling ... i just had this feeling ..."

"maybe she wants dinner"

(2013)

Aliens as a Form of Life:
Imagining the Avant-Garde

Written for and published in The Force of What's Possible: Writers on Accessibility & the Avant-Garde, *edited by Lily Hoang and Joshua Marie Wilkinson.*

Hey Lily,

Isn't it funny that before I knew you, I wrote an epistolary review of your book *The Evolutionary Revolution* for BOMB, and now I know you and am writing an epistolary essay for your anthology? It's always been difficult for me to write to an abstract audience, to write into a void without a specific occasion for enunciation—some kind of performative context, a person toward whom I am permitted to speak.

I write to you because you are coediting this book on the avant-garde, because you are my "alien sister" and aliens have a lot to do with the avant-garde. The other day you came to my house with a gift—a little boy's blue T-shirt, depicting an astronaut. The T-shirt made you think of me because you know I like space and I like space because I like aliens. I like aliens, not only because I am one but also because I enjoy imagining other forms of life.

In the photo I am with my kind, fellow travelers of universes yet unknown.

Right before I left New Mexico, I went to the International UFO Museum and Research Center in Roswell with D. Though the museum itself was shitty—cluttered with information, disorganized—I left feeling that representations of aliens are an index of the human imagination: they represent our desire for *new forms*. But what has always confused me about depictions of aliens in movies and books is this: aliens could look like anything and yet we represent them as creatures close to humans. The aliens at this museum had two legs, two eyes, a mouth—their form was essentially human. I wondered: Is this the best we can come up with? Is it true that all we can do when imagining a new form of life is take the human form, fuck with the proportions, enlarge the head, remove the genitals, slenderize the body, and subtract a finger on each hand? Is it out of narcissism that we construct their image in our likeness? From an evolutionary perspective, there is a statistical probability that any aliens that might be out there don't look like us, as they have been evolving apart from us, in a different environment and under different conditions, for many years. We strain to imagine foreignness, but we don't get very far from what we know. But my alien is more of what's possible—it is a shapeshifter, impossibly large, and yet as small as the period at the end of this sentence—>. My alien communicates in smells and telepathic song and weeping and chanting and yearning and the sensation of failure and empathic identification and beatitude. My alien is singular and plural and has the consciousness of fungus, and every night, instead of sleeping, it dies and in the morning is resurrected, and all of the aliens of the species I have just created live on edge because they never know when the death of their loved one is the real death … the final death.

The alien as it exists in our imagination is a liminal creature, existing at the threshold of what is familiar and what is imaginatively possible but not-yet, both formally recognizable and always somehow *strangerly*.

Sometimes, sitting before a blank page, I get a rush just thinking, ANYTHING IS POSSIBLE. Why is it that everything I write fails to capture the range of what is possible? I think, *We could write anything and yet we don't.* Whenever I am at poetry readings, I think the same thing: *We could do anything and yet we dutifully perform this boring ritual.* Why is it that we piously adhere to these stale forms? Why, when you encouraged me to submit to your anthology, did I draft two other essays that were dreadfully boring?

I could write anything here. I could be whacky as hell! I could go outside, kick over a garbage can, speak in numbers, and call the whole thing a poem. But something stops me. The question WHY stops me. I used to live my life according to WHY NOT and things were much more exciting. Today I practiced WHY NOT. After waking up this morning I had a thought: *Should I go to church?* I haven't been to a Catholic Mass in over ten years, but I figured I'd check it out, as I have been thinking lately that it's a good idea to believe in God. But what is the form of the Everything-Entity from whom I desperately desire a warm embrace?

God could look like anything, and yet we make her into a white man.

God, like the alien, reveals our inability to stray too far from identifiable forms.

When I was a child, I believed I was an alien. I think it had something to do with being mixed-raced. If I was the progeny of beings of two discrete forms, then what was I? I felt I did not belong anywhere. I know you have felt this too, particularly around white people of a bourgeois upbringing. I know we have sometimes felt like two aliens stranded on an island of normality. This world is a hostile place for aliens, but we must not wear humanoid bodysuits to dodge attention. We must inhabit our alienness!

I could write anything here, and yet I can't. I cannot hand you an egg and say, "Hey Lily, can you put this in your anthology? It's cosmic."

I am constrained by the task and the people involved in it, because my work is relational, and art that is relational is determined, in part, by what it is in relation to. It is out of love that I clarify myself, that I find a form to transmit these scattered nothings to you. Some writers eschew accessibility on the grounds that it imposes a consensus reality and is thus tyrannical. But there's tenderness in the impulse to clarify ourselves (for an-other, *for you*), even if it means that, in anticipating what forms might be legible to an-other, we are circumscribed. I call this THE PARADOX OF THE AUDIENCE: the creator is both profoundly limited *and* animated (read: enabled, opened) by the receiver(s). The constraints are more pronounced when the audience is abstract because in such situations the creator must adopt the lowest-common-denominator form. Every situation that is concrete involves some measure of negotiation. Therefore it is *not* true that anything is possible. But we can always do better, cultivate wilder and more feral imaginations by building spaces that open us, creatively.

Though the avant-garde is generally conceptualized in terms of formal innovation, I prefer to think of it in terms of space. Our mad pursuit of the "new"—of aesthetic originality and novelty—has made us neurotic. Perhaps it is time we redirect our energies into collaboratively creating material, psychic, and symbolic spaces where nonnormative activity and artistic production can take place. These spaces will constantly need to be fortified, and to properly fortify these spaces, we must identify which forces, mechanisms, and institutions foreclose possibilities.

To create a space for the imagination is to create a container for the uncontaining and unleashing of desire. The container should facilitate generative encounters and provide a ground on which energizing and magical experiences can take place. For me, art is always what happens during an encounter, for writing is first and foremost ENERGY and CONNECTIVE TISSUE—*a relation*. It's not the textual objects *but the bonds* that matter. So long as we think of artistic production in terms of the individual rather than collective body, then the isolated *product* will be prioritized over the *relation*.

I want to create this space with people. With you. Because without it, I am lost. My whole life I have been looking for a place to call home. Where's a whacky Brown femme dyke gal like me to go? I keep hoping the aliens will come back for me and take me home. When they beam me up to their ship, I will look into their bug eyes and ask, *Why did you leave me behind?* And we will travel by wormhole to a place light years away ...

I don't want to go out on a sad note.

So I must remind myself that the astronaut on the T-shirt you gave me is not a weary traveler, but an explorer of the unknown: *the Possible.* When I think of outer space—the scale, the distance between galaxies and stars and celestial bodies—it really puts things in perspective. From Big Bang to me there is a path, but it could have gone in any number of directions, never to arrive at me sitting in my little adobe house at this moment in time. What is the statistical probability that I should exist? It is almost impossible that I should exist, and yet I do. I should not be alive. It is a miracle that I am alive and that you are alive and that whoever is reading this is alive. It is even a miracle that out of all the sperm that could have won the race to the egg, I WON. I was only half an "I" then. I think it might be my greatest achievement—winning the race so that I might live.

Though the actualization of one out of everything possible will always exclude every other possibility, and though everything that is-not is always greater than what is, *we are.* You *are* this primary potential, manifest and true.

Love, Jackie

(2013)

Alien Daughters Walk Into the Sun

My presentation (via Skype) for the panel Bitches of Color in a White Boy World: Innovative Others and Identity Aesthetics, which was presented at &Now 2013: Off the Road, University of Colorado Boulder, September 27, 2013.

I am writing this on the subway in Glasgow, Scotland. I don't know why I want to see if I can write this whole talk on the tube. (Perhaps I want to prove to myself that writing and life happen at the same time, that they are not separate.) There is an old woman sitting across from me. Her nose is pink. I watch her touch the band-aided thumb of her grandson while her daughter speaks to her two young children in French. I could get off at the next stop and go to the university library, but something inside me says, "Stay." I will stay. I will stay on this train and try to figure out what it means to be a woman of color who writes. Is *this* what it means, this insistence on being in the world? To be integrated, by necessity. To speak from a place, always, even when I am not speaking of myself.

Last night I dreamed I made a home for myself in a beachside bungalow. As I looked out of my wide window at the marvelous ocean vista, I thought to myself, *My life is going to be great.* I imagined that I would finally be able to feel comfortable, but something stopped me from feeling comfortable. I lived in a town where people loved to throw flamboyant themed parties and though I knew I was lucky to be among those allowed to bear witness to these glitzy spectacles, I always felt weird and excluded. At one party I volunteered to be "the sober one" just to feel myself in relation to the crowd, thus making my sobriety a "duty" and not just Asian flush.

Most of my dreams can be put into two categories: dreams where I am out of place and anxious, or dreams where I am at home and comfortable. The "at home" dreams usually appear to me as touch, a feeling of warmth that fills the body when I am embraced by a human who wants to love me. Their touch makes me feel so safe I don't want to leave. In the other type of dream everything is dangerous and threatening or conspiring against me in more innocuous ways. The paranoid logic of these dreams can make banal, everyday situations—like eating dinner with someone else's family—terrible. In these dreams I always find myself inside someone's house, fumbling to figure out how things work while the residents quietly judge me for my bad manners and ignorance of house etiquette. The unnerving feeling that something is off, the incommunicable sense of being out of place: these paranoid dreams mirror the experience of being a woman of color who writes. In these dreams there is always something invisible lurking that makes me anxious: an ambient fear, an unnamable force that threatens to undo me at every turn, or even just a vague feeling that I do not belong.

I don't remember when I started being a woman of color or a writer, but claiming either has always been fraught. What is the woman of color's system of reality? Not any one thing, of course. But for me it has something to do with feeling that you are without a world, that the world was not made for you. (And because the world does not belong to you, you do not belong in the world.) Not belonging in the world is a peculiar place to occupy for it is not a place at all, but floating. It is kind of like being unable to put your feet on the ground ... yet nobody knows you are hovering six inches above the ground because you're always wearing really long pants ... everyone just thinks you have unusually long legs!

Though I've been writing my whole life, it has never been easy for me to claim the title "writer." That is why I call my writings "traces" and not "works": they are the remainder of a life spent in search of a place that does not exist, because the place where the woman of color lives and writes does not yet exist (she is making it all the time). As a queer woman of color I am a desiring-alien and this desire sometimes takes the form of a dream of wholeness, of home. Imagine a weepy alien who strolls through city streets with her suitcase, always carrying a suitcase because she is a go-between gal.

So many of these essays and talks are addressed to white people, in the form of a litany of grievances. But I would like to use this opportunity to address young women of color who like to write. I say "who like to write" because so many young women of color do not identify as "writers" because they feel illegitimate and unworthy.

Here's what I would like to say to them:

> Dear young woman of color who likes to write,
> I too am young, so this is as much addressed to me as it is to you. It is *with* you that I am trying to figure this all out.
> It was probably obvious to you from the moment you set out to write that training yourself to not be diffident is, as a woman of color, as much a part of the practice of writing as the

actual writing. It is a matter of making your voice louder than the voice of the proverbial white man inside you—the voice that says your writing is trivial, that you should feel bad about not making belletristic art, that you will never be Great. The cumulative space he and his system of reality take up in the world is proportionate to the loudness of his voice inside your head. Who is this white man? He is merely a stand-in for power, and we all have a relationship with power.

There are many things you can expect to encounter. In white circles you may feel profoundly misunderstood. You may be loved for your portrayals of reckless girlhood or even your rigorous engagement with communization theory but not, say, your interest in prison literature and the Black radical tradition, or the nuances of your understanding of girlhood, all the ways in which it is racialized. Your literary heroes may not be the heroes of the ones who claim you as kin. You will become extremely adept at occupying spaces where you don't quite belong, and while people may marvel at your grace and intellectual dexterity, you will dream of a space expansive enough to hold every part of you, a space where you won't have to bracket the things that matter most to you for the sake of others' comfort. Some people will tell you that to talk about your experiences or how you are positioned in the world is nothing more than vulgar identity politics, which should be avoided at all costs. It probably goes without saying that this is a clever way to recenter the white experience.

Though I don't want to make you paranoid, it's probably true that at some point you will encounter white women who view you as cultural capital and will try to use you to validate their projects. They want to include you, but only on their terms. If you are queer, straight women may be even more eager to befriend you because your sexuality makes you less threatening (i.e., you will not compete with them for male attention and validation, and therefore are not a rival). You may feel sincerely thankful for what they give you—adoration, publishing opportunities. But remember, you're giving them more than they are giving you, in the form of your value as cultural and institutional capital. Having a "down" woman of color around and on your side is the best defense against the charge of racism. You may feel disgusted when you learn friendship is never just friendship in a world where everyone is trying to get ahead—that even in the small-press writing world, human relationships have been reduced to professional advancement. You may be down on yourself for having been naïve enough to believe that it was all about building a nourishing creative community, for being eager and giving yourself and your work away for nothing. Your concerns were never perennial, your dramas were never central—or at least they were never as interesting as the tumultuous romantic lives of the white people around you.

When you finally become aware of the ugly inner workings of this symbolic economy, nothing will seem real. At this point you will have to decide if you want to play the game or preserve your integrity. I have no doubt that you could be an excellent player—that you may have already mastered the discourse, have all the proper reference points, and are proficient with white topics. You may have set out to develop fluency in this discourse unaware that in mastering the discourse—which is really much more like a habit of being—you are, in some way, validating it, even if you choose to reject it by writing a million angry tracts decrying the stupidity of these beloved books and political treatises. In some ways the choice is between remaining in close proximity to loci of power or resigning yourself to a nugatory existence and—if you are a lesbian—making a place for yourself in the world without having access to the material, symbolic, and psychic capital possessed by white men. You are worried that you are nothing without your white friends and this may, on some level, be true. Their recognition might mean everything to you. It is possible that your core sense of self-worth is bound up with their approval, and not having their love fills you with pain. You may feel trapped in the terrible contradiction of both needing them and wanting to run away to extricate yourself from their value system—to create space for your projects, your interests—in other words, to become the protagonist of your own life.

Wounded people act out and so might you. You will be tempted to wield your victim status against those you resent for being more popular, having more publications, for winning at the game you claim to reject. You want to become them; you want to destroy them. You want the power they possess because the only power you have is to create a morality out of not having power, to talk shit about their ways of having power as though you are somehow purer or more innocent. You think that the more you hate those who have power, the less ensnared you are in their way of doing and being in the world. But this just isn't true. You covet what you can't have and so you devote your time to making those who do have power feel bad or guilty about having it. They're never going to listen, and the closer you get to the centers of power you cannot access, the more infuriated you feel.

And you pray that nobody notices that the underlying motivation for battling these people is the desire for a few crumbs of recognition, or, if you can't get that, the desire to wreck their blithe and jolly rise to literary stardom (and perhaps to even make a career out of calling white people out). Besides, if anyone suggested that your political interventions are motivated by anything other than "good" politics and rectitude, you could just call them racist. They probably are. And you probably have a right to derail their "careers," especially when they are at your expense or built up using your emotional and material labor. The violence you feel when you recognize your life has been truncated is real. But there are also very real ways in which resentment can disfigure and mutate your spirit. If you get stuck in this reactive mode you risk developing a dialectical dependency on the "white man" (or woman), a dependency that will prevent you from growing and will use up all your creative energy. The more you hate people for winning the game, the more you will believe in the game yourself. In making the game "real" you reinforce an individualist value-system based, implicitly, on the idea that making others feel inferior or stupid indicates your literature is "good" (in other words, a framework where artistic genius is predicated on making people feel like shit).

The main advice I would give young women of color who are also writers: Protect your souls at all costs. A little bit of righteous anger is psychologically necessary and can make life more bearable, but don't let the compulsion to speak these self-serving truths turn you into a caricature of yourself. You're more dynamic than that. If no one else sees this, I do. Give yourself permission to be weird. It sucks that white people have a monopoly on weirdness, while we are always forced to exist on a "rational" wavelength by virtue of always having to explain the conditions of our lives, or because we are so used to making space for and accommodating other people's realities that we don't know how to insert our own.

My friend Joohyun just got on the train. When she saw me she started laughing and said, "Why are you still on the tube?" We left the same place, but I left much earlier and so she was surprised to see me on the train, typing on my iPad. I said, "I am trying to write a speech about being a woman of color who writes. I thought writing it on the tube would give my writing … a sense of motion."

Here is a poem I wrote today. It is called, "I Found my Soul at the Bottom of the Pool." THANK YOU CODA AND JOOHYUN FOR YOUR LOVE AND INPUT ON THIS ESSAY.

I Found My Soul at the Bottom of the Pool

PART I

i found my soul there

i found it at the bottom of the pool

she saw

no i saw

no she saw

no i saw

i saw my soul vibrating at the bottom of the pool

i saw my soul just out of reach

i saw my soul go for a swim

i found my soul in rainbow diving sticks at the bottom of the pool

i found the years i lost to sleep at the bottom of the pool

i found my mother's womb at the bottom of the pool

i found my mother's watch at the bottom of the pool

i found my focus in chlorinated water

i found a feast spread out on a dining-room table at the bottom of the pool

i found 2 cups of coffee and waking up at 6:00 a.m. at the bottom of the pool

i found the world at the bottom of the pool

there is water at the bottom of the pool

there is a comfortable bed at the bottom of the pool

i found the continuity of dust and mommy at the bottom of the pool

i found my manuscript at the bottom of the pool

i found centuries of strangled mirrors at the bottom of the pool

i found the first day of my mother's fall from grace at the bottom of the pool

i found unnamable deities at the bottom of the pool

i found particles of my past repeating themselves at the bottom of the pool

i found Nietzsche at the bottom of the pool

i found directions on how to say no to your tongue and walk away at the bottom of the pool

i found the reason why it is so easy to forgive everyone except myself at the bottom of the pool

i found the mystery of gravity at the bottom of the pool

i found myself untamed and inside the feeling at the bottom of the pool

at the bottom of the pool there is a basket of loneberries

and the pool is the spreading out and becoming full of the pool

the pool is tautological

the pool is at the bottom of the pool

the pool is a hum that settles blood and everything terrible

at the bottom of the pool there is the choice to get mad or just be a silent witness

at the bottom of the pool there is a house that can't get rid of the stench of animals

at the bottom of the pool there is a body that inhabits itself without the fear of being common

at the bottom of the pool there is a rocking chair and an old woman in it, waiting for her friend to return at the bottom of the pool there is a way back to the fever pitch of receiving your letter

at the bottom of the pool there is a way back to the joy of writing and the discovery of eyes you never knew were hiding beneath your hair

at the bottom of the pool there is an eye opening for the first time, a furry creature prodding its babe alive

i am creaturing at the bottom of the pool

at the bottom of the pool there is a cocktail of all the best drugs

at the bottom of the pool there is here

at the bottom of the pool there is a way to be here

at the bottom of the pool there is a toilet and the toilet is a portal to heaven

PART II

the Haymarket oracle whips her hair to the beat of the bleeding toes

we are as we should be, she says, even after swaths of our inner topographies are swept away by the flood

be quiet and admire the way other people strain to exist

let there be nothing inside your head except the image of women walking into the sun

you're looking for a fancy way to shoulder the night while knowing nothing of the night you wish to speak, the way the undertones chime like the voice of a distressed woman on the phone the woman on the phone says the red dress crumpled and limp on the wet street is what it means to suffer as a daughter suffers, 14 hours a day

her phone is not plugged in

and on she goes about how she would like to crawl into the dress and sleep and sleep and sleep for a fierce arrival tomorrow

"i am a blackberry covered in spider webs" she says

but all you take away is a passing impression of being *caught*

"i am a shrill bride anxiously anticipating the moment of negation,

which is also the moment of being made into someone normal enough to be a lawyer"

what do you know of the way lawful people count the days left to have a baby?

or the way people devote themselves to being vegan or a poet because they're not normal enough to be a lawyer

let them laugh a little because they are sick and need to feel unrestrained

the sun is rising over the hill and there's no question about it, you have reserved your tenderness for the WRONG people!!! for the people who deserve it least

oh Haymarket oracle, will you be a reason for me to take note of where i am?

he'll never love the crack and the way the world flows out of it as blood spurts from the mouth of the one who is a little too excited after having spoken to God!!!!!!!!!!

a word vibrating in the body is a way to know God

a gold coin glowing at the center of a damp street

or the way you knew, at the end of the night, that the truth of God was to be simple and kind to yourself

the gift of the word has been given to women who are not afraid of the rapture of turning themselves inside out

you weren't afraid of dying but only of being ejected from your life while alive

don't let yourself not be in your life

let there be nights spent at your desk, howling ecstatic

howling—oh Haymarket oracle of pithy mystery!

oh trains! oh how many people carry the hideous Metro rag!

oh spectacles of bodily disfiguration!

oh nose grown on the forehead of the one who weeps for a new face!

when the body is undone, some words are released

inauguration of a state whose book grows cosmic in scope

in a cup that says "relax" there is the juice of life

i'll be near God, from now on the pieces of the world will spring luminous into this vision

the way Karl Marx's words sprung luminous into the mind of the drugged-out Jewish boy reading in the library

you'll know yourself not afraid and so confused you know everything, *finally!*, which is to say nothing at all

there was always a Bible in the silence of the room

pursue that state until it becomes dream and you are a young man
on your way to study abroad, top hat and valise

eyes huge with money

what the desert did to your dreams

what the desert did to you

never had you felt more true to the state of waiting

buried alive

when i look in the mirror now i think, *the desert aged me*

i feel this haunt in my neck bone, where i carry everything left
behind

i said, "dimension"—i want to know life in all its dimensions.

come down and see me

witness my slaughter oh world felt in a gilded instant,

when we step out of unhappy rooms

into the sun we are shredded into our sons

tell him we will become what we never thought we'd have the
courage to become

tell him the sky is waking up to the finitude of tomorrow's coming

and we are to receive the memory of our childhood bedrooms

i remember the room, the way it bent down to meet me in my sorrow

and how many nights spent in bed drowning because, i don't know
where my head is

i don't know where i am

there are two ways of drowning in fire and i am the way of blood

i am the tiredness of this room, its low lighting

the way i bent down to meet the room in its sadness

you are the hypocrisy of light when your soul is dark

the sanguine countenance that betrays your inner disorder

together we dreamed of drifting down the river

and because it is a day, we are this miracle of day

the way we kneel and beg the day to shine its mercy on us

i was drawn to what i believed was his self-possession

and i used this to punish myself

because i will never be a man—

i'll return to the Caspian Sea with a book on how to begin

out of this we are born

we are born on the train

watching the morning spread out across the earth

i like the way the frumpy girl wears her headphones and never takes
off her jacket

i like everyone and everything

i like you

i like my life, my whacked-out way of being

but i can't say for how long

and when i didn't care about being smart, it was easy to just you know kind of be a person and there was the love i wanted to be and i had a mission on how to be, did my emotions go flat? no no, there was the desert but um i think that was more sad than euphoric but there was psychic yes i am losing my psychic powers because i don't remember the dream, and the dream has nothing to say to me when i am not bending down to meet the dream in the creek. what there was: profound appreciation like crying because the world wakes every day even though you are never ready to be in it. or how the ocean makes an infant of you, or the moon becomes "i appreciate your big hands" because of the way they remind me of the moon remind me of a pale heart remind me of the butt in *Butt* magazine remind me of the cheeks of my father or a passing cloud

soon it will be cold. there are too many directions inside you. finish your books. be an amorous dolphin. remember the way everything fired at once but you have some pills to curb your mania you have jolts of awareness you have a way of unstating everything that matters. you have a way of sitting on the floor, falling asleep you are sad on the train because you remembered the way you'd weep on the train at the beauty that was the feeling that life was coming rather than receding. now, only the feeling that life is falling away from you, like clumps of hair fall from an unnourished body. yes there was the swelling and a way of being more and more in the space until you were the space while at the same time you could see every little thing that constituted the space, in that moment and beyond. mistakes were exciting, inroads in the art of unknowing, the rush of not rushing, of just being, how marvelous!, this appointment: to be alive.

let your mistakes be a way of remembering what it takes to be free.

in the dream i discover the origins of the film

i return to where i began, in pitch black, at the bottom of the pool

i return to feel life coming

i return to where there is still someone waiting to meet me and be changed

to where the mystery of lost objects is audible

yes i live inside the feeling of embarking

and i have finally come to terms with the fact that i will never be the kind of person who can read on airplanes

accepting this, i let myself daydream of inverted skies

in transit the world is too large for demands to narrow my attention

my life becomes distinct and spontaneous

i go to the place where i become pure transmission

transforming, sensual and holy

at the bottom of the pool

(2013)

Queering Jackie O, American Royalty / American Outcasts, Lana Del Rey's White-Girl Archive of Female Suffering, and Graceless Lost Girls

This originally appeared on my Tumblr blog.

Jackie, oh Jackie oh, you never got an answer about where you came from. Your relationship to white femininity is doomed because you are named after Jackie O and you can't think of anything more ridiculous: little Brown lost girl named after American royalty. You could say you are from a nation that would never let you feel royal, but you don't know, sometimes you feel royal, but in a freakish, inverted way—not materially royal but spiritually royal. By spiritually royal you mean a certain feeling after you have given up, after you accept your failure and go for a walk. On this walk you feel the world becoming yours—not in a way that is possessive or projective but a way of just *being* that nobody can take away from you. In the woods beneath the viaduct at sunset, the river to your left: the whole scene *makes* you by unwriting you and drawing you into the landscape. Your feet sink into the mud. The world opens.

* * *

In Chicago you asked your friends five times who Miley Cyrus was and they explained but for some reason it didn't stick. The next time she came up you asked again, and every time you would say, "Ohhhh, Hannah Montana!" You, bona fide troglodyte—you ask them about Lana Del Rey: "Who is this woman whose sad voice captivated me in *Gatsby?*" And they explain and you say, "Ohhh, I know the type. A Plath girl!" And how elegantly she suffers, how operatic and finely clothed, arrayed in tulle, eyeliner running down her cheek … pearled, cinematic. When you cry you just look like E.T. and you wonder: *Does E.T. in a red dress look glamorous?* Does her red dress make you care that she's so far from home, or that she doesn't even remember where home is, or if she's ever felt at home anywhere?

Lana Del Rey just wants to be free yet she's a racist. You'll listen to the songs for their half-truths, because you're so fractured you no longer expect things to speak to you fully. You accept pieces of everything, there's no other way. You're as much a road dog as the white brunette in her cut-off denim shorts, waving her American flag, in search of a mythical American outsider caste—for you it is the punks, and your anti-American Americana, your new weird America, is the queer one, maybe the one Allen Ginsberg wrote about: unproductive, abject. Why is the American canon so damn queer, and does it make you more American to be (aesthetically) loose and gay and searching? James Baldwin says that if you don't accept this contradiction—the fact of being from the land you despise—you will never be able to develop a sense of where you are … whence you come. Sometimes you think about how curious it is that the only modernist poet who wanted to write an epic that was uniquely American was a fag—you are thinking of Hart Crane's *The Bridge*, and how his America was constituted by all of those purged by America: train-hopping tramps and other remainders of American capitalism … gay sailors cruising beneath the Brooklyn Bridge and the prophet-outcasts that guide the reader across the continent and back again, through New York's purgatorial subway system and up toward the light on heavenward-arching paths.

Do the punk rock vagabonds see themselves as part of an American nomadic tradition? And where are you in all this? Wandering, always. When you told her you were named after Jackie O she said that maybe you should change your name but you wondered what it would mean to claim this name, a named tied to American royalty. Jackie O, gay icon—could she be a gay herself? Could you be a better Jackie O than Lana Del Rey and where do you fit in this white-girl archive of feelings—their ways of suffering?

Lost girls just wanna be free—you can meet them that far but you're not sure you could make a pillbox hat and blood sexy. The baby dyke who courted me in New Mexico just wanted to be free, was always getting into trouble with the law. She let you borrow Lisa Crystal Carver's autobiography *Drugs are Nice: A Post-Punk Memoir* and would love to cruise around with you blasting those feel-good songs. Marie Calloway has reblogged your writings; what's that about? *It's cool*, you think. The lost girl's way of finding herself in being lost … is cool. She explores the process by which no-core becomes a core in itself. Call it "inverted power," "negative capability," whatever: this way of giving life by making yourself dead because you "are" for others. And you write in the letter that when there is no one to write to, you don't feel like writing at all. Where are you in these narratives of lost girls? Her work is an anatomy of feminine negation and the place where the chameleon soul has more sub-stance than the self-constituting soul because it is everything, like how Whitman made a place for himself as the greatest American poet by becoming everything. But not everyone can make a career of making themselves nothing to become everything—some are *made* nothing. Some are better at being nothing than others. Can suffer with grace. Can lose themselves with grace. Can lose themselves and still have: a story.

Where are you in it all? An ungainly lost girl. An uncouth dyke. You were never American—you were always America's nightmare, an enemy of the state and self-described anarchist since age thirteen—your mom even accused you of being a terrorist. Your older brother is not an American—he is property of America, a prisoner. You never possessed the pulchritude or social grooming or poise or skin color to live up to your name. Jackie O: America's tragic Queen. What would it mean to claim this name? To steal the crown. To say, *I am what constitutes this name, this boundary,* however contradictory—to say you are what you were never supposed to be.

* * *

"*Our crown*, you said, *has already been bought and paid for. All we have to do*, you said, *is wear it.*"—Toni Morrison quoting James Baldwin

(2013)

IV.

2014–16:

THE GETTING-MY-SHIT-TOGETHER YEARS

Somerville and Cambridge, Massachusetts, with trips to Martinique, France, Iceland, Italy, and Russia.

Is it any surprise that my first semester of graduate school was an absolute train wreck? My depression and suicidal ideation had gotten so bad that by my second semester of grad school I had stopped checking my emails and turning in my schoolwork, and was often unable to get out of bed. I read books and research papers on depression, hoping to find a cure. *Anything. I'll try anything.* And I did. Neurofeedback, CBT, DBT, therapeutic yoga, mindfulness meditation, fish oil, ketamine. I even tried to sign up for experimental treatments for depression but was rejected from all of them because I'm left-handed. The winter of my first year of grad school I decided that I needed to, once and for all, exorcize the demons that had a stranglehold on my soul by doing intensive psychoanalysis four days a week. People often say, when it comes to psychoanalysis, that it gets worse before it gets better. That's how it was with me. I guess that's what happens when you blow the lids off your tightly sealed trauma jars.

For a long time, after C., I was on a "love strike." How strange, when I started dating again, that I went from being a gold-star lesbian to dating two Russian mathematicians in a row. Those relationships didn't last long. Soon after things ended with the second mathematician, I found a lover with a true heart.

I suppose these were the years I finally got over my unconscious desire to sabotage every project or endeavor I initiated. A newfound sense of resolve came to me, finally, in 2016, soon after things ended with D., the second Russian mathematician. I was reading Christian

Marazzi's Semiotext(e) book *The Violence of Finance Capitalism* when it occurred to me that I was sitting on enough unpublished writing to make a book. I had put the Semiotext(e) book I was solicited to write on the back burner while transitioning to graduate school. Putting that book in the world was a lesson in how to let go, to not be eternally beholden to a neurotic perfectionism that made it impossible to complete any project. No doubt it was psychoanalysis that enabled me to get over my debilitating hang-up around completing work.

Who knows how psychoanalysts do their magic. It's shocking to me how many people, when comparing my past self and present self, joke that psychoanalysis cured me. Yet I'm suspicious of this saner "me": Whoever she is, has she lost that streak of wildness? No longer flayed alive—but was it that flaying that broke me into speech?

Lonely Wolves on the Floor of the World

This essay originally appeared in the Claudius App *literary journal. I was solicited to write a "negative review," but I decided to review "the negative" instead.*

> *Are you sick and tired of running away?*
>
> *Then lie down.*
> —Bhanu Kapil

In *Treinte Ban*, Bhanu Kapil writes, "I wanted to write a novel but instead I wrote this." She wanted to write the race riot from the perspective of the Brown girl on the floor of the world but instead she wrote the luminous edges of the girl's inverted body. Antenarrative told in color. A delirious study of the body at the expense, as she writes, of the event. I read *Treinte Ban* on my iPad sitting on the futon of a queer punk house in Boston and by the end I must make my way to the bathroom to cry because I feel embarrassed about crying in front of my hosts. Bhanu writes, to my friend Coda and me, "I hope that some of the black and silver edges of these rudimentary notes make contact with your own work, whether germinal or accomplished, making it possible for you—also—to write again with what—in other cultures—is called joy."

Here. What comes after this benediction? The desire to become lovely again so as to recirculate the gift. Grief at what I now acknowledge has been this inability to write joyously for the last two years. Neither joy nor that feral punk-girl fuck-you spirit. We must begin somewhere but I've grown tired of being someone who only knows how to begin from the place of not knowing how to begin— to only speak around the unspeakable instead of sinking into it. "I wanted to write an essay about the texture of the negative but instead I wrote this." "I wanted to write an essay about Fred Moten but instead I wrote this." Are you so solipsistic that you cannot see outside your inability to write? But how can you write anything without meeting yourself where you're at? I accidentally typed "meeting yourself where you're out" because I Freudian slip into my own displacement—I'm outside myself. What if I said, *It's okay to begin from your self-hatred, to really fail the task, to really not give a shit.* Would everything open up?

Here. I slow. Again, I must ask: *What comes after Bhanu's benediction?*

After a desultory effort to effervesce: the desire to give up, to go to sleep. The staccato stop-and-go that eventually succumbs to fear. A litany of all the ways you have failed. Contrivances to get outside your head: (1) imagine a person, (2) imagine a place, (3) imagine an action, (4) hold it there. What follows in my notebook is a hasty description of walking in the rain to see Jack Frost, Evan Kennedy, and David Brazil read in San Francisco—a scene poorly painted that quickly dissolves into gibberish and self-recriminations. Waiting. Waiting. This mess I've made. Wanting to be any other way. Wanting to be you. Wanting to be ecstatically destroyed and rebirthed with a new pair of eyes.

A person: the girl. A place: the steps of the library of the fanciest university in the world, Widener Library at Harvard. An action: She is born of shit and tears and she must fight her way alive. Crawls from the forest to where she doesn't belong, still covered in dirt, raw and unsocialized. Hannah: *You still have twigs in your hair when you walk into the library.*

She's asleep beneath the books. Her name appears in none of them, but many are bound in her skin. Anthropodermic bibliopegy becomes a way for the unwritten ones to slyly enter history. Their flesh—history's condition of possibility.

In this way the one from nowhere becomes the body of the world.

This feeling of nothingness or being made nothing is not the nothing some people glorify in their theories. It's not the hollow on its way to becoming pure receptacle. It's not the wild abundance Fred Moten speaks of when he says, "We come from nothing, which is something misunderstood." That was the youthful "nothing" of a queer-punk youth spent toiling deliriously in the penumbra of society, making zines unseen while the world got on with its important business and didn't bother me. The nothing I'm talking about is not loose and free but something more shameful. The embarrassment of an anhedonic depression that leaves you insensate, or an existence that finds equivalence in a list of synonyms for the phrase "out of focus": blurred, indistinct, blurry, fuzzy, hazy, misty, cloudy, lacking definition, nebulous.

How to be in the world? I attach to the one who cannot love me and make her the addressee of all my thoughts. Through her I know the scarlet nail polish my mother gave me—there is someone for whom I am permitted to *see*, and I live by the belief that I can only exist by rising up to become as forceful as the one I love. To enter history through this love for someone better, as Alice entered through Gertrude. In the dream Lauren Berlant drives up to my seedy Albuquerque apartment in a modest compact vehicle. We cruise around a vacant parking lot at night while they tell me about all the books they want to write before they die. I write to my friend Coda, "I don't think I said much. Probably stammered like a stupidhead or maybe was just sunk in that wordless feeling you get when someone voluble says something insightful and—after a long, gorgeous soliloquy—pauses to invite comment ... but all you can muster is 'I like it' or 'That sounds very good.'"

Before I have a chance to get into the rhythm of conversation (because I'm never very fluent in the beginning), Lauren drops me off and I must enter my apartment through a series of doors that won't click shut. A crazed woman tries to attack me and I can't shut her out. After Lauren drives away I no longer have a feeling for existence because my feeling for existence was in the moment of being seen seeing the one who is better. Like when Avital Ronell noticed I noticed her when I asked a question at a Valerie Solanas panel about madwomen who prop up male fantasies. Or maybe she just noticed I noticed that so many feminists hate women, that I am an initiate of a secret most dare not utter.

In the dream of being left wanting more, I overwrite loss sensations with a new experimental benzo that—instead of inducing amnesia—helps improve dream recall.

There's the pill. Then, the waiting not to feel. But wanting to feel—just not feel *bad*. Just not, uh, limerent and carried along by a revolving "one" who has a stronger feeling for existence.

But attachment can only be sustained for so long in the absence of a response. Because I cannot love forever—I am returned to myself. In my indistinctness I drift in and out of daydreams of becoming the kind of person whose intensity of vision gives flesh to words. Somewhere there is a future me who closes her eyes and, through sheer muscular concentration, manifests the body of poetry.

When I met Dana Ward, I felt sad about being in the world as I am. There was something about his style of being—his manner of appreciating the everyday in ways I never could because everything exhausts me. My poetry is merely the remainder of this perennial fatigue—traces of a flight from the self or the vibrating document the wolf-girl leaves behind when her forest has been leveled and she cannot find language for the landscapes that have left her. Which is to say: the disordered stammer of the psychically deracinated.

So you hover. Nobody likes pure abstraction but you're neither here nor there. Just beside yourself. No desire save for the primal pangs of hunger and this wanting toward sleep, somewhere between the wolf-girl of Bhanu's *Humanimal* and a lonely astronaut or maybe a wolf abandoned to outer space. A nothingness that is without redemption, that is not even freed by its antiteleological insistence, its tendency toward no goal no future no reason. Just the extension of flesh. Flesh narrowly alive enough to want to make a body for poetry so as to believe. (*Zero's neighbor*, Hélène Cixous writes of Samuel Beckett.)

I write Lauren: *I want to be persuaded.* In this desire to be persuaded—not yet fully dead.

Maybe the texture of *this* negative (the melancholic one?) cannot be spoken *of* but only spoken *in* a voice whose timbre bespeaks an exilic existence.

The voice has a certain quality.

She sounds like she's talking to herself.

Half-asleep. Half-human. Half-sick. Half-shimmering in her illness.

Half-happy to have written something (thanks for pestering me), even if it's mostly nothing.

[THANK YOU HANNAH BLACK FOR LETTING ME USE YOUR ROOM TO WRITE THIS!]

(2014)

Entropy Magazine Interview

This piece was originally part of Entropy's You Make Me Feel interview series curated by Gina Abelkop.

Tell me about one particular song/film/book/poem/piece of art (made by a peer in the last five years–ish) that has recently undone/inspired you. What about it was so striking to you? What in your life made you so open and receptive to this particular piece of art at that time?

I am ashamed to say—Lars von Trier's *Nymphomaniac*. I was in New York when I saw it. A man I have known (from a distance) for ten years, M., invited me, and we got noodles and bubble tea before going to the film. He picked the dish for me, which was a relief since I was too emotionally agitated to make any decisions. I went out knowing that at some point during the night I had to come up with a title for an essay I had just written for the *Claudius App*. It was a response to Bhanu Kapil's chapbook *Treinte Ban*, so I was thinking of girls on the floor of the world. Right before the film I sat on some park steps with M. discussing codependent relationships. Five or ten minutes before the film was scheduled to start, I tried to frantically come up with a title for the essay. It was the night of the blood moon. While I was wracking my brain for a title, a friend invited me to meet up at a bar called Lone Wolf. And then it clicked (with a little help from M.): the essay was to be called LONELY WOLVES ON THE FLOOR OF THE WORLD. Much better than the tentative title the editors had assigned the piece, which was something about a sloppy transference. "Imperfect Transference," I believe was their suggestion.

To my surprise, *Nymphomaniac* opened with a scene of a woman on the floor of the world. Joe, the film's heroine, was on the ground in an alley covered in piss and blood, but we don't know how or why she became a lonely woman on the floor of the world until later in the film. We find out quickly that she was an odd girl. A pervert. A little observer, as most lonely girls tend to be. Her sexual perversion was inaugurated by a mystical experience, which increased her sensory awareness to the point of existentially singularizing her. So she walks. She notices things while she walks. Ash trees, her father's favorite. A torn photograph of an old lover.

I don't spend much time in movie theaters and maybe that's why my sensorium lit up. The dark space is primal or primeval, a place that gives birth to primeval desires, a cave where projected unrealities captivate the viewer's mind. Watching films in the theater often has the effect of making people forget their bodies, but sexy films make you feel more in your body. Sometimes the exposure is too much. I don't want to think of all the boners in the theater during the film that night but I cannot deny the stirring of desire in myself, not necessarily at the sex. But where would I put my desire? I was looking for an object but this was desire without object. Did everyone in the theater feel a little bit self-conscious? To be publicly aroused. Actually I don't find images of heterosexual penetrative sex erotic at all. Apparently only 1 percent of women my age have not had this kind of sex, which makes me a statistical anomaly. But petting, on the other hand, between any genders ... maybe I can imagine whatever I want. There's just something about two bodies making contact. Maybe I'm just lonely ...

What was it that made me receptive? I don't want to credit Lars von Trier! It could have been the blood moon. It was also the night before I had to make a decision that would determine the course of my life. What a fucking headspace, right before having to make a big decision. It's its own kind of madness. The dizziness can create an opening. Time accelerates. Life moves in leaps. Everything was moving very fast beneath my feet and the film caught me in that moment. The smallest cinematic details were so vivid to me. When Joe was walking in the woods with her father in winter looking at the ash tree, I remembered a winter walk I had gone on with my ex-girlfriend in the woods on her mother's berry farm. Some naughty beavers had totally rearranged the landscape and the trunks of the trees near the lake were hourglass shaped in the places where the beavers had gone to work with their teeth. In the woods there was an ancient turtle made of stone. Not too long ago I took off a turtle necklace another ex-girlfriend gave me as a gift. She stole it from an aquarium. It was the first time I took the necklace off in five years. (This is another example of: a leap.)

Joe's walks reminded me of the walks I would go on when I lived outside of Glasgow, Scotland. Whenever I'd walk beneath the viaduct, I always felt, as I emerged from the tall concrete arches, that I was being reborn. The film made me think about lonely women and their walks, everything they notice. There was a man who ate rugelach with a fork. My ex-girlfriend was particular about how people ate her rugelach. I realized that the more particular a film or a text is, the more generalizable it becomes! My ex's favorite wasn't the ash tree—it was the birch. But my mind wants to constellate these details anyway.

In one scene, Joe is a child drugged on a stretcher waiting for surgery and then there is a chilling image of outer space. I found it horrifying—this image of the cosmos. Imagining child consciousness and the panic of abandonment in such a vast, empty space. I remember what I told someone a year ago when I tried to describe my loneliness and depression. "It feels like being an astronaut abandoned in outer space—untethered." I felt Joe's isolation. An isolation that maybe could be called "feminine," but hers was less self-pitying than mine because she was able to externalize aggression rather than turning it against herself. Lately I feel that female aggression is a necessary antidote to the disease of guilt—a highly feminized form of guilt that prevents women from freely experiencing pleasure or getting what they want.

In the film, Joe's sexual masochism is eventually replaced by a compensatory sadism. But she must pass through this phase of masochism first. The sadism doesn't exactly free her and maybe she's too sympathetic to torture others without experiencing guilt. Or at least she can't torture the pedophile. Their fates are too close. Like every woman seeking pleasure, her psychosexual relationship to power is always shifting. She is either acting against another or acting against herself. She reacts against feeling weak. She weakens herself. Maybe at some point she decides that violence against another is the only thing that will save her.

It happened while she was running away. Something told her to walk up the mountain—her soul tree was calling her, and she could not resist its magnetic force. In Lars von Trier's Depression trilogy, women are always having erotic experiences in nature, communing, on a soul level, with trees or the moon or forest creatures. Oh how I loved this moment of her finding the tree! But I was not in the theater. No, the guy I had gone with to see Vol. 1 forgot to invite me to see Vol. 2, so I had to download it and watch it on my tiny-ass computer.

The tree was bent.

After finding her soul tree—well, I won't give anything away.

I feel very sad writing this because I thought I wrote a lot more here about the discovery of the tree. Did it disappear or did I merely imagine writing it? And now all I seem to be able to say is, I love the deformed tree. But I must have written it? I remember quoting Fred Moten. I remember writing that love of the bent tree is love of the swerve. Fred: "I love mispronunciation. Anyone who can't help but deviate can pretty much tell me anything." The tree is for all the souls that can't help but deviate and must grow sideways.

I remember going to the library with notebooks full of scattered fragments about the discovery of the tree, the way it seemed to be reaching for her. The meaning of being "bent"—of failing to grow upright. Wayward trunks, wayward daughters. Did I type it up on another computer? Was I distracted because I'd gotten into an argument with M. on G-Chat about sadomasochism and gender in *Nymphomaniac*? He said I was wrong to view it through a gender lens. I wanted to ask why Lars von Trier had chosen women to represent his suffering in all three of the films in his Depression trilogy.

Tell me about three of your favorite contemporary artists (writers/film-makers/musicians/theorists, etc.): What makes each one of your favorites?

How did you discover their work? Did you discover additional artists/art via these people?

The zines of Vicky Lim (for their hilarious treatment of the neurotic mother-daughter dyad).

Emmanuelle Guattari's *I, Little Asylum* (for its insight into the radical French intelligentsia from the perspective of a child).

Valerie Mejer's *Rain of the Future* (for creating a language for emotion without speaking the emotion directly).

Hélène Cixous's *Three Steps on the Ladder of Writing* (for helping me [un]understand where I go at night: the School of Dreams).

Everything by Fred Moten. I once joked on Twitter that looking up everyone Fred references in *B Jenkins* has been my real education. I learned about so many things through him. Mostly I discover things through people.

Tell me your favorite things about the loose community of artists that you're a part of, if you're a part of one in some way, shape or form. What is most exciting about the work you see coming out of this community? Do you make work in response to any of it? What do you wish to see coming out of this community that you feel is lacking or underrepresented?

I'm not really sure what loose community of artists I'm part of. The poetry community? The feminist blogger community? The queer literary community? The Semiotext(e) community? I started out writing zines, criticism, political theory, and experimental fiction, but then was christened a poet by other poets. They have kind of become my community, though I can only tolerate being physically immersed in this world for short periods of time (it can sometimes be overwhelmingly white and hetero). Ultimately, I don't feel like I fit squarely in any single world. When I'm at the Kundiman Retreat, I am an Asian American poet. When I'm at Digital Desperados, I am a woman-of-color filmmaker. When I am with the postpolitical insurrectionist boys, I am of the anarchist milieu. As a PhD student I will be part of the Black studies and prison studies community. When I'm at the Alice Notley reading, I am a poet. When I am with my NY, Bay Area, and Baltimore political crews, I am a militant feminist. When I'm at Idapalooza, I am a radical queer. On Twitter I am a relentless chronicler of dreams. I float in and out of all these worlds. Each speaks to a different part of me. But it's not easy to code switch this much. Can I be a punk and a Harvard grad student at the same time? On the phone I tell Joohyun Kim, "I feel very fractured."

What do you find to be the greatest challenge in discovering new art/artists in the current cultural landscape?

I am allergic to the internet, which makes it very hard for me to be a part of the literary milieu, or the world at large. I feel too porous to engage with the internet too much—it makes me totally nuts. My head gets filled up with nonsense and then there's no room to notice the sky or wonder if time-lapse footage of geraniums blooming might look something like exploding fireworks. Of course, the answer is probably on the internet, but it's by not using the internet that the thought can exist at all. In other words, I try to maintain space inside me that is empty or isn't wholly consumed by the stimulus-reaction feedback loop of digital culture. Silence is my church, the library, a sacred refuge from the onslaught of stimuli that makes me feel like a shuttlecock getting tossed around in a techno-capitalist game of badminton. No, I want to *extend* the emotion. To sit with things. I'm not saying that everyone who uses the internet lives on the surface of things. It is precisely because I have a hard time focusing that I need such extreme conditions to go to the deep place, to feel real and alive and in touch with the mystery of everything swirling around me.

Some people wake up and immediately check the internet or look at their phones instead of trying to remember their dreams. This, to me, seems a great loss. There is so much wisdom in dreams. If we must use the internet as soon as we wake up, the least we could do is use it to remember our dreams (by tweeting them when we wake up).

With that said, everything circulates on the internet these days. The people I love put things on the internet. My friend Ryan knows about all the cool things because he is good at the internet (good at the internet and still a fantastic reader). I should probably learn how to deal with modern life instead of avoiding it. But at the same time, I must do what I need to do to protect my sacred space.

But. But. I want to know what my friends are doing! I want to read what they are writing, to know what is going on in their lives. Because I am so incompetent at modern life, I have often unfairly relied on them giving me things they have made as gifts when we see each other in person. Most of the things I discover seem to discover me. "It fell into my lap." Sometimes I browse certain sections at the library. If people want to mail me their work, they can send it to me.

How do you build and/or define your community?

Overall I feel a kinship with outcasts, lost souls, wayward daughters, feral poets, emotional misfits. Anyone who might have been sent to the school counselor as a child for Oppositional Defiant Disorder. Anyone bent, uncontrollable, excessively desirous of life. Fringe dwellers. Dream seekers. Reality breakers. The details of our interests hardly matter. What I'm talking about is a comradeship formed in nonconformity—belonging in the shared experience of displacement, of not belonging. A community of lone wolves and aliens (odd girls).

On Twitter, Hannah Black recently asked me, "When is the feminist commune?" Her tweet was apropos of a tweet I made about how conversations with her and my friends Joohyun and Caitlin filled me with longing for the feminist commune. When I first read her tweet, I read WHEN as WHAT: "*What* is the feminist commune?" I would like to take up *that* question—what I mistakenly read—here.

At the feminist commune we feast and talk all night. Fast. Irreverent. Real. Smart. We do nail-art divination and theorize and watch music videos on YouTube and critique Lana Del Rey. The conversation moves with ease from the everyday to the "global." Politics is always imagined according to a range of scales: cellular, psychological, social, economic, earthly, cosmic—even the "invisible" must be thought (what is imperceptible or not yet thought). Everything that is said comes from a place. Here are femmes who are intellectually sincere: genuinely curious and concerned with figuring shit out and not trying to prove anything. Not trying to master knowledge for the sake of mastery.

At the feminist commune there are a lot of beds and rooms for people to work in. There are books everywhere, gardens outside, herbs on the windowsills, fruit trees in the yard. The back wall is all glass so as to let sun in. There is a river behind the main house, and we are always swimming in it. If you walk north on the path that runs alongside the river there is a waterfall, on top of which sits a bent tree. There are caves nearby where some of the residents go to light candles and meditate.

Everyone is very different! The nonbinary nerd of the commune is never without a book, and they have a very rich and imaginative inner life. One woman is always making herbal tinctures or recommending remedies for the residents' respective ailments. Another is always gardening. Another is busy on her computer counterhacking the NSA, doorway lined with powerful magnets in preparation for that fateful day when the FBI kicks in her door and seizes her hardware. Though sleep schedules sometimes diverge, the residents converge around the sharing of food. Conflicts get intense. Some leave. Some return. Some try to form alliances based on the exclusion of so-and-so—not everything can be worked through. Some residents have been to college, and this affects how they communicate. Some have not been to college. Some have been with cis men and still have ties to them. Others don't. Some can't stand not being the best all the time though they feel bad about it. Others feel too timid to talk and get quiet around the residents who are voluble and loquacious. Their weird or witty side might come out when they are talking to someone one on one, or when a gregarious mood strikes in the form of a mysterious confidence.

We have been made by this fucked-up world. And so, are flawed. But we interact in good faith. It's hard to know why we do what we do but we are smart enough to admit when we are wrong.

There's a lot more that could be said about the feminist commune but I will leave it at that, half-mapped. There must be something left for the imagination …

(2014)

Desiring Defectively as a Form of Life

This originally appeared on my Tumblr blog.

"Anything that happens is probably fine."

It was the last thing I wrote in my journal, probably minutes ago, yet when I look down at the page I already feel as though I have drifted so far in my head from this point of view. How rapidly life shifts between feeling totally unlivable to deeply humorous. The people around me seem fine. Even when their lives are a mess, they can still make jokes about television shows and shopping the pain away by buying platform shoes. M. says, "I have to keep my hair short now because I'm getting old, and shaggy hair doesn't look good on aging men." The absence of any distress in his remark surprises me. "How do you talk about aging so casually, with such cool detachment and acceptance of the fact of aging?" His rotting teeth don't even seem to faze him. But I can't seem to think the phrase *we age* or look at the scars on my body without feeling deep existential dread about the inevitability of death. Becoming unlovable. A worthless woman.

I am surprised that it is possible for anyone to acclimate to living. To wake up without feeling intense psychic friction or mental anguish about having to live another day. To go on dates. To make dating profiles. To move the record player from the bedroom to the living room. To check their email. To have friends over for dinner. To answer phone calls. To get haircuts. On a hot summer New York day, I sat outside M.'s barbershop on the curb drinking a can of Arizona iced tea, wondering if I could one day be the kind of person who gets haircuts. Everyone seemed to want to tell me about their love and sex lives and I listened with the curiosity of an anthropologist. People get drunk, have sloppy sex, scream WHY DON'T YOU JUST GO GET HIS COCK in Washington Square Park. They throw knives. Hit each other. Cheat. Get jealous. Cruise. Have make-up sex. Break up marriages. Cry. Want more. Fuck their friends. Get suspended from hooks every weekend. Give lap dances to the men of Wall Street. Get tied up. Learn how to navigate being just friends. Fall in love at the wrong time. Know whether they are a "top" or a "bottom." Feel exhausted by polyamory. Get out of bad relationships. Get into good relationships. Know what they want. Don't know what they want. Say they want one thing then do another. Feel gendered in different ways in different contexts. Think about relationality. Don't think about relationality. Don't tell their old lovers they have a new lover. Get obsessed. Keep getting back together. Dry spells. Transitions. Spraying the terrain. Accept that things change. Don't accept that things change. Protracted break ups. Not wanting to lose one's object. *"Come get your cat." "I don't want to get the cat because that would mean that things are really over."* Desire strikes, an unforeseeable bolt cleaves a life. It's not the instability or irrationality of human relationships that surprises me, but people's orientation to fluctuation. The ongoingness of life. The capacity to endure the devastation.

While sitting in the garden with M. he asks what Hannah asked when she was visiting. He asks, *What do you want?* To which I reply,

I don't know. He says, *Make a mess. If it's not going to completely destroy you in the end, it's fine. You're young. Experiment.*

When M.'s haircut is finished, we walk back to his apartment, talking about crushes, cybernetics, teeth, whatever. He stops abruptly to take a selfie of his new haircut, but unable to get the lighting and angle right he hands me his phone to take the picture for him. I joke, "The selfie is the user's attempt to assert its subjectivity against the collapse of all Western metaphysical systems." He smiles because in some small way he sees that I see him and being seen seeing also constitutes me too. Maybe in the same way someone feels they have shape only when they are caring for another. Maybe it's the shape I'm given when I stop into a corner store to buy M. Cherry Garcia–flavored Ben & Jerry's ice cream when we are all walking home from the bar drunk, because I know what he wants in that moment. Small gestures.

The day before I left for New York, Dana and I talked about what it means to have shape only in relation to another. He started texting me while I was sitting on the perron of Widener Library at sunset rereading *My Walk with Bob*, feeling devastated about Bruce's loss of Jonathan, his sense that he was being replaced, that it was the most natural thing that a relationship should collapse and with it, the domestic language that was formed during the encounter. "How am I going to get along now, who's going to take care of me?" Dana: "… and with no one to care for—how will I be real to myself?" I told Dana that I have not yet figured out how to orient myself to loss in that I stubbornly insist on living with absences, presentizing them because I can't let anything go—*but that's not entirely true*, I think, as M. and I converse with the tenderness and familiarity of close siblings. I feel silly about my old sadomasochistic fantasies involving M., though perhaps to indulge the irrational fixation further would have been fine too. "You're fine," M. says to my neurotic self-analysis. "Am I?" I ask. "Yes." "But why do I feel so ashamed?" "Maybe you can play with that shame. Maybe the shame can be erotic."

Is that the Chris Kraus approach? To not necessarily strive for shamelessness but affirm one's abjectness, or at least reconcile one-self to the possibility that what might register as a personal defect in the way that one relates to or loves others may actually be a site of potential? Anyway, M. won't indulge my usual line of thinking. You can't convince a self-described pervert that any way of desiring is defective.

(2014)

Life Shit

This originally appeared on my Tumblr blog.

The way the song finds its way to you, your friend Ben singing Paul Celan ecstatically: "A rumbling: truth / itself has appeared / among humankind / in the very thick of their / flurrying metaphors." You're biking down Oxford Street with your new sunflower helmet. Next up is Ros Sereysothea and you think that you would like to live inside the sensation of biking in the sun to Ros Sereysothea forever. Inside the sun you feel as though it is possible that you are approaching a Cambodian beach, but this is Cambridge, MA—there is almost no place on earth more distant from Cambodia than Cambridge, MA (though they do share a *Camb-*). It's a quality of sun that warps time and geographically dislodges you—you are nowhere, you are everywhere. You are inside the love you lost as you observe some leaves it is a love without object or ego, just pure perception, enlivened senses and waking up to life this latent life always with you but buried beneath anxieties and wound-reactions and everything you want to be but are not, you're not enough. In the sun such thoughts fly away. A truth rumbles in the song. But this truth is the absence of metaphor, it emerges when human systems of thought peel away and language suicides to lay bare the world in its fecundity and raw materiality.

You? You is me and me is you. For a second I felt proud. I have to switch to the "I" to take ownership of the proudness I felt in that moment. For there was a future I could sense though I could not imagine it. I thought about my life trajectory to prove to myself that despite all those moments I believed there was no future, I did indeed eventually arrive at some new place I could not imagine in moments of despair.

Time is running out. Went to a 7:00 a.m. spin class and then a meditation class because I'm trying to be a human. I am sitting at a computer in the Lamont Library café, brain somersaulting because today is a full day from 6:30 a.m. until 8 p.m. A new life tempo. After living so long in the doldrums I feel myself entering the temporality of being a grad student.

There was something I came here to say and I feel I have to say it now or I will never say it, because this is my last hour before school starts, how strange. Life. I've barely had a second to stop and look at the ground and say, *I'm here*. How did I get here? After drifting around broke and aimless for four years post New College, between punk houses and shitty relationships, Scotland and the desert, misplaced obsessions and epistolary insanity, I am now about to start my first day as a Harvard PhD student. In the deepest depression of my life, I applied to PhD programs. This was soon after dropping out of an MFA program. I was living in Albuquerque for two months in a shabby apartment supplied by the editors of Semiotext(e). They thought if I had a little geographic stability for a couple of months I could write, but instead I applied to grad school because I needed a fast way to get my life on track … some intellectual stimulation, some money, a base. I wasn't expecting to get into any schools but I was proud to have at least done it, as an exercise. It was amazing I was able to do anything at all given the state I was in psychologically.

But then in February the acceptance letters started coming. First was Harvard, and then five minutes later NYU. This was the week of my older brother's hearing, the hearing we had been anticipating for almost nine years. I hardly had time to process the good news because of all the familial trauma. Court rooms. Judges. Then the morning after the hearing I found myself on a plane to San Francisco to speak on a panel with Lauren Berlant, Kathi Weeks, and others. I didn't sleep. Thank God the flight was delayed. The next few months were spent drifting around the Bay, Chicago, New York, and Cambridge—visiting schools, agonizing over which program to select. For most of the time I was leaning toward CUNY geography's program and studying with Ruth Wilson Gilmore and the other CUNY Marxist geographers, but New York was making me feel overwhelmed and I couldn't imagine living there as a grad student. I went with Harvard to do African and African American studies and history, but cried for weeks over the decision, particularly passing up the opportunity to work with Ruthie.

Now here I am. The immediate class ascension has been jarring—not that I'm making *that* much money, but I guess the Harvard brand is worth a lot in social capital. Now when people ask me what I do I don't have to shrug and say, "You know ... living the bullshit bohemian life." Have I been bought out? I hope not. No institution will ever be able to steal my soul because I have been against institutions since I was in middle school. But they can drive me mad. How can I protect myself? I'm trying to figure that out.

Sorry this is shitty; I'm trying to write fast. I just wanted to put my values down so I can come back later and analyze the discrepancies between where I was before starting a PhD and wherever I am in the future. But now I'm blanking at this very simple assignment. Do I really have to say it? I don't want to become an academic. I don't want a normative life. I don't want heterosexual monogamy. I want poetry to remain part of my life. I want my research to be relevant and committed. I want to continue to roll with the queers and militant feminists and insurrectionists and poets—or maybe less the poets at least the apolitical white kind. I wanna take time to be present with plants and sun and sky and water and to maintain the same level of intimacy with and love for my friends. I don't ever want to be an elitist. I don't want to make anyone feel stupid or not good enough. I want to remain epistemologically porous. I want to continue to pay attention to my dreams. I want to give life and make people feel strong but also to know when to not use up my energy on people who can't receive what I give. I don't want anxiety to replace joy as the primary affective space I occupy. I don't want to default to a secure/comfortable life because it's easier. I don't want to be neutralized, either actively by Harvard or indirectly by my new material situation (which could shift my priorities).

Out of time. There is more to say. Later gators.

(2014)

What Is This Orgy of Song

This originally appeared on my Tumblr blog.

What is this conspiracy of voice, the friend's voice who sings, this time, William Blake's "Laughing Song": "When the painted birds laugh in the shade, / Where our table with cherries and nuts is spread: / Come live, and be merry, and join with me, / To sing the sweet chorus of 'Ha Ha He!'" What is this orgy of song in the canopy above my head? What is the lightness of walking alone outside, or what I find when I force myself to stop reading and walk across the bridge over the Charles River at sunset? The breeze becomes an analgesic, the cop inside my head is gagged, and the light on the water mimics a fourth of July sparkler that sparkles forever as a loop of light growing in the mind of the universe—a pulsating mass of iridescent cerebral matter which any of you can plug into at any time just by accepting that perdition is not where you are condemned to dwell, that at any moment you can will the cosmic umbilical cords to drop from the light-mind for you to plug into your foreheads.

So it was all just a joke my head played on me? Hell. Hell was just a joke I could unbelieve? In the poem, what was it I said? *You do / you do undo.* My being, invaginated by the levity of stealing all the food I can while sauntering through the party in my machine-gun leggings. What is the nature of your being? Joohyun describes me as a "comedian," but why is it that some know me as a dour, joyless depressive? White people? Well, I guess not *all* of them. Memory of a conversation I had in Clair's car about substance, Spinoza, friendship, and bad mixtures. What mixes well with me is sun, but it's difficult to reconcile this with being a creature of the night. On the nighttime walk to the library, I close my eyes and am impaled by the light. The streetlights are false moons. Behind the tree, the real moon. Through a window in the Science Center I see a man looking into a microscope. Above him, a room in which the sign LASERS AT USE is plastered. The bio- and cyberneticians are at work. I feel them everywhere in Cambridge, engineering our collective death. Around the corner a teenage boy folds his apron in the Bon Me food truck. His shift has just finished and soon he'll be home or in the bed of a lover.

I remember … feeling inside my head but then getting hit by the sun from behind a tree. I look up, into the song. The wind breathes yellow rain, it falls from branches as bits of yellow confetti cut out of construction paper, shards of yellow littering the campus; the leaves stick to the bottom of the shoes of students and are dragged into the library. *The trees cry light so that we may be happy.* Are you happy? The German mathematician walks by; he seems not to recognize me. I want to find L. but I haven't got my phone on me. The yellow leaves transport me to the backseat of Nat's car, sitting next to Dana, pointing out the leaves to him, the way they catch the light on their way down.

To be on the road—it felt like an adolescent summer! "My last week of freedom." But for the punks, the summer never ends. There's no back-to-school to punctuate leisure time, for time does not revolve around the beginning and end of a semester, and so on the same day I start school I receive a postcard from Steve of a picture of him and Julian hopping trains across the BC Rockies. But these short train-hopping and sailing excursions are just a precursor to Steve's main adventure: sailing to Hawaii, where I'm sure Moxie will meet him on an app-coding trip. I want to write *Steve, TAKE ME WITH YOU*, but there is no return address—he's on the move.

When Dana asked me what I wanted to be when I grew up, I said, *A traveler.*

In the postcard photo both Steve and Julian are wearing black jackets. Steve is doing a peace sign and Julian is flicking off the camera. Are they caricaturing their respective temperaments? I remember the summer I met them both. I remember somehow finding my way to Julian's house—via Moxie, as I didn't know him then. As we sat in his living room talking, he told me stories about his travels across Central America and then it clicked—he was the author of the only zine I brought with me that summer, a zine I randomly plucked from the New College zine library, *One Way Ticket*. "31 and 32 years old and still oogles," Steve jokes in his letter. Julian is in a PhD program now, studying continental philosophy, still falling in love like it's the first time.

Maybe it's okay to take a break from concepts, theories, ideas, even literature. To try to find my way back to the nonteleological event of writing. A writing that is comfortable enough with itself to be simple, to just feel out the texture of a walk, or being with others. Small observations. So when people ask me what I'm working on

I can say, "Nothing." I have no grand statements for you. I am a life, like you, and this is about that. As I observed the uneven brick sidewalk of Oxford Street, I remembered the sensation of what was once the most distinct of all feelings for me: gratitude.

It seemed to radiate from everything. I loved strangers. I loved to watch the way they were present with each other. The more confused they appeared to me, the more I loved them. I loved the backs of their heads while walking down crowded streets. I loved Mátyás for sitting with me in the Kunming cafés, letting me in against his better judgment. I loved the dog shit-paved streets of Govan (Glasgow), the majesty of Buchanan Street and the thoroughfares of foreign towns, walking down them in the warped consciousness of toothaches. "Busby Station"—when Joohyun said it, our train rides came back to me. The timbre of a certain accent heard over an intercom, seared into our minds. I even loved when Nemo the Dalmatian (RIP) stole the fruitcake in Nosh and Cloudberry's living room. I loved the steam rising from the old houses on a rare sunny day in Glasgow. Today the sun was bright but it rained, for only an hour, and this hour of rain was synchronized exactly with my counseling session. From the fourth floor of the Harvard University Health Services building, I watched a storm rage and violently whip the leaves of a tree while the psychologist asked me questions about my depression. "I even loved everything bad, for it was part of the whole of life." But this mentality also manifests as a self-destructive inability to stay mad at anyone. "Because she was real to me, I could not hate her."

Was the rain sent to cleanse me?

Genuflect because there is gratitude—an all-pervasive feeling of contrition. Look at how my hatred softens. It is supple like silken tofu.

My skin betrays me by failing as a barrier.

But what does this ineptitude of skin allow me?

I loved coasting down the bridge into Lido Key.

I loved the weeping willows of Mesilla. I loved my spice shelf in the house I lived in with P. I loved the smell of the cool air coming through the cracks of my Good View porch room, walking down the snowy Hampden street on my birthday.

I have no grand statements for you. I have a bowl of pennies ... some sentences and half sentences. Scraps of patterned origami paper. I have ... the parti-colored lights on the bridge into Poughkeepsie. Whispers in the backseat of a car. Daydreams of lives epically lived, but epic in feeling, not wealth or importance. I have ... a pigeon crashing into a glass walkway, falling to the ground, and dying. Twitching on the ground. The death throes. The way it stared at me right before dying. L., my dad, and I were all deeply disturbed. As we pried ourselves from the distressing scene, my father told us the story of the man who killed the last passenger pigeon, how these pigeons were once so abundant they blotted out the sky. We were looking for a place to eat ...

There is history in every microtransaction, in glances exchanged between strangers, and even in the tear I left on the Woodberry table, the way the reflection of the light in the tear made it look like an eyeball with a laser pupil. The night will be good to you if you can resist the urge to blot out feeling with molecules that will make life bearable but less round. There is a night waiting for you, where you kill the fear that has been holding you hostage.

Loving as an owl, watching, at night, from a tree. Arboreal creature. We are made of feather, bliss, borrowed light. Write yourself into a state, again. Love and then sleep, some backtracking but all is not lost. "You are free"—but for how long? Life becomes this mythology of the everyday, made by freaks on their lonely, unscripted journeys.

(2014)

Mask Magazine Interview

Hanna Hurr: When did you decide you wanted to be a writer?

In middle school, I decided that I wanted to be a music journalist. I taught myself HTML so I could make band fan sites, and my dad would take me to shows. In high school, I was the editor for the entertainment section of my school newspaper. I would get free concert tickets, free CDs, and I would interview bands and write music reviews.

I wrote to the music editor of the weekly newspaper in Tampa, Florida. I remember writing him, saying, "I want to be a music journalist when I grow up! What do I have to do?" I don't even know how I figured out the logistics of it. I would contact the bands' PR agencies, send them clippings, and would tell them the circulation of the publications I was writing for. I would write for local magazines and online music magazines too.

Did you get money for it at the time?

Probably not? I did make money doing a few freelance gigs for a local magazine, but I was internally driven. It's confounding to me now—What the hell was I doing? I remember watching *Almost Famous* with my dad and him saying, "Oh that's you!" 'Cause I was chilling with all these bands.

It seems there's a period between thirteen and nineteen when certain people are incredibly prolific for their age, and sometimes their careers take off and they become somebody like Tavi Gevinson. I feel like many of us struggle to maintain that level of productivity in our twenties.

Yes, I was way more prolific as a teen than I am now. Something happens once you start writing for a defined audience or when you're closer to spheres of legitimacy—you psych yourself out and internalize expectations. When you're young it's very playful, and it's enough to just be curious and motivated.

Were you close with your peers in Florida?

I was kind of on my own tip. I remember wearing Chuck Taylors in middle school when no one else had those shoes. People would call me a Satan worshipper, but I was like, "I'm emo! I'm not a Satan worshipper." I was also vegan.

When I went to high school, all the older indie kids would ask me, "Where are you from? Who are you? How do you have such good taste in music?" Because I had all these band patches on my backpack. They thought I was a freak from another planet.

And then I became friends with people who were mostly older than me. My circle of friends primarily consisted of people outside of my school. I befriended a lot of local bands. The guy I dated in high school was the singer of an experimental grindcore band called Shed for You.

When did you start becoming more interested in literature?

My interest in literature developed alongside my interest in politics. I read a lot of zines, some of which were very literary. The bands that I liked were also literary. So I guess that sparked my interest in literature.

I got really into bands like Milemarker. One of the singers of Milemarker, Al Burian, made a zine called *Burn Collector*. It's a classic zine that started in the mid-'90s. Al Burian's *Burn Collector* was the fucking shit. His zines were collected into books and I read them over and over and over again. It started to frame the way I thought about the world. I would sometimes think to myself, "What would Al think about this situation?" He had a very funny way of perceiving people and events. Little things were very profound for him, and funny, and tragic. I liked conjuring him when I was moving around in the world.

Burn Collector opened up the world of zines for me and then the world of zines opened up the world of politics. So then I got into feminism and anarchism.

Do you remember any books that were especially significant at that time?

In terms of feminism, *Feminism is for Everybody* by bell hooks was one of the first feminist texts that I read, and it was formative for me. And then I got really into Samuel Beckett, the playwright and novelist. In high school I worked at this grocery store Kash 'n Karry, and I would recite lines from *Waiting for Godot* to myself while working at the checkout.

How did you get into radical politics, beyond private reading?

A lot of the friends I have now I met through the anarchist LiveJournal community. When I was fourteen–fifteen years old I became internet friends with Moxie Marlinspike. He would mail me zines, and his CD *A Hitchhiker's Guide to the United States*, which consists of audio interviews with people he met while hitchhiking. I loved reading his sailing stories, his hitchhiking stories, and his writings about postscarcity anarchism.

Through the LiveJournal community I found out about things that were going on in the area. I got involved with the St. Petersburg Food Not Bombs. This is the standard trajectory, right? You get interested in CrimethInc., and then you find the local Food Not Bombs, or you start a Food Not Bombs. When I was eighteen, I started the Sarasota Food Not Bombs, in Sarasota, Florida. And I would organize protests, but I would always have to goad my friends into going to them. At sixteen, I tried to start a feminist group at my school, but it was basically my friends humoring me. I would print out articles for us to discuss, screen films, and so on.

So your role within your group of friends was to take these influences from elsewhere, things you read on the internet or by people in other cities, and bring them home.

I guess so. I was importing ideas, culture, political models, and veganism into my suburban friend group. I radicalized some of my friends and some of them became vegetarians and vegans.

When I was sixteen, I went on a road trip with one of my friends who's a little bit older—she had a car, and I had gumption. I told her, "Let's go stay with these anarchists!" We'd just show up, we didn't plan anything. At this time, that was the culture; you'd just find the infoshop or the local Food Not Bombs, you'd ask around and find a place to stay. It was very porous and open. I don't know if it works like that anymore; maybe the internet has changed the way people find each other.

We'd drive to Asheville, NC, and meet anarchists there. One time when we were there, I remember reading this zine, *Hot Lead Is Medicine*. Did you ever read it? Oh my gosh. It's just a perzine, but my memory of it is still very vivid. In it the author "Texas" uses his personal experiences with addiction to analyze the violence of capitalism. The zine advocates revolutionary violence, discusses beating up cops—it is super extreme. I remember wanting to write the author and argue with him about the politics he was promoting in this zine. He was very chic and all violence and sex appeal, while I was nerdy and cerebral. It represented the world of anarchy that I wanted to be a part of.

The anarchist world that zine represented was very seductive. I always resisted the cool-kid brand of anarchism, particularly its aesthetics. I feel like the aesthetic that certain graphic-designer anarchists popularized is kind of *cold*, a little bit American Apparel. It has this very commercial, inhuman feel to it. And I was really into the sloppy, cut-and-paste, warm-fuzzy aesthetic. The pre-graphic design, anarchist-punk aesthetic.

It's interesting that Rookie, Tumblr *culture, teenage-girl producers tend to be much more in line with the punk cut-and-paste aesthetic than former punks who could now be described as insurrectionary anarchists. Who they speak to is more of a suburban nobody.*

Subjects without attributes. I was always the opposite in that I've always been invested in the personal voice, speaking from a place, or imbuing my writing with emotional qualities, cultivating a sense of intimacy rather than distancing or being cool or coy. My sensibility was always pretty different. But I'm open to everything.

Did you go to college?

Surprisingly, yes. When I was in high school I kind of stopped caring about school, even though I did alright. I was always in advanced classes. But I would skip class a lot. I always went to public school so I didn't have a spectacular education or anything like that. I had a lot going on with my family when I was in high school. My brother went to prison when I was sixteen—he was seventeen when he got arrested. My brother was allegedly selling marijuana when a group of white kids attacked him. These guys were known to jump people. They would call and act like they wanted to buy some weed and then they would rob drug dealers. Whatever happened on that day, my brother got jumped by these kids; he ended up being charged with shooting and killing one of the guys.

The juvenile-sentencing laws in Florida are extremely harsh. He was sentenced to life without parole. In most countries in Europe, the maximum sentence you can get as a juvenile is eight years, and the cut-off age for being a juvenile is twenty-one or twenty-three. The sentencing laws in the United States are exceptionally harsh in general, but especially in Florida.

I often say graduating from high school is my greatest accomplishment, because of how totally chaotic that period of my life was. My dad was also laid off from his job soon after this happened, so everything was unstable and precarious at the time. I missed a lot of school around that time. The kids who jumped my brother were threatening my family. They broke one of our windows and came to the door with a gun and threatened my dad, so my parents said it was not safe for me to go to school or to be at home. I had to stay at friends' houses for a while. It was a very difficult time.

My brother's case became a local spectacle. There were all these sensational stories about it in the newspapers. Kids from the high school also came to the trial.

This must have had a huge impact on you, experiencing the corrupt legal system from the inside at such an early age.

Not only did I learn how racist the criminal legal system is, but also how theatrical and performative it is—it's just a charade. I guess they call it "Cowboy Justice." The prosecutor had all these antics; he was known for being corrupt. At many of his trials he gets jailhouse snitches to testify, which is something sleazy prosecutors do. He does this performance during the trial where he brings out the jailhouse snitches and, after they give their testimony, he proclaims, "Ladies and gentlemen, there is an honest man in the house of thieves! Why would this man lie?" The prosecutorial antics were unbelievable. He used all this racialized terminology to refer to my brother. Repeatedly, he would call my brother a gangster, a thug, and he would reference rap culture.

All of this relates to the politics of innocence, which I wrote about in my essay "Against Innocence." The way that the white kids were portrayed in the media was so different from how my brother was portrayed. The media emphasized that they liked baseball and video games, and generally humanized the white kids, even though they were known in the area for jumping people. One of the kids who jumped my brother killed multiple people and eventually killed himself. One of them is missing. In some ways, I'm like, "Well, if my brother did get out, it's possible that they would've tried to kill him."

It definitely shaped my thinking. I mean, I just have such a visceral reaction to prisons and courts and the criminal-justice system in general. The ways that these systems operate are so unsettling. You feel totally powerless when you're ensnared. Once you're caught in the bureaucracy it's difficult to disentangle yourself from it. The appeals process is totally maddening as well. My brother had an appeal in February—an appeal that had been in the works for nine years. It basically took nine years for him to even get a hearing after the incident happened.

Not surprisingly, the appeal for a retrial was denied. The evidentiary hearing was bleak because the judge worked with the man who prosecuted my brother. Everyone in these local courts has all worked with each other or is in cahoots with each other, so it's basically impossible to get an unbiased hearing or trial. Even if you do, the courts in these smaller counties in Florida are conservative and harsh when it comes to punishing people and locking them up.

But you still managed to go to college?

Senior year I decided that I did want to go to college. I wasn't doing very well in high school, so I had to turn everything around very quickly. I decided I wanted to go to New College of Florida, which is this small, liberal-arts school in Sarasota. That was my fantasy. I went to New College, which was a great place for me. I was very happy there, actually. It's very small, 750–800 students, so you know everyone there. It's basically a giant family. People are pretty radical. I felt like I belonged somewhere for the first time. I mean, I had friends in high school, but I had a lot more intellectual and political stimulation in college.

I had a girlfriend whom I lived with from freshman year of college to senior year of college. That was my social world, being holed up with my girlfriend P. and my other lesbian friends. I lived in a house with P. and my best friends, Cindy and Jaclyn, who were also dating each other. We had this little lesbian enclave near the bay. We even had chickens. It was probably the most domestic my life has ever been, which is funny because people are usually the opposite: when they're in college they're unmoored and free, but I was tied down and holed up.

I had a great undergraduate mentor: an old woman, Cris Hassold, who was a strict art historian and psychoanalytic feminist. She had no children, no husband or family or anything. Her students were like her children. She was hard to please, so you had to prove yourself to her before she would give you her attention. I had to go through the process of proving myself to her, and then she loved me and took me on as a student. She kind of turned against me at one point when I outgrew her analysis. Her knowledge of feminism stopped in the '80s, and I got more interested in race and postcolonial theory, which was outside of her field of knowledge. I wanted to do a more experimental thesis project. She didn't know if I could pull it off and threatened to fail me, but ultimately, she said it was the best thesis she'd ever advised.

What was the thesis on?

It was on race, gender, and the practice of writing. I was reading theory as literature—lyrical and poetic theory—and talking about feminist and antiracist discourses that resist a phallocentric, masculine discourse. I was really interested in the work of Trinh T. Minh-ha, who's a Vietnamese postcolonial feminist theorist, and also Audre Lorde, Gloria E. Anzaldúa, Hélène Cixous, Luce Irigaray, bell hooks. I was interested in writing that merged the theoretical and the personal.

LIES: A Journal of Materialist Feminism *published your essay "Against Innocence," which later got picked up by Semiotext(e) as part of their Whitney Biennial pamphlet series. What was the process by which you ended up writing it?*

I wrote "Against Innocence" while living in Baltimore, where I moved after I finished my BA. I was part of a really nurturing and stimulating feminist and antiracist political community that I found through the Baltimore Feminist Reading Group. I became friends with a lot of super badass feminist intellectuals there.

The people in the Feminist Reading Group became my best friends. Some of them had gone to the Feminist Summer Camp that happened a few years prior, where a lot of the feminists involved with the LIES journal and the New York Feminist Reading Group all met each other. The Feminist Summer Camp seems to have generated a lot of the feminist projects that were happening at the time.

I knew some of the people who were involved with the LIES journal, and they asked me to write an essay. Initially, I wrote a spatial-feminist critique of the books *Rape New York* and *The Femicide Machine*. The editors of LIES liked the book reviews but asked me to write an essay instead.

I had already been thinking about a lot of the things that I wrote about in "Against Innocence." At this point, they were just nebulous ideas that were floating around in my head. Occupy was popping off at the time, Troy Davis had just been executed; there was a lot of energy, but it was also a very depressing, politically bleak time. The year 2012. It was simultaneously the most hopeful and the bleakest of times.

I wrote the essay from a guerrilla office in the Johns Hopkins library. Someone who had two offices gave me a key to one of his offices. I had no personal space in the punk house that I was living in, so I would do my work in this office that didn't even belong to me. Multiple people gave me feedback on the essay, there were several drafts. A lot of the ideas were developed in conversation with other people—the Baltimore Feminist Reading Group members, and my friend Lawrence Grandpre, with whom I would discuss Afro-pessimist theory. My conversations with him helped me clarify my thinking about race, incarceration, and the politics of innocence, particularly anti-Black racism in the United States. I'd thought about prisons for a while because of my brother.

What about Afro-pessimism interests you?

My thinking on Afro-pessimism and social death has changed a bit over the last couple years. At the time, I was really interested in the work of Frank B. Wilderson III. I've read everything he's written—both his academic and autobiographical work. He uses film to analyze racial structures and anti-Blackness, not just in the United States but globally. He advances a critique of civil society and a theorization of the psychosexual dynamics of anti-Black racism; it starts from the conviction that slavery was an event that has implications for and continues to live in our present moment, because slavery, ontologically, has restructured the world. He argues that there is a global anti-Blackness that produces Blackness as social death. And he understands slavery not as a historical event, but as an ontological event, a rupture. So when he talks about anti-Blackness it's not just an economic critique, but it's an ontological critique, it's a psychological critique, it's about how anti-Blackness structures white subjectivity, and how whiteness and civil society rely on the disposal of Black bodies to constitute themselves.

He's very pessimistic in his view of politics. To him, all politics proper reinscribe the structure that he's critiquing. In most of his essays and books he makes the same analytical gesture: he'll point to someone's effort at critiquing racism or anti-Blackness, and then demonstrate how it fails, because everything anyone does on the terrain of civil society just reinforces anti-Blackness.

The Afro-pessimists, especially Jared Sexton, have been engaged with people like Fred Moten in debates about Afro-pessimism and Black optimism. Fred Moten takes a Black-optimist stance that emphasizes the improvisatory socialities created in Black music and poetry; I've since become obsessed with Fred Moten's work. I don't see Moten and Afro-pessimism as diametrically opposed or mutually exclusive; I still find value in both perspectives, so I wouldn't say I've switched sides or anything. They're operating on different registers and have different affective dispositions.

When I wrote "Against Innocence," I was deeply engaged with the works of Frank Wilderson and Saidiya Hartman. Occupy, Trayvon Martin, Troy Davis, Oscar Grant, also the London Riots. My housemates and I followed the London Riots closely. We'd read articles and argue about them. We were constantly having these debates about politics, critiquing insurrectionist thought, and we kept up with the news religiously. And, like I said, I was having all sorts of other conversations with people in Baltimore as well.

Do you have any mentors?

I feel like I actually can't have a mentor because I would probably "cathect" onto my mentor and it would be too psychologically consuming. Although I've always fantasized about having a mentor. However, I do have a lot of people I would call "fairy godmothers"—

they're not really people who mentor me, per se, and they're not even people who are motherly, but they are people who come through in times of need, which is the role fairy godmothers play for what I call the "Lost Girl." Chris Kraus is one of these people for me. Bhanu Kapil is another. And then I have some older lesbians who sometimes take care of me. There's this couple in Glasgow, Scotland—Nosh and Cloudberry—who took care of me when I lived in Scotland for a few months.

I've always wanted a mentor, though, someone who cares about me enough to invest a lot of time and energy into me, sees my potential, and wants to turn me into an intellectual baller.

Maybe you need to find a partner who's a few years older.

I definitely have the fantasy of being in a power couple, or being psychically fused with someone who'd want to work through ideas and scheme. That's the goal, eventually. Not to be in a power couple, per se, because I'm critical of the couple form, but to be in an environment where I'm around a lot of motivated people who want to take it to the next level.

I've become accustomed to sharing my life with other people, whether it's through collective-living situations or long-term relationships. That's how I operate—I feel like I need a high level of intimacy and exchange to feel charged and motivated, so it's kind of weird to now have this monadic (but also nomadic) lifestyle. I miss having a crew to roll with and feeling embedded in some group or social formation.

Does that exist in the poetry world at all?

There is a community feel in the poetry world but there's not an emphasis on sharing your life with others, like in the anarchist scene.

You started a PhD program in African and African American studies and history at Harvard this fall. How have these first few months been?

I still have moments when I pause and think about where I am and how I got here; being at Harvard is hard to get used to because it's in contradiction with my internal sense of self. It's a paradox. I could never have imagined that I would end up at Harvard. When I started getting depressed over the last couple of years, it was always hard for me to conceptualize one day into the future, let alone think of my life having any kind of trajectory whatsoever.

I've liked it more than I anticipated I would. It's been a while since I've been really busy and intellectually stimulated, and I kind of need that to exist. I need to have intense conversations with people about what I'm reading, to be thinking with people; it's also nice having a fixed schedule. It's so different than the structureless lifestyle I've had for the last four years. I like it, and I'm surprised that I like it. I like my classes, I like my professors, I like sitting in the library reading books. I know I'm kind of a freak in the Harvard context, but it's whatever. [*Laughs*]

You've previously talked about being plagued by writer's block. How it gives you anxiety, and induces a sense of failure. It's fairly typical for writers to go through periods when writing becomes really painful, or impossible. It's horrible to be incapacitated in that way. At the same time, many of the writers I admire have politicized their writer's block, repurposed it as something connected to their other struggles.

Writers feel illegitimate claiming the identity of "writer" when they're not producing work. They might feel, "I'm not even a real writer, I'm not writing right now! I can't write."

Writing has become very fraught for me in the last couple of years—anxiety-inducing, perhaps even the source of my depression. I'm not sure exactly what precipitated it, although I have some theories. I think being uprooted and removed from my social circle, lack of political meaning in my life since moving to New Mexico, and being removed from the things that were sustaining me in Baltimore. I also got out of a three-year relationship that was physically and emotionally abusive and destroyed my self-esteem. At the same time I was trying to grapple with the end of that relationship and moving across the country, I was also trying to work on a Semiotext(e) book.

I received a lot of recognition in my early twenties and have been approached by four different publishers about publishing a book with them. I'm constantly receiving solicitations, invitations to do talks, and it has totally fucked with my head. Not in the sense that I've developed this big ego or anything, but I'm paralyzed by the expectations of the audience. The more I come into contact with these spheres of legitimacy or respectability, the more I feel a disjunction between how I identify and the contexts that I exist in.

I don't know how to reconcile other people's expectations with how I perceive myself. I feel afraid of disappointing people, I feel like they're gonna find out that I'm not the real deal. There are all these neurotic, negative thought patterns that emerge when I try to write or think about writing. So I've become pathologically avoidant of writing. Since becoming really depressed I've basically stopped writing for the public.

The way I thought and lived a few years ago has basically become unintelligible to me. A few years ago, my default was writing and creating things—I was constantly producing. After I finished my undergrad, I wrote a draft of a novel, two poetry manuscripts, and would write an essay a day about books, current events, films, whatever. And now I feel like I can't even look at my emails. Hopefully it's just a phase.

I never used to be afraid of failure; I was just doing my own thing, outside an institutional context, without any expectation of recognition. But the stakes were lower then, things were more playful. I was free to experiment because I was toiling in the shadows. There are no stakes when you're not trying to be someone great or do something profound or amazing. You're just doing your thing because you *enjoy* it.

And it's not like my work has been systematically rejected by the literary world or the radical world. I consistently receive positive feedback from people, and they tell me my work inspires them and has a positive influence in their lives. So that's good, that's why I like writing and sharing.

Do you feel that poetry comes to you more easily?

I've always been lyrical in my thinking and approach to my work. I'm kind of intense and I value emotionality in writing. And I like trying to find the register that feels natural or comfortable for me. I tweet my dreams on Twitter. I'm always half-conscious when I'm tweeting my dreams, but I value that headspace and feel like I can access something different when I'm writing in the oneiric register. In that sense, you could say it comes naturally.

I guess I do have a confidence or a level of trust in myself and in my writing that enables me to write in a way that sounds self-assured even when I feel like I'm overwhelmed by self-doubt. I don't acknowledge the validity of anything I do and constantly cut myself down and beat myself up and feel unfree. I should be freer. I think that I have an unconscious willfulness.

Self-doubt is usually the point of departure for a lot of my work. I always have to write through that doubt. Sometimes I sit down with an idea for an essay, and I'm so paralyzed by self-doubt that I must incorporate the doubt into whatever I'm working on in some way, or else I can't move beyond it. I resent that I must do this, but I also question the motivations for bracketing that experience because the excision of self-doubt is political (in that it's gendered and racialized). A lot of women are plagued by self-doubt and specifically anxiety around writing or asserting any kind of authority in their writing. Owning that doubt can be a political gesture.

In "Against Innocence" you write about white space or colonized space as a place where certain stories just don't matter or aren't interesting. It seems this fraught relationship you have to yourself and to producing your views of the world is so intimately connected to that. That is the experience.

I guess it can be generative in some ways. I've always been suspicious of writers who feel comfortable in language, which is why I've been drawn to Samuel Beckett, Hélène Cixous, Clarice Lispector. All these authors have a fraught relationship to language. Kafka as well.

Really hating the writing and still having to do it.

Right. There's this Samuel Beckett quote: "The writer is like a foetus trying to do gymnastics." Writing is the impossible yet necessary task. In some ways maybe this friction is the lifeblood of my writing, this struggle to utter anything. Maybe I resent people who don't have self-doubt because they seem like they can get to a place that I can't because I have to wade through the quagmire of self-hatred before I can even begin to start doing the thinking and the work that I want to do.

Since moving to New York, I've become more aware of how many freelance writers in this city rely on various cocktails of stimulants and benzos for work. I mean, the same was true in college, but after growing up in Finland where pharmaceuticals are less common I'm still surprised by the extent to which people do drugs on a daily basis. What's your relationship to drugs and work?

I actually think prescription stimulants are bad for creative writing, although they can be good for philosophy. I remember reading an exchange between Simone de Beauvoir and Sartre about Sartre's writer's block. De Beauvoir tells Sartre, "You used stimulants for decades to write your philosophy books," and he's like, "Yeah but I can't write novels on them."

There's also an interesting interview with Susan Sontag that was published in *High Times* where she talks about drugs and writing. She was also on stimulants but tried to regulate her reliance on them, because she's skeptical of the quality of writing that she produced on them. Derrida also relied on stimulants.

I've known a lot of people who take Adderall recreationally and find them annoying when they're on it. Not that they aren't wonderful people, but it's hard to have a conversation with someone who monologues at you while on amphetamines. I tend to feel anxious on anything that's an upper—coffee, other stimulants ... Maybe if I weren't so anxious they would be more appealing to me.

Benzos—I try to stay away from those as well because I know people who've had serious issues trying to quit benzos, though I understand the appeal. Sometimes I'm like, "Fuck, I wish I had Xanax right now so I could just shut off this thought loop."

I do think people should talk about drugs more. Drugs are ancient—they're a fundamental part of the human experience. I don't know why there's a gag order on talking about drugs. Everyone's on pharmaceuticals, and recreational drug use is so common. I mean, I understand why people hide their drug use. But it seems that in the past people wrote and talked about drug use and altered states of consciousness more. We're all becoming pharmacological monsters—it's a mark of our time. I've relied on Ambien to sleep since my early twenties because I've been an insomniac since I was twelve. And I've taken antidepressants in the past but I'm trying to survive without antidepressants, so I'm exercising and taking omega-3 supplements. [*Laughs*]

You've mentioned that some of your intimate relationships that were simultaneously creative/work relationships were similarly exploitative or abusive. How do you navigate your various identities as a poet and writer in these literature worlds that so often are dominated by misogynists?

Oh my gosh. It's totally maddening—the world, the writing world—especially as a woman. I feel like the only way to not let it corrode you psychically is to not be embattled with these patriarchs and gatekeepers, to not seek recognition from the white-male literary establishment. That's a lot easier said than done. There's an erotic dimension to this power dynamic, and the women who are embattled with these patriarchs sometimes have intimate relationships with the men who are in positions of power. The closer you get to that power, the easier it is to be taken advantage of. Proximity can destroy you. It's easier for me to maintain distance because I'm not very interested in men romantically.

I don't really put my hopes in the literary world. I'm never surprised when it comes out that there's sexism in it. I have one foot in the literary world and one foot in another world, the political world maybe. I've never really felt that the forms of life that I am looking for or that I'm trying to create will emerge out of the literary world. Oftentimes I feel like it's full of people who only care about social capital. There's nastiness in *any* world or subculture, but I never really felt that the people in the literary world are *my people* even though I probably spend more time in a literary context than anywhere else. Maybe my disidentification with the literary establishment enables me to maintain a healthy distance.

What has enabled me to maintain my sanity over the years is being part of a strong feminist friend group, especially since living in Baltimore. I really don't know where I would be without that grounding in my life. If it weren't for my feminist crew, there would be no way for me to confirm that what I think and experience is valid or real. It must be hard for people who don't have that, because the psychic isolation can alienate you, can make you feel that you don't exist and that none of your problems are real.

(2014)

The Fragility of Friendship (and Everything Else)

This originally appeared on my Tumblr blog.

have i forgotten how to write? i've forgotten how to write.

that night, when the thought occurred to me to write, i wanted to write something entirely different from what i wrote.

as i sat at the kitchen table sipping on the holy basil tea, i thought about all the people i have known

people lost to time and space

people falling in and out of relation

the inscrutability of it all

Lily called that morning

a college friend she had not spoken to in ten years had just died of AIDS-related complications

that morning she started to write an essay called "The Geography of Friendship"

an essay about distance and estrangement.

she couldn't get over the fact that this person she had known so well

fell out of her life completely and now does not exist on this planet at all.

who was the person who died

and who was the person she knew?

i have sometimes thought about this when thinking about the brother i knew before prison and the brother i cannot know now because i am not privy to his universe

because we live in two different worlds

the world of the free and the world of the unfree

me on the side of the free

but bound to the world of the unfree by a blood relation

what does it mean to grow apart

to evolve on separate islands

into the creatures you become mostly by happenstance

the finch or the bird of paradise

on the phone Lily and i congratulated ourselves for staying friends across the distance.

i assured her that it is possible to remain in relation

though the quality of the relation is sometimes altered when you try to resync after being apart for years.

when i wanted to write that morning, i was thinking about an essay i wrote a few years ago about traveling to Budapest to visit Mátyás, a Hungarian man who had been my best friend while i lived in Kunming, China. i probably would have forgotten this piece of writing completely had Dodie Bellamy not spoken of it glowingly.

though the piece of writing is only a skeletal description of a neutral encounter,

the piece has remained dear to me

perhaps because in writing it i learned two very important lessons:

that human connection is all about timing

and that staying in relation is all about rhythm—

remaining in sync, or *becoming* synchronized

inhabiting a similar tempo

or being near each other when your daily tempos get thrown off beat and you suddenly find yourself experiencing each other through that rupture

through the cuts in your lives

"swerve with me"

observe

who comes into your life

during those moments

you lose

control

observe

what happens to the texture of your writing

the moment you are

without

addressee

(do you even write at all?)

i opened the post with the question

have i forgotten how to write?

perhaps i have forgotten how to write *you*

to say anything to an-other

or to conjure the object of memory by tricking it into presence

you:

the "self" understood through a linguistic relation

because there is only relation and no self

only the "third body" created between entities

i thought about the loss of the *you*, and the structure of apostrophe, as i thought about a letter my best friend Matthew sent me for my birthday.

when we lived together we would go to a local gay bar and write letters to people on our DIY stationary.

we were compulsive in our desire to connect

always dropping our whimsical musings into everyone's mailboxes

getting all twisted up inside over abstract crushes we had probably idealized.

Matthew's letters are always nostalgic

no matter where he's at, he starts from the place of loss

from the belief that his life once contained a magic that is now irrecoverable.

in this letter he reflects on the domestic traditions that were developed by the New College queers as they were caring for a dying friend.

one of these traditions was using the *Joy of Cooking* as a kind of Bible.

cooking was practiced as a form of care, as queer homemaking.

in the letter, i wrote to Matthew that i also mourned the loss of socialities that revolve around the sharing of food

"i no longer have anyone to cook for. what feels better than cooking for friends? almost nothing. it is terrible to have no one to cook for."

writing to Matthew made me think about the last time i cooked with someone

though i was just getting to know them, the act of cooking with them created a feeling of familiarity.

in the kitchen i thought about the slipperiness of relations

and sunk into the "objective" view of my life

where everything i've ever experienced has meaning simply because it happened and i am made up of all these encounters.

to inhabit the memory is to move beyond good and bad

the interpretation is silenced by the raw sensory experience of it.

in such moments the self that wants to ward off hurt, abandonment, and loss dies

and all that is left is a bundle of mysterious relations

the facts of a life, which i experience as pure dissociative joy,

and my body: a trace of everything that has been lived

like my words

which together do not constitute my "work"

but rather

are an extension of my body:

a trace of relation

when the memory becomes vivid there is truth and nothing else

you understand everything by forgetting who you are

you become who you are by forgetting who you are

the last night the new friend was at my house, we stopped by the grocery store because they wanted to cook me eggs Benedict and fried polenta as a gesture of appreciation for the generosity i had shown them during their stay.

i drifted through the grocery store in a sleep-deprived daze while they plucked the ingredients from the shelf with grace.

they accidentally grabbed crumpets instead of English muffins.

when i heard "crumpets" i thought of Holly saying "would you like a crumpet?" in her English accent.

because i was so sleep-deprived and emotionally agitated from processing so many intense situations, my mental filters were malfunctioning.

memories kept firing at random

and i continued to slip deeper and deeper into this universe of private associations

sometimes laughing to myself at the tragicomic absurdity of existence

evidenced by the twisted thoughts that were marching through my brain.

as we were listening to music in my bed the flashbacks grew more intense and vivid.

when the Bulgarian State Radio and Television Female Vocal Choir came on i was transported back to one of my Mesilla nighttime walks along the arroyo

beneath the moon and stars

the desert night was so emotionally charged.

i remember the pony i would see on my walks

how it would come to the fence to greet me

and how seeing the pony would put a stop to my crying

because the pony was just hanging out beneath the full moon.

when Kiki d'Aki's "El Futuro" came on i thought about the beginning of my relationship with C.

dancing to the song together in the kitchen of the Copycat Theater in Baltimore

how strange it is to have this beginning-to-end view of a relation

how impossible it was to be so in love with someone so abusive

i looked down at my hands

the watch Ashley gave me

the garnet ring my mother gave me when i was 11

who was i, in that moment, when i was filled up with everything i had ever lived through?

i was nothing at my core

an assemblage of encounters and the marks left by them.

the accessories i had received as gifts seemed proof of this

how did Hanna know, when she wrote the *Mask Magazine* article, that all my accessories are gifts from friends and lovers?

i started to ramble manically as the force of the memory deluge intensified i wanted to say

that at the end of it all

there is light

and i thought, perhaps ...

perhaps it is necessary to travel through violence to reach the "exalted frequency"

to enter the illuminated world through the blood-stained gate screaming

("the wailing that accompanies entrance into and expulsion from sociality")

what had i learned from reading Fred Moten and Bhanu Kapil

about the space opened up by trauma?

the space where everything becomes terribly proximate

but are you touching anything?

are your limbs falling off as you enter the earth's atmosphere?

is your hair on fire?

embarrassment brought me back to earth

the weird dissociative state i was in—my manic ebullience—put enormous distance between me and this new friend, who was waiting for me to let them cook the dinner they had planned with care

i sensed the distance

and felt ashamed of the way i acted

though they were not trying to shame me

i had simply fallen through a mental wormhole that led me to a different world.

when i returned to my "self" i felt terribly alone

doomed to dwell in a world that no other being could ever possibly penetrate or understand

is this the survivor's universe?

in all the books i read on trauma there is reference to survivors not feeling human

they think of themselves as aliens, monsters, witches, vampires, dogs, rats, snakes, cyborgs.

before i read the books, i already knew this from Bhanu.

but i did feel

that the new friend

could meet me that far

(the space outside the human.)

when we got to the kitchen their mood shifted

they came out of their silence

and i was happy to again be occupying the same world as another sentient being they moved through the kitchen with the finesse of a ballerina, for they were practiced in the art of making eggs Benedict.

i stood near the refrigerator watching the dance

drifting in and out of human consciousness.

i was mesmerized by their demonstration of how to poach an egg

and they were excited to show me

because they knew that i was a lover of eggs.

to poach the egg, they made a whirlpool in the pot

and carefully dropped the eggs in.

as i stared into the pot at the floating eggs, the pot opened up into a whole universe

each egg became a coagulating celestial body.

when they started to make the hollandaise sauce they said, "come here. check this out."

they were separating the egg yolks from the whites with their hands.

i was impressed.

"i thought you would like it," they said.

after working in food prep for years, they could crack eggs with one hand.

the blueprint for making diner food seemed to reside deep in their unconscious sometimes bubbling up to the surface in their art or in the form of surrealist food imagery

children's-book drawings depicting floating food and trapdoors.

the morning they left my house, their glasses broke.

i woke up to them frantically trying to fix them, and then running out the door to catch their bus.

in the corner of the room they left a little pile of things

a sweater, some tights

the objects are themselves—

a tableau of absence

or trace of an encounter

poorly understood

why write all this?

why write anything

except to document all the ways in which experiences accrue to a body that does not know how to make sense of them.

no matter how much ink we spill we will never be able to get at it

the enigma of relationships

these invisible microtransferences

the impossibility of ever knowing where someone else is at

or the weird doubt you sometimes feel upon reflection

when you wonder if you ever really knew someone at all.

what Lily wanted to understand on the phone was the process by which a friend becomes a stranger

the fragility of the categories "friend" and "stranger"

and how the transmogrification of the friend into stranger throws your being into crisis

because who i am is only ever in relation to (you)

* * *

what have you become, passing through this life

and who are you in relation to who you were

after you have been mutated by everything you've ever touched.

some damage

some joy

or the way joy can never exclude damage

why do you keep putting your hands in the fire?

to touch the fire—

it was worth it to get burned

(2015)

Writing the Fool

This originally appeared on my Tumblr blog.

i have been given an assignment: to write a poem about the Fool on the day of the black moon, February 18, 2015. today. but i don't know how to do assignments because something in me only wants to do the thing i'm not supposed to be doing. because something inside me resists the notion of laboring toward an end, though i like contemplating the Fool and being given the chance to think about what the Fool means. this is not a poem, but maybe i can just keep writing and something will emerge that i can pull from the muck and call a poem.

for the Fool, there is only the nonteleological event of writing
writing with one's eyes closed
writing on the go
writing in a crumbling shack on the side of the road in the middle
    of nowhere Pennsylvania
the Fool is in it for the ride
reading about the Fool made me feel that my biggest problem right
    now is that i've lost my foolishness
it's a paradox
i've made it to where i am right now by embracing madness
by staying open to everything
cruising through life with no plan, doing what i wanted to do because

it was fun
stumbling into bad and difficult situations because it's inevitable when
    you keep all the doors of your skin open
things were exciting! very exciting
i could experiment because i wasn't trying to be anything
recording my first song with the Copycat Theater kids in Baltimore
    was a delight
to feel out the texture of my singing voice was a delight

what did i care if people thought i was stupid?
i was free
and there were friends
and there was improvisation
and of course, lunacy
rambling performances about bugs and worms
long bicycle journeys in the rain
sweat
trials
laughter
letters
energy
typos
not giving a fuck
doing it because i enjoyed it, because it was what i wanted to do

this is all very abstract
what i'm trying to say is, i think i've lost touch with the crazy-wisdom
    of the Fool
the girl who just gets up and goes, over and over, blind to tomorrow,
    in love with the unknown, hungry for experience

the girl documented in zines like *The Adventures of Loneberry* and *The Vertigo of Falling*
now i type this out knowing i need to wrap it up
because i am a PhD student, and there is work i have to do tonight
is this domestication?
is domestication the death of me?
i can't just stay up all night waxing poetic about the black supermoon
writing odes to the Fool
bathing in the mystery of the moment
feeling on the edge of life and loving it
vibrating on the precipice
on the cliff
my dog in tow, protecting me
while i dance in the sun
spinning the white rose between my fingertips

i want to follow the thread of my desire to the end of the world

when you meet a fool, you'll know her
she's never doing what she's supposed to do
sometimes it looks as though she's doing nothing at all
because what is walking alongside the river in the winter sun to the one who is always busy?
the Fool doesn't know the phrase "i'm busy"
she doesn't know how to protect her time or plan for tomorrow
she is a force of chaos in the world
but if you can handle her, you'll realize that her chaos is also a gift
it dislodges people from their habitus
gently
disorganizes &

makes possible
something
that wasn't possible

what do i do with my chaos now?
feel bad about it because i am a serious student at a serious institution

i loved being a fool
i didn't need people to believe me
i was generating meaning, by living it
i loved not being sought after by publishers and Harvard
i loved when i was only surrounded by those who are true
no matter how small—we liked living off the radar
i loved the time before there was an "idea of Jackie Wang" circulating
    in the world
i loved chillin' all day long
all-night diners
kitchen talk

there is still a lot of this
like when i got food with Nat, Ariana, and Joohyun after the Akai
    Gurley benefit reading
and we laughed and laughed at our frozen brains and the flaming
    heart on the wall
i may have even let platitudes like "this is the stuff of life" spill from
    my mouth
because i was happy
and there was nowhere else i wanted to be

(2015)

Peplophoros as the World with Her Head Lopped Off

This piece originally appeared as a limited-edition chapbook produced by [2nd floor projects].

I. The Isthmus of Memory

Begin, begin. How does she begin? She doesn't know how to begin. Only gather. Fragments of dream and affective filament. The twigs she hoards always for the nest to come. How does one create a container for writing? An abode to write through what you don't understand? I light the blue-sage and red-sandalwood smudge stick given to me by Bhanu Kapil, using a leopard-print lighter Dana Ward bought for me at a gas station we stopped at on a drive from Poughkeepsie to Boston.

Go to the place where it is okay to not understand. What Hélène Cixous says of Derrida: *Should I think of you as a convert to dreams?*

Today. Where was I when I woke up?

In the dream there is an isthmus or maybe a narrow peninsula on which I encounter my ex-girlfriend.

Her life has taken a turn for the worse—she was arrested for carrying 1.5 Xanax pills because I took the Xanax before going to sleep. I ramble excitedly to her about all the things I'm reading and she says she misses my truth rants.

Do you remember, in Steak 'n Shake, how your soul was on fire because you saw the world naked and essential? And you believed you could never be depressed again.

We are trying to get hot water for green tea. The isthmus is now somehow China. I see my old Korean friends at a table drinking soju. M. says, *Jackie, is that you?*

In every room on the isthmus there are old friends and lovers from a different period of my life.

Is this narrow stretch of sand-land my past rolled out and still living? Every chamber is a section of my life, enshrined. The Sandbar of Memory or the lair beneath Isabella Gardner's mansion with a single window illuminating baubles of the East: the Chinese Room.

And at the end of this thread of land there is a slide that launches you into the ocean. From memory, to ocean.

I knew it would be too cold. Could I survive that chill?

Without knowing where I was, I had a feeling I was very north.

But when it's my turn to launch into the ocean I'm at the bottom of a slide trying to crawl up it to see, but I keep sliding down.

It's insurmountable. I collapse in exhaustion.

Retreat into the memory isthmus …

The headmistress of the memory isthmus yells at the girl who reencounters herself in the Room of Forgotten People.

It felt like a cruise. (But this was land.)

I wanted to buy popcorn. (To watch my life?)

Like every dream, I cannot figure out the etiquette of my inscrutable environment.

It's like constantly being on trial.

You never know when something you do will warrant recrimination.

Then the memory isthmus becomes elsewhere, another dream of a lost shoe.

Another dream of a lost purple platform glittering-satin studded shoe.

Because I am missing a heel, I limp around the party in search of my balance.

I see Jasmine, a woman I used to know, wearing similar shoes and I think maybe she stole mine but close up I see they're subtly different.

I ask the old friends, *Have you seen my purple platform shoe?*

I am back at New College. Giant cookies are being served and I want to grab one to bring to Persephone on the isthmus of memory.

The shoe is never recovered.

In the film *The Last Time I Saw Macao* by the two Joãos all that's left of the murdered woman is a platform shoe. Then there's the other João Pedro Rodrigues film *To Die like a Man*—I remember all the things Tonia loses. Does she pray to St. Anthony? Only when she's dying does she realize the dog has been playing a trick on her and has been stealing all her things and burying them in The Garden of Lost Objects. At the end all the objects are returned to her, including the shoe she wore during her first drag performance. After she saw the witch in the forest everything went harmonious.

The lost objects had to be returned, because the world is now such that the one you love loves you back.

(What did I write João, about the shoe and the structure of queer longing? *I make R. replay the graveyard scene, after Tonia finds Rosario on the ground, poking at the dirt with a knife. Earlier that day when R. & I were walking down Mass Ave in Harvard Square we passed an unhoused man who was digging up the dirt between the sidewalk bricks with a stick.*

R. didn't notice. But some of us have our heads turned toward the ground …

Oh Rosario. I am your mother. You can't live without me. In the forest there is a witch who recites Paul Celan with the "doctor." Nothing stays in sync very long until they listen to Baby Dee's "Calvary" beneath the blood moon. Her body is falling apart. Leaking, infected. My head is not okay. Few more pills? He puts his head on me, or his hand on my back when I start to get upset.

Light rain after the film. The streetlight orange and the blinking lights— bike lights?—reflected in the window of a car. Dragging my possessions in the mist. Pizza and Sanpellegrino (blood-orange flavor) for me, gin for him. Outside the bar the clouds were moving rapidly in front of the moon. I wanted the equilibrium that came with the blood moon, but why, I wonder, is harmony only possible when dying? People falling in and out of sync.

He liked the way she sang to herself in the car.

Be guided by the emotion. "But how were we supposed to get there?"

"What does this street look like in winter," I asked, out of nowhere, remembering my birthday, walking to Golden West with my housemates, streets covered in snow.

He covered me with the blanket. While he was asleep, he had wrapped himself with the purple fleece blanket, leaving me with no cover. "You should have punched me," he said.

Where is my head?

Tonia singing to herself about loneliness. Radio transmission. Queer melancholia. Made nonsovereign by love but that's not me. Where am I? Simple lovers, jealous of the dog. A story of lost souls.

At the end of the film, all the lost objects are returned to her. What is the significance of the shoe? Libidinal attachment to that which triggers the memory, her drag debut. I said, "There is a recurring dream where everything lost is returned to me. My older brother, in a grocery store." Was I talking to myself?)

The dream comes full circle.

A few years ago, I dreamed I took a pair of purple platform shoes out of a pile of discarded things left inside a temple.

Today I lose half the gift.

In a poem I wrote,

waiting to see what will be left behind
a pair of beautiful purple platform shoes
something very personal

The ocean was not as cold as I thought.

When I write to J., autocorrect changes "nasturtium" into three different words. The mistake becomes poetry.

II. The Cake Corpse and the Daughter Possessed by an Alphabet of Funeral Flowers

The morning of my grandma's wake I dream her corpse comes flattened and cut into three pieces: the head, the chest, and the body below the waist.

You can see cross sections of her body where the cuts were made. Like Damien Hirst animals. Layers of flesh, a zoological specimen.

Grandma's body becomes an ice cream cake.

Her face is not her face, but a face sculpted out of whipped cream and icing, with maraschino cherries for eyes and a creepy clownish smile.

A week later. What did I see? I was at IHOP with Leah, Brandon, and Ryan after psychoanalysis. When I looked at the IHOP menu I saw a frosted smiling pancake in the kid's section: the face of my grandmother's corpse. The cake corpse I dreamed right before seeing the corpse-corpse. I think I nonchalantly said, *This smiling pancake has the exact same face of my grandma's corpse when it appeared to me as cake.* Quickly, I changed the subject, not wanting to be so macabre before people even had a chance to consume their morning coffee.

The fantasy of melancholy cannibalism, according to Julia Kristeva in *Black Sun: Depression and Melancholia*, is a way to maintain an attachment to the lost object in the face of death. The body of the other is literally consumed in many of the dreams of depressed persons:

> Better fragmented, torn, cut up, swallowed, digested … than lost. The melancholy cannibalistic imagination is a repudiation of the loss's reality and of death as well. It manifests the anguish of losing the other through the survival of the self, surely a deserted self but not separated from what still and ever nourishes it and becomes transformed into the self—which also resuscitates—through such a devouring.

I wasn't ready for the call. I wasn't ready to go back to Florida. To face my old room or my aunt. Where was I when the email came? "Grandma died" was the subject line. There was no text in the body of the email, just a blurry picture of a half-eaten cake. Was this cake Grandma's flesh, the food we make of death, or the way we eat to avoid writing, to avoid utterance? The sign leaves me. I was never ready and could you see it in the way time collapsed in my syntax? Because melancholia is the inability to *sequentialize*. The dread is punctured by the rambling bullet of life that goes on and on like the life of the bullet in the Korn music video for "Freak on a Leash."

I am at a graveyard in the rain sitting in a car behind a hearse amidst an alphabet of funeral flowers

The coffin is on wheels like a gurney. No pallbearers.

The oak trees are covered in Spanish moss and a young couple is planting fake flowers next to a bench in the pouring rain …

My mom doesn't attend the funeral; she says it would "upset her too much." The few of us who have showed up leave before the body is interned. But why? I never saw the burial of my childhood parakeet and because I believed he was still alive in the garage I would hallucinate his caw at night as I would pace the dark and quiet house. I never saw the body put to rest. I shrieked. My little brother said it was unsettling, the way I shrieked when that bird died. But nobody knew about my private hallucinations or midnight rituals. Pacing. *He's not dead!* I hear him crying in a shoebox in the garage. I want to ask, what did you do with the body? Did you throw it away? Did you treat my bird like trash because … of what use is a dead thing to the living?

My aunt touches the corpse as she walks away from the casket. "She's cold," my aunt says. "She always hated to be cold but now … she's so cold." I stare at the details of the hand of the Hans Holbein painting *The Body of the Dead Christ in the Tomb*. The skin around Christ's hand is black in the place where he has been nailed to the cross and the black hand becomes the hand of my grandmother in the casket, holding the wooden rosary.

The hand of the corpse was black

where the IV had failed to meet the vein.

I am writing this on Easter Sunday.

In *Black Sun*, Kristeva says that the Christ of Holbein's *The Body of the Dead Christ in the Tomb* is a truly *dead* Christ, so final it lacks all promise of resurrection and redemption. There's no waking up. Christ has been made carnal and turned into a corpse modeled after an actual corpse fished out of the Rhine. Something about the painting forces us to confront the nothingness at the core of being.

Is that why it's so hard for us to look at the corpse of Christ rendered with such reality? Dostoyevsky wrote that while looking at the painting some "may lose their faith."

I couldn't approach the corpse. More than facing the singular absence, it was time I feared—the gradual erosion of life and the draining of vitality. A family unraveling. Why does one collapse at the thought, *Once I was a girl and Grandma would drive me to school.* Randy is still in prison and cannot attend the funeral. Once, Randy was not in prison. Grandma could drive. Grandma came to the trial. A couple days before grandma died a nurse tried to explain "selfies" to her and she laughed.

> *What if*
> *the last concept*
> *added to the repertoire*
> *of this singular existence*
> *was "selfies"???*

I don't want to get on the plane because on the other side of the journey is a finality without end. An end that, hereafter, will always have ended. But surely life will eventually become something I can face? For now the question becomes: *How can I continue pretending I am living in the same world as everyone around me?* When I read Jamaica Kincaid's email—"take care of your grief"—I started weeping and then passed out in an alcohol-allergy fugue, after taking a few sips of a White Russian purchased for me by S. Shaking. Two little girls in tulle skirts were singing Lorde's "Royals" during karaoke at the Southwestern dive bar called MineShaft and Lara sang the Cure's "Letter to Elise." Elise, Elise … the name of the girlfriend of the painter who tried to court me. I remember perching on various stones overlooking desert valleys. To cogitate. Sitting on the rock, I close my eyes and feel myself withdrawing. *To gather strength?* I wonder, feeling no guarantee of return. With my eyes closed I face the sun. The world becomes a tunnel, pure blood red, and when I open my eyes the red remains because I have colored the landscape with my grief—the juniper trees also become totems of my sadness. *There!* I could be that rived and withered trunk, struck by black lightning and burned to the ground. I could be ...

There were two perches: the one before I knew and the one after. The valley between them is the caesura, a rupture that upends my basket full of glittering signifiers and places me in the backseat of a Toyota next to a pile of funeral flowers.

What did I smell, when I climbed down from my perch and crushed the creosote leaves between my fingers? It was the rain. All this time, the smell of tar and burnt pavement that came with the desert rains was the oil of the creosote plant. When I opened Dylan's package of dried creosote, I was opening the rain. Do you remember? Glued to your bed next to the makeshift pink-zebra-print curtain—there's that smell again. Pitter-patter to unlock the scent that colors the feeling of wanting to die. At some point I must have fallen asleep. At some point living must have felt easier until it didn't, again.

III. Oneiromantic Flowers

The question of how to begin is not a question of what you have to say but where the dream places you.

I sleep to know what I can't let myself know awake.

A couple of days after receiving the haunting image of the half-eaten cake, I have a dream I replace my dead grandmother in her nursing home but the nursing home is also a mental hospital and I don't know why I'm there. A pretty boy waits for me in the vestibule of the asylum but I don't see him. I'm too fixated on the one who has wounded me to see anyone. Leonardo DiCaprio (which autocorrect wants to change to "diva prop") walks out of the asylum in metallic gold pants carrying the lovelorn boy. In the "activities" center I am visited by a friend. She has made an alliance with the one who wounded me, and I'm so pissed I throw a deck of tarot cards into the air. The cards explode and fall like confetti. *Have I made a scene?* Good! Maybe for the first time I know the meaning of uncontrollable anger—the gesture was benign enough, but you cannot imagine the raw violence behind it. With D. in alliance with G. (Deleuze and Guattari?), I was truly alone. With my cards. Warming the seat of my grandmother, feeling like I was going to fall because I couldn't count on anyone …

A man walks into the elevator with his wife. He says, "Don't cry. It will pass." Am I still in the dream? No, this is the *hyperdream*. You see it all began in the courtyard of the Isabella Stewart Gardner Museum, sitting beneath a statue of Persephone overlooking the garden while reading the book. The hanging nasturtium vines were spilling out of the Venetian windows like black mouths vomiting flowers in a cascade of orange. The memory crypt becomes the hyperdream that sends me back to New England summers peppered with nasturtium, on my ex-girlfriend's mother's farm. We'd put the flowers in our salads for color and tang. Every day until the chill came I would eat a nasturtium flower while walking down Oxford Street. Did I tell Ryan and Hannah Black to eat one? Did they believe me when I said, *These flowers are edible?* But why would any-one want to destroy something so beautiful? A laminated booklet informs me the vines are nursed for nine months before they are draped over the balcony. The gestation period of a human fetus ...

Stepping out of the museum and into the park, a branch breaks inside your chest. There. What emotion crescendos and dislodges to become the shimmering SIGN made flesh, in perfect pulsions to find THIS rhythm, a rhythm to match the dream of every cell of your body turning into solar flowers which bloom for a single April of one girl's lonely life? What was the feeling you had walking to the park bench to eat your salad, the day grey with ruin like the final scene of Tsai Ming-liang's *Vive L'Amour?* It was the feeling that despite the ruin or maybe because of the ruin, something could be said. Did you start to cry? Did you stop dissociating from your pain? And weep and weep all that day, and the next, this flood, on the subway, in Starbucks, in the library, in the elevator, on campus—the scrim of water separating you from the world of the living. Did you cover your face with your hands when spoken to in public? Did you think that if your words were truly gone and this stupid life has once and for all upended your basket of shimmering signifiers, your alphabet of funeral flowers—did you think, *That would be the end of me?* What of you wants not to end: you approach. Collapse. Approach again. Circle the question. Masticate it. And return ...

Why did the flood begin in Isabella's garden? Because Cixous too has stared into the icy visage of "the world lopped off" and resur-faced, *with language.*

Your faith was enough.

But how could you maintain it?

Even Cixous could not always maintain it. In *Hyperdream* she writes, "I get up. The world's not there. Day does not dawn. I don't believe. Six a.m. Belief does not show up."

What was it Jamaica Kincaid said when you were sitting in her class, about how every time you wake up and put your feet on the ground in the morning you are making a leap of faith? You are operating under the assumption that the ground is still there, that the world has shown up, but a part of you wants to blurt out, *Not for me ... on some days, the world does not show up.*

"There is no world, I say. It makes me ill."—Cixous

J. says, *It must have cost her something*, to write it, the way it reads, you know by the way it reads that it must have cost her something.

IV. Peplophoros as the World with Her Head Lopped Off

She says, *I am here*, and I believe her. She makes herself here by saying, *Here I am. Hear me, how I come into the moment by announcing it.*

Is it Persephone? Or is it the statue of Peplophoros with her head lopped off?

Observe

how the headless woman

watches the garden

without a face

You feel the auric force of her glare coming from her body.

Just as you hear the laugh of a woman echo in the atrium, you read,

"A laugh resounds, creeps, ricochets, coughs, floats."

In the dream the echo solders the heart to the instance of word and soon the whole will pronounce the fade of standing on the train platform, thinking the voice transmitted directly to mind

Until the turn of breath focuses her laugh on the reality of the other

Finding again the voice at the other end of a vanishing flame ...

Losing one's skin to the day's burial to make time for the kiss of words ...

When she arrives to Penn Station, it's like the whole world is breathing, like the flows of people themselves are the cosmic breath of life

A hard crystal blooms in her mouth and the sky opens, dragging her into the earth through a wound.

(2015)

Venus as a Bull:
Notes on Björk

This essay originally appeared in Asphodel *magazine.*

For Lara Lorenzo and Melissa Buzzeo

One minute of presence becomes precious and elusive. I worry. I worry. I kill pleasure with worry. Then I fall. I was circling the Thing. It flickers. I fall. I spent the whole day in the Björk womb at MoMA and still I kept falling out and into my worries. When I watch Björk I want to be an unstoppable force. But what is between me and the force I could be if I could just kill what is killing me: myself.

She's moon and glowing in her love nest, pink bed, head thrown back in New York City. She can be a '90s club girl. She can emerge from a crack in the earth. She can own blue lava and robots like there's no contradiction. She can roll the egg across her face, can shriek in pain and endless delight. She can whisper and explode with ecstasy. Her emotions are a geological event. The way she pulsates, the way she stands and pounds her chest and sheds her gold petals as she rotates in the air. What kind of person can withstand the one who will not or cannot submit to your will? But it's only with such people that you will come to know the deeper pleasures in life. I love Björk because she cannot be tamed. She will surrender to his touch, but she will not give up her power.

Now the train rushes toward the heart of things, with strings making the chorus flutter as I pass some lights, pass the memory, on my way from NYC to Boston, a fog hangs over the city, makes night precise by making it imprecise, like atmosphere. Lara and I held hands in the Björk womb. With Lara there is a sense of safety that is total.

When any emotion peaks, there is clarity. When the voice goes from singing to screaming and the earth cracks, raw emotion is released. For a second my pleasure goes from mental to physical. He teaches me how to smell the bread, to sit in the sun, to let the water rain on my face while we touch. The snake and the lily. "Oceania" is a song of delight and water bliss. Shiny creatures dance in the golden water while blooming orchids pirouette toward the sun. I love Björk covered in sparkles ("Oceania," "Lionsong," "Venus as a Boy"), hearts spilling out of her mouth ("Triumph of a Heart"). Together the videos for these songs are a feminine epic. In pieces.

* * *

The flower of Lara's poem is also my escape into beauty, but it's only the illusion of being inviolable. Then I look inside myself and see: "I want to die." It seems lodged in the core of my being. At the Björk cinema I cried while looking at the death drive, remembering how I would sing a live version of "Possibly Maybe" as a teenager when no one was home.

Björk was the feminine hero's journey, making her own bliss and rising above the bullshit to become the voice of landscape and arctic desolation and the elements and the earth with its cracks and eruptions—she simply could not *not* sing. She was born to sing. She can sing about the everyday in a fiercely direct way, but is also capable of great poetry. Not the kind that obfuscates but clarifies. She's too real for games of mystification. She is a world unto herself, or maybe my personal guide to the universe. She is the full range of emotional experience, and she embraces the strength of her emotions with animal-like vigor. When she pounds her chest, I understand: the woman's ancient lament is being released from the body. By pulsating, by screaming and singing. I love the way she touches herself—maybe it's a self-soothing touch or maybe it's a way for her to remember the touch of the Beloved. A way to revive the memory. When she grabs a chunk of earth and starts pounding a rock, I understand that she is trying to obliterate herself so she can be reborn. When she falls onto the damp dirt and wakes in the mossy rolling field, draped in gold, spinning with her mouth open, she has transformed her suffering into something else. At the end of "Black Lake" her back is toward us, and she is walking away, toward the mountain. Yes, I cried. Because the arc of the video was so familiar. I felt I understood her style of suffering and saving herself from the darkness with her art. It's the same emotional (not narrative) arc of my film—the Tsai Ming-liang clip that bleeds into a sequence of release, a person backflipping on a trampoline in slow motion. Is this levitation a defensive mysticism that overtakes the oceanic subject in times of great distress? Do suffering people always want lightness and beauty? Is Björk a rocket or a flower? Why is the lava blue? Is that the blue mood finally erupting? There it goes. The beat comes in to help the body find a rhythm to expel the blue mood. She crawls on her hands and knees. She hobbles barefoot—it is necessary for her to be barefoot because of the raw vulnerability of the song. After the purge she is upright and strong. After strength, she floats.

Earth bears witness to her transformation. In Björk videos, the man who delights her or makes her suffer never appears. Eggs appear. The city appears. Cats, snakes, iguanas, bears, robots, and sea creatures appear. The moon appears but the man does not. It's not about him, though this man in absentia is her muse. Sometimes he's a death-obsessed destroyer. Often he's boring and too cowardly to accept her limitless emotions ("5 Years," "Black Lake"). Other times he's a master of arousal who fills her with infinite delight ("Venus as a Boy," "Cocoon"). He's somewhere in the background, frustrating her, tickling her fancy, and she goes and takes these emotions and turns them into vibrations that merge with the cosmos. Björk is nothing less than a cosmic force. Serious and silly, she's all of the universe in a girl.

> *It takes courage*
> *To enjoy it*
> *Big time sensuality*

* * *

Where was I, after analysis, the trees of Commonwealth Ave. half-covering the sun. It flickers as Björk's "Moon" plays. It is a song of being rinsed by the universe. She sings, "As if the healthiest pastime is being in life-threatening circumstances and once again be reborn. All birthed and happy." She gets lost just to reexperience finding herself. She fails just to experience this rebirth—reconnecting with the universe. How to begin, again, as though everything were possible, as though my body doesn't clench to brace for something bad. My body stays supple. I stay in the world, in the fault line, the tears are not enough to wake up, but who will be there when I open my eyes, a tree, did I laugh in the cinema when Björk sang about her stubborn tree-trunk legs, like the body has a will, my legs are so willful they carry me even when the head has given up. Write over the decaf-coffee spill in the notebook. Will anyone retrace these steps? At the end of yoga, I am traveling toward a purple light. Is this the seed of the universe? Did I see you?

She runs to the edge of life, and there, at the threshold, the moon swallows her adrenaline pearls. Now she is in the comedown. Now the world rains down on her failure. The lights go out. There are some breaths in the darkness, then a road, at night, illuminated by a single streetlight. A light in the void, then the Kwanzan cherry tree, then a wind to blow the petals off the tree. The world grows around this scene, but there are no people in it. There are the lukewarm hands of the gods, making the buildings, making the clock that will put time into the world. To be alone in the world is to be without a witness. She imagines the world this way because it is safer to be alone.

First the screen is black, then a woman sways in the cave. "My shield is gone." She is the wound, geologically active. The body supine on the rock, the heart exposed, the heart pumping lava. In the cave: first there is silence, then strings. Then the beat, so she can fall into time. The beats are the body. Throb long enough and the door opens. It is your passage.

(2015)

T Clutch Fleischmann and Jackie Wang
on Queer Essays

This interview originally appeared on Essay Daily.

So we were at a reading at the Poetry Project a couple of nights ago and afterward you turned to me and said, "You know, I really just think Eileen Myles shines in the essay form." Which I totally agree with, I like them best as an essayist, but they're certainly considered more widely as a poet. When you said that it reminded me of the fact that we met through poetry—we really became close when we organized a queer poetics gathering (Mad Cap) together. But I don't really think of myself as a poet, and a lot of your work is as closely aligned with the essayistic as with poetry. Anyway, what I'm wondering first is if you think of yourself as a writer of any particular genre, as someone that moves through genres?

Clutch, thank you for giving me this opportunity to think about form, and my relationship to it, which I don't do very much. Or maybe everything I do is about form and, in some sense, is a meta-commentary or meditation on my relationship to form. I don't know. I usually rely on other people to see the "structure" in what I'm doing. To label it. To put it in relation to a school. To see the genre in it. I have always been promiscuous when it comes to genres and disciplines because I rely on my intuition to guide me during the moment of writing. Whatever protocols I'm adhering to while writing are unbeknownst to me though I don't doubt they are operating on me on an unconscious level. With academic writing it's a little clearer to me—especially as I try to transition into becoming a "historian." When I sit down to write a paper I have a much clearer sense of what I'm doing. With creative writing the structure or genre either emerges in the process of writing, or is specific to the occasion of the writing itself.

Did we meet through poetry? I believe we met first through "the essay," then reencountered each other and developed a relationship around poetry. We met when you solicited an essay from me for the literary journal *DIAGRAM*. I wrote you a poetic essay on the relationship between writing and silence, and poetry as incantation.

Maybe our relationships to poetry are similar. Before I wrote poetry and fiction, I wrote essays. Later I was christened a poet by other poets and I just kind of rolled with it. Poets are very enthusiastic about identifying as poets (they're kinda cliquey), and maybe are also eager to fold others into the tribe. Why are poets so into parading their poet identity? I think it has something to do with the fact that most people don't give a shit about poetry, so we've gotta self-valorize. I used to have this ongoing joke about the "ontology of the poet." When poets were super self-aggrandizing about the Poet and her being and role in society, I thought it was silly. I still do, but now I embrace the grandiosity ... strategically? Hmmm. Do I believe that we poets are a special breed of visionary creatures endowed with linguistic and sensory superpowers? Are poets, as Shelley says, the unacknowledged legislators of the world? Maybe at one time I believed that such statements were elitist. I was mad when Genet insisted on labeling George Jackson a poet first and revolutionary second ... because I have so much more respect for revolutionaries. Now I see that the occupations of the poet and the revolutionary are closer than I initially thought—they both require a visionary mode of being and working.

When I talked to Douglas A. Martin he said he doesn't feel like he owns his interpretation. This really appealed to me because I feel like a lot of people do want to own their interpretation, like it's really vital to a lot of people to have some ownership over that, especially in terms of queerness or gender or whatever, but he was kind of just chill about it, which seemed to sidestep a lot of narrowness to make room for more openness and more questions. How do you relate to your interpretation?

I can't own my interpretation, and that is a thrilling thing. I cannot control how my words circulate in the world and how they live in people. My words are like a baby I place in a skiff and send down the river. My words are out in the world to have adventures of their own, and I try not to be like an overbearing mama when it comes to controlling what my words do. I might check in every now and then because I am curious about where my words have been and what they have seen, but if I wanted to be all proprietary about interpretation I would have kept my words to myself, shoved them up my vagina instead of setting them free.

After I published some poems on *Fanzine*, I had a funny talk with Dana Ward about his interpretation of one of my poems. In some of my writings I have used "Kant" as a pseudonym for someone I was platonically obsessed with. In the poem Dana read, I am at a party to celebrate the publication of a leftist journal titled *Deathnotes* and am surrounded by factious Marxists who are fighting about the nuances of value theory. Kant shows up to the party and saves me from the horrid scene. When I told Dana that "Kant" was a pseudonym for the Professor he was like "Aww, but it was so funny to imagine the philosopher sauntering into the party." I like to imagine Dana imagining me chatting with Kant-the-philosopher about sea turtles against the backdrop of a petty feud between academic Marxists. So his reading of the poem was thrilling and in no way "wrong."

That said, I also do hope that people engage my work thoughtfully and at least try to develop a sense of what I'm about. I have, at times, felt maybe a little "used" in terms of how people position me and my work. Like sometimes I find people aligning my work with projects that I feel no affinities with, and using my name to validate their projects or their literary camps. While I don't feel proprietary about how people interpret my work, I also don't want to be used as social capital by people who need a little Brown queer sidekick to look legit.

You spent the night at my place last night and then today all we've been doing is reading Maggie Nelson's The Argonauts *and talking about it and reading Claudia Rankine's* Citizen *and talking about it. Well I've been sleeping all afternoon but you've been reading. You talked about how Maggie Nelson's life feels very informed by what she's reading, like the life and the reading feel one in the same. Is that an experience you have, too? Who are the writers you carry around with you?*

One of the reasons I was so set on becoming your friend when I met you was because I got a very good feeling about you based on the books you had on your shelf. Maybe that's a somewhat juvenile way to relate to people (through literary "taste"), but you seemed to like many of the books I liked—I knew I had a lot to learn from you too. We could probably write a history of our friendship using the books we encountered through each other. I hope it's not terribly boring that I spend so much time reading when I'm around you! It appears every time I see you, I always borrow a little stack of things to read. Did I borrow Jenny Boully's *The Body* the first time I met you? You had two editions! After we parted I read more of her books. Before you moved out of IDA I remember how at the music festival Matthew and I commandeered your house while it was empty. I wanted to stay in your bed forever and read. When you and others came back to the house to "pregame" I was still in your bed reading. Everyone was in the mood to party while I was in raptures reading *Franny and Zooey*, a book I had not read since high school. In that moment the book seemed genius to me but maybe I was intoxicated. I was shocked by how little of it I remembered. Did I falsely remember a scene where Franny cried and rubbed a tear into the table? Eric, on the other hand, remembered a great deal. Perhaps his memory could even be called Proustian—ha! My episodic memory is not very good so most novels that I read quickly just kind of wash over me—rereading them is basically like encountering them for the first time.

Though I did not want to pry myself from the book, everyone convinced me to go check out the party. People teased me about being a nerd and you told Israel they would be into Dennis Cooper. Matthew agreed. We joked about how our Mad Cap email password was Dennis-Cooper-Loves-Emos. While you were trying on cute clothes for the party (Eric was being playfully bossy and you were lovin' it), you gave me a rabbit-fur coat to try on and someone took a picture of me in it to show me how good it looked on me. I wore it to the party with zebra-print flip-flops. At one point during the party, I found myself near the snack table (typical!) and accidentally leaned into a little puddle of melted butter. I felt sad about getting butter on the new fur coat you gave me. When I went back to your house to get my backpack an exciting orgy was taking place, so I watched from the sidelines with a couple other people. Rose came and I convinced them to climb over the pile of writhing bodies and retrieve my backpack. This story seems to no longer be about books.

But if books can bring us back to the body, that is a good thing.

Yes, reading is life, and life is reading. I don't claim to be a good reader. I'm slow and unsystematic and don't take as much time as I should to *fully* absorb a text after I read it (as in, I move on to the next book too quickly). But reading is such a huge part of my life. Books and libraries are the only things that have consistently been there for me throughout my adult life. Mommy may or may not love me (depending on the day), I may or may not have a home, life and all my relationships may be in flux, but so long as there is a library nearby I can restore myself. When there is no ground, the written word becomes my ground. When I am without a home, or am vagabonding, the library is my sanctuary. It was nice getting to hole up with you in New York that week, to ignore my phone and read the wonderful books you had around while you restored yourself through sleep.

Lately the main writers I've been carrying with me are Saidiya Hartman, Jennifer Tamayo, Bhanu Kapil, and Fred Moten. Jennifer makes me want to be fierce and unapologetic and to really own all the fucked up parts of myself. Saidiya makes me feel less bad about dwelling in the space of trauma and maintaining a political fidelity to wounds. Bhanu and Fred both give an exhilarating feeling that anything is possible, and a sense of what the body (flesh) can do under pressure. The "pressure" is always terrible, violent even, but the effects of the violences they explore are paradoxical.

Was the Serena Williams section your favorite part of Rankine's Citizen*? It was mine and I think it was yours, and I've heard quite a few people talk about it. And it's also maybe the most essayistic bit in a book that a lot of people read as poetry. That seems queer to me, to come to essay within a poem.*

Like I told you, the Serena Williams section of *Citizen*, more than any other part of the book, gave me the feeling that I was losing my bearings. Without coming out and stating her analysis, I think Rankine is trying to "give" readers an experience—to psychically induce in them the unsettling feeling that, as in the case of Serena Williams, the rules do not apply to you. As we discussed on the train—Black Americans (and, to varying degrees, non-Black people of color) inhabit this experience all the time. So maybe it is true that *Citizen* is written primarily for a white audience, though the people on my Twitter feed who have received the book most enthusiastically have mostly not been white.

Regardless of who the "intended" audience is, I think Rankine is trying to make a paradoxical experience legible: that of psychic erasure and being brutally called into presence through address. Our innate addressability makes us vulnerable, but the violence of the address varies according to how others experience our bodies. This is a dimension of anti-Black racism that is explored much less than the material, economic, and political aspects of racism.

But back to your question. In the Serena Williams section Rankine is able to induce the feeling of going mad in a more total way through sustained repetition (of slights against Williams made by referees). In a way the genteel atmosphere that is cultivated around tennis makes it the perfect setting to explore racism. You really get a sense of how white people manipulate reality by selectively applying "the rules," and how maddening and disempowering it feels to have your reality systematically negated and to not be able to do anything about the arbitrary application of the rules because those who control the game and have institutional power are white.

Overall, what Rankine is illuminating in her book is the psychic dimension of racism, and she does this by creating a text that is essentially a litany of anti-Black microaggressions. The book works by accrual, but the Williams section works a little differently, through suspense and the gradual unfolding of a story: narrative? The logic of the book unfurls and reaches its fullest realization during this section. The appearance of "the essay" amidst the poetic vignettes disrupts the tempo of the book. I think its appearance enhances both the poetic and essayistic parts of the book by playing with our formal expectations. It's kind of like this mostly silent film I made a while ago—the film is completely silent until the end, but because the viewer gets so accustomed to silence, the appearance of audio is that much more jarring. Rankine is more subtle than that, but when she switches modes, it does force the reader to pay attention. The manipulation of tempo in writing is all about guiding the reader's attention, and alternating between essay and poetry is one way of messing with the tempo of a book. Of course, in *Citizen* it's not just these two modes she's playing with—the book is working on many registers, including film, performance, criticism, media studies, and visual art.

And then related to that earlier question, do you connect yourself with any traditions? If you were going to make a (maybe queer) lineage that leads to the work you're doing now, who would be in it?

Oh god I'm not much of a literary school-maker. Remember when we joked about doing a workshop called the New Queer Sincerity that was about writing, creepiness, projection, and queer sentimentality? Maybe that's kinda in the New Narrative lineage of Robert Glück and Bruce Boone or something. I dunno. I'm not a gay man. I was just solicited for the new *Gurlesque* anthology and it never occurred to me that I might be read as a "gurlesque" poet, especially since I feel like my relationship to felinity I mean *femininity* (autocorrect) is quite a bit different than how it's been previously articulated in the poetics of the gurlesque. My lineage? I'm not sure. I feel a certain affinity with aliens and Asian lost girls. Feng Sun Chen, Joohyun Kim, Vicky Lim, Oki Sogumi, and Christine Hou definitely feel like literary kindred spirits. And of course, I am so on board with Bhanu Kapil's decompositional method, which is maybe related to Deleuze's description of Beckett's "exhausted" mode of writing. My School? The School of Exhaustion.

(2015)

The Future Is Now: Speech for the 2015 Pen World Voices Festival Opening-Night Panel

The prompt for this panel was to imagine worst- and best-case scenarios for the year 2050.

I'm gonna do this the only way I know how, even though everyone's leaving because Tom Stoppard just finished talking. See you one day. [*Waves to audience members leaving the venue*]

I want to start with a short exercise that my friend Anwar shared with me from Dante Barry.

I want everyone in the audience to close their eyes.

Keep your eyes closed and imagine a space where you feel safe. [*Pauses.*] Hold that image in your head. Take note of the things you are doing in the space, and the people you are with.

Raise your hand if there were police in the place you went to in your mind.

[*Pauses*]

The now-moment starts here, at the moment I pull up the shades. The sun is rising over Manhattan and with each passing minute my room gets brighter. The day is too bright to stay inside so I go to

Madison Square Park to write. This is the only way I know how to begin, in the moment of writing, pale pink petals falling from the trees and getting caught in the tangle of my hair. This morning when I opened my eyes I was dreaming of the ocean. Some friends and I were trying to find water but it wasn't difficult because the oceans were growing. I remember thinking, *The ocean is so much closer than I thought*, but I knew it was because the water levels were rising and soon we would all be underwater. I could not ignore it, though everyone around me seemed not to notice that the shoreline had moved.

When I woke up today, May 4, 2015, I wondered—was the dream a worst-case scenario for 2050? Over the phone I solicit my friends for predictions.

By 2050 there will be more coconut water than water in California.

By 2050 the United States will be one giant cybernetic prison controlled by biometric technology developed with funding from the Department of Defense.

Ecosystems may collapse and the cities may be reduced to dust.

But what are the best-case scenarios?

Last night I walked up Fifth Avenue on my way to my hotel from a sushi restaurant, rewriting this speech in my head. Walking is the only time that the scope of my thinking is wide enough to meet the requirements of this exercise. Time unfurls. I look behind me and see everything left in my wake. And in front of me, a path I carve with each step. I observe the alien-like paper flowers in the window display of Anthropologie. *Is this the best we can do?* I wondered as I stared into the shop windows, thinking about my freedom to walk around New York City while my older brother languishes in prison, where he has been since he was seventeen. I thought about my friends, some of whom are working three jobs just to pay back the interest on their student loans. "My generation is fucked," I thought, though I knew that I would have to say more than this in my speech. What could I say? Financial precarity alone is enough to remove our capacity to imagine the future. The present becomes so overwhelming that—psychologically and materially—we are merely treading water, or worse, are being dragged into the past by what we owe.

Three years ago, when I was writing my essay "Against Innocence" and reflecting on the significance of Occupy Wall Street, the execution of Troy Davis, the murders of Trayvon Martin and Oscar Grant, and the 2011 London riots, I was trying to understand how the structures of grievances shape and limit the forms of revolt that are imaginatively possible. So much has changed in the last several years. Now, mainstream media outlets such as CNN and *Time* are publishing articles that reframe the discourse around recent antipolice riots to highlight the violence of the state, white supremacy, and capitalism rather than the destruction of private property. At the time I was writing that article, a police- and prison-abolitionist position was not intelligible, though these new abolitionist movements have been around for decades. The struggles of the people against police violence, anti-Black racism, poverty, and incarceration have shifted the discourse so much that even Hillary Clinton has been forced to acknowledge racialized mass incarceration. This is a strange admission considering she supported her husband's tough-on-crime legislation, such as the Violent Crime Control and Law Enforcement Act (the 1994 "Crime Bill") and the Prison Litigation Reform Act, which put more cops on the streets, gutted social and educational programs inside prisons, imposed harsher sentences, and systematically dismantled prisoner rights by giving correctional administrators the power to oversee prisoner complaints. Politicians are opportunistically seizing this moment by co-opting the issues that have been forced into the public consciousness by the people who have contributed their labor and marched in the streets.

Given how much has changed in the last year alone, it seems possible that by 2050 the institutions of prisons and the police will become obsolete. For the last several weeks I have been thinking about how to convey the message of police and prison abolition to you, but I knew on my walk last night that as a poet it is not my job to win you over with a persuasive argument, but to impart on you a vibrational experience that is capable of awakening your desire for another world.

Solidarity with Baltimore.

Thank you and good night.

(2015)

The Distortion Principle:
On Sickness and Perception

This originally appeared on my Tumblr blog.

In Jamaica Kincaid's *Annie John* the protagonist Annie falls ill at the beginning of a three-and-a-half-month deluge of rain

From her sickbed she listens to the rain

The world is warped by the delirium induced by her illness

In my writing I have sometimes referred to this as THE DISTORTION PRINCIPLE

The world seen through pain

The world seen through the eyes of the sick or the traumatized

The disorganized thinking of the dying

One of Kafka's last phrases—"lemonade everything was so infinite"—as remembered by Hélène Cixous

"I write to you in disorder, I well know. But that is how I live." —Clarice Lispector

No other text captures the consciousness of sickness better than Lispector's *Água Viva*

> How can I explain it to you? I'll try. It's that I'm perceiving a crooked reality. Seen through an oblique cut. Only now have I

sensed the oblique of life. I used to only see through straight and parallel cuts. I didn't notice the sly crooked line. Now I sense that life is other. That living is not only unwinding rough feelings—it's something more bewitching and gracile, without losing its fine animal vigor for that. Upon this unusually crooked life I have placed my heavy paw, causing existence to wither in its most oblique and fortuitous and yet at the same time subtly fatal aspects.

The oblique life is very intimate.

Do you see the world through an oblique cut?

Through emotions so intense they threaten to undo your body?

It is what Jamaica Kincaid captures in the chapter "The Long Rain" when Annie John falls asleep on her sickbed and dreams of drinking the ocean dry

As I fell asleep, I had no feeling in any part of my body except the back of my skull, which felt as if it would split open and spew out huge red flames. I dreamed then that I was walking through warm air filled with soot, heading toward the sea. When I got there, I started to drink in the sea in huge great gulps, because I was so thirsty. I drank and drank until all that was left was the bare dry seabed. All the water from the sea filled me up, from my toes to my head, and I swelled up very big. But then little cracks began to appear in me and the water started to leak out—first in just little seeps and trickles coming out of my seams, then with a loud roar as I burst open. The water ran back and made up the sea again, and again I was walking through the warm

soot—only this time wet and in tatters and not going anywhere in particular.

In the morning, I was bleeding. Was I bleeding the ocean I dreamt
last night?

This crack called my cunt, out of which flows the ocean I swallowed
in the dream

Perhaps I was trying to imagine Antigua

a secret place in the sea between Florida and the islands of the
Caribbean

a place I wanted to reach, where the waters were crystal clear and
neon coral reefs lined the seafloor like a majestic glittering city

a crooked city, without right angles

I remember entering the waters by way of Miami

and thinking, "The waters aren't clear here. I will have to swim
farther out."

When I woke, it was snowing outside.

I did not want to get out of bed.

I told myself, I don't have to.

I told myself, I am convalescing.

I will let the snow set the rhythm by which I rest and wake

I thought about Annie John convalescing during the rain

dreaming in bed

attended to by her parents, the doctor, the obeah woman, and her grandmother

how everything was different after the rain

after she destroyed her family in effigy

But what if this Long Rain, this feeling of everything being crooked, never ends?

On my whiteboard in my little adobe house in New Mexico, I wrote the María Sabina quote HEALTH IS COMING

Dylan reminded me of it on the phone and I felt sad because the health I longed for never came

I wrote, *What if health never arrives?*

What if health never was, and everything has always just been *distortion*?

The oblique life.

Wayward daughters with wonky circadian rhythms, bad teeth, tinnitus, poor affect regulation, and broken senses

Could I learn to reorient myself to THE NOISE?

Could I learn to celebrate that which corrupts, degrades, corrodes, destroys, bewilders, destabilizes, inverts, perverts, and derealizes?

When I woke all I wanted to do was stay in bed and write

Outside the window next to my bed were ominous icicles

The stalactites of the cave of my forgotten dreams, I wrote

I looked at what I had written late last night

I had spelled *mold* "mould" (the British spelling?)

and knew it was because I secretly wanted to make *mold* more like *mourn*

(2015)

Some Thoughts on Writing Platforms, Extemporaneous Thinking, Speed, Sparrow // The Shape of a Day Is Liquid

This originally appeared on my Tumblr blog.

If all worthwhile thinking is extemporaneous thinking, then why have I disavowed blogging?

Chris Kraus once introduced me to a handsome European Graduate School cinephile as a "blogger"

At first, I caviled at this label

But now I would do almost anything to reinhabit the subjectivity of the blogger

The blogger in all her mania and unapologetic joy

This blog was once the inevitable byproduct of one thinking girl's life

A trace—

A document of thought in motion

At the time it seemed that the length of a blog post was the upper limit of how long I could sustain a thought without getting bored

Has the limit shrunk to 140 characters?

Does technology shape the length of a thought?

The death of Google Reader killed the blog but I still treat Tumblr like a blog by keeping it text-heavy, image-light, probably too prolix but still proximate … like a diary—that "talking to myself" quality—but analytical like a blog, some weird combination of LiveJournal meets Blogspot meets perzine 2.0. I have traveled through these forms, not knowing where I belong but maybe now I'm passing through Twitter and still using everything all wrong.

The form was meant to be broken.

I don't know how to get myself to write.

I mean I never stopped writing in my journal but I've become so plagued by anxiety when facing my hypothetical audience that my thoughts shatter as soon as I sit down to conjure language

Language leaves me at the moment I set out to write

My journal entries are reduced to lists: half thoughts, frustrations

In the past I could start writing without knowing what I was going to say

But now …

"I haven't got anything to say" has become a reason to never begin

I've stopped taking that leap of faith

The leap into the darkness of the thought-yet-unthought, the words yet unwritten—that prebirth moment—oh how I miss—sinking—getting to know a day by discovering it later—in language—some honey on my lips—I loved the way writing made everything I lived that much sweeter

Now that I have a few very long papers under my belt it is clear it is possible for me to sustain a thought beyond 140 characters but that form seems so unfit for me

So untrue to the way

The thought

Keeps falling

Apart

Adam Phillips has some interesting things to say on this topic apropos of the essay as a genre, which he compares to psychoanalysis

Maybe I like psychoanalysis because it's one of the few places where we are given permission to free-associate

You may have noticed that my "blog posts" are sometimes punctuated by rhapsodic lyrical interludes

This is me trying to get loose

(Sometimes by going into the dream …)

Phillips says for him an essay is successful if, when after you've finished reading it, you don't remember what it said

Because you were witnessing thinking in action, witnessing someone "trying out" different ideas

The thinker rarely knows where she's headed when thinking commences

Are you brave enough to follow her there?

To nowhere

To where there is no point

It is the nonteleological event of writing, as I say.

Essayer: "to try" (in French)

I have a theory on class and speed, on the velocities at which classed bodies travel

And this theory is largely informed by my observations of what the people on the Harvard shuttle do while commuting vs. what the people on the public bus do

It's clear that the Harvard shuttle people are traveling (rushing?) through the world with a clearly defined purpose

All downtime is instrumentalized so that productivity is maximized

Even on the bus they have their laptops open and their highlighters out

While the people on the public bus are much more inclined to go with the flow, chat with the bus driver, stare off, or maybe listen to music on headphones (the younger ones)

I am among the people who move at a leisurely pace

But here—I've forgotten where I wanted to go with this point

Then out of nowhere I remember a bird I saw outside of Mass General Hospital today

A house sparrow, which I had just seen in sticker form at Trident Books in a little sticker booklet of common birds

How does one go from bus to bird?

By moving slowly enough

to see

(2016)

Notes on the Cosmic Yes:
Paris and Beyond

This originally appeared on my Tumblr blog.

My time in Paris has come to an end. Today I fly to Rome. I meant to see more of France but I could not bear to leave this city—it was the people I met here that made me stick around. I am so grateful to have been warmly received by everyone I met in Paris, especially Rona, Alex, Laura, John, Camila, Freddie, Lise, Nathaniel, Matt, and everyone else I got to hang out with. How marvelous it is that you can land in a new city and so quickly discover a way to move through it. To be with people.

While walking from Pigalle to Barbès I remarked to M. and J. how strange it is that in a little over two weeks, Paris has come to feel more "home" than my home—How is that possible?

What goes into making a place feel like home?

People to hang out with and talk about politics, psychoanalysis, philosophy, and poetry.

A feminist crew.

A poet crew.

A commie-anarchist crew.

A QPOC crew.

A place to study and read the newspaper.

Good public transit.

Parks to hang out in.

Late-night kitchen and living-room banter.

I found that in Paris.

Iceland was brief and go-go-go. I encountered people rhizomatically, connecting and diverging, connecting and diverging—always a new vista around every corner, a gorge or waterfall or lava field or glacier or volcano or soul-searching traveler. Whom I encountered was largely left to chance. I remember the moment I decided not to sleep in a drainpipe and keep moving, how I walked along Route 1 a few miles east of Jökulsárlón trying to hitch a ride anywhere. The violent wind whipped my hair as I walked near the ocean in the pseudosetting midnight sun. There were almost no cars, but eventually a manic, bald Midwestern American man picked me up in his rented car. The interior of his car was a hilarious tableau of Snickers bars, bottles of soda, candy, and snacks. For the duration of a night, I shared a world with this whacky amateur photographer from Wisconsin. We drove for several hours through the pouring rain during the "night" and talked and talked and talked and by the end of our fortuitous encounter I had a general outline of his whole life story—his trajectory and path through the world. The years he spent in Thailand and Venezuela. How he courted his sassy bartender girlfriend while she was dating someone else. The people he knew became vivid characters to me. Oh how much I liked this weird middle-aged man (for being open to everything?). I napped in the passenger seat of his car while he walked 4 km to photograph the Sólheimasandur plane wreck at "sunrise." When he returned he thanked me for not stealing his car.

* * *

Clarice Lispector opens her novel *The Hour of the Star* with the lines: "All the world began with a yes. One molecule said yes to another molecule and life was born."

Rona says, "Death is the last thing." But would Spinoza say death is also a YES? How marvelous and terrifying—that you can't stop becoming, even when you are becoming toward nonsentience. A soul never goes away, it just continues being part of the substance. YES YES YES. The Lispector novel ends with the YES of death, which is also the YES of life. Molecules saying yes to other molecules. Same substance, different form. YES. The fungal theory of (de)creation.

When you meet someone, space is created in your mind. Your world grows a little larger. Every encounter puts you on a new path. You can't even know what is made possible by each encounter.

For instance, one spring night while reading at the Emmanuel College library where Ryan worked I decided to see the Polish film *The Hourglass Sanatorium* at the Harvard Film Archive. In the theater I encountered someone from a country very far away and as we were walking through Harvard Yard after the film, he invited me to follow him to the Math Department. I hesitated before submitting to the cosmic YES—we fell in and out of love—and that was that. After a great deal of damage was done, I was ready to curse my submission to the YES—only to discover later that this YES also had a purpose—that it would make something possible—new love?—or maybe it was also a lesson on how to live in my body. To be a body, fucking on the beach and in the woods …

Before being set on a wayward path by that misplaced YES it would never have occurred to me to go to France. That first trip to France was so terrible that afterward it would make me feel sick to see or hear anything having to do with France. One year ago, my love miscarried on a bathroom floor in France. One year ago, I landed in Nice. I was there on Bastille Day. I walked with the Russian mathematicians to the Promenade des Anglais, where Mohamed Lahouaiej-Bouhlel ran over revelers this year. I swam in the ocean at night by the Promenade des Anglais. We took a BlaBlaCar to Lyon to watch the fireworks in the evening.

Here some people have asked me why I am visiting Paris and I'm always unsure how to respond. "The first time I came to France I had a very bad time so I'm trying to create new associations."

Of course it seemed possible that I could have a pleasant visit to France, but I never imagined that I could make the connections I've made here in Paris. For this reason, at 5:30 a.m. on the day of my departure, I bow to the universe. I sing my YES and vow to keep on singing my yes until the golden age of the universe is over and our sun burns out or is swallowed by Fenrir the wolf of Norse mythology.

It is night. The heads of the sunflowers are bowed in a pose of supplication. For now. For now the sun will come, the guarantor of my yes.

(2016)

Blood-Moon Notes: Saint Petersburg and Beyond

This originally appeared on my Tumblr blog.

A boat trip on the Neva River at night. And beyond a bridge—what was it in the distance? A giant dome glowing orange? No, it was the moon, low on the horizon, crowning the city of Saint Petersburg. Why did I believe it was called a "blood moon"? As it climbed toward the sky, it grew smaller and whiter and in the street beneath that shrinking rock, little girls danced and made enormous bubbles. Onion domes were sprouting out of their heads. A block away I said a prayer for a great poet, Dana Ward. This was at the Stray Dog Café, the old haunt of the Acmeist poets of the Silver Age. At my table across from a painting of Mandelstam, I closed my eyes and had a vision of Dana moonlit and swaddled by a peace like no other. Beneath the blood moon, pain was transmogrified into something larger than itself: I saw the light create this new path. "Let him find …" It's the same moon staring at me now as I look out the window of the sleeper train on the journey from St. Petersburg to Moscow. "A rhizome called Jackie Wang," I thought on the boat, bobbing on the water, imagining my strange collisions, detours, and zigzagging path through the world. Now my thoughts branch before the abundance of everything lived, all these associations. Peter the Great's two-headed boys become a Neutral Milk Hotel song mournfully sung by adolescents cruising in an aeroplane over the sea. There was the St. Petersburg of my Florida youth, the city I would go to in high school for indie concerts and Food Not Bombs. There was…falling in love with a smile in the park. A funeral by the ocean. I could go on all night like this beneath the moon-egg above me, but my phone is dying and I'm traveling pleb-style surrounded by unroomed sleeping bodies on a train. In darkness.

Suddenly my morning dream returns to me. We had to shit in front of an audience. There was a marvelous inflatable island, a floating amusement park made of brightly painted metal. I was looking at it while swimming and told a boy, *I have been to that island*. It was like a Soviet funhouse with steampunk mechanisms. As I type this the man next to me is snoring. I see the crags of my dream. A cascade of orange nasturtiums looming above me. I see the trees outside the window of Anna Akhmatova's room. The ceiling becoming a cupola of light becoming the hydrocephalus girl with the swollen head who can't help but be the scribe of the universe, even if it costs her her life.

(2016)

Twists and Turns in the Bowels of the Neon Dragon: A Dream Maze

This essay appeared in the "National Corpse Month" series of blog posts edited by Brandon Shimoda for the Poetry Foundation.

Have you ever

in the space of a page

registered the shadow of what you could not say

and saying nothing, all you could say

was the gesture of turning away?

My circumlocutions went nowhere. While talking to my analyst I was unable to finish my sentences. I report to her, "I have not been in the right emotional space to write this essay. I don't feel it. This mood is not lyrical."

"It sounds like you haven't found your way in," she replies. But for weeks I've been collecting possible points of entry for this essay on corpses.

Can one write oneself toward the border one feels so far from?

I'm not living on the border. What I mean is: my connection to the other side has become weak. Without intending to, I've silently rejoined the community of the living. By that I mean I've haphazardly erected a fragile bridge over a black ocean.

I report to my psychoanalyst: "Yesterday, nothing moved."

Would this essay have been easier to write if I were writing it a year ago, when I was still in the depths of a depression that lasted for years? During those years my mind was full of corpses. When I looked into an empty sarcophagus at the Isabella Stewart Gardner Museum I saw myself, my corpse, resting in the marble coffin decorated with a scene of Bacchic revelry. The corpse I saw was not my body as it existed in that moment, but my corpse as a little girl— I had a feeling I had died long ago.

Do you ever feel that you were not meant to live through something, but the murder was incomplete, so you continue to live as a ghost of yourself?

Hélène Cixous: "It's as if they've botched beheading me."

Face to face with death...

I wanted to write the brutal fact of absence, the corpse that does not signify, but also the impossibility of grasping this absence, which jams our thoughts when we attempt to cogitate death and sets into motion a marvelous play of presences that dance on (or around) the corpse-void. Observe: all this circling (the empty thing at the center). Dead people are phantom limbs. Maybe at one point I wanted to write about the ethics of calling lost ones into presence through a million emotional, mental, and spiritual tricks, but now it seems to me that it is not a question of whether or not one should speak with the dead or can claim to have made contact with them. We do and we will. These conjurations seem to be a primal part of the human experience. What remains to be understood is how absence structures the present, and the conditions under which some are permitted temporary border crossings.

I'm not living on the border. I mean I'm no longer looking in the direction of the border, which I once felt as a temptation or beckoning. When the other side beckons, I turn away. When I think I'm not on the border I'm still on the border. We're only ever one misstep away from becoming corpse. This, I hide. What is the nature of this truth, which I have consigned to secrecy? Once everything was weighed down by death, and it was almost impossible to move. I did a little trick. I said, "I'm not on the border," so movement would again become possible. That is why today I must start with the structure of the maneuver that conceals the corpse and not the corpse itself.

* * *

A year ago, there was a dream I circled for a few sessions in psychoanalysis. At that time I only registered one death but there were three, three dead things, seen from three different angles: the event of death (the moment when someone passes over), the corpse, and the resurrected object. All I remember seeing was the corpse on its way to losing its shape.

In the dream M. dies in my arms and seeing death makes me believe in God.

Death was everywhere. In grandma's old house full of Italian baubles and knitted blankets …

A band played new-wave covers as we slow danced for death.

The brass band played in a circle with their horns pointed to the center.

In the dream the dead dog returns in a shaggier form and is incapable of peeing outside.

The corpse has been liquefied. We try to leave it out for a week to slow dance around the plastic bag of soupy chop lover I mean liver.

But the plastic bag of liquefied corpse will not close.

The interminable mourning made me sad so I left to go investigate the educational cult.

I "drove" but it was not driving for my body was the car and I was moving on my stomach without getting burned by the pavement.

So euphoric, to glide through the night like this.

I said to myself, "Driving isn't so hard after all!"

Then I happened upon the warehouse of the educational cult that had just been busted by the cops.

They told me to leave or they would kill me.

That's when I saw M. Did I know he was about to die?

He was backing out of a driveway in a mini Corvette but he hit something and slammed his head against the windshield.

Yes I knew he was going to die before he died. I was so relieved that I got a few words with him.

He said, "Tell X. I love her." Then he joked, "Will we still be able to have our fun conversations?"

I said, "Yes of course. When I'm dead too we'll resume our fun conversations."

Right as he died a halo of light surrounded him.

When M. died I thought, "I guess it ultimately didn't matter that he was a smoker."

Who will take care of the reincarnated dog?

She's full of ghosts and phantoms,

She sleeps with them
and takes them into her dreams.

The dream starts with the event of death—the death of the friend, at the moment he passes over. This friend first drew me in with his death-drive nihilism. Once in the back of a cab in Brooklyn he told me it was a shame I didn't smoke because "every cigarette is a dance with death"—he was that kind of person. I used to have romantic feelings for this friend, but these feelings were aggressive and not tender; I wanted to reach some kind of limit experience by destroying or being destroyed by him. Nothing came of the crush but here he is in my dream, still repping death though this time not as its spokesperson, but through the act of dying itself. So he dies. And after witnessing the proverbial flame go out I undergo a religious conversion. Why his death made me a believer, I do not remember. Was it a need for eternality in the face of a finitude I could not accept?

But the dream didn't start with M.'s death. It started in the House of Death, surrounded by Grandma's Italian baubles and knitted blankets. Her liquefied corpse was in a plastic bag on an altar in the center of the room, and this fleshsack magnetized my attention. No matter what was happening all around me I was hyperconscious of a certain threat, that the plastic bag would topple and spill the contents of my grandmother. So for a week I stood at the altar trying to prevent the corpse from leaking out of the bag while relatives milled about around me, publicly (and perfunctorily) performing their grief. From time to time the fleshsack would sort of wobble as though sentient and I would rush to catch the bag, saving liquid Grandma from further disintegration. It was my duty. I kept trying to position the bag such that it would stand upright and not fall over, but both the bag and its contents were formless, my attempts to stabilize the situation were futile. I had to stand watch for the duration of the wake, but my attention was divided. Why was I the only one paying attention? Did no one else care to prevent the splatter of Grandma? I hated the indifference of my relatives and their irreverent attitude toward my grandma's corpse.

I don't remember the brass band that played new-wave covers. I remember the dog, which was a reincarnation of my childhood dog. When the reincarnated dog arrived on the scene, the task of containing Grandma became more challenging. This dog, which did not resemble my childhood dog at all but indeed was the essence of the deceased dog, was not potty-trained and so he pissed and shat on everything. But no one paid any attention to the leaky dog; it was on me to manage both the dog and Grandma's liquefied corpse. How could I contain both? My task was impossible. There would soon be a huge mess on our hands, one that, no doubt, I would have to tend to. Bodily fluids would cover the House of Mourning. Everything about the situation fatigued me, especially my relatives, so I left.

I remember almost nothing about the educational cult, except the conspiratorial atmosphere of the warehouse and a looming sense of danger. In fleeing the House of Death I was trying to escape a duty I could not fulfill, but instead I became an accidental witness to a criminal operation. I knew something, and this knowledge meant I would henceforth be a hunted woman.

M. and I tried to escape in the mini-Corvette, but I knew he would die. How? Because I was the dreamer? Did I need him to die? I experienced his death as the consummation of a love that had been denied me, because what is more intimate than witnessing someone's death? Still, duty governs me. As an accidental death shepherd, it is my task to comfort the dying friend, to facilitate the transition—in a sense, to soften this abrupt death. In real life M. and I would always have very stimulating conversations about philosophy, politics, relationships, etc. We would spend hours walking around New York, rubbing our brains together. Did I believe we would continue our conversations, or was I just telling him what I thought would bring him the most peace of mind? Did I need to believe that as an *interlocutor* I was somehow *more than a lover?*

June 17, 2015

The city is alive tonight but I am in bed trying to wind down so I can wake up early tomorrow and prepare for my reading. So many things to do tomorrow—Clair is going to introduce me to new people. I have to stop by an art exhibition I am in to see the exhibit and pick up a check and copies of my chapbook PEPLOPHOROS AS THE WORLD WITH HER HEAD LOPPED OFF, *which I wrote in March around the death of my grandmother after dreaming her corpse came to me as an ice cream cake with a pancake head and whipped-cream death smile. In* The Hourglass Sanatorium *I kept crying every time there was a corpse because I was dreaming of the corpse in so many forms: food, a plastic bag of liquefied flesh. Two nights ago I dreamed of a row of corpses in ostentatiously decorated open mini caskets that small people slept on as a kind of grieving ritual. I wanted to ask,* Why? Why this parade of death? *There was a painting of Jesus in a whorl of color rendered roughly, like it was made by a child. The next day the poet Brandon Shimoda sent me a random message that said the corpse is saying* fuck you. *Maybe if you met me at another time you would have overlooked me because I wouldn't have been leaving the Harvard Film Archive in a dazed state of emotional agitation. How did I start talking about this when I was just trying to list what I will do tomorrow? See different groups of people. Gallery. The big reading. Radio-show appearance. Then I will fly to Detroit and my tree brain will forget these dreams of corpses and the bowels of the glowing dragon and the field where the distant poetry professor appears suddenly full of love and dying to profess that all this time he has wanted to tell me that I am someone truly special, and with this love that suddenly completes me I can travel to a land very far north and produce beautiful Björk music videos full of gold sparkles that sway in water. Everywhere I go there is so much love waiting for me yet why do I wake up from these dreams feeling loveless? Bereft. Could anything ever possibly repair this deep feeling of motherlessness? My friend Hannah Black always used to joke that I was raised by the universe. What does that mean?*

I saw your dream.

And I saw yours.

In the dream there was a Korean spa with a dirty tub and a hero's journey through the guts of a glowing dragon.

Did you see the face? No, I didn't see the neon face glowing in darkness.

We saw the seams of the performance. What was behind the curtain …

It was all commerce. The amusement-park spa ended with the desperate woman trying to sell me jewelry.

I remember all the rings and earrings. She knew I wanted a glam butterfly ring but it was too small and heavy.

Bling butterfly …

Cheap jewelry from China. Earrings made of fake fingernails.

Then there was a performance behind the curtain. Did we miss part of the show?

Was everyone performing death?

We left through the back door

Past a lonely piano in the secret chamber …

In the alley behind the spa were grieving people lying on extravagantly decorated mini caskets.

How had so many died at once?

I asked about the death ritual because it was unique.

The dead bodies were visible. It could have been a stationary parade of death, crucifix in a swirl of colors.

But how was everyone so small?

Why was it important for me to distinguish between commerce and authentic ritual?

The spa cost $68.

Why was it so hard for me to disappoint the capitalist? She guilted me.

The ritual of commerce …

I slept only a couple of hours, if that, and dreamed a little boy was exposed on a table and I climbed on top of the table to cover and protect the boy with my body. I was confident that I could soothe him and lived only to soothe the exposed child. In the distance was his mother, who was trying to transmit messages to him with her facial expressions. Did the boy want to go back to his mother or did he want to stay? The mother was staring at me. We were in the middle of a poetry war. L. was trying to recite an Audre Lorde poem and forgot the words on stage, and then A. tried to upstage her by reciting the poem from the audience while gesticulating wildly. The war was between the white and non-

white poets. *I did not participate in the poetry competition because I was too tired, so I stayed near the child. Everyone was reading a zine of my work, which was assembled by one of my fans (in my dreams it is always others who "assemble" my work, for I have no motivation to do it myself). I was not who they thought I was. I made a joke. I was not in the mood to make a joke but I made it to make everyone else feel at ease. It made me feel terrible.*

When I woke up I was very confused. Didn't want to get out of bed. Everything seemed wrong. Wrong wrong wrong. Then the attack. I won't say anything else about it. I looked out of the window at the rain. It's too much effort to turn a light on. I take a long bath when everyone has left for work. Masturbate. It's later than I think, so I must rush out of the house. Tried to take a bus to the house of the woman who gave me a ride to Chicago to pick up Hélène Cixous's Dream I Tell You, *which I left in her van. Run to the bus in the rain. Get on the bus. Realize I'm going the wrong way on the bus. The bus driver is angry that I got on the bus and then immediately got off. I stand in the rain while waiting to get the bus going in the other direction, but the bus never comes. I can't wait any longer because I have to meet Lauren Berlant, so I walk a mile in the rain to the train. Before meeting Lauren I go to the bathroom and look into the mirror. My eyes are bloodshot (from crying?)— little red demon marbles to match my red lipstick. And I am completely wet. We sit through an artist talk by Wu Tsang. After the talk they say,* Do you want to eat at Russian Tea Time? *Oh yes, I might go to Russia one day, I should learn how to drink the tea. At dinner—cried into my vegetarian sampler. Before we parted they said they wished they could give me something to carry, a keepsake or stone or talisman that would make me feel safe in the world.*

When I got back to the house, Ben and Holly were playing and singing labor-union songs. I made Ben play all my favorite Great Tap Root songs for me on a banjo. Everyone sang and rolled around on the floor together like we did when we all lived in Baltimore. I kept making Ben play his song based on the William Blake poem "Infant Sorrow":

My mother groand! my father wept.
Into the dangerous world I leapt:
Helpless, naked, piping loud;
Like a fiend hid in a cloud.

Struggling in my father's hands,
Striving against my swaddling bands;
Bound and weary I thought best
To sulk upon my mothers breast.

When Lauren says "protection," the word ricochets off my morning dream and is shot through the Blake poem. It is an infant feeling. You get lost in it. How can I live, so lost in it, but then I ask myself, What can anyone know about life without knowing the extremes of joy and death, without experiencing that moment when emotional anguish becomes so unbearable that the Self detaches from Being and you find yourself at the center of the mystery, in the middle of the night, staring out the bathroom window of a crumbling Detroit house listening to the breeze gently blow some wind chimes while everyone sleeps. Why did I think, I will hear that twinkle at the moment of my death, whether or not it is objectively there—it's the Breath of God. I don't know how the nighttime wind chimes could produce absolute knowledge of death, or why, in that moment, the truth of death is felt as the ultimate peace. I dread the moment the Self floats down from the sky and reinhabits my body.

I... I don't know where I am!

On the outer edges of subjective experience—"It's lonely out here." I walk through the Ukrainian forest in the dark. And on the other side: an unbearable light. The fear, the fear, the beheading—then, grace. Suddenly the luminous world emerges from behind the veil of darkness.

INTO THE FOREST, WHERE LOST THINGS GO

What didn't I see the first time I watched the film *Shadows of Forgotten Ancestors* by Sergei Parajanov? Ivan is dying, stumbling through the razed forest, which is still on fire. He looks into the river. He is bleeding into the water and the dead Marichka appears. She taps the water. His blood disappears. He looks up and the forest is whole again. But now the song of Marichka is echoing all around him. Where is Marichka? Has Ivan lost his mind in the birch and poplar trees? "I shall sing to you so that you won't understand." What is the song or chant that accompanies this passage?

I shall sing for you so that you won't understand.

I remember what Édouard Glissant said about borders, how he likes borders because he likes the way the atmosphere changes when crossing a border. He said that borders should be about marking a passage—a change in air—and not about keeping people in or out.

What is the world between worlds, when Marichka returns, and the forest is restored, and the song is suddenly everywhere, the forest is singing the lover's song to the lovers as they stare at each other, confused about what is happening. Ivan wants to know: *Am I dead? Is this the Grim Reaper's siren song, summoning me to the other side?*

What changes when she taps the water: it is a border crossing.

The sound changes

and Ivan is reborn in the forest.

"And when we parted the lilacs withered."

Nothing grows in a world without Marichka.

On the edge of death: the return of lost love. When you are about to die you meet the ones who are already dead. They facilitate the passage. One touch and you turn to silver, which is cinema's way of saying "corpse."

A week ago, Dylan called me in the morning, 8:00 a.m. his time. What could it be? He had just woken up from a dream in which he was visited by a dead friend, and something about the visitation made death seem softer, more peaceful. "If anything happens to me, Gui Gui, you know …"

I want to say that every dream is a little death … a visit to the liminal space, where it is always raining silver in the forest.

[Film stills from Werner Schroeter's *Malina*, Wojciech J. Has's *The Hourglass Sanatorium*, Akira Kurosawa's *Dreams*, Apichatpong Weerasethakul's *Cemetery of Splendour*, and Sergei Parajanov's *Shadows of Forgotten Ancestors*]

(2016)

Acknowledgments

It's impossible to truly account for all the precious souls who make a book possible, for single authorship is always an illusion. I will try. First, this book would not be possible without my wonderful team at Semiotext(e). Robert Dewhurst was a punctilious reader who saw this manuscript through from beginning to end. Hedi El Kholti and Chris Kraus helped bring this book into existence with their vision and generous stewardship.

Lily Hoang has always been a steadfast alien sister. Dylan Retzinger took the cover photo and even washed my dishes when I was too depressed to take care of myself. All my friends at the Baltimore Feminist Reading Group helped me out in my darkest hour: I would especially like to thank Emilie Connolly and LaKeyma Pennyamon. I am especially grateful for my fairy godmothers, particularly Bhanu Kapil, the late Cris Hassold (my undergraduate mentor at New College of Florida), and Chris Kraus (again!).

Special thanks to my beautiful students and colleagues at the University of Southern California and The New School, especially the students in my Lang course Lost Grrrls: The Poetics of Waywardness. I would also like to thank my dear friends: Sherah Bloor, Christopher Soto, Nat Raha, Jack Frost, Molly Steele, Er(ic)

Linsker, Lara Lorenzo, Fred Moten, Matthew Polzin, Rosie Stockton, Cyrus Dunham, John DeWitt, Laura Silverman, Rona Lorimer, Hanna Hurr, Banu Guler, T Clutch Fleischmann, Kate Zambreno, Anne Boyer, Moxie Marlinspike, Tyler Reinhard, Steve Stevens, Lane Zajac, Adrian De Leon, Jonathan Leal, Joan Flores-Villalobos, Hannah Black, Maya Singhal, Michael Ralph, and Clair Voyance. I'd also like to give thanks to my friends at the Museum of Jurassic Technology, that marvelous beehive of artists who have created the most magical place in the world!

I'm also grateful to my analysts, Dr. C. and Dr. L., as well as my literary agent, Ian Bonaparte.

Huge thanks to Alexander Moll—you are my rock. Thanks to my family: Mom, Dad, Danny, and Randy.

Jackie Wang is a poet, scholar, multimedia artist, and assistant professor of American Studies & Ethnicity at the University of Southern California, where she researches race, surveillance technology, and the political economy of prisons and police. She is the author of *Carceral Capitalism* (Semiotext(e), 2018) and the poetry collection *The Sunflower Cast a Spell to Save Us from the Void* (Nightboat Books, 2021, National Book Award Finalist). Her current book project, *The Carceral Laboratory: The Rise of High-Tech Prisons and Police*, is forthcoming with Princeton University Press.